Julie Shackman is a feel-gc
journalist.

She lives in Scotland with
little Romanian rescue pup, Co

julieshackman.co.uk

twitter.com/G13Julie
instagram.com/juliegeorginashackman
facebook.com/julie.shackman
bookbub.com/authors/julie-shackman

Also by Julie Shackman

A Secret Scottish Escape

A Scottish Highland Surprise

The Cottage in the Highlands

A SCOTTISH COUNTRY ESCAPE

JULIE SHACKMAN

ONE MORE CHAPTER

One More Chapter
a division of HarperCollins*Publishers* Ltd
1 London Bridge Street
London SE1 9GF
www.harpercollins.co.uk

HarperCollins*Publishers*
Macken House, 39/40 Mayor Street Upper,
Dublin 1, D01 C9W8

This paperback edition 2023
1
First published in Great Britain in ebook format
by HarperCollins*Publishers* 2023

A catalogue record of this book is available from the British Library

ISBN: 978-0-00-859518-0

Printed and bound in the UK using 100% Renewable Electricity
by CPI Group (UK) Ltd

Chapter One

'Are you sure this isn't a knee-jerk reaction to all that's happened, Elle? You've been to hell and back these past twelve months.' She gulped back tears. 'We both have.'

I shook my head at my grandmother, almost dislodging my haphazard bun, which I'd secured in a creamy blonde ball at the nape of my neck.

I stared round with damp eyes at the empty newspaper racks and the plastic jars with their circular screw-top lids that previously housed everything from rainbow-coloured sweeties and pastel-shaded mints to sherbet-sprinkled lollipops.

A couple of lost-looking envelopes were still poking out of the greetings card display.

Further up the shop floor, on the right-hand side, lay the vacant space where Mum had stocked magazines, ranging from fat, glossy women's monthly publications to those aimed at the train, fishing, and golf enthusiasts.

I leant on the dark wooden counter and dragged my attention away from the inactive electric cash register to the two bottle-glass windows.

I could still see my late parents bouncing ideas and jokes off one another behind the counter, greeting everyone like old friends.

Mum's imaginative shop displays had been the talk of Fir Haven. So many locals would comment on Dana Cassidy's Easter-inspired window extravaganza with its yellow and cream daffodils, arrangements of lemon-coloured confectionary and cute cuddly toy rabbits.

Then she would lace silver Christmas lights, like shards of twinkling stars, around the window frames and use everything from Christmas crackers, cotton wool, and glitter to make a festive scene that any high street store would have been proud of.

Cassidy's was nestled halfway down the cobbled high street, sandwiched in between Mr Monteith's antique business, Through the Ages, and Mrs Campbell's pet shop, Paws for Thought.

It seemed inconceivable even a year on. Dana and Gareth Cassidy, much-loved and respected members of the local community, killed outright in a car accident whilst on holiday in the heather-studded beauty of the Scottish Highlands.

Another vehicle, tackling a bend too wide, had veered into them.

Emotions raged inside of me, white-hot and raw. I bit my lip. Life would never be the same again. I had tried to convince myself that after their funeral I might be able to get my life into some semblance of order, but it hadn't happened. I hadn't been able to face coming into the shop, but I couldn't leave the business sitting like this, echoing with the ghosts of them, through layers of dust.

'Elle?'

I blinked over at my grandmother and tugged at the hem of my jacket. 'Sorry.' I cleared my throat. 'I was lost in my own world there for a minute.'

I forced myself to concentrate on Gran's question. 'I know what needs to be done. I won't put things off any longer. Mum and Dad wouldn't have wanted me to give up on the shop.'

I studied the shoulder-length sweep of her silver-lilac bob and her sorrowful pale-grey eyes. 'They never gave up on me.'

I moved around what used to be our family newsagent's, my leather heels clipping against the rustic oak flooring.

The May sunshine had toyed with us all at the cemetery the day of their funeral, dipping and weaving in and out of rinsed puffy clouds. Now it was spooling in through the windows, like tiny gold necklaces, draping themselves over the counter and looping across the floor.

'I want to do this, Grandma,' I appealed to her, 'but I can't without your blessing.'

She let out a ragged breath and moved towards the counter. I watched her as she trailed her veined beringed right hand along the edge.

I swallowed, keen not to upset her. 'The supermarket already stocks so many newspapers and magazines. The town doesn't need a traditional newsagent any more, given the size of the place.'

I had considered leaving Fir Haven and its wealth of memories behind: our home; the shop; the gorgeous expanse of our local nature reserve, where we would ramble as a tight-knit little family unit of three. Even the thought of going to the reserve now without either of them made my breath stall.

The local nature reserve was like the beating heart of Fir Haven, with its throbbing wildlife, feathery expanse of trees, and tangles of streams that slithered and danced over the rocks. It was a sweet little Scottish town situated on the gateway to the Highlands, only a short train ride away from the likes of Perth and Inverness.

We even had our own Fir Haven Rose Garden, located up one of the cobbled lanes from the main street, where an assortment of beautiful paintbox-bright roses, mulberry trees, and cypress bushes bloomed and made for a very popular setting for tourist and day-tripper photographs.

Mum, Gran, and I would often go and sit amongst its frilly blooms during the summer months, putting the world to rights, moaning about Dad having his rugby matches turned up to full volume on the TV, and inwardly cursing the odd tourist dawdling along the pavement or parking where they shouldn't.

There were numerous rumours about the historical legacy of our little town, ranging from it being a bolt-hole for William Wallace to it once being used by smugglers to stash their spoils before transferring them on by boat. The latter would have been a very appealing explanation if Fir Haven were close to the sea.

It was even rumoured to be where a local nineteenth-century artist, Stratford Miller, sat and painted his most famous work, *Little Town*.

The local library had a blurry black and white photograph of the painting hanging in its reception area, showing layers of snow like fondant icing covering the bare branches of the trees before travelling across the hazy winter fields and down to the stippled roofs of Fir Haven itself.

Rumours swirled for years about who might be in possession of Miller's most lauded work, but it remained officially lost. That was another tantalising tale which lured culture vultures to the town.

Miller was said to have found great inspiration up at the reserve, and I wasn't at all surprised.

I might enquire about having a commemorative bench or a tree planted up there in my late parents' honour. They would both have loved that.

I hauled my attention back to the shop. One thing at a time. I offered Gran a reflective look. 'Remember how Dad was always popping in and out in his builder's overalls and Mum had often just swept the floor.'

We shared a fleeting, reflective smile at the memory.

'If I can turn this place into a sweet little stationer's, we'd still be carrying on the business, but just in a different guise.' I stared around myself, conjuring up images of the shop as it could be. 'I've contacted suppliers already to obtain rough quotes for stock and I've also been thinking about colour schemes for redecorating the place.'

I hadn't been able to face the prospect of continuing to work for Dad's old building firm when his best friend Stuart offered to buy it from us. I had been my father's PA, girl Friday, and confidante all rolled into one since quitting the marketing job in Perth I'd had up until about five years ago.

I had worked for a successful family of magazine publishers and was supposed to have been their marketing and advertising manager, but had instead found myself carting around posters, tables, and flip charts whilst the publisher's daughter had been shoehorned into my team and had taken great delight in undermining me.

Needless to say, after four years of study that had resulted in me pouring endless cups of coffee for colleagues and placating frustrated members of the public over the phone as to why their latest copy of *Golf Now* magazine hadn't been delivered, I reached boiling point. I quit after sticking it out for a painful eighteen months.

That was when Dad had swooped in to the rescue and asked if I could put my organisational, creative, and social media skills to good use and work for him at Brick by Brick. Seeing the impact I had on his business and the harmonious way we worked together had made the past five years one of the happiest and most rewarding experiences I could have had.

I set up social media accounts for the company, regularly updating them with news on the latest designs, offers, and competitions; made sure Brick by Brick advertised and was featured in the relevant trade magazines, and came up with ideas for radio & TV campaigns, as well as managing Dad's work diary.

I had loved it.

But things had changed beyond all recognition for us now. Cassidy's newsagents was no more and I realised I had to do something. I'd always had an obsession with pretty stationery and there were no other businesses like that in the surrounding area.

Grandma sensed my attention was elsewhere. 'You don't want to live your life in your mum and dad's shadow, Elle. They wouldn't want that for you.'

I dashed a weary hand down my face. 'You have to admit that my parents are a tough act to follow around here though, Gran.'

Mum and Dad had been Fir Haven's answer to a real-life Disney couple. Not only had they made a strong marriage together, they had been best friends too. Coupled with their friendly little business, my parents had been respected stalwarts of the local community.

Grandma's lips twitched. 'It's not easy, is it, when folks expect you to live up to your parents?'

'And that's why I won't even try,' I explained. 'I want them to always be proud of me, but I know I have to do this in my own way.'

She inclined her head. 'You have to be you, Elle, and if that means you turning the shop into something new, then so be it.'

My heart zinged with a mixture of hope and apprehension. 'Seriously, Gran? You're OK with it?'

She squeezed the tops of my arms. 'I don't need this place as it is to remind me of my daughter and son-in-law. They are up here and in here.' She raised one finger and tapped at her temple and then at her chest. 'And, most importantly of all, I have you.'

I buried my face in her shoulder, breathing in her lavender-scented perfume and blinking back more tears which were clustering on my lashes.

'Come on,' she managed after a few moments. 'Let's lock up the shop and go home. You're going to be busy.'

Grandma buried herself deeper into her billowing black velvet cape which she wore despite the pleasant temperature. We made our way out and I gave the empty shop another forlorn look, before rattling the key in the lock of the heavy, knotty wood door behind us.

We negotiated the sun-washed cobbles in silence. Children were being ferried past us in buggies and mums had sunglasses propped on top of their highlighted heads. As we walked, the shadows of the trees licked across the dry-stone wall that ran along the other side of the road. How could all these people be brandishing smiles and telling jokes to each other when I was still mourning the loss of my parents?

I'd parked my car, a lilac Mini, up a lane which led to the library. Grandma settled herself in the passenger seat and I slid on my smoky sunglasses. It was a relief to hide my tear-stained face. I caught a glance of my reflection in my rear-view mirror. I looked haunted. My fair, freckled skin was washed-out and my dark-brown eyes and slightly bemused-looking mouth were all blurred at the edges. Still, it was a relief, in a sense, to have come to a final decision about the newsagent's, and the fact that my grandmother was being so supportive was a weight off my mind.

I'd only just fired up the ignition when Marjorie McDade, one of Grandma's oldest friends, appeared at the side of the Mini. I switched off the car engine and wound down the driver's side window. A cooling breeze, carrying the rich aroma of cherry blossom from the nearby park, danced in.

That took me straight back to Mum and Dad's funeral, when the heavy cherry blossom trees had bowed their heads in the church grounds. It was as if we had all been surrounded by pink candy floss as we stood there by the graveside.

Marjorie and her husband, Graeme, were two long-standing friends of my grandmother, though Graeme was nowhere to be seen today.

Marjorie delivered a kind smile as she approached the car window.

'So, what have you two ladies been up to? Are you both heading home?'

Grandma craned her neck forward in her seat to get a better view of Marjorie. 'Yes. We were just in, taking a look around the shop.' She reached over and clasped my hand.

Marjorie shifted the weight of the straw bag she had slung over her shoulder.

She explained that Graeme was at home watching the cricket while she popped out to pick up some milk and a few other essentials.

'Well, we'd better get home,' said my grandmother, her voice weary.

Marjorie insisted we let her know if we needed anything – which she always did and for which we were both so grateful – and were about to rumble our way out of the car park, when she rapped on my window. 'Oh, I meant to say that if you've got time, take the longer route back to Pebble Brook.'

She offered Grandma a quizzical rise of her overplucked eyebrows. 'I think you might be interested, Councillor Blackmore.'

Gran rolled her lined, light-grey eyes. 'Ex-councillor, if you don't mind.'

Marjorie gave a small smile. 'You'll never stop being a councillor, my lady, and don't pretend otherwise.'

I wound up my window and prepared to tug my sunglasses back down over my eyes. Grandma observed her friend bustling down past the glinting shop windows, all coiffed burgundy hair and expensive loafers. 'I wonder what she meant when she said to take the longer route back?'

'What would you like to do, Gran? Do you want to take the scenic route home? See what Marjorie was talking about?'

Grandma turned around in her seat. 'Yes. Let's do that. We haven't got anything to rush back for, have we?'

The thought of rattling around at home, consumed by thoughts of Mum and Dad, was too much to deal with right now.

'No,' I admitted, flicking up the indicator to turn right and wishing I could change everything back to how it used to be. 'No, we haven't.'

Chapter Two

The snaking road, sandwiched between frothing trees either side of it, led us out of the centre of Fir Haven.

As I arrived at the junction, my attention flew to the red and white 'For Sale' sign strapped to the balcony of my former second-floor flat situated on the corner. It was one of twelve that occupied a beige Edwardian building.

I'd lived there with my long-term solicitor boyfriend, Lloyd, up until a year ago, when he'd failed to be any kind of support to me when I lost my parents. Instead of offering words of comfort, he had put his law firm ambitions first and would work consistently late in the office, insisting that if he wanted to succeed, he had to be seen to be a 'go-getter'. I was left to cope with all the shock, grief, and anger on my own. Lloyd would vanish out of the flat at half past six every morning with his briefcase and gym bag and not get back until late.

I realised then that he wasn't the man I'd thought he was, and after three years of being together I finished the relationship – such as it was. The last I heard; he had taken himself down to London to join a law firm there.

One of his parting shots had been, 'You don't seem to realise there is more to life, Elle, than Fir Haven. If I never see one more sodding tourist leaflet about red deer or hear the call of a reed bunting and tufted duck, it'll be too soon!'

Needless to say, Lloyd hadn't been able to process that I loved living here, 'in the back of beyond'.

I was born and bred in Fir Haven, whereas he had moved into the area from Edinburgh because he had managed to secure a job as a solicitor with a local firm. We met when my dad and I dropped by his office to ask for some legal advice regarding a client's proposed house extension. Lloyd Mullen had been all teeth, smooth charm, and floppy fair hair and after providing us with the information we needed, kept dropping by Brick by Brick's offices on a series of pretexts.

In the end, he asked me out, I said yes, and our relationship took off. I'd really thought we could make a go of it.

Bereft at our relationship dissolving so fast after three years, I had finally got myself together. I arranged the clear-out of our flat and put it on the market only a few weeks ago, and moved back in to Pebble Brook, my family home, with Grandma.

My grandmother had a gorgeous little annexe, the building of which Dad had overseen, which offered her company but also privacy when she wanted it.

Thoughts of what had happened to my parents clutched harder at me. I gripped the steering wheel.

My knuckles became blocks of white marble as I drove on. The visit from the Phil, our local policeman, in the middle of the night, to tell Gran and me what had happened; the wails and screams coming out of both of us, like two wounded animals…

My imagination conjured up images of their buckled car; them laughing and joking together right before the smash—

My grandma's husky voice from beside me in the passenger seat, made me flinch. 'Do you miss him?'

I blinked back at her through my sunglasses. 'Who?'

'Lloyd.'

Her lavender-painted nails glinted as she laced her fingers together in her lap.

'I did,' I confessed after a pause. 'I mean, I'm still bruised by the split, but it's more resentment and anger about how unsupportive he was when Mum and Dad died. I couldn't believe he could be so self-centred and uncaring.' I ground my jaw. 'I'm much better off without him.' That was the last time I would lay my feelings out there for someone to stomp all over, as if they didn't matter. If I couldn't have the relationship my parents had, then so be it. I was better off on my own, anyway. At least I could rely on myself!

I jerked my head at what surrounded us as we drove on: the plumes of sage-green Scots pines and my particular favourite tree, the ash. I remembered Mum telling me that the ash tree was shrouded in mystery. In Norse mythology, it was called the Tree of Life, believed to possess healing powers and it could be burnt to drive away evil spirits.

My parents had undertaken one of those ancestry tests years ago and it had transpired that there was Viking blood on my mother's side. I suppose I shouldn't have been that surprised. Apart from inheriting my dad's dark eyes, my features were of the Scandinavian variety, what with my blonde hair, fair skin stippled with the merest dusting of freckles over my rather snub nose and a slanting, winged angle to my cheeks.

'He never really belonged here,' remarked Gran, staring out of the car window. 'Lloyd never understood what Fir Haven means to us country bumpkins.'

I indicated left, taking us past a crop of fields that were changing colour under the bobbing sunlight. 'He never tried to make a connection with the place.' I made a dismissive noise. He always compared Fir Haven to Edinburgh, and in his eyes it was usually found wanting. 'Well, I'd rather be a country bumpkin than an unfeeling knobhead.'

She smiled for a moment, while she revelled in my features.

'You're getting more and more like your mother and I don't just mean your looks.'

I dropped down into second gear as we slid past another car on the narrow country lane. 'I'll take that as a compliment.'

The crops on either side of the road waggled their heads and the grass waved like long jade fingers.

'Good grief!' exclaimed Grandma, shifting herself bolt upright. 'What on earth is going on here?'

She indicated an elegant hand ahead to where shards of bright yellow were peeking through the trees. As we drew closer, we realised it was construction machinery. There were also flashes of lime, which we realised, as we drove on, were from the jackets worn by builders.

'This must be what Marjorie was talking about,' said Gran. 'Do you mind if we go up and see what's going on?'

I shook my head. 'Not at all. My curiosity is well and truly piqued now.'

As we drove towards a steel fence, Grandma's eyes widened under her plucked brows. 'Oh, you have got to be joking!'

I shot her a curious sideways glance as I swiped off my sunglasses and perched them on top of my head. 'That's where your council offices are.'

'You mean that's where they *were*.'

I drew up and stopped in a crude parking area beside two white transit vans splattered with mud.

I watched my grandmother hurry out, slam the car door shut, and scurry towards the site fencing.

Under the marmalade May sunshine, I locked my car.

'Elle!' hissed Gran. 'Come and have a look at this.'

I negotiated the small grassy incline in my heels to stand beside her.

My mouth fell open as I took in what was happening. 'Bloody hell!'

Chapter Three

Grandma had been a councillor up until around ten years ago and she had been based in the distinguished headquarters of East Carwood Council.

It boasted spectacular surroundings of woodland, a carpet of fields, and was in a prime location to enjoy the abundance of the local nature reserve close by without being intrusive. It was all arched windows and turrets – an architectural reflection of its Victorian influence.

It was where we were standing. Or at least it had been.

What had once been occupied by a member of the local judiciary in the mid-1800s, had now been transformed into an elaborate Gothic-style mansion, complete with new pointed windows and ornamental flourishes.

The flying buttresses of rearing horses complemented the wrought-iron balconies thrusting out from beneath several of the windows. It was dramatic; over the top, but spectacular.

Two excavators were parked close by the house and there were a couple of Portakabins with their doors flung open. A few site workers milled around, pointing at parts of the sprawling pile and engaging in animated discussions.

My grandmother made a strangled noise and whipped her head round to look at me. 'I don't believe this! It's gone! Carwood House has been replaced by… by that monstrosity!'

I wouldn't have described the mansion in those terms, but it did carry a bit of a haunted house vibe. Whoever it was who was moving in, had certainly gone to town re-establishing the Gothic vibe of the place. It must have cost them a fortune. 'Did you know this was going on, Gran?'

Her mouth set in a line. 'I'd heard the odd rumour about building work taking place up here and stories of security guards being seen around, but I didn't take much notice. There were even stories it was just a film crew, on location for *Outlander*.'

We fell silent, both staring through the wire fence at the bustling site workers. It definitely wasn't a TV crew filming. 'Do you know who might be moving in here?'

Grandma rolled her eyes up to the sky, and somewhere behind us in the trees a blackbird flapped and fizzed its song. 'I've no idea, but no doubt it will be one of those obscenely wealthy YouTuber types.'

I was just thinking how impressed I was that my seventy-seven-year-old grandmother was au fait with the social media generation when I was interrupted by a terse male voice. 'Excuse me? Can I help you, ladies?'

My grandmother and I started at the sight of one of the builders barrelling up to the other side of the wire fence. He was kitted out in a white hard hat, the obligatory fluorescent jacket, and had his shirt sleeves rolled up to his elbows. He was carrying a red clipboard.

His narrow eyes appraised us out of his ruddy, jowly face. 'Are you selling something?'

I bit the inside of my cheek as my grandmother delivered one of her best glares. 'Indeed we are not, young man. My granddaughter and I live here in Fir Haven.'

She craned her lavender-grey head past his shoulder towards

the gothic mansion. 'I see someone has been busy. New owner, I take it?'

The middle-aged man puffed out his chest. 'Yes.'

Grandma folded her arms, making her cape ripple. 'I used to work in that house as a councillor back in the day. Well, in the house it used to be. Not the Dracula's castle you've turned it into now.'

The insulted foreman's jaw clenched. He cocked one eyebrow so high it threatened to push his hard hat clean off his head, so I decided to try an alternative tack. 'It looks beautiful,' I insisted. 'And you guys must have worked flat out to do so much work so quickly.'

Grandma narrowed her gimlet eyes up at me.

The foreman basked in my praise. 'Thank you. We've got a good team here. Our client insisted they wanted the renovation work completed as soon as possible.'

'Renovation?' gasped my grandmother beside me. 'It's unrecognisable!'

The foreman shot Gran a sharp look and appeared to be on the verge of saying more, but a shout out from a young lad in a yellow hard hat distracted him. 'Sorry, ladies. If you'll excuse me.'

Gran watched his retreating back with suspicion. 'That's why most of the locals won't know about this,' she muttered out of the corner of her mouth. 'You heard Bob the Builder just now. It's all supposedly "renovation work", so whoever the new owner is, they won't have had to ask planning permission from the council. Very clever.'

I studied the landscaped rolling grass and rejuvenated ornate wall of mini Corinthian-style columns surrounding the property.

Grandma sniffed and peered again through the lattice wire fence that towered over us. 'No doubt it will be some ignorant townie who thinks a crested tit is a porn star.'

'Gran!'

She made a grunting noise in frustration. 'As long as they

don't do any damage to the wildlife round here, they can do what they ruddy well like, as far as I'm concerned.'

We took one last look at the triangular roof, soaring up to pierce the expanse of China-blue sky.

'Come on,' I urged. 'Let's go home.'

She nodded and I linked my arm through hers to make our way back down the slope.

'I'll ask around,' she said. 'Someone must know who will be moving in there.'

Chapter Four

I indicated left and took us down the sweep of lane that boasted 'Pebble Brook' in black writing on a painted white sign.

Grandma and I sat for a while, listening to the car engine fade and surveying the gold lights Dad had strung along the garden fence at the front of the house. She slid a freckled hand across to clasp mine in hers. 'Let's go in,' she suggested. 'We've got lots to do.'

I blinked away pictures of Mum's empty newsagent's. 'What do you mean?'

Grandma's silver eyes crinkled. 'Well, this new stationery shop of yours isn't going to launch itself.'

Pebble Brook, formerly my childhood home and now where Gran and I lived together, was built from eighteenth-century Cornish stone. My dad had called on many of his building trade buddies thirty years ago when he and my mum had bought the old mill and had it renovated.

It was situated in a peaceful location, at the bottom of Pebble Brook Lane – hence the name. A wild rock-tangled brook gushed up and around the bend, held back by a grassy stone wall and topped off by the lit fence Dad had erected. There was a wooden balcony at the side of the house, where you could stand like a Scottish Juliet and oak-panelled doors to fit in with the natural ambience. Dad had installed a pillared entrance, which gave the former mill a more majestic air and two large ceramic pots, housing hot-pink cross-leaved heather, sat either side of the door.

Inside, the house boasted a rustic farmhouse-style kitchen. Mum had been keen on the unusual and had insisted on an antique apothecary cabinet in distressed pine as the centrepiece and breakfast table. Even the range hood above the stainless-steel cooker made a statement, as it was constructed of barnwood to conceal the basic vent. The walls of the kitchen were slicked in paint the colour of distressed cream, making the flagstone floor of smoky grey pop in contrast. Ceramic mugs and flower-stippled dainty saucers were distributed amongst the three pine cabinets that sat between the two sash windows. They boasted old-fashioned shutters to match the walls and ceilings.

The sitting room was opposite the kitchen – blonde wood fixtures, vanilla fireplace, and dashes of various shades of green cushions and ceramics.

Grandma's annexe was located on the ground floor, towards the rear of the house. Dad had ensured she had her own en suite bathroom, furnished in white and claret, and her bedroom itself was a sea of pastel lemon and duck-egg blue, with a brass double bed. Billowing curtains in daffodil yellow and charming wooden furniture gave it a homely feel.

Opposite the downstairs cloakroom was a winding polished staircase that led up to what would now be my bedroom – again. I twitched my nose at the thought. I had intended to move back out again once the flat was sold and I could get rid of the last vestiges of Lloyd for good by giving him his half of the sale.

Just a day before we lost Mum and Dad, Mrs Fraser's cottage, that overlooked the local rose garden, had been put up for sale. She had decided to move into residential care and it would have been perfect; still close by my family and to work at Brick by

Brick, meaning I could help out Mum in Cassidy's whenever she might need it.

But nobody could have predicted that Mum and Dad wouldn't return from their holiday.

Mrs Fraser's house sold quickly, as I suspected it would. But even if the property had still been available, I knew I couldn't leave Grandma on her own here. Pebble Brook was gorgeous and would always be my family home, but now it would be like she was trapped, alone, living in a museum to my late parents.

At the moment, I had assorted chiffon scarves draped over the oval mirror in my bedroom and boxes regurgitating assorted bits and pieces that I hadn't had the time or compunction to do anything about since moving back in.

When Lloyd and I split up, he wasted no time in suggesting we sell our furniture and magnanimously stated we would split the cost of whatever we made. At least that meant I hadn't had to concern myself with storing furniture.

Mum and Dad's bedroom was located across the hall from mine. Their door had eased itself open. I straightened my shoulders and took the briefest of glimpses inside, before closing it again.

I didn't want to transform Pebble Brook into a mausoleum, but I knew I still wasn't ready to head in there with Grandma and start sorting out Mum's perfume and jewellery and Dad's collection of rugby shirts. It was painful enough, seeing their holiday photographs and sage and butterscotch satin bedding.

Even Buster, Mum's cuddly toy bulldog that Dad won for her at the local fair six years ago, was still propped up against their pillows.

One step at a time. At least I was galvanising myself to finally deal with Cassidy's.

The house resonated with silence as Grandma and I tapped our way into the kitchen. I tugged off my heels and tossed them into the hall. My feet let out a sigh of relief as I gave them a rub.

'You sit down,' instructed Gran, indicating one of the high-backed chairs. 'You look shattered.'

I shook my head, almost dislodging my haphazard bun. 'I'm all right, Grandma. You take a seat and I'll make the tea.'

I watched her throw off her cape and drape it over the back of one of the kitchen chairs. She looked drained, but tried to disguise it with an element of positivity in her words. 'Things won't be the same again, but we are slowly learning to deal with it. That's all anyone can do.'

I filled the teapot with gurgling water from the tap and watched the bubbles jostle against one another. 'I need to keep busy,' I managed to say, spotting one of Dad's favourite mugs on the sideboard, 'otherwise I'll lose my mind. I think that's been the problem the last year. I've just let the business fester, but not anymore.'

I busied myself with seeking out two mugs from the crockery cabinet. 'I'm going to make a start on getting the shop knocked into shape. I've already made a to-do list and will work my way through it. I've got a couple of numbers for painters and decorators and I'll give them a ring. I've started thinking about stock too and a suitable name for the business. I want to sell stationery that's unique—'

Gran interrupted me as she materialised at my shoulder. She looked small and delicate, but insisted on bundling me into her arms. 'Come here, darling.'

I propelled myself into her arms and buried myself in her shoulder.

'I know you want to keep occupied, Elle, but I'm not prepared to see you exhaust yourself in the process.'

I pulled back and we exchanged watery smiles.

'I've lost them, and I'm not prepared to lose my granddaughter well.' She squeezed my bare upper arms. 'Right then. One thing at a time, OK?' She pointed one finger at our forlorn-looking mugs sitting by the teapot. 'Tea first with a slice of that carrot cake you bought the other day. Then we get to work on turning Cassidy's into a rival for Smythson.'

Chapter Five

The next week evaporated in a tornado of actioning and ticking off items on my to-do list for the transformation of my parents' shop.

I was frantically making notes on what I wanted to do with Cassidy's, arranging the delivery of stationery supplies and finalising paint colour schemes to revamp the look of the business and give it a makeover.

I knew Gran was appalled at the way I was suddenly throwing myself into everything, zooming from one thing to the next, but it was the only way I felt I could handle things.

She would pin me to the spot with those marble-esque eyes of hers and tell me to slow down, or materialise at the shop in her little avocado Volkswagen Polo, armed with a flask of tea and a Tupperware box steamed up with warm scones she had baked or sandwiches she had made, to keep me going.

In some ways, it didn't seem like a year since Mum and Dad's funeral and the weather was in stark contrast to what it had been then. Instead of golden sunshine dangling through the branches of the trees, the late May sky today was a washed-out grey, weighed down with solid patches of cloud.

There were moments when I wondered about my own sanity; taking over Cassidy's and launching my own business, and then at other times I drew on the self-belief my parents had instilled in me, convincing myself that I was capable of making a go of it.

I left the shop door open, to allow the cool breeze to wash over the tired interior.

I had already cleared away most of the remnants of any stock that had been lurking there, piling it into large cardboard boxes and donating them to charity. These had consisted mainly of children's toys, like mini tennis rackets and balls, dinky cars, and tubs of plasticine.

Now I was dealing with the last of it, which was just a few pocket diaries from Christmas that had been reduced and a couple of puzzle books.

I planted my hands on my hips. The bare white shelves looked so forlorn. I knew I should have done all this sooner, but my heart hadn't been in it.

Still, once the whole place had been cleared out, I could concentrate on giving it a good dust throughout and then it would be ready for the decorators to work their magic.

'Reporting for duty, madam.'

My best friend, Cate, was beaming at me through the shop doorway, her white even smile flashing out of her ebony skin. She had tamed her cloud of black spirally curls back from her face with a red dotted bandana.

I took in her denim Capri pants, navy boat shoes and loose white shirt. 'I told you not to bother coming. I can manage.'

Cate rolled her wide dark eyes up to her hairline. 'I know you can, you stubborn mare, but Lucy is taking a Skype work call in the flat, so I thought I'd make myself useful down here.'

Lucy Montgomery and Cate Dyer had been an item for three

years, after Cate had moved here when her parents, both jewellers, had decided to leave Glasgow and retire to the countryside.

Cate was an accomplished jewellery designer in her own right and had meandered into Cassidy's one winter morning in February three years ago, asking if she could place an advert for an accountant in our shop window.

Mum had said she would be glad to and while she was putting it in a prominent place, Cate and I got talking and soon became firm friends. Not only that, but Lucy, a gorgeous redhead with an impressive accountancy pedigree, responded to Cate's advert.

I therefore liked to remind Cate at regular intervals that I was instrumental in getting her and Lucy together.

Cate dismissed my protests about her showing up to help out. 'I can't be all soldering and hammering in the spare room when Luce is discussing diversification and trial balance.'

'Perish the thought.'

As she strode towards me and gave me a hug, I noticed drops of shimmering silver diamond earrings nestling against her hair. 'Oh, they are gorgeous. New design?'

'Yep. I was inspired by the triangular shapes in the local church stained-glass windows.'

I stood back and marvelled at the way the shop light sparked against them.

Cate grinned. 'OK, OK! I get the hint. I'll make you a pair of rose-gold ones.'

'Was I that obvious?'

'In a word, yes.'

We both leant against the shop counter to survey the empty surroundings of what had once been a treasured family business.

Cate asked how Gran and I were bearing up and listened, soft flecks of understanding in her dark eyes, while I explained how keeping occupied seemed to be the only way of keeping myself together. Then I went on to expand about my plans for the shop.

'Gran is really supportive about the whole idea. I think she understands that we couldn't go on as we were. Even I've realised that.'

I stared down at my sparkly trainers. 'The business was starting to lose money and although there is so much nostalgia attached to this place…'

Cate nodded. 'I get it. Your mum and dad would too.'

She reached over to squeeze my hand. 'You don't need Cassidy's as it was to remember them. You've got all your memories up here.' Cate reached a finger up and tapped her temple.

Then she nodded over at the bare shelves. 'I think in a town this size, you're doing the right thing by diversifying.'

'That's what I said to Gran.'

I reached behind the counter to my shoulder bag and pulled out my phone. 'I think we could make a start on some brainstorming.'

Through the open shop door, I spotted a couple of inquisitive older ladies hovering, before exchanging charged glances and moving on. I let out a sigh. 'I know my decision won't be popular with some folks around here, but I'll just have to ignore any negativity and make a go of it.'

'That's what I meant to tell you!' erupted Cate beside me, her eyes wide.

'Bloody hell! You startled me.'

Cate apologised, but was suddenly bubbling with news she wanted to share. 'It all seems to be happening up at what used to be the council HQ.'

Cate folded her arms. 'Looks like a house-warming party is taking place. Connie from the library was up there with her dogs this morning and saw everything from circus acts and musicians to ice statues being ferried in and out.'

She tried to hide a smile. 'Connie said it all looked rather ostentatious and common.'

'Yes, Gran wasn't impressed. We overheard two of the construction workers chatting and someone is definitely moving in up there.'

'So, who's our new neighbour? Any ideas?'

'Lord knows.'

I clapped my hands together in what I hoped was a decisive action. 'Right. Enough talk about ostentatious new neighbours. I suggest we go and grab a takeaway coffee from the bakery and then we can get cracking.'

We wandered out of the bakery, followed by the rich scent of freshly baked crusty bread and the tang of lemon icing that reminded me of summer.

Cate and I clutched our paper cups of dark, silky coffee and made our way back to the shop.

I caught sight of my wavering reflection in the window of the chemist's, all messy blonde ponytail, nautical-striped T-shirt and old jeans. There were traces of weariness under my dark eyes. It was Monday morning and I wasn't sleeping well. I hadn't since the accident. My head was also churning with concerns and apprehension about my new business venture. After everything that had happened, I could hardly expect to look like Margot Robbie.

As we sauntered back to the shop, I spotted a figure standing only a few feet away from it. When Cate and I drew closer, we recognised the ankle-length hessian skirt and floppy straw hat of Mrs Carlucci.

We hadn't known who she was at first and hadn't thought too much about the handsome-featured older lady who had begun appearing occasionally on the high street over the last few days.

It was surprising that she seemed to have returned to the area, after having moved away years ago. Or at least, that was what young Campbell, who worked in the local fishmonger's, had told me. 'One of our customers said her first name is Linda and she's in her seventies,' he remarked, stopping to chat in his lunch hour. 'Other than that, I don't know anything about the woman. Cheerio now!'

Armed with her usual mini bouquets of assorted heather thrusting out from between her ringed fingers, she smiled at us as we approached her. 'Good morning, girls.' Then she dazzled me with her lined green eyes and curtain of dyed dark hair.

Cate and I noticed that not many of the locals engaged much with her. In fact, she appeared to be a rather solitary character.

Mrs Carlucci's expression softened. 'I was so sorry to hear about your parents, Elle.' She let out a sigh. 'Such a tragic business.'

I bit my lip and nodded my appreciation. 'Thank you.'

Mrs Carlucci gave a flicker of a smile and handed me one of the miniature posies of heather, so I delved into my shoulder bag. I located my purse and went to give her a five-pound note.

She refused to take it and thrust it back at me. 'No, you keep the heather. I hear you're re-launching the family business. I hope it brings you luck. You deserve it.'

I nodded and thanked her, placing it inside my bag. 'Thank you. That's very kind of you.'

Cate and I started to move away from Mrs Carlucci, but the next few moments became a sudden tangle of noise and confusion.

Mrs Carlucci had nodded good day to a gentleman in a flat cap and I was jangling the shop keys in my hand, ready to unlock the door. I had only just eased it open and was remarking to Cate about possible new names for the shop, when a grinding noise erupted behind us.

I spun round. 'What the hell was that?'

But Cate was already marching away from me, gesticulating wildly. 'This is a pedestrianised area, you prick!'

My jaw dropped open at the sight of a smoky-grey Jaguar F-type charging along the cobbles. The windows were blacked out, so it was impossible to make out who was driving.

I waved my arms in the air. 'Sorry, you can't come down here. No traffic allowed.'

But whoever was driving either couldn't see me or had decided to ignore what I was saying.

The car kept coming.

'What the hell?! Stop! You can't drive down here!'

But the car continued to move at speed, the milky sunshine glancing off its bodywork.

Everything felt like it was moving through treacle.

Pictures of Mum and Dad, driving along in their car, marvelling at the majestic Highland scenery, lodged themselves behind my eyes.

Panic and burning anger fired up inside of me as I watched the car continue to move.

Something made a strangulated noise from somewhere close by and I jerked my head round.

I realised that the terrified noise had come from Mrs Carlucci. She was rooted to the cobbles just a few feet away from me, her hooded green eyes wide and unblinking as the growling car squealed towards her in a raging spin of tyres.

Oh shit! The car was going to hit her!

Chapter Six

Without thinking, I lunged to the right and threw both my arms out, grabbing her and bundling her against me. Shocked, Mrs Carlucci let out a cross between a cry and a moan, as she recoiled back against my chest. We both tumbled to the ground.

There was a rush of air hissing out of my throat as my back and bottom connected with the cobbles. Shit! That hurt. I let out a groan of pain.

Mrs Carlucci was now sprawled on top of me, all thick black tights and battered straw hat barely clinging to her head. Her posies of heather lay scattered around us.

From where I was lying in a crumpled heap, I could hear Cate's frightened screams rising into the air. 'Jesus! Elle! Mrs Carlucci! Are you both OK?'

When we both groaned, Cate turned her ire on the car and faceless driver. 'You utter prick! You could have killed them!'

Mrs Carlucci struggled to her feet and stretched out her hand to help me up too, still wild-eyed and pale as she stared at the fast car. She couldn't pull her attention away.

The car engine had now died and the vehicle was sitting at an angle, casting a dark shadow across the cobbles of the main street.

Its glinting bonnet was facing the three of us, but the doors remained closed, concealing whoever was driving behind its blacked-out windows. It was unnerving that they could see us but we couldn't see them.

I smoothed back stray hairs which were clinging to my hot, flushed cheeks. Shock and surprise were giving way to fury and relief.

'What the hell did you think you were doing? You can't drive down here!' My voice was quivering as I dusted down the front of my old denims. 'What's the matter with you? Can't you read the signs? You could have killed us!'

Cate and I delivered the full force of our death stares upon the vehicle, with its huge tar-black wheels that reminded me of spiders' webs with their fancy silver trims. Mrs Carlucci was white and shaking. She stood rigid beside me.

I reached out one trembling hand and patted her arm to reassure her.

Was the coward going to get out of the car and apologise? Who the hell was driving this thing? Didn't they realise the power of a car?

There was a pause before the driver side door of the stranger's vehicle finally eased open with a decadent *whoosh* and two long legs emerged.

They belonged to a tall, handsome man with swept-back collar-length raven-black hair and a set of startling blue eyes that were topped by thundery black brows. His wide mouth carried an air of arrogance.

He was dressed in a moss-coloured T-shirt and dark-blue jeans.

My eyes travelled down to his dark-brown lace-up boots.

Everything about him made him look as though he'd just

stepped out of some lavish magazine photoshoot at an abandoned LA viaduct.

I opened my mouth to deliver a verbal tirade, but Cate's hissing voice in my ear made me stop. 'Hang on! I know him from somewhere. I'm sure I've seen him before.'

'On the front cover of *Knobhead Weekly*?' I hissed under my breath.

Beside me, Mrs Carlucci was still examining the man and his beast of a car with a pale, wide-eyed expression. Upon seeing the man, she shot out her hand and clung to my arm. She stuttered something in frantic Italian. The poor woman must be in shock. And no wonder!

I continued to glower at him, but he was too preoccupied surveying our main shopping street with a combination of disdain and bemusement.

He angled his very attractive aquiline profile, and all at once I experienced the same jolt of recognition that Cate had. His face was familiar. But where from?

'I recognise him!' blurted Cate, sudden triumph in her voice.

Mrs Carlucci attempted to steady herself. Her voice sounded odd. 'Who is he?'

'That's Dexter Grayling,' hissed Cate to both of us. 'You must have heard of him. He's that crime writer everyone's been talking about.'

I gave my throbbing arse a tender rub. Adrenaline was still pumping through me.

Cate nodded her curls. 'It's definitely him. He's been described as the rock star of crime writers.'

Fleeting images of him that I'd seen in a Sunday newspaper supplement the other week shot though my head. There had been a set of arty black and white photos of him and quotes about the infamous louche parties he was always throwing. Yes, it was him.

I took in his flash car again. 'More cock than rock.'

He must have heard what I said because he snapped his head

round from critically examining the street. I found myself on the receiving end of a thunderous glower.

He swung his car keys around one finger before locking his car door by pointing the fob at it. The vehicle lit up like a firework, bleeping and flashing. Then he strode towards us.

'Is there somewhere I can get some decent notebooks around here? And I'm not talking about the cheap, thin variety with paper you can spit peas through.'

His voice was deep and educated, but arrogant.

His attention landed on me again and he allowed his gaze to trickle over me, in no hurry to look away.

My cheeks felt like they were suddenly on fire and I almost forgot that he had been seconds away from totalling Mrs Carlucci and me with his car.

My indignation rose again. *Was this man serious*? Was that all he could say after what he'd just done? Mrs Carlucci and I had almost been pinned under his wheels!

'Are you joking?' I finally managed, struggling to control my voice. 'You just sped down here and almost knocked us over and yet you stand there and ask where you can buy notebooks? Have you been drinking?'

'I happened to take a wrong turning, that's all, and I most certainly have not been drinking.'

Mrs Carlucci stared open-mouthed at him. It took her a moment to collect herself. I could see she was still trembling. Her voice quavered. She muttered something else in Italian. 'You shouldn't have been driving round here. It's pedestrians only!' Her breathing was ragged. She illustrated what she'd just said by repeatedly jabbing a shaky finger at the necessary signs. Her eyes glowed a furious green. 'I take it you can read, young man?'

He blinked at her through thrusting dark lashes, as if she had interrupted his train of thought. 'Of course, I can. Oh, never mind.'

Cate and I exchanged disbelieving stares as he continued on, unabashed. Had we just imagined the whole thing?

'I've just moved in to the area. You might know it. Hawk West Hall?'

The three of us sported vacant, confused expressions.

'Well, that's what I've named the place,' he continued on. 'It used to be the local council offices or something.'

He surveyed me, Cate, and Mrs Carlucci in turn. 'I've just moved in up there.'

It took a few moments for my brain to catch up.

Dexter Grayling narrowed his cobalt eyes. 'So, anyway… as I was saying, is there somewhere round here I can get leather-bound notebooks? A Smythson's perhaps?' He grew more irritated by our shocked silence. 'Look, I'm in a hurry. I've got writing deadlines to meet and I'm hosting a house-warming party tonight.'

He scanned the high street. 'Well, if there's no Smythson's, I doubt there's anywhere round here where I can pick up some gold disco balls?'

Mrs Carlucci was incandescent beside me.

I frowned at her and said, 'Are you all right?' But she didn't seem to hear me. She was too preoccupied, pinning Dexter Grayling to the spot with the full force of her ire. 'No, there isn't anything like that here!' she ground out, trying to gather herself together. 'I suggest you pop into the local supermarket. They stock jotters in there.' She hoisted herself up to her full height. 'And as for your balls—'

Horror at Mrs Carlucci's suggestion shot across his face. 'Are you kidding me? Jotters from the local supermarket?'

Mrs Carlucci flapped one hand that wasn't clutching her collection of heather. 'You still haven't apologised for careering down here and almost running us over!' She gestured again at his car. 'Those things are death traps.'

His mouth tightened. 'I did not career down here, as you so

colourfully put it. It's not my fault if you don't look where you're going.'

What?

A bubble of anger burst inside of me. 'We weren't in the wrong, *you* were! And as we've just told you, this is a pedestrianised area anyway.'

Bored with our conversation, he peered up and down the cobbles again. He was muttering to himself. 'Dear lord, is this it?'

Cate's mouth twisted. 'Sorry?'

'Is this the extent of the shops around here?'

Adored crime writer or not, my skin was sizzling with indignation. The sight of Mrs Carlucci, still so distressed, fired up my annoyance even further.

Cate whirled to look at me, as if to say, *Bloody hell! He really is a prize prick!*

I ground my teeth together. 'Well, if your impression of the town is so poor, why are you here in the first place then?'

Dexter Grayling blinked and Cate prickled on the other side of me.

As threads of sunshine appeared and rippled through his dark hair, he indicated to himself, completely ignoring what I'd just said. 'I don't know if you've heard of me,' he announced, attempting to sound bashful and failing, 'but I'm Dexter Grayling.'

The three of us raked him over with disbelieving stares.

'Yes. We know. You're that crime writer,' commented Mrs Carlucci, her voice still raspy and odd.

'That I am.' He struggled to sound self-deprecating.

Dexter Grayling appeared momentarily startled as Mrs Carlucci edged closer to him. She swallowed hard, drinking in his features for a few moments. 'So, am I to assume we won't be receiving an apology from you?'

He made an exasperated noise.

Well, I thought, *when I do stock fancy notebooks in my new business, I won't be rushing to sell them to him, the conceited sod.*

After reading Mrs Carlucci's annoyance, Dexter Grayling muttered an unconvincing apology. 'Look, sorry, OK? No harm done.' He began to move back towards his car. He examined the row of main street shops, deciding that he wouldn't find his extravagant notebooks or disco balls within the immediate vicinity.

But Mrs Carlucci moved after him, shot out a hand, and snatched at his arm. Her emotional green eyes were trained on him like searing radar. Her other hand reached up to her throat and held a silver crescent moon pendant dangling around her neck.

Cate gave me a nudge. 'What is she doing?'

'I've no idea. Maybe she banged her head.'

He frowned down at her hand first and then into her face, before snatching his arm away, as though he had just received a third-degree burn.

The poor woman was still shaken. I knew I was. I also knew I would be sporting a lovely rainbow of bruises tomorrow morning.

Dexter Grayling's eyes grew larger. He stared down at Mrs Carlucci and at her hand gripping at his bare arm. He tugged it away and took a few awkward steps backwards. 'Right,' he coughed, blinking after a few moments of charged silence. 'I guess it's a journey into town then.'

Cate and I gawped at him in disbelief. He stopped to open the driver's side door, glancing over his shoulder at Mrs Carlucci with an odd expression. That was it? No enquiries about how we were?

We watched him take off in a fizz of exhaust.

'Can you believe the audacity of that man?' I gasped. 'He didn't even have the decency to apologise.'

Cate shook her corkscrew curls. 'Talk about up your own arse.'

I offered to make Mrs Carlucci a cup of tea with sugar – I was sure her odd behaviour was due to shock at almost becoming road kill – but she refused.

'Don't you think you ought to see a doctor, Mrs Carlucci?' I suggested gently. 'You still seem rather shaken.'

She was watching the space on the cobbles where, only minutes before, the sleek sports car had been careering along. 'No,' she managed, after a considered pause. 'No thank you. I'm fine, dear.'

I re-entered the shop, with Cate following behind. 'Do you think Mrs Carlucci is OK?' she whispered. 'She was behaving really oddly just now.'

'Well, can you blame her? We were almost totalled by that idiot.' I pulled a furious face. 'Someone like him needs to be taught the meaning of humility.'

I shot her a look, but Cate was pensive.

'What is it?' I asked.

'She was clutching her pendant around her neck as she was staring up at him.'

I shrugged. 'She was most likely worried it had come off when we fell on the cobbles.'

Cate didn't look convinced. She was on the verge of saying something else when Mrs Carlucci appeared in the doorway as though on castors, making us jump. She blinked at both of us, and there was a certain haunted inflection in her handsome, older features.

I asked her again if she was all right and insisted I would make her a cup of tea with a good couple of spoonful's of sugar. Mrs Carlucci thanked me and Cate guided her to one of two old foldaway chairs I'd brought in to the shop that morning.

My attention fell on the large silver pendant dangling around her neck. 'At least you didn't lose your necklace.'

Mrs Carlucci's freckled hand shot up to it. 'Pardon?'

'Your pendant,' clarified Cate. 'I saw you clutch at it when you were talking to that cretin just now.'

All at once, Mrs Carlucci sprung up out of her chair and gathered herself together. She flashed us both nervous glances. 'Thank you for the offer of tea, Elle, but I must be going.'

And with that, she scurried out of the shop and vanished along the street, leaving Cate and me with our heads in a spin.

That evening, I pulled up Dexter Grayling's name on the internet.

Curiosity was gnawing at me and my bottom was letting out intermittent stabs of painful protest. What on earth was a successful author like him doing almost knocking people over in Fir Haven?

I tried to block out the screams and gasps from Mrs Carlucci as I bundled her into my arms and we landed in a heap together on the cobbles. It had been an unwelcome reminder of what had happened to Mum and Dad. Blazing anger lit up in my throat. What the hell did he think he was doing?

I jabbed at my laptop trackpad, grim-faced. Various headlines leapt out of the screen. The first one – 'DELECTABLE DEXTER'S LOVE CRIMES' – was one of the headlines in a recent gossip column and gave, in delicious detail, a string of names of well-known women who had, apparently, been wined and dined by him before being relegated to the status of a 'dear friend'.

A couple of photographs appeared underneath two women with impossibly white teeth who declared that they were still close to Dexter Grayling. 'He stays friends with all his ex-girlfriends,' cooed the first, whose name was Ginger Miller. 'He remembers all our birthdays and we always receive presents at Christmas.'

Good God! Really?!

I could feel my eyebrows rising to my hairline as I read another headline, which trumpeted 'DEXTER GRAYLING – THE ROCK STAR OF THE WRITTEN PAGE'. This article had featured in a newspaper supplement and was not only extolling his ability to write, but also his apparent penchant for leather jackets and rock music.

'CRIME WRITER SLAYS THE OPPOSITION' talked about his phenomenal book sales, not only in the UK, Canada, and Australia, but also in Europe. Then there were assorted glowing reviews of his novels, all of which seemed to feature covers of shadowy alleyways or blurred street lights and his name marching below the titles in huge gold lettering.

I fired through an assortment of photographs of him either escorting various long-haired lovelies or of him alone, staring moodily into the camera. Then my attention was drawn to the latest headline: 'BESTSELLING AUTHOR MAKES SCOTLAND HIS HOME'.

I cleared my throat and began to read.

Dexter Grayling, the crime writer who has burst onto the literary scene and shaken the genre to its foundations, is leaving his native London for Scotland.

The handsome 36-year-old, who has captivated readers with his gripping plots set in museums, airports, and banks, has today announced that he is relocating to Scotland in order to immerse himself in the culture for his next novel, Killing Time, *which is set there.*

Representatives for Grayling would not be drawn on the exact location of his move, however, his agent, Angie Carson, did say that he had discovered a 'simple little place, where [he] feels he can concentrate on his book. If he settles there, he may consider staying permanently.'

I struggled to contain my irritation. 'A simple little place? The bloody cheek! How dare he?!'

'What is it, Elle?'

Gran emerged into the sitting room, her spectacles dangling around her neck and a book thrust under one arm.

She had just returned from her weekly book group and was

unaware of today's events. I pointed at my screen and relayed the story to her about Dexter Grayling moving to the area.

Her eyes almost popped out of her face. 'Are you serious? *The* Dexter Grayling? Living here? Oh, my word! His books are wonderful. So atmospheric!'

'Yes, well, please forgive me, Gran, if I'm not as enthusiastic about our new arrival as you are, but I don't think mowing down the locals is the best way to ingratiate yourself with your new neighbours.'

Gran sank down on the chair opposite me. 'What? He almost knocked you down?'

'Not just me. Cate and Mrs Carlucci too.'

'Bloody idiot!' she snapped, giving the book in her lap a frustrated thump. 'You could have been killed…' She paled at what she was saying. Then she drew herself up. 'Did you just say "Mrs Carlucci"?'

I waggled my bare feet as we sat together in the sitting room at Pebble Brook. 'Yes. She happened to be on the street outside the shop, selling heather.'

Gran shot forward in her chair. She looked stricken. 'Are you sure it was her?'

I blinked at her reaction. 'Yes. Campbell from the fishmonger's told me her name.' I smiled over at her, but Gran didn't reciprocate. She took in a sharp breath.

I leant forward in my armchair. My concern grew. 'Gran, what is it? What's wrong?'

She avoided my gaze and tried to brush away my concern. Her fingers gripped the book resting in her lap. 'Nothing,' she faltered. 'Nothing at all.'

Chapter Seven

It was the beginning of June and the next few days saw me losing myself in preparations to turn the shop into my new stationery empire.

Thanks to the money I had inherited from my parents, I was able to channel funds into the business in the hope it would breathe new life into the shop.

Rose was my mother's middle name, so the idea of calling the shop Paper Roses had jumped into my head whilst I had been browsing merchandising catalogues and agreeing a price with a local artist to have a new sign designed for above the door.

I had never run my own business before, but I had worked for Dad and helped Mum in the shop when it was the newsagent's, so I hoped this would stand me in good stead. Also, Cate, although not a premises owner, was self-employed and instructed me to ask her anything I wanted. 'No question is a silly question!' she had beamed.

It had come as no surprise to me that Grandma had teared up and enveloped me in her arms when I told her of my shop name idea. 'That's beautiful,' she had managed, gazing up at me. 'Your mum would love it.'

Now we were sitting in the shop on the first Friday of June, with a summer shower drizzling down the windows.

We were sitting behind the counter, surveying the painting job that Pete, one of my dad's old tradesmen buddies, had finished the day before.

To reflect the new name, I had decided to go for a palette of pale carnation-pink on the walls, with macaroon cream painted on the shelves and counter.

I'd retained the rustic European oak floor Dad had put in only a couple of years ago, as it complemented the new colour scheme so well.

As for the shop door, I'd decided to be more adventurous and this was now a gleaming shade of deep French rose, with the exterior of the shop now in a simple pale ivory.

The walls were currently bare, but I decided to buy some prints of various types of roses I had found on an art shop website. In the end, I opted for four, one for each wall, which depicted images of cherry parfait, tea roses, prairie roses and a dogrose. They were expected to arrive within the next few days.

With regards to what I wanted Paper Roses to stock, I had opted for more nature-inspired products, which I hoped would not only be more original but which would also reflect the abundance of wildlife that Fir Haven had to offer.

Grandma had enthused when I showed her the butterfly-studded pens and pencils and the hardcover notebooks embossed with flowers, wild birds, and assorted species of trees. Goodness knows if they were posh enough for that idiot Dexter Grayling! As long as he didn't run someone else over though – that was my main concern!

Then there were the vanilla-coloured envelopes and writing paper for the traditionalists, with a selection of rose-gold, mint, ice-blue, and bold Day-Glo designs for the more adventurous stationery aficionados.

I had also ordered a range of funky, modern stationery

(exercise books; pencil cases; sharpeners and erasers) for the local school children. Additionally, there would be a selection of greetings cards and pretty picture frames made out of shells and dried flowers. I planned to expand on these if they did well.

I looked at Grandma sitting beside me as she surveyed the newly painted interior, the bare shelves pleading to be filled with exciting new stock. 'What are you thinking?'

She put her tea cup down on the counter and laced her fingers in her lap. 'How about speaking to that retired lady who runs the painting workshops in the town hall? Maybe she could come up with some bespoke bookmark designs for you? It would be a great USP for you.'

I grinned at her over the rim of my cup. 'Get you! USP? You'll be turning into Gordon Gekko next and shouting about greed being good.'

She fired her silvery bobbed hair back from her face. 'Something tells me you're being sarcastic.'

I smiled and was about to reply when the shop door clattered open, delivering a burst of summer rain onto the wooden floor.

Grandma and I jumped in alarm.

Dexter Grayling was framed by the doorway, his black hair tumbling forward and glistening with raindrops.

I rolled my eyes. Who would he try to run over in his vulgar car today?

I rose up from behind the counter and folded my arms, ready to give him a verbal lashing if his attitude was anything like it had been before.

I waited for some caustic quip or condescending remark, but neither was forthcoming.

Instead, his troubled expression darted from me to my grandmother and then back again. He lifted a hand and swiped his agitated brow.

'You have to help me!' he pleaded in desperation. 'You have to help me!'

Chapter Eight

My grandmother blinked at the long-legged, dark-haired man who had just barrelled through the shop door. Dashes of raindrops were glinting on the sleeves of his black hoodie.

Her appraising silver eyes travelled down the length of him to the drips of water hitting the wooden floor.

Recognition reared up in her face. Grandma rose to her feet and rearranged the sugar-pink chiffon scarf draped around her neck. 'That's him,' she croaked out of the corner of her mouth. 'That's Dexter Grayling.'

I gave a bored sigh. 'Yep.'

He rivered an agitated hand through his damp hair. 'That woman the other day… the one selling the heather…'

'You mean Mrs Carlucci,' I said. 'The one you almost pinned under your wheels.'

From out of the corner of my eye, Gran's body stiffened at the mention of her name. I hadn't imagined it. That was the second time I had seen her react oddly. What was it with my gran and Mrs Carlucci?

But I didn't have an opportunity to consider the possibilities, because Dexter Grayling was scowling again from under his brows. 'Oh, not that again. Look, that was a misunderstanding and we've already been through all that.'

I arched one brow.

'I need to speak to this Mrs Carlucci. Do you know where she lives?'

More charged glances between my gran and I were exchanged. Before I had time to say anything, she marched up in front of Dexter Grayling and shook her head. 'No, I'm afraid we don't.'

'But you must do! I thought everyone in all these parochial little towns literally knew how many fillings their neighbours had!'

What an arrogant shit! One of my feet tapped on the floor in irritation. 'If you mean, do we have a community spirit here, then the answer is yes. If you mean, are we all nosey beggars who pry into each other's lives, then it's a no.' I narrowed my eyes at him. 'You don't get that type of support in big cities.'

Dexter Grayling's square jaw jutted out, but he didn't reply.

Grandma's mouth, slicked in her favourite shade of berry lipstick, twitched with irritation. 'Mrs Carlucci doesn't live here in Fir Haven, that much I do know.'

'So, where does she live then?' he persisted, thrusting both flailing hands into the pockets of his zipped-up hoodie. 'There must be someone round here who knows.'

'Not that I know of,' I shrugged. 'She's only just begun reappearing here again. She turns up from time to time to sell heather and crafts. She keeps herself to herself.'

He sighed in disbelief. 'What sort of bloody place is this?!'

My dislike for him was ramping itself up, even though I grudgingly had to admit he was very good-looking.

Grandma frowned. 'Did you want to apologise to Mrs Carlucci? Is that why you're so anxious to speak to her?'

He fidgeted. 'Yes. No. Er, I mean…'

I surveyed the well-known author and struggled to

comprehend how someone who wrote such successful crime novels was now standing in front of us babbling incoherently.

'My granddaughter and her friend deserve an apology,' sniffed my gran. 'It's not every day you're almost knocked down by a Formula One racing car.'

But Dexter Grayling was too entangled in his own dilemma. He suddenly looked rather lost and pale.

'Are you all right?' I asked, puzzled.

'Of course I am! I'm fine!' he barked. Then he thought better of it. 'Actually, I'm not too sure that I am.'

'Well, excuse me if I don't extend much sympathy,' countered Grandma, 'but you did almost put my granddaughter and two other people in hospital – or worse.'

Dexter Grayling didn't argue. He fidgeted from foot to foot in his charcoal Merino wool trainers.

He took a few steps closer to us, leaving a vivid trickle of rainwater stain on the floorboards. 'This Mrs Carlucci,' he began, swallowing hard, 'I need to find her. I need to speak to her.' He rubbed at his stubbled chin. A hint of pink bloomed on his cheekbones.

'Whatever for?' asked Gran.

Dexter Grayling cleared his throat. Conflicting emotions charged over his face. He was struggling to decide what to tell us, if anything at all. There was a long pause. 'Look, I know this might sound… well, actually, there's no might about it…'

I shot him an irritated look. 'Mr Grayling, what are you trying to say?'

The author swallowed and tilted his chin. 'I think that woman,' he said, the words struggling to leave his mouth, 'this Mrs Carlucci… well… I think she put some sort of curse on me.'

Chapter Nine

What was he talking about? Had he just stumbled out of one of his own flamboyant parties?

It took a few seconds for what he had said to be digested and even then I wasn't sure I'd heard him correctly. 'Pardon?'

Dexter Grayling shuffled in front of us, as the raindrops continued to chase each other down the bottle-glass windows of the shop. 'I know it sounds crazy,' he rushed out, 'but she's done something to me. I can't write; I can't come up with any ideas…'

I lifted one amazed brow. 'I think it's called writer's block?'

He narrowed his bright-blue eyes at me. 'I'm only too aware of writer's block and what that feels like.' He raised his chin. 'I'm very fortunate not to experience writer's block very much at all.'

'Of course you don't,' I whispered under my breath.

'But this isn't that.'

I watched him throw his hands up in the air and let them fall back down by his sides. 'I know it sounds ridiculous, but this feels unlike anything I've ever experienced before and it started just after we had that… er… altercation a few days ago.'

'What exactly did Mrs Carlucci do? Can you explain?'

interrupted Gran, lacing and unlacing her suddenly anxious hands.

I swung my head to look at my grandmother so fast I almost gave myself whiplash. What?! Why was she asking him that? If I didn't know any better, I'd think she almost believed him! She had been so tired and was still grieving just like I was. That must account for her rather odd behaviour.

I continued to stare at her in disbelief. Surely this conceited writer with the rock star swagger wasn't charming her? It wasn't like her to be taken in by appearances.

A flicker of relief crossed Dexter Grayling's chiselled face, that someone was prepared to listen to him.

My grandmother remained silent as he described his lack of creativity, inspiration, and motivation. 'I don't have any compunction to write and that isn't like me at all.' He rubbed furiously at his forehead. 'I'm waking up every morning with just this feeling of emptiness. I feel like I'm not me anymore, as though I'm some sort of imposter. And it's been happening ever since I met her.'

'You didn't meet her,' I corrected. 'You almost ran her over. There's a difference.' I glanced again at my gran. 'Perhaps you're feeling a bit run-down, Mr Grayling?'

His gaze flashed at me. 'If that's your attempt at a joke, I'm not finding it very funny.'

This was ridiculous! I was supposed to be pressing on with preparations for Paper Roses, not talking magic spells with a man who no doubt winked at his own reflection every morning before leaving the house.

What was even more frustrating was that my grandmother seemed to believe him!

Turning his attention back to my gran, Dexter said, 'I felt fine until that woman touched me on the arm.'

I gave my head a mild shake. Was this man for real? First he criticises Fir Haven and its lack of modern amenities, and then he's accusing someone of using the dark arts on him! And he only moved into the area five minutes ago.

Dexter's voice broke through my thoughts as he emphasised again, 'I was fine before I arrived here.' He cleared his throat. 'As soon as she spoke to me like that and touched my arm, I didn't feel right at all.'

'You did almost put the poor woman in hospital,' I pointed out.

Cue more scowls from beneath his arched black brows. 'I did apologise.'

'Excuse me! You most certainly did not. If you think what you said was an apology, you're sadly mistaken…'

It was at that point that my grandmother raised her voice. 'Elle. Please! Let him speak. Mr Grayling, do carry on.'

Dexter Grayling looked grateful. 'Please call me Dexter.'

My mouth flopped open. She believed him. She was actually taking what he was saying seriously!

Oh, good grief. He was a piece of work.

My grandmother acknowledged him. 'I'm Clara.'

What is this? Some sort of love-in?

Ignoring the waves of disbelief I was emanating, Dexter Grayling continued to tell Gran that after returning to his sprawling pile, he had been overcome with strange, almost flu-like symptoms. 'And then things just got worse from there.'

His eyes bore a desperate glint. 'I'm supposed to be well into the first draft of my next novel by now.'

'Well, there you are then,' I pointed out. 'You've likely had some sort of virus and it'll take a few days for you to throw it off.'

Dexter growled something under his breath. He flicked me an undiscernible look. 'She muttered something too,' he went on, addressing Gran again. 'I couldn't make out much of it and didn't give it too much thought at the time, but over the last day or two it's been playing on my mind.'

'What did she say?' asked my grandmother, paling.

Dexter crinkled up his eyes in concentration. He hesitated. 'Some of it was in Italian and then she said something about Fir Haven, but I couldn't make out the rest of it.'

Oh, this was crazy!

I turned to my grandmother, deciding I would get her to rest and have a cup of tea, but the conversation screeched to a halt when my grandmother's knees buckled and she reached out to grab hold of the shop counter.

'Gran!'

Chapter Ten

'Grandma! What's wrong?'

I snatched at her with one arm, while Dexter leapt round and pulled forward the chair she had risen out of.

'Are you ok?' I asked her, my heart sticking in my throat. 'What is it?'

She took a few breaths and flapped away my concern. 'I'm fine, dear. It's just a little warm in here, that's all.'

I frowned down at her as she scooped back some of her hair behind her ears. The June rain was splattering against the windows, and the radiator that heated the shop wasn't on. 'It isn't that warm in here, Gran.'

She delivered one of her gimlet-eyed looks and patted me on one worried hand. 'Stop fussing, Elle. I was standing up a little too long, that's all.'

'Maybe you should get checked over by a doctor,' suggested Dexter. 'You did turn very white.'

'What, whiter than normal?' she joked, tugging at her chiffon scarf. 'I'm Scottish, young man. We're not known for being sun-kissed.'

I shook my head in exasperation. 'You almost fainted.'

'Rubbish! My legs got a bit tired. You wait till you're my age.'

I fetched her a glass of water from the kitchen and she sipped at it. 'So, go on, Dexter,' she prodded after taking a long drink.

Oh, good grief. Must we?

He eyed us both. 'I know how all this must sound – nuts.'

What's nuts about telling us someone's put a curse or spell or some other such nonsense on you in twenty-first-century Scotland?

I wanted to say as much, but the last thing I wanted to do was upset my grandmother further, so I bit it back.

Dexter eyed me with blatant suspicion. His voice was deep and rumbly. 'You seem to be friendly with this Mrs Carlucci.'

My eyebrows travelled up to my hair line. 'I don't know her.'

Grandma took another shy sip of her water.

'But you're local,' he pushed on. 'And you must have so much knowledge about the local history of this place.'

'Yes, I have some,' I admitted after a pause, 'but I don't know about every single family or all the comings and goings around here…'

'Can you help me?' he interrupted, his eyes glittering. I found myself admiring his impossibly long and spikey black lashes, before reminding myself that I didn't care for him.

'Can you help me find this Mrs Carlucci?'

Was it Gran he was speaking to?

I followed his gaze. *Nope.* Shock registered inside me. *He's talking to me.*

It took a few moments for me to form some coherent words. 'So let me get this right: you're asking me to help you locate Mrs Carlucci so you can ask her to break the curse she put on you?'

Grandma eyed me from her seat, clutching her glass of water. She still didn't say anything.

'I'm desperate,' he admitted.

'Gee. Thanks for that.'

'You know what I mean.'

I gestured to my empty freshly painted shop with its bare shelves. 'I don't know if you've noticed, but I'm trying to open a business.'

'I think you should help this young man.' My grandmother's voice pricked the air.

My mouth popped open. I stared down at her, incredulous. 'What?'

She shifted in her chair. 'I can help you in the shop with anything else that needs doing and you've Cate's offer of help too.'

This was worrying. Really worrying. I'd never seen her like this before. 'Are you serious, Gran?'

'Very.'

I shook my head, unable to comprehend what she was saying. 'Gran, I'm not being rude but are you feeling all right?'

'Perfectly fine. Why?'

My cheeks pinged under the gaze of Dexter Grayling and my grandmother.

'So you believe me?' Dexter asked, in a way that made it sound like an appeal.

She didn't respond, but there was an odd angling of her mouth now, which she got when she was thinking about something. My mum had been the same.

'Grandma?'

She made an exasperated noise. The silence was heavy until she spoke again. 'Yes. I believe you.'

Her tone was grim. Hesitant.

I must be dreaming all this. Hallucinating. My head whizzed from my gran to Dexter and back again. 'How can you?' I half laughed. 'Gran?'

She shifted her grey gaze away. 'Nobody would make up something like that.'

Dexter's panicked expression was now one of temporary but tense relief. 'Thank you.'

'That's why I think we should help him.'

My eyes rolled in their sockets. Then a sudden feeling of foreboding stole over me. '*We?*'

Grandma's expression was pinched.

'But the shop,' I argued, drinking in the bare surroundings with rising concern. *Is she ill? Has this Dexter Grayling character manipulated her in some way? No. He can't have done. This is the first time she's met him.*

I struggled to keep the concern out of my voice. 'No disrespect, Mr Grayling, but we barely know you. I'm sorry but as you can see, I've got other priorities right now.'

Grandma straightened her back as she sat there. 'I've just told you, Elle, I can deal with any issues about Paper Roses on your behalf. I'm not senile – yet.'

I couldn't conceal my shock. Dexter Grayling had managed to work his magic on my gran within the space of twenty minutes of meeting her. Frustration and worry gnawed at me. 'But, Gran, this is crazy!'

I shrank backwards when she turned in her chair and appraised me with a hard stare. 'No, it isn't.'

There was something about the way she spoke to me; I had never seen her looking so rigid and intense before. 'Elle, have I ever lied to you or misled you?'

'Don't be silly, Gran. Of course you haven't.'

'And I'm not about to start now,' she announced, flicking back her hair. 'So, are you going to help this young man or not?'

Chapter Eleven

I stood, bewildered, in front of Dexter Grayling and my grandmother. Both sets of eyes pinned me like lasers to the shop floor.

Gran had never mentioned anything about Mrs Carlucci, so why the sudden interest now? But as soon as the literary world's answer to Ian Somerhalder had burst in and dialled up the pleading charm, she'd experienced some sort of personality bypass. And then there was that odd moment when I'd thought she was going to faint. Was she ill? Was there something she was reluctant to tell me?

Her voice disrupted my skittering thoughts. 'You're always talking about the importance of community spirit and how we're so inclusive here in Fir Haven, Elle.'

'Yes, I know, but…'

This wasn't like her at all. What the hell was going on here?

I pushed my hands into the back pockets of my jeans. I would speak to her again later, when we were on our own. Confusion flitted across my features. For some reason, this seemed to mean a great deal to her. What if she was harbouring some serious illness after all and didn't know how to tell me? Perhaps this was her way of trying to come to terms with things in her own mind?

Random questions leapt into my head. This was ridiculous. Surely she knew she could confide in me about anything? But she looked so pleading now; so intense. She had always been there for me.

I felt like I had no option. And the way Dexter Grayling was appraising me was unnerving. Frustration, worry for my Gran, and irritation battled away inside of me. 'Yes, all right,' I snapped, after a protracted pause. 'I'll see if I can help, but this place comes first, OK?'

'Of course. Thank you, sweetheart.'

Dexter Grayling murmured something which I think might have been an attempt at a thank-you, although it could also have been a hiccup. He placed his business card on top of the counter. Like him, it was on the ostentatious side.

I examined the white card with its gold lettering. It bore his name and his email and mobile number. 'Give me a call once you've had a chance to think about how we should proceed with this, OK? But I would appreciate it if we can get going on finding this woman as soon as possible.'

I fired a stony look at him. Who did he think I was? His PA?

I scribbled down my contact details on a piece of old envelope at the bottom of my bag and thrust it at him.

He vanished back out of the door and into the rain-slicked street.

As soon as the shop door clicked closed behind him, I turned to my gran. 'What on earth is this all about? Have I stepped into some alternate universe?'

She remained seated and dashed some imaginary dust from the top of the pristine counter.

'You believe him, don't you? You really do think there's something in what he says about Mrs Carlucci.'

I folded my arms across my chest and sank back down into my

chair opposite her. 'Why are you so keen for me to help him, Gran?'

She didn't make eye contact with me.

'What is it? What's going on?'

She didn't reply.

'Gran? I'm totally confused by all this. You actually believe what Dexter Grayling said about Mrs Carlucci?'

'We need more investment in Fir Haven,' she insisted. 'Dexter Grayling is wealthy. He can inject some much-needed cash into the town and raise our profile.'

I examined her. 'And that's why you insisted I help him?'

'Yes.'

'No other reason?'

Gran shifted uncomfortably in her seat. 'Like what?'

I shrugged my shoulders. 'I don't know.'

I watched her rise to her feet, eager to kill off this particular conversation. 'I'll brew a fresh pot of tea and then we can make a start on pulling together ideas for your grand opening!'

Chapter Twelve

'And Clara wouldn't elaborate on any of it?' asked Cate over the phone that evening.

I pushed my mobile closer to my ear. I had retreated to my bedroom.

I dropped my voice lower. I could hear my grandma pottering around further down the hallway.

'No. She assures me she isn't ill. I've asked her a few times today why she was so adamant I help Dexter Grayling, but she just changes the subject or makes light of it. She insists she's only being neighbourly.'

I played with my ponytail. 'I don't believe her. There's something she's not telling me.' I shifted on my bed and pushed myself upright against my pillows. Outside, the milky early evening June sky was being buffered by clouds. 'She's keeping something from me, but goodness knows what it is or why.'

I waggled my bare toes, which were dipped in a slick of baby-pink polish. 'We've always been so close. Sometimes, when I was a teenager, I would tell her things that I felt I couldn't even tell Mum and Dad.'

Cate's dusky voice was a welcome distraction. 'And she will

confide in you again. Whatever's going on, Clara will tell you. She must have her own reasons for not saying anything.'

I grudgingly admitted she was right.

'She'll tell you in her own time.'

Cate then advised me in the meantime to focus on Paper Roses and to give some thought to what would be the best thing to do about Dexter Grayling.

'He must think I wear a trilby, raincoat, and dark glasses,' I ground out, picking at the corner of my duvet cover. 'I've got no idea what he expects me to do. I'm not experienced in the dark arts.'

Cate laughed into my ear. 'Well, he has only just moved here, so my guess is he wants you to speak to some of the locals and see if they know anything about Mrs Carlucci. And please try not to worry about Clara's little turn today. She was most likely a bit tired and dehydrated.'

I made a noise. I wasn't convinced by that explanation.

'Remember,' reminded Cate, 'I can help you out in the shop and that will give Clara a break.'

My to-do list was expanding at an alarming rate. As soon as I ticked something off, another urgent task would take its place.

'If you don't push Clara to tell you what's troubling her, you might find she suddenly confides in you anyway.'

I wished I had Cate's belief. My grandmother and I each possessed a streak of stubbornness that ran in the family. Mum often joked that the word *determination* was stamped behind our ears.

'Anyway,' smiled Cate down the phone, 'until that happens, I think you're just going to have to accept she's not going to divulge anything until she feels ready.'

'That's always the case with my gran.'

'And in the meantime, let me know what I can do to help.'

'Thanks, Cate. I appreciate that.'

I tried to pull up ideas and images for Paper Roses in my head, but right now, thoughts and concerns about my grandmother were cancelling out everything else.

I had only just finished my conversation with Cate when my mobile trilled again and a number I didn't recognise glowed up at me.

Before I had a chance to say anything, a gruff male voice made me blink. 'So, any thoughts about what we're going to do?'

I sat up straighter on my bed. It took a few seconds to realise it was Dexter Grayling. He obviously didn't go in for small talk. 'Excuse me?'

His voice was weighed down with frustration. 'I can't let this situation slide.' There was a heavy pause. 'I've got deadlines; I've got my agent pressing me to deliver my next novel…'

I bit my lip. 'I'm sure you can appreciate, Mr Grayling, that you aren't the only person around here who has work commitments.'

'Yes, I'm aware of that,' he snapped, not seeming to be aware of anything else other than his own predicament. 'But I'm telling you, that bloody Carlucci woman did something…'

I pulled a dismissive face and drummed my fingers on my jean-clad legs.

'Your grandmother believed me.'

That was a low blow.

My attention moved from his voice to the sound of my gran's digital radio humming away from her annexe.

I had to find out what was going on and, while I was certain Dexter Grayling's author's imagination was overruling his common sense, that couldn't explain my grandmother's odd and surprising behaviour.

'Paper Roses opens next Friday,' I said. 'I've been thinking… it might be a good idea for you to come along to the shop opening. It would be a good opportunity to meet some of the locals.'

Dexter was indignant. '*Next Friday*? That's a week away. I can't wait till then! Ms Cassidy, I don't think you fully appreciate my situation.'

I sat bolt upright on my bed, rattled by his attitude. 'Shouting at me won't resolve anything!'

Good grief! If he wanted to make an effort to fit in here, he was going about it the wrong way!

I rolled my eyes at his unenthusiastic grunt down the line.

'I suggest you *walk* to the shop on Friday morning,' I said calmly after a beat. 'I wouldn't try to take out any more of the locals, if I were you.'

I could hear him grinding his teeth. 'Very funny. When's your Netflix comedy special coming out?'

I stuck my tongue out at my phone. 'Well?'

'OK. OK. I'll be there. It seems I don't have much choice.'

Chapter Thirteen

It was the day of our official opening and Paper Roses reminded me of a decadent candy-pink and white cupcake.

Both its exterior and interior sparkled, with its newly erected sign and stripy pink-and-white canopy.

Gran, Cate and I had constructed the inaugural window display out of lilac and ballet-slipper-pink notebooks. I'd placed them on top of sheets of tissue paper in the same shades and sprinkled rose petals over and around them.

Arranged beside them were an assortment of rose-gold and silver pens and pencils I'd chosen to stock.

The interior of the shop was now bursting with everything from glittery greetings cards to handmade bookmarks depicting wildlife, as designed by the local artist my gran had suggested.

On the shelves I'd dotted some fancy photo frames, as well as unusual paperweights I'd spotted on the internet, which were made by a glass-blowing artist on the coast. They ranged from extravagant snow globe designs to ones that contained sea creatures and miniature shells.

I'd decided to offer complimentary pink champagne and

cupcakes decorated with edible roses to all the locals who came along to the opening.

The cakes had been supplied by our local bakery and rested on cerise platters beside the elegant flutes of popping champagne all neatly arranged on trestle tables just inside the shop.

I'd secreted my iPod underneath the counter and chosen a selection of recognisable classical pieces, such as Vivaldi and Mozart, to play in the background.

I took a breath as I hovered in the doorway, my nerves and excitement tumbling around me.

As if reading my merry-go-round of thoughts, my grandmother edged up to me and gave me a warm hug. 'Dana and Gareth would be so proud of you, darling.'

'You think?'

'I know.'

I smoothed the sides of my hair, which I had piled up on top of my head. I adjusted the collar of my oyster-coloured pussycat-bow blouse. I'd teamed it with my favourite pair of black fitted trousers and, hoping to be swamped with customers, I had slipped on my jewelled ballet pumps, which were very comfy. No heels today!

Grandma looked resplendent in an ankle-length wine-coloured dress with a long matching cardigan. Her hair swung about her jawline in its trademark shimmery bob.

'Are you ready?' she asked.

I nodded and watched her tap over to the door and swing round the pink wooden sign to proclaim us open. My stomach pirouetted.

The clock on the far wall struck 9 am.

I had experienced a fitful night's sleep, worrying about how Paper Roses would be received by the community. Then my thoughts would career in the dark to my gran. What was it that had troubled her that day, when she had almost passed out? And why had she been so adamant that I help Dexter Grayling?

I had tried to raise the subject again with her in the last couple of days, but she had brushed my questions aside, insisting it was because of what he could do for the area. Then she would attempt to distract me further by discussing Paper Roses.

I had sent Dexter a text, reminding him of what day we were opening and what time. To be honest, I'd imagined him to be one of those louche individuals that didn't surface until noon.

Instead, he made me flinch in surprise as he bounded through the door as soon as Gran had unlocked it, his blue eyes concealed behind aviator sunglasses. He did look very attractive, but I pushed that to one side.

He stared around him, disappointment weighing down his shoulders. He swiped off his sunglasses and then his attention settled on me. His gaze lingered for a few moments. 'Good morning, Ms Cassidy. You look… very pretty.'

It took a moment for his compliment to sink in. 'Oh. Right. Thank you. So do you… I mean, you look very dashing.'

There was a quiver of a smile at his mouth. 'Thank you.'

There was an oddly charged silence and then he flipped back to being brusque again. 'So, where is everyone?' He pushed his mirrored sunglasses into the pocket of his crisp white shirt and they dangled there. 'We need to get on with this. The sooner we locate this Carlucci woman, the better.'

I flicked a look at Gran, but she was distracted by a few expectant faces appearing at the windows. 'Oh, here are your first customers, Elle.'

A steady trickle of locals came into the shop, eager to see what the 'Cassidy girl' had been up to. They partook of the swirling flutes of pink Champagne and savoured the fat iced cupcakes.

I tried to conceal my initial disappointment as they indulged in the complimentary treats, but only Mrs Cavendish, one of Gran's book club buddies, bought one of the sea shell picture frames within the first hour. The others mooched about, picking up items and then putting them down again. It was only when one of the book club ladies recognised Dexter that half the female population of Fir Haven suddenly besieged Paper Roses.

Dexter eyed me from where he was swigging champagne and being polite to a gaggling throng of admiring ladies, clutching copies of his various novels which they had brought with them and asking him to sign them. He fought his way through. 'Dear god! I might not get out of here alive!' Then he pinned me to the spot with his intense gaze. 'I've had no bloody luck finding out anything at all about Mrs Carlucci. I can't get a word in! If I'm asked one more time if I'm married…'

I lifted one brow. 'Yes, all that fawning adoration must be awful.'

Dexter eyed me over his half-empty champagne glass. 'It depends who's doing the fawning.'

My cheeks flushed pink as Grandma stepped up. 'Isn't this wonderful? More customers!' she trilled.

Dexter pushed himself away from the counter and drained the last of his champagne. 'Time for me to mingle. We have to find that woman.'

Gran edged closer to him. 'Please be tactful. And watch what you ask and how you ask it. Some of the folks round here can be rather… protective of their privacy.'

This whole situation was laughable. More admiring gaggles of women attempted to flutter around Dexter, asking for his autograph. It was like something out of Cinderella, when the prince was clutching the glass slipper and gaggles of women were eager to see if it fitted.

Dexter nodded. 'I will be circumspect, Clara.'

She flushed a little pink and lightly touched his sleeve, before he was swallowed up by more autograph hunters.

What on earth had I let myself in for?

I didn't even like the man!

Chapter Fourteen

Dexter's gaze followed mine as a cluster of recognisable locals buzzed through the shop door and each took a glinting champagne flute before starting to meander around.

Grandma, who was putting a picture frame and a couple of postcards through the till for two backpackers, eyed me with intent. Then she returned to what she was doing.

Mrs Davenport, the retired art gallery receptionist, wandered in with her husband. They were exclaiming about how lovely the newly painted Paper Roses was.

From what I could remember, May Davenport's knowledge of everyone and everything connected with Fir Haven was bordering on encyclopaedic. If she didn't know anything about the Carlucci family, then it was unlikely anyone else would.

A glimmer of optimism crept through me as I thought about what I was going to say while I began to approach her and her husband Douglas. If, for whatever reason, my own grandmother was reluctant to tell me anything about Linda Carlucci, then they might.

Both were immaculately turned out as usual. May was in a pair of slate-grey linen trousers and a crisp white shirt that fluttered loose, while Douglas was wearing a mustard polo shirt and beige trousers. They looked like they'd just been for a relaxing jaunt around the golf club.

Their sweeps of soft white hair gave them both an added air of authority.

I complimented May on the delicate pearl earrings she was wearing and enquired after their three grandchildren. Once May had enthused about their various skills at cello, ballet, and basketball, I mentioned Linda Carlucci.

My eyebrows rocketed up when I noticed the charged look Douglas aimed at his wife.

May became suddenly fascinated by the swilling soft-pink liquid rocking against either side of her glass. 'Why are you asking about her?'

I glanced over my shoulder at Dexter, who had desperation etched into his expectant gaze. He was bobbing his dark head up and down over the sea of the increasing number of visitors, in an attempt to get a clearer view of what was unfolding.

'I was just curious,' I went on to explain. 'Mrs Carlucci has been seen again recently in the area.'

I clung to the hope that May hadn't already been informed of this by the Fir Haven gossip brigade, who, although few in number, moved with impressive speed and stealth.

The response I got wasn't the one I was expecting. 'Elle, you don't want to get involved with the likes of her,' blurted Douglas, taking a swig from his glass.

May delivered a sharp dig of her elbow and it connected with her husband's side. He winced. 'Ow!'

I pretended not to notice. 'What makes you say that?'

Chatter and sweet classical music mingled with the scent of iced cupcakes and new stationery.

May's long face tightened. Now it was her turn to gulp her champagne and avoid eye contact with me. What on earth were all the meaningful glances and pinched mouths for? Where Linda Carlucci was concerned, it seemed to be catching.

During the couple of times I'd come across Mrs Carlucci, she had seemed a very pleasant woman.

'Oh, you know what this place is like,' May forced out. 'If folks around here don't know something, they make it up!'

Douglas Davenport dropped his eyes to his leather loafers.

'Like what?'

May clutched at the stem of her flute. 'Fanciful nonsense.'

'Yes, but what?'

They exchanged more glances before turning back to me with forced smiles. Neither of them answered.

What on earth did the charged looks and strained smiles mean? And why all the secrecy and mystery?

I shrugged, still channelling what I hoped was a casual air of interest. 'Nobody seems to know where she lives. I know she used to stay here in Fir Haven.'

Douglas and May didn't reply. They waggled their flutes at the other curious shoppers milling around them. 'You've got a wonderful turnout.'

Like my gran, they were trying to move the conversation on.

But why?

'The town needs some cheering up after the news about the nature reserve. Isn't it terrible?' Douglas Davenport's voice interrupted my thoughts.

A feeling of foreboding reared up inside me. I blinked at him. 'Sorry?'

May frowned at her husband beside her and took a genteel sip of her champagne, while she admired one of the new rose prints hanging up on the walls. 'From what we've heard, unless the footfall improves, the council have said they will have no alternative but to sell off the land for holiday homes.'

Chapter Fifteen

My mouth formed a series of odd shapes, but nothing came out.

I stared, wide-eyed, at them both. Had I heard them correctly? 'No… that can't be right.' The nature reserve was the beating heart of Fir Haven.

May blinked at me. 'I have it on good authority that it is.' She shook her head. 'All those suits – all they care about is money.'

Douglas nodded in agreement. 'You can forget about flora and fauna where profits are concerned.'

My stomach lurched. I felt like the floor underneath me was shifting. All that tumbling, gorgeous woodland and the wildlife it protected shimmered through my mind. The ferns, waggling their inquisitive fingers; the carpets of soft bluebells; the proud soldier oaks, willows and ash trees; the glassy streams trailing over slick rocks.

Images of me with Mum and Dad, rambling through the grass, made my heart thud faster. The skittish grey squirrels racing up the tree trunks and the exuberant throb of birdsong.

If you were fortunate enough, you might even glimpse a flank of red deer melting into the undergrowth or catch sight of a lithe fox.

Anger and trepidation surged through me. I struggled to keep my composure. I'd already lost both my parents; I wasn't prepared to lose a place where the three of us used to spend so much precious time together. 'We can't allow this to happen,' I croaked, staring wildly at both of them. 'We've got to do something.'

They didn't look convinced that I would be able to do much, but nodded anyway. 'There's talk of the locals coming together to form Save the Reserve Action Group.'

They drained their glasses and sauntered off, leaving me standing there, shock, fury, and determination waging war inside my chest.

Dexter had been examining my stock of wild bird notebooks close to the till, but abandoned it when I approached. 'Well? What did they say? Did you manage to find out anything?'

I could feel myself quivering with rising frustration and rage, unable to answer. 'About what?'

His bold blue eyes bore into mine. 'About the ramifications of Brexit. What do you think? This ruddy curse or whatever it is that I'm under.'

My brow furrowed up at him. 'What? Oh. Yes. That.'

Dexter's stubbled jaw throbbed. 'That *is* what you were talking to that couple about, isn't it?'

I fired my ponytail back over my shoulder. 'Yes. No. Well, I did ask them about Mrs Carlucci to begin with…'

Dexter made a grunting noise as a couple more customers squeezed past him to read the verses in a stack of handmade wedding cards. 'But what happened then? Did you veer off on a tangent?' His tone was one of building frustration. 'Did you find out that the local milkman had given someone the wrong change? Or perhaps the fishmonger closed half an hour earlier than usual?'

I folded my arms. 'For your information, I've just found out that the local nature reserve is under threat.'

I waited for the enormity of this to sink in with him.

Dexter pushed his hands into his trouser pockets. 'Look, I do sympathise. Really. I know the town prides itself on its wildlife.' He flashed me a look. 'Can't something be done to stop the plans?'

I rubbed at my temple and fought to keep my stunned bubbling temper under control. All I could think of right now was that beautiful reserve being wiped out for some naff development – and going with it would be the soul of Fir Haven.

Frustration pumped through me. 'You probably haven't been up to the reserve yet.'

The lilting music in the background was now Mozart, soaring and bobbing around the clusters of curious visitors to Paper Roses. I bit my lip. 'It's beautiful; like something out of a water colour painting.' I tried to read the flashes in his eyes. 'As a writer, I'm sure you would be able to appreciate it.'

'But that's the bloody point, Ms Cassidy. I'm not a writer. At least, not right now, thanks to that ruddy woman, Carlucci.'

More pictures of the nature reserve, all burgeoning with pastel colours and dew, prodded me.

Out of the corner of my eye, I could see Gran observing our exchange with concern.

'I'm telling you,' he ground out a little louder this time, 'that woman has done something to me and I need to find out what.'

I blinked and stared incredulously up at him. 'Is that all you care about? Yourself?'

Dexter moved to protest but the combination of pink champagne and the awful news about the reserve was firing up my fury. 'That reserve means so much to so many families here.'

'I'm sure it does,' he replied. 'And I'm sure it's beautiful. But right now, I need your help.'

I took a faltering step backwards, one hand fluttering to the bow of my blouse. Oh my God. I felt like everything that was dear to me was slipping away. And this man, handsome though he might be, was more concerned about his own predicament.

My little world felt like it was imploding. Who had I been kidding? I honestly thought I could make a future for myself after the mess with Lloyd? After the way he hurt me and let me down? That I could move on from what had happened to Mum and Dad?

I pressed my lips together. 'I'm sure you do, but I'm afraid I can't.'

'Pardon?!'

I knew I'd promised Gran I would help, but right now, what with opening Paper Roses and the loss I had experienced, everything felt like it was about to tumble down around me.

I dropped my voice while my grandmother chatted to a couple of her chess buddies. 'Priorities, Mr Grayling. It's called priorities.' I stared around at the pink and macaroon-white walls of the shop. 'I can't be everything to everybody. I just can't.' Dexter stared down at me with concern. 'I'm sorry but I can't help you.'

And with that, I marched back towards the counter.

Chapter Sixteen

Dexter stormed out of the shop, oblivious to the admiring glances of two teenage girls.

Grandma thanked a dapper gentleman in a Panama hat, who had deliberated over a sparkly birthday card for his granddaughter before opting for the one with a unicorn made out of tartan fabric. 'What was all that about?' she asked.

I could feel a guilty blush staining my cheeks. *Oh no.* Now I had to explain it to her. I cleared my throat. 'Sorry, Grandma, but I've decided not to help Dexter after all.'

Her pale-grey eyes clouded. 'Why? What do you mean?'

I lowered my voice and explained the concerning rumours I had just heard about the nature reserve. I could hear myself saying the words, but not believe they were coming from my mouth.

Grandma processed what I'd just told her, her mouth slack with shock. 'I don't believe it about the nature reserve, Elle. I mean, I've still got council contacts and I haven't heard a thing. I'm sure it's a lot of nonsense, anyway.' Worry stole over her. 'Isn't it?'

I admitted I wasn't so sure. 'If there's any truth in it, I'm not prepared to sit back and let it happen.'

I gave my ponytail a firm shake, as though to reassure myself. 'And I'm certain a lot of Fir Haven will feel the same way.'

Grandma's shoulders dropped. 'So that's why that young man marched off like that? Because you said you're not helping him after all?'

I flushed under her studious gaze. 'All that stuff with Dexter pales into insignificance when you compare it to a threat to the reserve.'

I glanced over at the pink and white crumbs dotted on plates, like discarded confetti, where the tower of decadent cupcakes had been. Now, there were only about half a dozen left, and a handful of half-empty bottles of champagne.

'But you promised me, Elle.' Gran's voice was so heavy with disappointment, I shot out my arms and hugged her.

She was worrying me. This wasn't like her at all. She was usually such a stoical woman. 'But why? Why is locating Linda Carlucci so important to you, Gran?'

She didn't answer.

'Look, Grandma, we've never kept secrets from each other. At least, I hope we haven't.'

'Of course not.'

I sighed and waited a few more moments, until Paper Roses had emptied out further and all that remained was Mrs Carter and her tartan shopping trolley.

She nodded over and wrapped one of the fat cupcakes still remaining into a napkin, before darting out of the open door.

I resumed my appeal to my grandmother. 'I'm really worried, Gran. You haven't been yourself lately and that's understandable after what we've been through, but all this—'

'Just trust me, Elle,' she pleaded, snatching my hands and sending a surprised tremor through me. 'I promise I will do all I can to help if the nature reserve is in danger, but in return you must promise to help that young man.'

I opened and closed my mouth. 'But why, Gran? Why does it

matter so much to you that I help Dexter Grayling? You haven't told me anything.'

I moved to speak again, but Grandma raised one freckled hand. 'You're right. I haven't told you everything, at least not yet. But I'm going to now.'

She fidgeted with her yellow-gold wedding band. 'But first of all, I suggest you ring Dexter and tell him you've changed your mind and that you will help him after all. Then I'll stick the kettle on and we can talk.'

When I hesitated, she picked up one of my hands and gave it a squeeze. 'Please, Elle.'

'All right,' I murmured. 'I will.'

'Good girl. Thank you.' She moved into the small, bright kitchenette at the rear of the shop. 'You call him now.' Her eyes glittered with renewed optimism. 'Then we can also talk about what action we can take to save our reserve.'

When Gran vanished into the kitchen in a swirl of citrus scent, I rubbed my weary eyes. A new business; a grandmother who was being secretive; a crime writer with a chip on his shoulder the size of Loch Ness, convinced he'd had his writing mojo torn away from him; and now our gorgeous nature reserve was under threat.

So just another ordinary day then.

Ringing Dexter back to tell him I would help after all and that Gran had come up with a suggestion for a starting point for our investigations was not something I was relishing.

While Grandma prepared a pot of tea in the kitchen, I took my time serving a young family and insisting their two little girls avail themselves of a cupcake each.

Their wide doll-like eyes threatened to fall out of their faces as they cupped the domes of baby-pink and white in their hands and their happy but exhausted parents helped themselves to the last of the champagne.

I just wanted the customers to vanish for a bit so Gran and I could have some time alone and then she would open up to me about all this.

They had only just bundled back out of the door when Gran reappeared, grasping two ceramic mugs of builder-strength tea. 'So, what did he say?'

I dropped my eyes to the counter and fiddled with a notepad. 'I haven't rung him yet.'

Her expression fell. 'May I ask why?'

'We've been really busy the last ten minutes.'

She surveyed the now-empty shop, her attention sweeping from the wooden floor to the glossy white shelves. 'Yes, I can see that. We can hardly move in here right now.'

I rolled my eyes good-naturedly. 'I was serving a young family and they only left a second ago.'

Gran set down my mug on top of the counter. 'Well, you aren't occupied at the moment, are you, darling?'

Oh, for pity's sake! I made a frustrated sigh. 'Point taken.'

I rummaged in my shoulder bag under the counter and pulled out my phone. I dragged up Dexter's number and Gran disappeared back into the kitchen, sipping her tea.

This is ridiculous! Why am I so reluctant to ring him? What is the issue here?

I know, whispered a teasing voice. *You're trying to keep your distance from him.*

Why is that? the rational voice inside my head asked.

I'll tell you why: it's because you find him attractive.

The realisation gave me a jolt and I tried to force it out of my head. It wasn't that at all. After Lloyd, getting involved with another man was not on my list of priorities. Perish the thought! Dexter Grayling was louche, famous, and had a reputation to boot. Yes, he was also very good-looking and talented...

Oh bugger!

I refused to dissect my thoughts any more about Dexter. Part of me hoped he wouldn't answer and that he would be too busy staring into the middle distance, looking moody and struggling to conjure up his next chapter. But just as I was about to ring off, his deep rumble rang in my ear.

Shit!

I studied my jewelled pumps and gathered myself together. 'Look, this is against my better judgement but my gran has pleaded with me to help you look into all this crazy business, and I'm not prepared to let her down.'

There was a weighted silence, then he spoke again. I could have sworn there was a hint of bemusement in his gravelly voice. 'So what you're saying is you're doing this solely for your grandmother's benefit?'

I straightened my shoulders even though he couldn't see me and pushed out my chin. 'That's about the size of it.'

'Well at least you're being honest,' he answered wryly. 'So, where do we start?'

'I'll talk to Gran and take it from there.'

'So you do have a lead? What is it?'

'My grandmother said she would have a chat with me now about something specific. I'll call you back later, once we've talked.'

The sooner this ridiculous situation was resolved, the better. Then I might actually be able to concentrate on Paper Roses and fighting this awful nature reserve business.

I shoved my phone back into my bag 'Thank you, lovey. You have no idea how much I appreciate what you're doing.'

I pushed out a smile, despite my reservations. 'Don't worry, I'll remind you often about how selfless I am.'

She indicated the two chairs behind the counter and we settled ourselves.

The shop was still empty, so Gran wasted no time in talking to me about Mrs Carlucci. 'I didn't want to rake over all this again, but it looks like I have no other choice.'

Her words vanished as the background music in the shop morphed into melodic panpipes.

'Gran, you're scaring me now.'

She shook her head. 'There's no need to worry. It's my embarrassment, not yours.'

I leant forward and placed my mug beside me on the counter. 'Whatever it is, just tell me. Please.'

Her beige-slicked eyelids flicked up to the ceiling, which was now dotted with circular white-gold spotlights. 'You should speak to Adam Fraser,' she managed after a few moments of contemplation.

'Who is that?'

She swallowed and tilted up her chin. 'Adam Fraser,' she replied, her dusky voice cracking, 'was... was someone from my past.'

Chapter Seventeen

I leant forward. 'When was this? Is he connected to Linda Carlucci too?'

Grandma's cheeks developed two strips of colour. 'It's all tied up in our younger years,' she confessed. 'It isn't an era that I or a lot of my contemporaries in this town are very proud of, though.'

She hesitated and was about to carry on when two more of her book club friends bustled in. 'Isabel! Dora!'

I watched her rise out of her chair and give me an apologetic smile, before embracing them both.

What did she mean by it all being connected to her youth in Fir Haven? Frustration niggled at me. Looked like I would have to quiz her about this former mystery man a little later.

The remainder of the day saw a visit from a reporter from our local newspaper, *The Fir Haven Herald,* who wanted to do a human interest write-up about Cassidy's transforming into Paper Roses, the loss of my parents, me starting over the business, that kind of thing.

The photographer who accompanied the reporter took a few inside shots of Gran and me, before photographing the outside of the shop in all its new sugar-pink and white glory.

Mid-afternoon saw a flurry of schoolchildren, who must have heard about the novelty stationery sets I'd decided to stock and had decided to purchase them prior to the school summer holidays which were just about to begin.

I had spotted the novelty stationery while I was trawling ideas online and saw they consisted of fruit-scented pencils, pens, erasers, and rulers. The strawberry and watermelon designs were the most popular.

I snatched up my block of notepaper from the counter and scribbled a reminder to myself to order more.

My curiosity was firing on all cylinders and I was about to ask my grandmother again about this Adam Fraser character, seeing as there was another lull in customers, when she emerged from the kitchen.

It was almost five o'clock and the mid-June sunshine was becoming lazy, pushing its weary, dappled fingers through our bottle-glass windows. She already had her straw bag slung over one shoulder as she shrugged on her linen jacket.

She stretched out her jewelled right hand and gave me a piece of lined paper. In her sweeping handwriting was a name and address:

Mr Adam Fraser
2 Mayfield Road,
Fir Haven

There was also his telephone number.

She moved towards the shop door and watched me scan the note.

'Gran?'

She stepped out of the door, causing a palette of late afternoon light to wash across the wooden floor. 'Please let me know if you need me tomorrow.'

'But, Gran—'

'I think Cate said she would be in tomorrow,' she cut across, blowing me a kiss. 'I'm so proud of you, Elle.'

She delved into her bag for her Jackie Onassis-style sunglasses and slipped them on. 'See you back at Pebble Brook, darling.'

Then she was gone.

Chapter Eighteen

When I rang Dexter to tell him about the mystery lead my grandma had given us, he did his utmost to persuade me to drive up to Hawk West Hall straight after closing the shop, so we could drive straight over to speak to Adam Fraser.

My legs felt as if I'd put them through two hours of frantic Zumba and my hair was escaping from its ponytail; add to that, the sticky, sweaty sheen on my skin and it was a definite *no*.

You don't want Dexter seeing you looking like that, whispered my inner voice.

I ignored it. *I wouldn't want anyone seeing me looking like that,* I qualified quickly to myself.

Ignoring Dexter's grunts of protest down the line, I locked up Paper Roses and suggested we go and visit Mr Fraser after work tomorrow instead.

'But that's another twenty-four hours away!'

I pulled a face as I rattled my keys. 'Yes, Mr Grayling, I can count. But you have to realise I am busy.'

He emitted a painful groan. 'OK. Tomorrow it is. I suppose another day won't make much difference.'

For the remainder of that evening, Gran remained tight-lipped about Adam Fraser.

I made several concerted efforts to find out more, but all she would say was that he too was Fir Haven born and bred and that she had known him when she was in her twenties, prior to meeting Grandpa Tony.

Any further questions were met with a guarded refusal. 'Speak to Adam,' was all she would say. 'I want to hear his side of things first.'

I folded my arms at the breakfast bar and pushed away my plate of half-demolished lasagne and salad. 'What does that mean?'

But she'd already changed the subject to the news that Mrs Thomson's grandson had qualified as a doctor.

I sat cross-legged on my bed and fingered the piece of paper Grandma had given me. I considered whether to ring Adam Fraser first. That would only be polite, wouldn't it? Two strangers turning up at his door might well alarm him.

But then there was the element of surprise that might be to our advantage.

Dear me. I sounded like I was involved in some covert criminal operation!

In the end, I decided that calling him first might be better. Steeling myself, I jabbed in Adam Fraser's telephone number. After a few rings, an educated, older Scottish male voice wafted back.

I took care to explain who I was and then mentioned my grandmother.

I pulled myself bolt upright on my bed when Adam Fraser reacted with a bark. 'Your grandmother and I knew each other a long, long time ago. I don't see the good of dragging up the past now.'

'Mrs Carlucci,' I countered, trying to salvage what I could from the phone call. 'Gran seems to think you knew about her, or certainly knew of her.'

'Well, I don't! Please leave me alone. It's all fanciful nonsense!'

'What is?' I squirmed on the bed. 'What's all fanciful nonsense?'

But the line went dead. I flopped back deflated against my pillow.

Gran's eyes widened the next morning at breakfast as we discussed Adam Fraser's reaction again. 'I can't believe he did that. Putting the phone down on you!'

I poured milk onto my cereal and watched it wash over my Bran Flakes. 'He made it clear he has no intention of talking about it. He said it was all a lot of rubbish.'

Grandma's speckled hand fluttered to her throat. 'That's charming. And did he make any comment about Linda Carlucci or her family?'

'Nothing. All he said was something about fanciful nonsense.'

She pressed her coral-slicked lips together.

'Maybe if you came with us tonight, Gran? If he saw you he might change his mind?'

'No!'

I blinked at her forcefulness.

Grandma collected herself together in our quiet kitchen. 'Just leave it, Elle. Forget I suggested it. I should never have urged you to speak to him in the first place. I should have expected as much from the likes of him.'

I was prepared to argue the point, but Gran was having none of it. 'Promise me, darling, that you won't speak to Adam anymore. Best to leave the past alone. I'm sorry I suggested it. Cranky old bugger!'

I dropped my gaze and played with my cereal spoon. I felt like the things I thought I knew were rapidly falling away from me. Secrets were bubbling under the surface and I was within touching distance of them. I couldn't just leave things like that. Especially not now.

'Gran, you need to tell me. Please. What is this all about?'

But she was already leaving the kitchen.

I thought again about Adam Fraser.

Frustration rose inside me. Well, if my grandmother wasn't prepared to tell me, I would have to try and persuade him to talk to me after all.

Chapter Nineteen

The day began slowly, but by mid-morning, a steady stream of locals and the odd serious hiker put paid to the quiet, which was punctuated only by Cate's musical choice of Florence & the Machine drifting ethereally from my iPod.

Gran had insisted she would come in again to assist me behind the counter, but I refused. Her distracted, pale appearance at breakfast had been a bit of a shock, so I had urged her to relax and reminded her that Cate was coming in to help me out. 'If things get too hectic, I'll give you a shout,' I had assured her.

I was sure she had tired herself out after the opening day and the Adam Fraser issue most likely hadn't helped. I'd tried again before leaving for Paper Roses to speak to her about Adam Fraser, but she had ordered me out of the house and vanished back inside, a blur of pink-checked shirt and navy trousers.

I planned to ring her a couple of times during the day, to see how she was.

I readjusted the band securing the end of my plait.

Cate handed a young couple their change, together with the Charles Rennie Mackintosh pen and pencil set they explained they were buying for his dad's sixtieth birthday.

Cate wrapped it in a sheet of silver paper and topped it off with a froth of black bow. I smiled in admiration as her fingers danced over the paper, arranging and folding. 'You can tell you're an artist,' I said, once the couple had offered their thanks and disappeared up the street.

'Hopefully not a con artist or even a piss artist.'

I laughed while she leant on the counter, her uninhibited curls bouncing against her black, clear skin, and cream V-neck top.

Cate rested her jewelled hand against her chin. 'Do you know, I could be sitting at home right now, finishing a jade pendant from eye pins.'

I made a snorting noise. 'I've got no idea what that means, but I'm sorry.'

She dismissed my apology. 'No, don't be. Look what I would have missed out on otherwise. And it's good to get a break from copper wire and seed beads anyway.' She surveyed me with her chocolate eyes. 'You're not here, Elle. I don't know where you are, but you sure ain't here.'

I blushed and examined my glittery trainers.

'Well, that's not exactly true,' she carried on. 'I think I do know where you are.'

Cate rubbed at her nose. 'Your thoughts right now are scattered between your parents, Clara, Linda Carlucci, this place, and that crime writer.'

At the mention of Dexter, I felt my cheeks flare and hoped Cate hadn't noticed.

'Not to mention the nature reserve,' said Cate, squinting from under her plucked brows. She observed my jaw clenching.

'I can't let the reserve go under. I just can't.'

Cate's eyes softened further. 'Look, Elle, I'm not trying to tell you how to feel or what to do. You and Clara have been through so much recently.'

'But?'

She reached across and took my hand in hers. 'But you can't

take on everybody else's problems. I get that you want to be busy and I get that you want to make Paper Roses successful, but I should point out that you don't wear your knickers over your trousers.'

'Only at weekends.'

A smile flashed across her face. 'I'm being serious. I don't want you taking on too much.'

I reached up to a stray hair and secured it back. 'I understand what you're saying, Cate, but the Dexter thing and now this Adam Fraser's reaction when I told him who I was...' I shrugged. 'You should have seen Gran this morning. She wasn't herself.'

'Well, that's understandable. Plus, she will be trying to look out for you.'

Frustration reared up inside of me. Of course my gran was distraught. She was doing all she could to get on with things, just like I was.

But every time we approached Pebble Brook, when just the two of us were rolling around inside that big, old converted mill with its achy smiling beams and rustic aura, the enormity of losing both my parents so suddenly and so tragically would descend like a heavy black cloak that I couldn't remove.

Gran's shoulders would drop, her mouth would turn down, and she would wear her grief like a mask.

Cate's words pulled me back. 'And you don't know what connection this Adam Fraser has to your gran?'

'None. He wasn't prepared to say and neither was she. At least, not yet.'

I listened while Cate advised me to leave things be. 'Let Dexter sort things out on his own.'

I didn't say anything. How could I? I had promised Gran.

She folded her arms. 'For a moment there you had me worried. I was starting to wonder if you actually believed all that crap about a curse!' She delivered a bright-white smile and I arranged my features into an *as if!* face.

Since Dexter Grayling had arrived, it was like a giant box of secrets had burst open and people around here were frantically scrabbling around, trying to stuff the contents back in again.

Right now, I wasn't sure of very much at all.

But what I did know was that I was even more determined to speak to Adam Fraser again – this time, face to face. I had to know what was going on – and what my gran wasn't telling me.

Chapter Twenty

Adam Fraser lived in Mayfield, on the outskirts of Fir Haven. It was a little hamlet, consisting of several miner's cottages huddled together with puffing chimneys and trellises dotted with blooming flowers.

There was a small supermarket and a post office, but that was all. It was as if Mayfield was a protected entity all of its own, working together to keep out the modern world.

Dexter eased his car to a stop outside the closed post office and peered over the top of his mirrored sunglasses. 'Good grief! This place is like something out of the Stone Age!'

I twisted round in the passenger seat, sending my plait flying backwards. 'Just because it doesn't have seven nightclubs, doesn't mean it's any less important.'

Dexter swiped off his sunglasses and stashed them in the pocket of his sage-green shirt. 'I don't care if you lot engage in weekly orgies around here so long as I get my writing ability back.' Then a hint of a teasing smile tugged at the corners of his mouth. 'You don't have weekly orgies, do you?'

'Only monthly ones.'

'That's a shame.'

Dexter clambered out and I eyed the plush interior of his vehicle. It was a deep-caramel leather, carrying splashes of black and chrome on the dashboard that lit up like the night sky on New Year's Eve.

As I got out of the passenger side, the golden glimpses of late June sunshine dissipated, to be overtaken by a pearly-grey sky.

My eyes travelled over the jean-clad Dexter. He had collected me from Paper Roses just before 5pm and I insisted to Cate that she leave me to close up for the day.

She'd blinked at me from under those sooty black lashes of hers and said, 'OK, if you're sure. Thanks!'

I had felt like an utter cretin not telling her where I was going and what I was doing, trying to speak to Adam Fraser again. I didn't know what to expect myself, so decided not to overcomplicate things for now.

Dexter surveyed the six cottages crouched together on the opposite side of the road. Number two, Adam's property, appeared to have been dipped in a box of children's paints.

The snow-white pebbledash was complemented by a tangle of apricot 'Teasing Georgia' roses snaking through the wooden trellis. The front door featured a French-blue hue, with the window shutters painted more of a sky-blue shade, reminiscent of the Mediterranean, rather than Scotland.

The carefully tended flowerbeds and modest but manicured square of grass, gave the whole house an idyllic chocolate-box aura. It was hard to reconcile this image before me with the gruff, abrupt gentleman who had damaged my ear canal yesterday.

The other five cottages, which ran the length of the quiet road, although sweet and well cared for with their net curtains and bobbing blooms of pansies and tubs of lavender, didn't quite have the same immediate impact as No. 2.

Dexter's drawl was sarcastic. 'Are you going to stand there, admiring their paint work, or are we actually going to knock on the door?'

'Any more wisecracks and I'll ask Linda Carlucci to make her curse permanent.'

He raised a thick, dark brow. 'That's not funny.'

I strode past him, eager to put some space between us, and up to the dark-blue door.

My stomach rolled. Was all this such a good idea after all? Adam Fraser wasn't expecting us and he had told me to sod off on the phone. I really hadn't thought this through at all. I had been so irritated by his rudeness that my impetuous side had taken over.

I took a breath and stared at the brass heart-shaped door-knocker. My hand rose and hovered over it.

'Oh, for pity's sake, Elle! Rattle the bloody thing!'

I swivelled round on my ballet pump. Dexter was looming behind me, his piercing gaze burning into my back. That was the first time he had called me by my first name. 'All right, all right! Keep your designer kegs on!'

'Kegs?'

I rolled my eyes up to the shards of dirty-looking clouds lurking overhead. 'It's Scottish slang for trousers.'

I lifted the pretty door-knocker and rattled it against the painted wood. There were a few moments of silence – which made me think we might have undertaken a wasted journey – until I thought I heard the creak of a door handle.

I took a nervous step backwards, bumping against Dexter's solid right shoulder. The feel of his warm skin made me shoot forward again. I tried to still my heart, which decided to take off at a gallop.

An older gentleman appeared in the door crack in checked waistcoat and brown trousers. He carried a dapper air about him, which was enhanced further by a thick white moustache and severely parted hair.

His mouth turned down. His attention shot from me to Dexter and back again. 'Can I help you? If you're selling anything, I can tell you now that I'm not interested.'

I arranged my hesitant features into a polite smile. 'No, we're not selling anything. I'm Clara Blackmore's granddaughter.'

His suspicious pale eyes blinked at me and then narrowed. 'You rang me yesterday.' There was accusation in his voice.

'Yes, I did, Mr Fraser, and I'm so sorry to trouble you again like this.'

'I've got nothing to say to you or your boyfriend here.'

I made an incredulous sound. 'Oh no! Good grief, no! He's not my boyfriend.'

'I don't care if he's Mick Jagger, I'm not speaking to you.'

'But, sir,' interrupted Dexter over my shoulder. 'Elle's grandmother seemed to think you might be able to help us.'

'It's about Linda Carlucci,' I went on in a desperate rush.

The mention of Linda Carlucci's name caused Adam Fraser to blink again several times. 'Yes, well, your grandma always had a tendency of saying a lot of things.'

What did he mean by that?

He grasped at his door handle, his knuckles transforming into blobs of white. 'All that Carlucci nonsense is an old folk's tale around here.'

'What nonsense?' pushed Dexter, his voice adopting an excited edge. 'What do you mean, sir?'

Adam Fraser's eyes grew large at Dexter's close proximity. 'I'm not saying any more. That was all years ago.'

I wanted to ask him more questions. They were crowding into my mind, jockeying for position, but my glimmer of optimism vanished as Adam Fraser pushed his front door closed.

'Please leave now, otherwise I will call the police. Now away with the pair of you.'

Chapter Twenty-One

'That went well,' said Dexter, dragging a frustrated hand through his hair. It now sat up in a black plume.

I marched past him and back down Adam Fraser's flower-lined path. 'You think you could have done better, do you?' My frustrated gaze swept the length of him. 'You haven't exactly endeared yourself to the local community since you moved here.'

Even though the sun had vanished, Dexter hooked his sunglasses out of his shirt pocket and slid them back on. 'Are we talking about the incident with my car again? You can't let that go, can you?' he answered. 'I didn't almost kill three people. I merely lost concentration for a few seconds.'

'And almost put three people in hospital.'

I could see a nerve twitching at the side of his strong jaw. 'I'm paying for it now though.'

I moved back towards his car, which was glinting charcoal under the pale sky. 'You don't even know that it is some curse.'

Dexter loitered for a few moments before whipping off his sunglasses and studying me across the glossy roof of his car. 'Why are you helping me, Elle?'

I stuffed my hands into my pockets. 'Like I told you, because my grandmother asked me to.'

Dexter's dark angled brows rose. 'And for no other reason?'

I could feel my stomach wriggle. 'Like what?'

He aimed his key fob at the car and it began to flash and bleep like an out-of-control microwave.

'Excuse me? Hello there!'

I looked up to see where the disembodied voice was coming from. An elderly lady in a crackly flower-print apron was hovering at the front door to no. 4. She had hair like a giant snowball.

'She's probably recognised me,' said Dexter.

I performed a comical eyeroll and strolled over to her.

'Please forgive me if I'm speaking out of turn,' she apologised, lowering her voice and casting a surreptitious glance towards Adam Fraser's cottage next door, 'but I had only just come out to collect some mint from my garden when I overheard you mention Linda Carlucci.'

Optimism sprung up inside me. 'Do you know her?'

She squinted out of dark-blue eyes, making her plump skin feather at the corners. 'Maybe you and your young gentleman should come in.'

I pretended to look around for the young gentleman.

'Very funny,' Dexter carped. 'And not very original.'

The outside of her cottage was similar to no. 2, but this one sported pillar-box red shutters and a white-paned front door, bearing stained-glass images of pink roses. Ceramic tubs of lavender thrummed with excited bees.

The lady introduced herself as Fran Boyd and led me and a puzzled-looking Dexter down her hallway. It smelled of pine polish and dark-wooden furniture.

She insisted we settle ourselves in her sitting room, which led off to the right. That also featured an abundance of dark wooden fittings, together with ornamental China dogs and printed yellow curtains.

Dexter and I eyed each other while Fran bustled to her chair.

We took up positions next to each other on her two-seater toffee-coloured sofa. 'Do you think she knows something?' he muttered to me out of the corner of his mouth, but before I could reply, Mrs Boyd's slanting deep-blue eyes glittered with appreciation. 'May I just say you make a very handsome couple!'

I flapped my hands in protest. 'Oh no! We're not a couple. Nope. Not at all.'

I slid an awkward side-eye at Dexter beside me. He offered me a look back that was indecipherable.

'So, you were saying about Linda Carlucci?' I prompted, eager to move the conversation on.

Fran took a couple of seconds to consider what she was going to say. 'There were always rumours about the Carlucci family,' she began. 'Strange rumours.'

Dexter shot forward. 'Like what?'

Fran dropped her voice, even though there appeared to be no one else around apart from us in her home. 'My own grandmother told me fifty-odd years ago now about the rumours of their so-called abilities.' She threw her delicate hands up into the air, before letting them fall back into her apron-clad lap. 'I know it must sound ridiculous, but so many people around here were saying the same thing.'

Dexter gave me a brief look of triumph while my mind cartwheeled with what Fran had just told us.

She continued talking, her gaze switching between Dexter and me. 'There were stories about the Carlucci women possessing some sort of ability after Maria, Linda's great-grandmother, discovered that her sister, Eva, had been treated badly by her then beau.'

'What happened?' I probed, my interest piqued.

Fran sat back in her chair and laced her fingers together. 'Some say it was an awful illness; others alluded to the possibility that Eva died of a broken heart after her beloved Jonathan cheated on her.'

We fell silent. All that could be heard was the rhythmical ticking of a green and gold carriage clock on the mantlepiece.

'Anyway, Maria swore revenge on Jonathan after the death of her sister and, soon after, his printing business failed, his new fiancée dumped him at the altar after discovering he had no money, and then he became addicted to gambling.' Fran shrugged her shoulders. 'I know what you're thinking. Many people did. It could all have been a matter of coincidence.'

Dexter and I listened, entranced, as Fran described Jonathan Swinson's sudden fear of the family and his insistence that Maria Carlucci had placed some sort of curse on him.

'He was adamant,' said Fran. 'He insisted that was what had happened. If the rumours are true, Maria visited his home three times immediately after Eva's death and it was said to be after the first visit that she wished him financial ruin and suffering as retribution for her sister.' Fran shrugged. 'The Carlucci family used to read tea leaves, make and sell arts and crafts, that kind of thing. I think a lot of the narrow-minded locals were wary of them from the off.'

Fran reached her fingers towards the base of her neck, as if to illustrate the point.

'The story goes that Maria clutched at some sort of pendant around her neck as she cursed him.'

From beside me came a loud intake of breath from Dexter. He turned pale and tried to steady himself. 'This pendant… do you know what it was supposed to look like?'

Fran blinked at him.

'Well, I don't know for definite, but it was said to be a silver crescent moon.'

Chapter Twenty-Two

Dexter had mentioned something about Linda clutching at a pendant when she spoke to him. I recalled Cate mentioning that too.

I watched his eyes grow wide with alarm. 'That's what was round her neck,' he mumbled in a rush. 'That's what she was holding when she spoke to me.'

I whirled back to Fran. Dexter had been adamant about what had happened to him, and now Fran was telling us this? My head spun with assumptions. 'So what happened after that? What did Jonathan do?'

'He still had a few influential friends in Fir Haven, despite falling on difficult times. They made sure the Carlucci family were driven from the area.'

'And they never came back?'

Fran hesitated. 'Folks said they did return to the area in the early 1970s and bought some farmland about an hour away from here.' She let out a sigh. 'Jonathan Swinson still ended up a lonely old man, despite having the Carlucci family frog-marched out of town.'

'But you don't know where they are now?' interrupted Dexter.

Fran shook her head. 'Nobody knows. They always kept themselves to themselves. After all those shenanigans, they never returned to Fir Haven.'

Dexter was in danger of falling out of his chair in agitation. 'We have to find out where Linda Carlucci lives now.'

Fran stared at him. 'My goodness, young man, you'll do yourself a mischief.' She gave a small smile. 'Don't tell me you think Linda Carlucci has put a curse on you!'

Dexter swallowed. He jumped to his feet, a long and towering figure looming over Fran and me. 'Yes. No. I mean, I'm not sure. I'm a crime writer, but now I can't bloody write.'

He lowered his bright-blue gaze to Fran's russet carpet.

Fran stared up at him. She raised an excited finger and pointed it at him. 'Hang on a second. I thought I recognised you. You're that chap who writes about Detective Dani Haines! Oh, I love your books!'

Dexter managed a smile. 'Thank you very much.'

'What about Adam Fraser?' I asked, while Dexter stood there, looking pensive. 'Why wouldn't he talk to us? My grandmother, Clara Blackmore, suggested we speak to him.'

Fran's lined expression froze. 'Did you just say Clara Blackmore? She's your grandmother?'

My heart was bumping against my ribs with apprehension. 'Yes. Why?'

Fran rubbed at her cheek. 'I used to work in the local solicitor's offices, which then became the library.' Her eyes grew hazy with recollection. 'My boss, Mr Archer, was always hanging around with his councillor friends and they were forever gossiping about local issues.'

She raised her brows at the memory and indicated her head to her grouchy next-door neighbour. 'Adam Fraser discovered the Carlucci family were living in Fir Haven. He was a young councillor at the time and had them evicted from their home. The story going around was that Fraser and his council cohorts had them accused of anti-social behaviour, but from what I heard, there was never any truth to it.'

I blinked. 'That's awful. But I don't understand what my grandmother has to do with any of this.' Then a thought came to me. 'Was Gran going out with Adam and didn't approve of what he did?'

Fran hesitated. 'No. She wasn't courting Adam Fraser, although he did have a major crush on your grandma.'

I frowned. 'Sorry, Fran, but I'm confused.'

She sighed, recalling her memories. 'Adam Fraser was jealous and that's why he got involved in having the Carlucci family evicted.'

I frowned at her. 'Jealous of what?'

'Not what. *Whom.*' Fran sat forward a little. Her jowly cheeks were carrying a hint of pink. 'Your gran hasn't told you any of this?'

'Told me what?'

Fran studied both of us in her chintzy sitting room. 'Adam Fraser was jealous because your Clara was in love with someone else at the time.' She flicked looks at Dexter and me. 'Clara was in love with Lorenzo Carlucci, Linda's brother.'

Chapter Twenty-Three

My head felt like it was spiralling.

So, had my gran lost Lorenzo Carlucci because of Adam Fraser's spiteful, jealous behaviour? I was struggling to rationalise any of this. She had never mentioned Lorenzo, let alone his sister Linda. She had been my grandmother for twenty-nine years and yet I knew nothing about this.

I glanced at Dexter, next to me. He had sat back down again, a concoction of intrigue and confusion charging across his features. He wasn't the only one. I had doubted his outlandish claims, but what if what Fran had just told us was true? I had no reason to doubt her, and my grandmother had believed him from the start.

Oh, this is ridiculous!

Dexter turned to me, a glint of quiet satisfaction and empathy in his penetrating gaze. Then he spoke to Fran. 'I need to find Linda Carlucci.'

Fran pursed her lips, which carried a trace of frosted-pink lipstick. 'Whatever did you do?'

'He almost killed her,' I interjected. 'And me and my best friend too. I suspect that probably annoyed her somewhat.'

I could have sworn Fran's mouth twitched at the corners.

'It was an accident!' insisted Dexter. 'I keep telling you that!' He angled his body away from me and towards Fran. 'Is there anything I can do to stop all this?' He rubbed at his stubbled chin. 'Since that accident happened, it's like I've lost my mojo.'

He stared past Fran. 'I can't even come up with any new ideas, let alone finish the draft of my next novel.'

Fran's round face read Dexter's desperation. 'I don't know if there's any truth in this. It might just be all a load of old hokum.' She steepled her hands in her lap. 'The story goes that there were two different people who did manage to have their curses reversed.'

Dexter's eyes promised to fall out of his head. 'Go on.'

'They had to show the error of their ways and prove they had changed for the better.'

'I can do that!' he exclaimed, leaping to his feet again. 'That should be easy enough.'

Fran studied him from the comfort of her armchair. 'It isn't enough to say the right thing. You have to genuinely mean it.'

Dexter appeared suitably chastened and sank back down again beside me.

'Do you know anything about these two people who were purported to have had curses put on them?' I asked.

Dexter's mouth flatlined beside me. 'There's no bloody *purported* about it.'

Fran delved into her memory. 'One was said to be Daphne Curtis. She lived in Fir Haven, but passed away a few years ago now.'

Dexter's broad shoulders slumped.

'But the other one is a gentleman by the name of Robert Masters, who still lives locally.'

Recognition pinged in my mind. 'Robert Masters? As in, Roberts Masters, the former provost?'

Fran nodded. 'He might not be willing to talk to you though. He can be a bit prickly.'

Dexter's head travelled between the two of us. 'Provost?'

'Like a Scottish mayor. Don't you know anything?' I teased.

Dexter pulled a sarcastic expression. 'It's not my fault you don't speak proper English.'

We exchanged teasing smiles, before remembering we were supposed to be on frosty terms with one another. I quickly turned back to Fran. She was examining us both, her head angled to one side. 'Are you two sure you're not an item?'

Colour flooded my face. 'Nope. No! No. Just acquaintances.' I cleared my throat. 'So, you were saying, Fran?'

'The Carlucci family,' continued Fran, choosing her words with care, 'haven't been treated well by some folks around here over the years.'

I listened, appreciating what she was trying to say. She raised a finger and indicated next door to Adam Fraser's cottage. 'He's a case in point.'

Dexter's attention followed Fran's jabbing finger. 'Can you tell us where we can find this Robert Masters, please? Anything's worth a try.'

Fran looked at both of us. Then she snatched up an old envelope and pencil sitting on top of her tea trolley and began scribbling on it. 'Here is Robert Masters's address. He was friendly with my Bertie. He was my husband, God rest his soul.'

She handed it to me with an absent smile, when a tall man with receding blond hair strode into her sitting room, emitting a cheery, 'Hi, Mum. Only me,' and taking us by surprise.

He drew up when he saw Dexter and me with his mother. Fran rose and patted the lapels of her son's navy pinstripe suit. 'This is my son, Joshua. He's a developer.'

Dexter and I stood up and shook hands with him. I noticed his hooded muddy-coloured eyes bore a fleck of appraisal as he said hello.

'Busy day, darling?' she asked, her voice brimming with pride.

Joshua Boyd smoothed his claret sliver of a tie and jutted out his chin with an air of self-importance. 'You know me, Mum. Always busy.' He let out a theatrical sigh. 'Tough decisions have to be made.'

Fran beamed up at her son, adding that he was employed with Atticus Development. 'Oh dear. Tough decisions about what, love?'

He puffed out his chest. 'Sorry, Mum, but I can't divulge that sort of information at the moment.' He pinned on an indulgent smile. 'But let's just say that Fir Haven will be attracting a different class of clientele in future. Luxury holiday homes are on the horizon!'

I digested his words. A spark of panic flared. The subject of holiday homes and their rumoured connection to the reserve shot through my mind. 'Excuse me, but are you talking about the nature reserve?'

Joshua Boyd's smugness evaporated. 'How do you know about that?'

I didn't answer him.

He sounded weary, as though he had trotted out this explanation a hundred times already. 'We've looked at all the options, but…' He allowed his pompous voice to fizzle away. He was savouring the attention.

'But what?' I asked, folding my arms.

Joshua Boyd raised his attention to his mother's Artex ceiling and held it there for a few moments. Then he deigned to look back at me. 'The council are in dire straits round here and supporting a failing nature reserve isn't doing them any favours.'

The breath jarred in my throat.

He surveyed our faces. 'Oh, I might as well tell you. It will be public knowledge soon enough anyway.' He couldn't conceal his delight. 'They've agreed to sell the reserve to us.'

Chapter Twenty-Four

My stomach plummeted to my feet. 'But they can't!'

Joshua Boyd's eyes slid over me like treacle. 'It's been a difficult decision for them, but sometimes you have to be realistic.'

'But the nature reserve is a huge part of Fir Haven's heritage!' I pleaded. 'The flora and fauna that lives there… it's been part of this area for generations.'

He tried to look sympathetic. 'It can't support itself any longer.'

I could feel Dexter studying me. To my surprise, he said, 'There must be some other alternative, surely, to destroying an area like that?'

Fran's anxious expression travelled from me to Dexter and then her son. 'It's not going to be a popular decision, dear.'

Joshua indulged his mother with a shark-like smile. 'Tough decisions never are, Mum.'

Oh, for pity's sake!

I managed to thank Fran for all her help before barging past Joshua Boyd. The thought of staying any longer in the company of that smug snake made my stomach heave.

So, the rumours were true after all. The nature reserve would be flattened to make way for some glass-riddled five-star monstrosities to attract weekenders with more money than social conscience.

Dexter emerged from Fran's cottage and eyed me from across the top of his car roof.

'Are you all right?'

Memories of rambling around with my late parents up at the reserve charged through my head.

'No, I'm not!'

I jumped into the passenger side and slammed the door so hard that Dexter winced. There was a prolonged silence.

'Are you OK to visit this Robert Masters guy right now, or do you want to go home and prepare for war?'

I twisted round to look at him, my face flushed with fury. 'I'm a woman. I can multi-task, you know!'

A ghost of a smile appeared on his chiselled face before vanishing again. 'I had noticed both things. I've lost my writing capability, not my eye sight.'

I focused my attention out of the car window. If the council thought the people round here were going to accept this, then they were very much mistaken.

Dexter kept shooting me side glances as we made our way back to Fir Haven, his car skimming past the winding country lanes and white blobs of grazing sheep in the myriad fields. He manoeuvred the steering wheel, taking us around the ornamental roundabout on the outskirts of town and back towards the main throng of Fir Haven.

I stared at the flashing black image on Dexter's sat-nav screen indicating that Robert Masters's house was moments away.

It was situated in close proximity to a couple of other impressive properties that sat opposite the church and up a slight embankment. I had passed this detached Edwardian home before on the odd occasion. It was an elaborately decorated building, built over three floors. It consisted of a combination of paler and dark-grey brick, with two ornate pillars on either side of the angular roof that protruded up into the patchy blue sky. The windows winked out of white painted frames, which complemented the glass-panelled entrance. The front garden was rather formal, made up of a curved moss-green lawn, with a belt of trees providing privacy from the main road.

Dexter clutched his car keys and we both stepped onto the pavement. 'It's pretty spectacular,' he said, of the impressive abode. 'If I had known about this place before, I would have made the guy an offer.'

'What? And turn it into some sort of theme park?' I scowled at him, still stung by the revelations about the reserve. 'Not everything is about money, Dexter.'

My cheeks flashed as he said, 'Do you know, Elle, that's the first time you've called me by my Christian name? And yes, you're right, not everything is about money.'

My blush deepened. I shouldn't take out my frustration and pain over the reserve on him. It wasn't fair. I moved ahead of him, easing open the claret-painted iron gate. 'I'm sorry. I shouldn't have spoken to you like that.'

Dexter brushed off my apology. 'Forget it. You're right. At times like this, you do realise that not everything should be about how much something costs or how audacious it is. I'm learning that the hard way.'

I flicked him a brief smile. 'You will get your writing ability back.'

Now it was Dexter's turn to deliver a fleeting smile back at me. 'Thank you. I do appreciate that – and your help. It's a novel experience to talk to someone who doesn't want something from me. Most folks usually do.'

'Ah. I'm the genuine article!' I laughed.

Dexter's expression softened. 'You don't need to tell me that. It's a refreshing change to meet someone who doesn't use you for what you have.'

There was an electric silence. Then a thought hit me. Oh hell! I hadn't even considered what I was going to say!

Good afternoon. This is the crime writer Dexter Grayling, and I own a new stationery business in town. He thinks he has been put under some sort of curse and we understand you experienced the same thing years ago. Can we come in and discuss it in more detail?

It sounded like I had indulged in one too many glasses of Glenfiddich!

Assumptions reeled in my mind. What the hell did I think I was doing?

Grandma materialised in my head and I swallowed. I was doing it for her.

While we hovered from foot to foot, eyeing our hesitant reflections in the glass panels of the front door, I slid a look at Dexter. He was solemn-faced, his blue-black hair ruffling in the breeze. He reminded me of a dark, brooding poet…

I snapped my head away.

'I don't think there's anyone at home,' I remarked, listening out for any noise from within the house.

Dexter's disappointment shone out of his eyes. He rubbed at his chin. 'This is like some second-rate farce. First, we're told to go to that Adam Fraser's address. Then we get a door slammed in our faces. Now we're told to come here.'

'I know you're getting frustrated, but moaning about it won't help.' Yes, this was the more familiar Dexter – moody and growly.

Dexter glowered. 'You heard Fran just now. There are people around here who have experienced something inflicted by the Carlucci family too.'

I hitched up one brow.

'My agent is having palpations over *Killing Time*, and my publishers are getting antsy.'

Our conversation screeched to a halt however, as a figure materialised behind the glass of the front door.

Chapter Twenty-Five

'Can I help you?'

The middle-aged man possessed an intense air, as well as unruly conker-brown and salt hair and an outdoorsy tone to his craggy skin.

This wasn't Robert Masters, who would occasionally pop up in the local press, awarding school prizes or hosting events at the local golf club.

The figure standing in the doorway in front of me was dressed in a light-grey sweatshirt and combats and looked like he'd been having a battle with the lawn. He seemed familiar.

'Hello. I'm sorry to bother you, but we wondered if we could have a word with Mr Robert Masters, please? I'm Elle Cassidy and this is Dexter Grayling. I own the new stationery shop in the high street, Paper Roses.'

His gruff expression shifted between us, like a creepy painting in a haunted house. Then he turned to me. 'Elle, it's me. Paul Reid. I used to go to the rugby club with your dad.'

It took a few seconds for me to place him. Then I remembered. 'Paul! Hi there. I haven't seen you for a while. How are you?'

'I'm good, thanks. Been away working in France for a while

and then I came back. I got the offer of more gardening work here, so I'm doing some planting for Mr Masters.'

From behind me, I could sense Dexter's agitation. 'This trip down memory lane is all very nice, but can we get on with this please?' he hissed into my ear.

Ignoring his impatience, I carried on. 'We've got no intention of taking up too much of Mr Masters's time.'

The man flashed a kind smile as he looked at me. 'I'm sure he'll be able to chat with you.' He paused. 'I heard about your mum and dad. I'm so very sorry for your loss. They were a lovely couple.'

I forced a smile. 'Thank you. That's very kind of you.'

From behind me, I could feel Dexter snapping his head between the two of us. His gaze stayed locked on me. 'What is it, Elle?' he whispered. 'What's happened?'

I flicked him a glance from over my shoulder. 'I'll tell you later.'

Paul changed the subject. 'Can I ask why you want to speak to Mr Masters?'

Dexter stepped forwards. 'It's about a local curse.'

Paul looked taken aback. I couldn't say I blamed him.

'It's about local history,' I cut across him quickly, with an embarrassed laugh. 'I know Mr Masters is a former provost of Fir Haven and must have a wealth of knowledge.' I knew I was babbling, but did my best to sound composed. 'I wanted to feature something on my new shop website about old businesses that used to be in the area.'

Dexter offered me an impressed glance. 'That's right. We only have a couple of questions for him. I promise we won't take up much of his valuable time.'

Paul stepped to one side, revealing a shadowy hallway slicked with buttercream-coloured paint. 'He's getting ready to go to the local bridge club, but I'm sure he can spare a few minutes. I'm just getting ready to head off myself.'

I smiled up at him gratefully. 'Thank you.'

'You're welcome.'

Dexter followed behind me, while Paul vanished down the hallway, his heavy boots thudding on the cool tiled floor.

Paul reappeared moments later and pointed to a door further down the long hall and to the right. 'Please come with me.'

He led us down the glorious hallway which was like something out of a period drama, boasting more gilt-edged paintings of military men and creamy-skinned women.

We were directed to a solid panelled door to the right and into a study, choked with books. In front of those was a heavy office desk, dotted with papers and the remnants of two cups of cold coffee. The window was south-facing, with a view of stretching woodland. In the distance, the trees reminded me of clumps of broccoli, thrusting upwards into the horizon.

Robert Masters rose up from behind his desk and shook our hands. He carried an air of quiet confidence, exacerbated by his open twinkling gaze and welcoming smile. His features were long and weather-beaten, but there was something dashing about him.

I introduced us both and was about to smooth a path towards asking him about Linda Carlucci, when Dexter lurched right in with a torrent of questions about the Carlucci curse.

Robert Masters's smile evaporated. 'I'm confused. I thought Paul said you wanted to speak to me about the history of some former businesses.'

I shot Dexter a look and then composed myself. 'It's actually about Linda Carlucci, Mr Masters.'

Robert Masters's clean-shaven jaw tensed. He remained standing and began to busy himself with papers on his desk. 'Sorry, but I can't help you.'

Desperation was creeping into Dexter's voice. 'Please, sir. We only want to ask you a few questions and then we'll go.'

Robert Masters fired an agitated hand across the top of his close-cut grey hair.

What's going on here? He clearly knew her – or at least knew of her. 'Fran Boyd gave us your name,' I tried again. 'She said you might be willing to talk to us.'

Robert Masters trained his concerned petrol-blue eyes away from us. He stood resolute; his tanned hands now stuffed into the pockets of his dark-brown checked trousers. His cheeks were flushed.

'Please, sir,' begged Dexter again.

A flicker of sympathy lit up in my chest. Desperation was evident in Dexter's downturned mouth.

'Mr Masters,' I began again. 'We wouldn't be bothering you about this unless it was important. I'm sorry that we misled you about why we are here, but we just weren't sure what to say.'

From the study doorway, Paul hovered, his brows gathered in confusion. 'Is everything OK, Mr Masters?'

Robert Masters moved towards his study window. Afternoon light glanced off his pensive features.

'We were worried that if you knew the real reason we are here, you would refuse to talk to us.'

Robert Masters made an agonised noise. Without looking back over his shoulder, he spoke to his gardener. 'Thank you, Paul. Everything is fine.'

'Are you sure, sir?'

'Yes.'

Paul gave us both brief smiles. 'I'll be off then.'

'That's fine, and thank you for your hard work. The lawns look as wonderful as always.'

Paul nodded, told me to take care, and closed the study door behind him.

Robert Masters gestured to us to sit down in two mismatched armchairs opposite his desk, before sinking into his black leather swivel chair. 'OK,' he conceded with a deflated sigh. 'I think you should start at the beginning.'

Chapter Twenty-Six

I sat and listened while Dexter explained to Robert Masters what had happened when he almost ran over Linda Carlucci and the aftermath of the incident, which, at first, he hadn't given much thought.

'That was until I arrived home a bit later that day,' Dexter carried on, twisting the leather strap of his chunky Tag Heuer, explaining his panic at finding he was suffering from a writing drought. He blew out a cloud of frustrated air. 'I know this must all sound crazy.' Dexter looked at me beside him for an instant, before transferring his attention back to Robert Masters. 'I know what you must be thinking, sir.'

Robert Masters gave the briefest nod of understanding. He regarded Dexter for a few moments. 'I've heard about you. You're the crime writer who had the old council offices renovated.'

Now it was Dexter's turn to nod. 'That's right.' Anxiety rang out from his bright-blue eyes.

Robert Masters continued to listen, while the pale sun teased the clouds outside the window.

'And you're sure it was her? Linda Carlucci, I mean?' he asked, his anxious stare travelling from me to Dexter.

I nodded.

Robert Masters rubbed at his clean-shaven chin. 'After all this time.' He sat forward in his study chair, his long limbs appearing stiff. 'What did she do? Did she say anything to you?'

An uncomfortable inflection crept into Dexter's deep rumble, as he mentioned her touching his arm and then clutching at her crescent moon necklace.

Robert Masters's Adam's apple bobbed up and down. I noticed him squirm in his chair.

Dexter carried on talking. 'It was as I was walking away that I began to feel a bit odd. At first, I wondered if I was coming down with something.'

Robert Masters had grown paler.

Dexter moved to speak again but Robert Masters cut across him. 'I believe you.'

Dexter and I started at his admission.

A concoction of relief and shock swamped Dexter's handsome, dark features. 'You do?'

I didn't know what to expect when we came here, but to hear him so emphatically agree with Dexter's unusual take on events still gave me a jolt.

'Linda Carlucci did the same to me,' he managed, rising up from his chair. It gave a leathery creak.

He wandered back over to his study window again; his gaze drifting out towards the rise and fall of woodland beyond. I could see his shoulders stiffen under his shirt. 'I haven't told anyone about this, apart from my dear friend Bertie Boyd, God rest his soul.'

Fran's husband, I reminded myself.

Robert turned away from the window, a slight shadow cast down one side of his distinguished face. He spoke with a sardonic smile. 'I suppose I was like you.' He was addressing Dexter now. 'I thought that if I did tell anyone, they wouldn't believe me anyway. I struggled to even believe it myself.'

He returned to his desk and stood there for a moment, his hands rising and falling down again by his sides. 'Sometimes when I remember about it, I think I must have imagined the whole bloody thing anyway.'

A release of something – like a bubble of pressure – permeated the study. Robert sank back down in his chair and toyed with a pen. His shoulders, under his white shirt, had shaken off the aloofness of before. 'I can't believe I'm talking about this after all these years.' He blew out a cloud of air. 'Still, I hope what I am about to tell you might help.'

He straightened his back in his chair as he talked. 'It was 24th September 1962, at Lakeland Manor, which was our family home. My father was forever throwing fatuous parties, which used to bore me to death, but he insisted I go. They cost a fortune, didn't achieve anything, and seemed to be nothing more than an excuse for Jacob Masters to illustrate his power and wealth in a goldfish bowl like Fir Haven.'

He gave a wry smile as he talked. 'I remember standing there, drinking champagne and deciding I would sneak off.' He carried on reminiscing, his eyes softer. 'I shrugged off my dinner jacket, loosened my bow tie and dumped them on the staircase when this figure flashed past me. I remember her hair was like a long black flag with burgundy strands.'

Robert Masters paused.

'Her eyes were a deep blueberry. She reached up to her hair and scooped it back into a tight bun at the base of her neck.' He smiled at the recollection. 'She was wearing a simple black dress, court shoes, and a frilly white pinafore. I knew she must be one of the extra members of waitressing staff my mother had recruited for this evening.'

He paused again, clearly remembering her profile.

'She was about to disappear into the dining room when I

found myself walking towards her. She was stunning.' Then he grinned. 'We said hello and she told me she had been warned that the master of the house was a tyrant. She had no idea who I was. I asked her what she had heard about Robert Masters. I suppose I wanted to find out what she knew about me.'

Robert Masters looked dazed, lost in the past, as he continued: 'I remember her glancing around herself and saying, 'I hear he has a reputation." Then his smile faded. 'She excused herself, saying she would be late for work if she didn't hurry. I couldn't take my eyes off her.'

Robert Masters sighed. 'I asked her, 'What's your name?' She stopped, reddening to the roots of her black hair. 'Marina, sir,' she replied, blushing at me. Marina Carlucci.'

Dexter and I swapped surprised glances.

'Marina Carlucci?' I asked.

'Linda's younger sister,' Robert clarified, memories clouding in his cool stare. 'Even in that waitressing uniform she was beautiful and outshone all those show ponies.'

My heart twitched for him. So, he had fallen for Marina, Linda's sister, over fifty years ago.

'What happened?' I asked, failing to conceal my desperation to know more.

Robert pulled a gnarled hand down his face and reached for a coffee pot behind him. We both declined his offer, keen to hear where his story twisted and turned from here. We watched him pour fresh, hot black coffee into a clean mug he produced from a drawer.

He took a measured gulp of his coffee and then placed his mug on top of a hessian coaster. His expression was weighted with regret.

'How did Marina take it when she found out you were Robert Masters?' I asked.

'She ricocheted between annoyance and embarrassment, I think. But she knew how I felt about her.'

Patchy sun strobed across Robert's desk.

'When I told her who I was, she refused to have anything to do with me... to begin with.' Robert's lips hinted at a smile. 'I did have rather a reputation in my younger years.'

'How did you manage to win her over?' I asked, intrigued.

'Marina made it bloody difficult for me, I can tell you. But I loved her. I refused to give up on her; on us.' His passionate tone surrendered to resignation. 'She was a proud young woman, who came from a proud family.' Robert recalled it with clarity. 'It was the 31st March 1963, and I can still see the pain in Marina's dark eyes, even now.' He swallowed. 'She begged me not to go ahead with it; asked if there was anything I could do, but there wasn't.'

'About what?' I asked gently.

Robert's sigh was pained. 'About making them leave their home so my father could use the land to build a five-star hotel.'

Robert laced and unlaced his fingers on his desk. 'Amore Cottage was their home, she was the woman I loved, and yet I was too weak to stand up to my father.' Robert shook his head in disbelief. 'I tried to reason with her that the hotel would be such a huge success and that it could set us up for married life.'

'And what did she say?' asked Dexter.

Robert's shoulders slumped as he sat there. 'She said that I could think again if I thought she would marry me after this.' He looked at me. 'I begged her not to go, but she took off across the lawn and that was it. I never saw her again.'

Robert Masters shifted in his leather chair, his attention still lost in the gardens spread out like a scene from a pop-up book through his study window. Myriad memories were clearly pulling at him.

'So what happened then?' I asked him.

Dexter flashed Robert a charged glance. 'Do you mean things began to take a bad turn?'

Robert's lips carried a faint, ironic tilt. 'Oh, the curse was reversed in the end. I threw myself into doing charity work for the local community. I found that it gave me purpose and satisfaction.'

'But…?' I asked, sensing hesitation.

'But since the day I lost Marina, I've never really felt lucky in love again – let alone anything else.' Robert Masters performed a watery smile. 'So, in a way, I think I'm still cursed for losing her – and always will be.'

Chapter Twenty-Seven

Dexter and I sat enthralled as Robert explained that his business decisions, and those of his father, took a disastrous turn from that moment onwards.

'Linda Carlucci arrived at Lakeland to see me the next day. She was furious about how I had treated her sister and said that I was an arrogant and overprivileged bastard who deserved to know what it felt like to be treated so badly.'

Robert drummed his fingers on his heavy cherry-wood desk as he talked. 'I went from having a strong and solid intuition for business opportunities to losing all confidence, and my father discovered that many of his friends and business associates no longer wished to be associated with the family name. When Linda said to me that I needed to learn I wasn't this immortal man but someone who couldn't even stand up to his own beast of a father, I chose to ignore it.'

Robert picked up his coffee mug.

'It was like someone had flicked on a light switch. I know it must sound preposterous, but it was a shock to go from being such a success one minute to a laughing stock in the local community the next.'

'So, you never saw Marina or her family again?' I asked him.

'No. That was it.'

Robert pressed fingers to his lined forehead for a few moments. 'Maybe there never was a curse. Perhaps it was me simply making awful life choices...'

He let his shoulders rise and fall. 'Curse or not – I've never been all that sure – but what I am certain of is that I realised over time what an arrogant arse I'd been and decided to do something about it.'

I raised my brows at Robert's response, as I sat in the velvet armchair.

Robert's cheeks blanched at the memory. 'I'd lost Marina, but the five-star hotel my father wanted didn't go ahead. I made sure of that.'

He steepled his hands together on top of his paper-strewn desk. 'It was too late to fight my father on having the Carluccis's cottage knocked down, but I ensured that the piece of land it stood on was left bare – apart from the roses, mulberry trees, and cypress bushes, that is.'

My eyes widened. Oh my goodness! 'Do you mean the local rose garden? That's where Amore Cottage stood?'

'Yes. Right there. The least I could do was arrange for some flowers and shrubs that were Marina's favourites to be planted there instead.'

He pushed out his legs from under his desk. 'I knew what I was doing was wrong, but I was so bloody weak-willed then, especially when it came to my father.'

I nodded. 'But it's easy to look back and decide how differently you would have done things. It's not so easy when you're all caught up in it at the time.'

Dexter was still digesting Robert's story.

Robert's shoulders set and he sprang forward in his seat, as though some sort of major epiphany had occurred. 'So, you saw Linda Carlucci?' He let out a breath of air. 'I wonder if that means she's back living in the area?' His eyes became distant again.

'Do you know what happened to her?' I asked him. 'Marina, I mean?'

'Yes. Unfortunately, I do.'

His stoical expression blanched. 'I hired a private detective five years ago. A friend of mine who was the same age as me had a health scare at the time and I suppose it made me think about things.' His face was haunted. 'It turned out Marina passed away in 2011 in London. Dementia.'

Dexter was sympathetic. 'I'm so sorry.'

Robert slumped back in his swivel chair. 'I like to think she never forgot me. I suppose it's up to me now to keep the memories alive of what we had.'

He flapped one hand after a prolonged pause. 'Please forgive me if I seem a little off-colour. This news has thrown me and what with my brother passing away just a few weeks ago, things have been rather hectic.'

I offered my sincere apologies. 'I'm so sorry for intruding. We had no idea. If we had known…'

Robert Masters nodded his appreciation. 'There's no need to apologise. I was glad of the distraction.' He rose to his feet. 'I will have to deal with Richard's affairs and then there's the joy of clearing out his house, but all in good time.'

Dexter extended his hand. 'Thank you for your time, Mr Masters. It's much appreciated. And I'm very sorry for your loss.'

I stood up too and prepared to leave.

Robert guided us out of his study and back across the hall. 'I would like to see her. Linda.'

'Believe me, so would I,' agreed Dexter grimly.

Dexter strode back to his car and was subdued on the journey back. There was only the murmur of Coldplay coming from his digital stereo. Well, I say stereo but it looked more like a piece of intricate NASA equipment to launch rockets.

'You're very quiet,' I observed, giving sidelong glances to the hedgerows studded with white flowers.

From the corner of my eye, I could make out Dexter's moody profile. He had thrust his sunglasses back on, even though the sun was tiring now and being swallowed by increasing clumps of cloud.

'Just digesting everything.'

I tightened the bands securing the end of my long plait. 'This… thing… writer's block… the curse…' I began. 'It will all come good in the end. You'll see.'

Dexter kept his attention trained on the country lanes. 'I wish I had your optimism.'

I picked up on the despondency in his voice. 'We will come good. OK, so it's not going to be easy tracking down Linda Carlucci, but we will.'

He gave me another long look as he negotiated the roads. 'You don't have to tell me if you don't want to, Elle. Just tell me to shut up.'

'Is that a promise?'

He pulled a face. Then there were a few seconds of heavy silence. 'Your parents… I heard Robert Masters' gardener say something to you just now. Do you mind me asking what happened?'

I angled my head to gaze at the emerald trees and cottages flashing past. It still sounded at times like it was someone else and not me saying the words. 'They both died a year ago in a car accident.'

Dexter inhaled. 'Jesus. I'm so sorry. I don't know what to say.'

'There isn't anything you can say. Gran and I are trying to just get on with things and be there for each other.'

There was another of Dexter's blue-eyed sideways looks from behind his sunglasses. 'And that's why you took over the family business?'

I nodded. 'I decided I wanted to keep it going in some shape or another. I couldn't bear the thought of selling it. My father's building business was bought by one of his oldest friends, but I wasn't prepared to let the shop go the same way.'

I twisted round in the leather car seat, aware that Dexter kept shooting me glances. 'Why are you looking at me like that?'

'Like what?'

'Like that.'

Dexter continued to stare out of his windscreen through his aviators. 'It's called admiration. You've been dealing with so much and just getting on with it. And now you're busy thinking about saving the small crested blue tit.'

'I'm glad the threatened destruction of the nature reserve is providing you with some entertainment.'

Dexter flicked the indicator and swept us left, past the Fir Haven tourist sign. 'I'm not laughing about it at all. It says a lot about you.'

His icy-blue eyes scanned me for a few seconds longer from behind his shades. 'Something tells me you're not going to have much time to help me find Linda Carlucci. Now I understand why. I'm so sorry again for your loss.'

I folded my arms and swallowed, touched by his genuine concern. 'I promised Gran I would help you and I will. I can do both; help you *and* fight the reserve threat.'

For the briefest moment, a quirky smile looked like it was spreading upwards on his face. 'And the shop?'

'I've got Gran and Cate to help,' I insisted.

Dexter controlled the large charcoal leather steering wheel. We were now winding our way past the chain of high street shops. The icing-pink signage of Paper Roses blossomed outwards.

Cate had closed up for the day and the shop was slumbering with the lights all switched off and the bottle-glass windows a hazy dark hue.

'All the more reason to concentrate on making it a success,' said Dexter.

I narrowed my eyes at him. 'Is this your not very subtle way of telling me you don't want my help after all?'

Dexter returned me to Pebble Brook, sliding down past the patchwork fields and dry-stone walls. He killed the engine. 'I never said that.'

'Mmm. You hinted.'

'No I didn't.'

I raised my eyes in frustration, up to the car roof. It was all thick leather too. 'Look, why can't you just accept that I'm going to help you?'

He swiped off his sunglasses and left them poking out of the top of his shirt pocket.

'Don't think I'm doing all this for you,' I said, his hypnotic eyes unnerving. 'I'm community-spirited.'

There was that sexy, quirky smile again. 'Sure.'

I reached down to my shoulder bag resting by my feet and got out of the car, thanking him for returning me home. I straightened my T-shirt while he pressed a button and the driver's side window slid downwards with a decadent *whoosh*.

'I don't give in easily either,' I pointed out through the open window.

'Now that I can believe.'

There was silence, except for the odd burr from a wood pigeon and the tinkling of the stream.

'You'll have your writing talent back in no time. You'll see.'

Dexter didn't appear convinced. He opened his mouth, but then closed it again.

'Thank you for the lift home.' I started off down past the stream that rolled across the stones. I turned around to see Dexter raise one hand and give a mock salute.

'I've had one or two more ideas about how we might track down Linda Carlucci,' I called, finding myself keen to reassure him.

'Great.'

Dexter poked his dark head further out of the driver's side window. He hesitated and cleared his throat. 'Maybe I can help you with brainstorming on the reserve… You know, ideas on how we can try and save it. You know… together.'

We? *Together?* I blinked back at him, surprised. 'Are you sure? Oh. OK. That would be good. Thanks.'

'I'll give you a call tomorrow.'

Then he was gone in a blur of silver wheel trim.

I stared up at Pebble Brook, the light from a couple of lamps washing out onto the path. The Carlucci siblings had reached into the lives of certain individuals in Fir Haven, leaving an indelible memory. Even after all this time, it seemed that their echoes persisted.

Trepidation took hold. It had been one hell of a day of revelations and repercussions. Now I had to speak to my gran about Lorenzo.

Chapter Twenty-Eight

Grandma examined me over the top of the breakfast bar later that evening. 'I fell in love with Lorenzo Carlucci in the summer of 1962.'

She traced a finger around the rim of her mug. 'It was before I met and married your grandfather.'

I noted a dreamy softness swim in her eyes.

'I was twenty years old and I thought I was such a modern young woman. I believed I was ahead of my time.' She let out a bark of fruity laughter. 'I was so ambitious then – fighting to be a councillor instead of marrying and having four children like many of my friends were doing. I wanted to give the world a bloody good shake!'

She cradled her mug of hot chocolate, which I had insisted on drizzling with mini marshmallows and a dollop of fresh cream. 'I enjoyed working as a doctor's receptionist at the local surgery, but answering the phones and making appointments… well, I felt like there must be something I could do to help the needy here in Fir Haven. That was when I realised I wanted to be a councillor.'

I sank down opposite her at the breakfast bar. 'Go on, Gran.'

She flicked me a charged look. Straight away, I imagined her as a determined, young force of nature, all idealistic and passionate.

'Lorenzo came to a town hall meeting. His family hadn't long moved to the area.' Gran took a considered sip of her drink. 'I remember I had been exchanging heated words with a few of the old stuffed shirts about providing a proper play park for the local children and had just got on my high horse about entering Fir Haven for the Prettiest Town in Scotland Award. Lorenzo had been a gardener in his native Italy and was starting to earn a bit of money providing gardening services here in the local area.' Her fine-boned cheeks conjured up a streak of pink. 'I was in the middle of my prepared speech about how the competition could really raise the profile of the area, when he walked in and took a seat. He was the most beautiful man I'd ever seen.'

Captivated, I pleaded with her to continue. 'And what happened, Gran?'

'We began working together on this little committee and quickly found we were very attracted to one another.' Then her wistful expression melted away. 'Fir Haven came second in the competition in the end but our relationship… well…' She toyed with the handle of her mug. 'Adam Fraser was part of the committee too. I always knew he liked me.' Gran shook her head, as if trying to reconcile everything. 'But he became so jealous of Lorenzo.' She puffed out her cheeks, her lacquered nails tapping away. 'Adam connived to have Lorenzo and the rest of his family forced out of the area.' She took a pensive sip from her mug and resumed talking again. 'With such pressure on us, our relationship couldn't last. Maybe if I had been stronger and more outspoken… I was weak,' she erupted, self-disgust evident in her voice.

'Gran, please don't blame yourself. You were only twenty.'

She stared down into her hot chocolate, lost in thought for a few moments.

'Was that why you were so keen for me to help Dexter? Because of the guilt you felt over Lorenzo?'

Gran didn't reply. Her preoccupied expression answered for her.

'Do you know what happened to Lorenzo after you split up?'

She gazed past my shoulder and towards the kitchen window. 'He returned to Italy and married a local girl. Then I heard several years later that he had three children and was running his own little gardening business near Lake Garda.' She shrugged. 'It was my own fault. I couldn't find my voice then.'

'Well, you've certainly more than made up for it,' I half joked, hoping to raise a smile from her.

It worked momentarily. Gran's lips slid upwards into a brief smile. 'The same can be said of you, young lady.'

I cradled my drink between both hands. 'Did you ever tell Mum any of this?'

Gran looked appalled. 'Goodness me, no! Lorenzo was part of my past. I didn't see any reason to mention it or drag it all up again. What would that have achieved?'

I studied her. 'Why did you want me to hear it from Adam Fraser?'

My grandmother's smoky-grey eyes now glittered with resentment. 'I wanted him to admit to his behaviour, although I wasn't at all surprised when you told me it was his neighbour who revealed everything in the end.' She sniffed. 'Even now, after all these years, he still can't face up to playing his part in the Carluccis leaving Fir Haven.' She eyed me with unease. 'It was a terrible thing. It wasn't just Lorenzo who upped and left. His sisters, Marina and Lena, ended up leaving too, along with their parents.'

I frowned at her. 'Lena?'

'That's Linda's real name. Lorenzo once commented that she was never keen on Lena. Apparently it had been her grandmother's suggestion when she was born, but she never liked it.' She took a longer sip of her hot chocolate. 'This might be a small and picturesque little town, but it has more than its fair share of skeletons, I can tell you.'

I paused, letting everything she had just told me settle between us. All these romances, intertwined like fine ribbon. 'It wasn't just you who fell in love with one of the Carluccis, Gran.'

She blinked across the breakfast bar at me. 'What do you mean?'

'Robert Masters told Dexter and me that he was in love with Marina.'

Her clear grey eyes popped. 'As in the former provost, Robert Masters?'

'Yes. It sounds like very few people knew about him and Marina either,' I confided.

Grandma's mug paused half way to her lips. 'Well, I never! Robert Masters is a surprise. I didn't think the likes of him lost his heart to anyone. He always came across as a bit buttoned-up. If Lorenzo knew about it, he never said anything.'

Her manicured brows climbed upwards.

Gran folded her freckled arms and leant on the edge of the breakfast bar. We both glanced around, still expecting my mum and dad to stroll in at any moment.

Dad would have peered over my shoulder at the pastel-coloured marshmallows in my hot chocolate and pinched one, while Mum would have tutted at him and bundled me into her arms. She always smelt of Coco Mademoiselle.

I arranged my lips into a forced smile and pushed my memories back into the corners of my mind.

I climbed off my stool and padded over the laminated flooring in my bare feet to tug down the beige hessian blinds. The spotlights under the kitchen cupboards, which Dad had fitted, shone out, highlighting his and Mum's favourite mugs, still swinging from the mug tree. Resentment burrowed in my chest. Tonight was not a good one. I was in danger of wailing in grief.

I rubbed at my gritty eyes and sank back down onto my stool.

'Are you all right, darling?'

I nodded at my concerned grandmother. 'I'm fine, thanks. I'm just a bit washed-out after today.'

I drained the dregs of my hot chocolate and moved around to collect her empty mug. She rubbed at my arms and I planted an affectionate kiss on the top of her head. 'More importantly, how are you?'

'I'm OK if you are.'

We were both doing our best to be strong and stoical for each other.

'If you don't mind, Gran, I think I'll go to bed now.'

'You and I both.'

I rinsed out the cups, losing myself for a moment in the warm sensation of the tap water sliding over my hands.

'And what about Dexter?'

Her unexpected question made me whirl round, splashing the front of my pyjamas. 'Bugger! Sorry. What about him?'

'He's very handsome. Quite the *bon viveur*, if the papers are to be believed.'

I turned away so she couldn't see the guilty colour blooming in my face and loaded the mugs into the top rung of the dishwasher. 'I suppose he is, but there's no need to worry on that score, Gran. After what happened with Lloyd, I'm done with relationships. They never live up to expectations anyway.'

She propped one arm by the sink and reached out for the cluster of germini flowers in hot pinks that were thrusting out of a vase on the window sill. She stroked the soft daisy-like petals. 'Your parents' relationship did. You said yourself what a wonderful marriage they had.'

'Yes, well, that was a one-off,' I insisted. 'They were lucky to find each other. Most people don't ever have what they did.'

Gran eyed me. 'That's a very pessimistic view for a young woman to have.'

I shrugged. 'I'm just being realistic.'

Gran considered this. 'Just be careful. I know I'm the one who's been encouraging you to help Dexter, but all the same…'

'Careful of what?'

Grandma moved towards me. She raised one hand and lifted a stray hair back from my cheek. 'Of losing your heart to a handsome man, despite your protestations. Believe me, I should know.'

Chapter Twenty-Nine

Lunch time rolled around fast, thanks to a morning that saw a harassed mum purchasing a job lot of animal-shaped erasers, mini notebooks and glittery pencil cases to put into party bags for her daughter's seventh birthday party. She also decided to purchase a pack of thank-you notelets for her daughter to write on after the festivities.

She had been followed up by middle-aged lady in ruby-red lipstick, who clutched a list of family birthdays and proclaimed she was eager to be mega-organised for once and would buy all the birthday and anniversary cards in one go, to save a panic later.

Then there were proactive school children dragging along their parents, asking for new pencil sets and colouring pens for the new school year, which was due to start again in a month.

I had only just managed to snatch a welcome cup of peppermint tea when one of the young apprentices from the butcher's darted in, anxious to get a special card for his fiancée for her graduation and Mr Conroy, a friend of Gran's, who was in search of a 'lovely but not too soppy' anniversary card for his wife.

I swished my ponytail back over my shoulder as I slit the brown tape of the next box open with scissors.

If business continued to be brisk (which I hoped it would be) I would have to think about taking on another member of staff or two. Even a couple of part-timers would be welcome.

I was just about managing at the moment, what with my grandmother popping by to serve for the odd few hours here and there and Cate also helping out. She insisted she would be available more in the autumn, once she had been able to satisfy her current jewellery demands.

The other box of cards I had just received were secured together by elastic bands and consisted of everything from cute felt, fabric, or embossed unicorns and trains, to designs aimed more at the teenage market, with birthday images of football boots, headphones, and designer handbags. Glitter speckled my fingers while I plucked them out of the box and began slotting them into the white wooden display.

As I glided then into their respective slots, I increased the volume on my iPod and hummed along to the rock tunes I had placed on shuffle. I wiggled this way and that, sashaying around.

So engrossed was I as I threw some shapes that I missed the dinging noise of the shop doorbell.

'I think you might have missed your calling.'

I leapt up, embarrassment flooding through me. I let go of half the cards in my hand and they skittered across the wooden floor.

Dexter stooped down and gathered them up.

I reached for my hair and hoped half my make-up hadn't slid off during the morning. I found myself also adjusting my shirt collar and dropped my hand in frustration. *What on earth was I doing?* Brilliant. Just brilliant. Dexter had seen me dancing around, making an utter tit of myself. 'Do you always sneak up on poor unsuspecting shop owners?'

He paused, still holding the cards he had picked up for me. He appraised me with his thickly lashed eyes. 'Only the very pretty ones.' Then he remembered he was holding the greetings cards. He thrust them back towards me.

I took them, the glitter and gloss designs rubbing against my skin. 'Thank you.' I felt my cheeks flame.

He was dressed in a navy-blue V-neck jumper, petrol-blue combats, and dark trainers. He sifted one hand through his blueberry hair.

My heart was starting to gallop against my ribs.

Grandma's words of warning pinged around my head, so I placed the greetings cards onto the counter. Heat crawled up my neck. 'Is there something I can help you with, Dexter?'

He blinked at me, recovering himself. 'Of course. Right.' He glanced over his shoulder, checking that the shop was still quiet. 'I wondered if we could have a chat about what to do next with this whole Linda Carlucci thing?'

I beckoned him to come behind the counter and into the kitchen area. From there I was still able to look out onto the shop floor to keep an eye out for any customers wandering in.

I had been thinking about the Linda Carlucci situation last night and all morning. I decided not to divulge what my Gran had told me about her falling in love with Linda's brother. It was all still fresh and new to me and I didn't want to betray my grandmother's confidence.

'I don't know if this will work,' I warned, choosing the chair opposite Dexter rather than directly next to him, 'but it could be worth a shot.'

Dexter's bemused attention flicked from the chair beside him to the one I sat myself down in which was at a safe distance. 'Go on,' he encouraged. 'I don't know how much longer I can carry on like this.'

A desperate edge took over his bright-blue eyes. 'It's not the financial security I'm concerned about. I mean, don't get me wrong. It's wonderful my books sell so well. But I miss not being able to write. It's not like I want to write. It's more that I *have* to, if that makes sense. It's all I know and all I've ever wanted to do.'

I listened, touched by his honesty and worry. 'It does make sense.'

He dragged a hand down his face. 'Maybe you're right, Elle. Perhaps this isn't a curse. Maybe I'm losing my touch and at the back of my mind I'm trying to find an excuse rather than face up to it.'

I stared over at him. 'Don't say that.' I leant forward in my chair. 'This doesn't sound like you at all, Dexter.'

He sighed. 'It took me a long time to get published. I have some real howlers stashed away and a pile of rejection letters from publishers and agents that could paper half of Hawk West Hall. It's all I ever wanted to do.' His shoulders sank further. 'I just can't begin to imagine not writing anymore.'

My breath lodged in my throat for him. 'We won't give up. Let's track down Linda Carlucci and take it from there. Sound like a plan?'

His full lips hinted at a grateful smile. 'It's a plan.'

I realised he was studying me again from under his lashes and I gave myself a mental shake. 'Right. So, I wondered if it might be worth putting an advert in the local paper, asking if anyone knows of Linda Carlucci's whereabouts?'

Dexter considered this. 'Anything is worth a shot.' He let out a long, slow sigh. 'And I'm more than happy to put up a generous reward for finding her.'

Oh god. He looked so forlorn and lost sitting there, his handsome, haunted poet's face etched with worry. Without thinking, I shot out my hand. My fingers closed around his. He had short, square nails and his skin was warm and welcoming.

Oh shit! What am I doing?

I snatched my hand back across the table, as if he'd just burnt me. *What's gotten into me?*

Dexter examined his hand for a moment, as if wondering

whether I did really just touch him there a moment ago. He took a few moments to answer. 'Let's give it a try.'

I ignored the long look he was giving me.

'Good! We can come up with the wording now, if you like.'

'Elle…'

Relief swamped me as the shop phone let out a series of sharp rings.

I felt sorry for Dexter. Yes. That's what it was. I had reached out my hand to comfort him, as I would have done with anyone else. I was being empathetic. That was all.

I kept my back turned away from him to conceal the scalding heat in my face. My grandmother's experience with Lorenzo played on a continuous loop in my head, like those concussion stars in a *Tom & Jerry* cartoon. She was still carrying hurt and regret, even after all those years. And look what happened between Lloyd and me. I had trusted him, loved him, and yet he hadn't been there for me when I needed him most. I wasn't prepared to put myself through that again.

I snatched up the silver and black phone receiver on top of the kitchen cupboard. My voice sounded as though it belonged to someone else. 'Good afternoon, Paper Roses. How can I help?'

I kept my back turned away from Dexter's charged gaze.

I spoke again into the phone, longing for something to break the tension in the shop. My voice was disembodied; strangulated. *Why did I have to touch his hand? Why didn't I make some understanding noises instead?*

My iPod was channelling some classic Sir Elton John, but the track was fizzling to an end, which made the atmosphere throb even more.

I snatched a glance over at Dexter before turning my attention to my pink and white framed cork notice board, bearing pinned reminders of the bin collection dates, phone numbers for our main suppliers, and ripped pages from a catalogue in which I'd spotted Advent beauty calendars.

His dark expression was unfathomable.

It was one of the greetings card reps calling to ask if I might be interested in checking out their new range of West Highland terrier themed products.

I turned around with an apologetic smile for Dexter and to reassure him I wouldn't be a minute.

I need not have bothered.

His chair was empty. Dexter had gone.

Chapter Thirty

'Elle. Elle? Are you still there?'

'Yes,' I faltered, disappointment at Dexter leaving searing right through me. *Why had he left so abruptly?* 'Yes. Sorry. I'm still here.'

I finished the call, making an appointment for Lisa at the greetings card company to pop by and see me with samples from the new range in a few days.

In the meantime, a determined toddler had got her way with the teddy bear card she had selected and grinned up at me as I rang it through the till for her mother.

Dexter kept appearing at the corners of my mind, niggling and haunting me.

Once the mum and child had clattered back out of the shop, with me holding the door open for them, I steeled myself and reached for my mobile.

I rang Dexter's number. Something inside me wondered whether he would pick up, but after half a dozen rings, his stilted voice made me start. 'Elle.'

The words rushed out of my mouth, before I had a chance to

stop them. 'Why did you leave the shop just now without saying anything? Did I do something to offend you?'

His silence irritated me further.

'Don't you think you owe me an explanation? One minute we were talking about ideas for tracing Linda Carlucci, and the next you had gone.'

His voice was heavy; faltering. 'I had to take an urgent call. Sorry about that.'

I decided not to conduct a post-mortem on it. It seemed he wasn't prepared to discuss the real reason for him disappearing like that, let alone go into details. It was perplexing though.

'Look,' I said, staring out of the shop window at the odd local wandering past, 'we really do need to talk over the wording for a notice in the local paper to find Linda Carlucci. That's if you still think it's a good idea?'

'Of course, I do.' There was a pause. Then he wrong-footed me. 'How about you drop by Hawk West Hall when you close up the shop tonight?'

I blinked hard.

Why was he inviting me to his home? My brain felt addled. One minute he goes AWOL on me and the next he's extending invitations? But Dexter and I couldn't keep dancing around one another. We wouldn't get anywhere otherwise!

I decided to accept his invitation, even though a tiny voice inside me was screaming at me to think again.

Chapter Thirty-One

I closed Paper Roses that evening before heading back down the street and around the corner to the car park so I could drive up to Hawk West Hall.

The street shone with the silver remnants of afternoon rain. I climbed into my car and examined my reflection in the rear-view mirror. My dark-brown eyes bore smudges of tiredness and a lot of my hair had worked itself free from its ponytail.

I neatened my hair before reaching into my bag beside me and dashing on some fresh rose-pink lipstick and blusher. I finished by flicking on another coating of black mascara.

I stopped.

Hang on. Why am I bothering so much about how I look? I was going over to Hawk West Hall to discuss our search for Linda Carlucci. End of.

I switched on my car radio to drown out the odd thoughts swimming around inside my head and set off for Dexter's home.

The hedgerows were fringed with pale droplets of rain from the earlier shower as my car flashed past.

There was already an abundance of wooden protest signs erected by the roadside in brightly coloured paint, with the words 'Nature Comes First', 'Save Our Reserve', and 'Wild about Nature – Stop the Closure!' emblazoned across them.

Good! So the other protestors hadn't wasted any time in being proactive.

I made myself a promise to do all I could to help. I flicked my indicator right and negotiated my way down a narrow country lane with banks of grass on either side.

My stomach performed an impressive forward roll as the woods opened out on my right and the Gothic splendour of Hawk West Hall soared up and above the tops of the trees. Branches heavy with an abundance of shimmering sage-coloured leaves dangled like giant arms.

I raised my chin and tried to concentrate on my driving. What was wrong with me?

The last time I'd been up here, there had been workmen bustling around in fluorescent jackets and hard hats.

I eased up to the wrought-iron gates. The council offices were just a distant memory.

I edged the car closer to a silver intercom system that had been installed. I admired the sharp pointed spires and flying buttresses as I leant out of the driver's side window and pressed the button marked 'Visitors'.

I sprang to attention as an older female voice barked at me through the intercom. 'Yes?'

'I'm Elle Cassidy. I'm here to see Mr Grayling. He's expecting me.'

There was a few seconds' pause.

'Welcome, Ms Cassidy. The gates will open now. Please drive into the grounds and take the first right. There's a visitor car park at the rear.'

I settled myself back into my seat and eased my car through the opening gates. My tyres spun on the rosy pink gravel.

There was an area with several parking spaces, three of which were occupied by what looked like tradesperson vehicles. I parked up beside a white transit van and collected my shoulder bag from the passenger side.

I locked the car, wondering where I should go next, when a figure approached. She extended one hand. 'Ms Cassidy? I'm Elsa Bennett, Mr Grayling's housekeeper.' She had a warm London accent and twinkled with friendliness.

I took her hand. 'I'm Elle. Nice to meet you.'

She indicated for me to follow her through the back door and I tapped up behind her. Her blue-grey expensively cut hair nodded this way and that.

Elsa led me up a coil of granite steps towards a door that opened out into a kitchen that was like something out of a glossy interiors magazine.

It consisted of a striking combination of a panelled blonde wood floor and avocado fixtures and fittings. The breakfast bar, which more closely resembled a Henry VIII banqueting table, ran the length of the kitchen in black and grey marbled swirls.

Sash windows occupied either side of the kitchen and suspended from the slate-grey painted ceiling was a fluted black and gold light fitting. It wouldn't have looked out of place in a sci-fi TV series.

Mrs Bennett, who insisted I call her Elsa, caught me gawping. 'Not bad, is it?' she said with a wry smile.

'It's certainly the poshest kitchen I've ever been in. It's gorgeous.'

I watched her reach across the chrome sink and lower the volume of the digital radio.

'Where did you work before?'

'I've been working as a housekeeper for twelve years now. It was after I lost my husband suddenly that I decided I had to do something different and have a change of scene.'

'Oh, I'm so sorry to hear that.'

Mrs Bennett smiled. 'Thank you. I still miss Kenny so much, but I enjoy what I do, so that helps. I started off working for an affluent businessman and his family in Chelsea and then for a well-known footballer who lived in Kensington. I was even a housekeeper in New York for Mr & Mrs Turner-Woods for a little while.'

Images of Mum and Dad appeared in front of my eyes. 'People who you love never really leave you.' For fear of upsetting her and myself, I moved the conversation back to her work. I couldn't conceal how impressed how I was. 'The people you just mentioned in New York. That's not Jackson and Mila Turner-Woods, the fashion designers, is it?'

'The very same.'

'What was that like?'

Elsa gave the briefest curl of her lip. 'Demanding. I'm much happier working for Mr Grayling.'

She urged me to follow her again. 'Mr Grayling is in his study waiting for you.' She cast me a long look over one shoulder. 'That's where he likes to sit and write, although he doesn't seem to have been doing much of that of late.'

I wondered if Dexter had confided in Elsa and then concluded that it sounded like he hadn't. She seemed a very approachable person though, with her gentle smile and enquiring gaze.

Elsa led me away from the kitchen and through a heavy door – another oak-panelled affair. This led out into the grand hall, which was a mismatched combination of silver-grey tiled floor, a dark wood winding spiral staircase I could imagine Cinderella sweeping down, and two velvet chairs in olive green that were accompanied by a matching sofa.

Two large black and white prints of horses decorated the white walls.

I studied the proud stallions, who were staring down their nostrils at the camera. Their long tousled manes flapped in the wind. 'Both those horses belonged to Mr Grayling,' said Elsa, folding her arms. 'That one is Byron and the other one is Wilde.'

Something made me conjure up an image of him riding along a windswept beach, his dark hair ruffled with salt. I pushed away the picture, realising my cheeks felt warm. 'Does he still have the horses?'

'His parents take care of them for him. They live in the Cotswolds.'

She beckoned me forward to another door to the right of the hall that was closed. 'It's Mr Grayling's dream to use the rest of the land here to have his own stud farm.'

'Hello.'

The door moved and we both jumped guiltily at the sight of Dexter standing there. He filled the doorway in a loose white cotton shirt and black jeans. His hair appeared to have been freshly washed and was falling back in damp layers from his face.

His attention travelled from my ponytail down to my jewelled ballet pumps. I realised I was staring back, equally as intensely as he was. I tilted my chin up. 'Hi, Dexter.'

'Thanks for coming. Please come in.'

He stepped to one side and I moved past him.

While he exchanged a few words with Elsa about what he fancied for breakfast the next day, I snatched the opportunity to take in the fluted blue drapes at the floor-to-ceiling window and his heavy polished writing desk.

It was positioned to the right of the window so that it took in the rear lawns and a burst of trees that fed down to some farmland.

The nature reserve was stippled beyond that, in amongst the army of forest and trickling streams. No wonder Dexter wanted to write in this room. The view was like a Constable painting.

'This is where I find I'm at my most creative,' he said from behind me. 'Well, usually.'

I spun round, a pang of sympathy for him hitting me in the chest.

He pointed to a quilted high-backed chair on the other side of his desk and I sank down into it. He sat down too, the top of his desk an array of notebooks and scribbled-on sheets of paper. His flatscreen computer was switched off.

Frustration was etched into every sinew of his features.

'Look,' I blurted, keen to say something positive, 'I don't know if my idea will work, but we should at least give it ago. Someone might see our notice in the paper and respond.'

I refused to believe that there wasn't someone somewhere who knew Linda Carlucci's whereabouts. 'And she can't live that far away from here since she has started appearing again from time to time.'

Dexter's lashes cast a shadow against his cheeks. 'I'm getting desperate, Elle. I really am.'

My eyes were drawn to a shelf behind him. Running along the length of it, were paperback copies of his novels. His name ran down each spine in gold lettering. There must have been at least a dozen books there.

He followed my gaze.

I set my shoulders in what I hoped was a show of confidence. 'Well then, let's give it a try.'

I reached down to my feet and plucked a small notebook out of my bag, along with a pen. I flicked it open. 'I hope you don't think I'm being too forward, but I did also wonder about you hiring a private detective…'

His voice was cold and abrupt. 'No.' He rubbed at his chin. 'Don't get me wrong, Elle. It's nothing to do with the cost. I have the money. It's just…'

I waited.

'It's just, I hired one a few years ago on a personal matter. I thought I could trust him, but he ended up trying to sell a story about me to the press.'

'OK. Then we do it our way. So I thought we could draft up an appeal for information.'

Something made me raise my eyes from where I had started scribbling on the lined paper. I could feel him watching me.

Dexter had steepled his long fingers together. 'Why are you doing this, Elle? Why are you helping me?'

My heart juddered and I placed the pen on top of my notebook. 'You know why.'

'Do I?'

'I'm doing this as a favour to my grandmother.'

'And that's the only reason?'

My fingers scrambled for my pen again in my lap. 'What other reason could there be?'

He sank back in his chair, his bold gaze refusing to leave my lips. 'You tell me.'

I cleared my throat, searching around for something witty and decisive to say, but my increasing frustration was starting to reveal itself. It had started off like that – as a favour to my grandmother – but the longer this went on, the more I realised I wanted to help Dexter. I wanted to be around him; to forget about all my protestations about not getting romantically involved with anyone again, after Lloyd and my insistence that I would never open up my heart to another man again. Something was happening and I felt as though I was at a loss to stop it. Perhaps I didn't want to.

The flurry of colour in my face made Dexter stare at me harder.

'Do you know what I think?' he said after a considered pause.

My breath stuck in the base of my throat. I couldn't drag my eyes away from him.

But then haunting images of the hurt and disappointment Lloyd had inflicted reared up again. The way I had assumed he would support me when my parents died, only for him to turn his back on me when I needed him most. *Shit*. I had to get a grip of my emotions here. What was I doing? What was I thinking? I'd promised myself I wouldn't allow myself to go through all that again. and yet here I was, teetering right on the edge. I was the only one capable of stopping this.

I cleared my throat. 'I think we should concentrate on finding Linda Carlucci.'

Dexter's black lashes blinked at me from across the desk. 'Right. Yes. Of course.' He paused, watching me, but all I offered, despite my internal turmoil, was a friendly smile. 'So, what about the wording for this ad?'

I was grateful to turn my attention back to my notebook. This was for the best. Whenever I loved someone, I seemed to lose them in the end or they let me down. I focused hard on my notes. I would be saving myself from more heartache in the long run. 'I also thought about having a broadcast put out on local radio.'

'Do you think it could work?' asked Dexter.

'I think it stands a great chance and anything is worth a try.'

I leant forward, rolling my glittery silver pen between my fingers. 'Someone must know something about where she lives now and all we need is one small lead to kick things off.' My thoughts gathered enthusiasm. 'I think we'll need to use these same mediums to protect the nature reserve.'

Dexter sat back in his chair and appraised me.

I narrowed my eyes at him. 'What is it?'

'Nothing,' he said through a small smile. 'Nothing.'

Chapter Thirty-Two

'He's offering how much?!' choked Cate the next morning.

I repeated the amount of the reward Dexter was putting up for locating Linda Carlucci.

Cate shook her corkscrew curls in disbelief. 'Bloody hell!' She turned her attention back to unpacking a new delivery we had received of photo frames decorated with dried twigs and leaves.

'What can I say? He's desperate.'

Paper Roses was gilded now with watery summer sunshine. It lay across the floorboards like a gold cloak.

Cate took a step backwards in her red and white trainers and admired the display of frames she was arranging on the shelf. 'And saving the reserve? What's the latest on that?'

I folded my arms and explained that as well as contacting our local MP and the regional media, I was going to run a photography competition on the Paper Roses website for the best picture of the reserve and have it printed up into a greetings card to sell in the shop.

I was also going to put up protest posters, sell badges with 'I Heart Nature' which one of Gran's local artist friends was organising, and speak to the other businesses along the street to see if they would also be willing to get involved. 'I also wondered if the likes of the garden centre would give a contribution from all proceeds of their tree sales and publicly support us too.' I pulled a horrified face. 'If this fight becomes protracted, we will need money for a court case.'

Cate gave me an encouraging smile. 'Sounds like you really are going for it. Good! Well, just let me know what I can do.' She wrinkled up her nose. 'Pity you couldn't get a well-known face on board.'

She walked into the kitchen and began clattering around with the kettle. 'If you could attract the interest of a famous name and have them voice their support for the reserve, that would be such a coup.'

She reappeared in the doorway as the kettle began to grumble behind her. 'I bet the national newspapers would pick up on it then.'

I pulled a face. 'But who could I ask?' I snapped my shoulders to attention. How stupid was I? The answer was staring me in the face. 'Oh my god! That's a brilliant idea!' I pushed my hands into the pockets of my denim skirt. 'I mean, I'm doing him a favour by helping him find Mrs Carlucci.'

Cate's mouth dropped open. 'You're going to ask Dexter? Are you serious? I was meaning someone more like Frankie McVey who has that holiday home up by the park.'

Frankie McVey was the drummer in a well-known Scottish folk band, who dropped by Fir Haven for the odd weekend break. 'Yes, but you just said it yourself. Frankie McVey has a holiday home here. He doesn't live in the area though, does he?' Excitement began to pump in my chest. 'At least Dexter does. He's got such a high profile too.' Then another idea made me gasp. 'Maybe Dexter's team could release a press statement, voicing his support for the reserve?'

I moved towards Cate, more ideas bubbling away. 'What do you think? Do you think he might get involved?'

Cate made a helpless gesture with her hands. 'I'm not sure, Elle. From the little I know of him, he doesn't come across as exactly generous of spirit. That's why Linda Carlucci took exception to him in the first place.'

Snapshots of Dexter speaking out in favour of the reserve and headlines proclaiming 'FAMOUS AUTHOR PROTECTS SCOTTISH BEAUTY SPOT,' lodged themselves behind my eyes. 'But that's the point,' I argued. 'If Dexter lets people see – especially Linda – that he's changed for the better, or at least is trying to, then it's all to the good.' I clapped my hands together. 'I'll ring Dexter now and ask if it's convenient to go and have a chat with him.'

While Cate furnished me with a mug of tea, I pulled up his number on my phone. She didn't appear convinced by my suggestion at all, judging by the long looks she was giving me.

When he answered, I didn't reveal in the call what I wanted to discuss with him. I thought it would be better face to face, in the hope he would agree if he could witness first-hand what saving the nature reserve meant to me and everyone else.

Dexter told me he had a Skype call with his agent at 10:30 a.m., but that any time after that would be fine.

Once I ended my conversation with him, I took a thoughtful sip of my tea. 'I can ring Gran and ask her to come in and help you out at lunchtime, till I get back.'

Cate said no, that wasn't necessary. 'I'm sure I can manage. You just concentrate on the reserve for now. Paper Roses is in capable hands!'

Chapter Thirty-Three

'What you said, Elle, about me being part of the community here now, well, you're right.'

Dexter cleared his throat. 'I'm in a position where I can hopefully do something.' His deep, lilting voice tailed off as he continued to search my face. 'It's the least I can do. Anyone can see how much this means to you, Elle.'

'Thank you,' I breathed. 'I mean it. I'm very grateful.'

I squinted across at him in his sunlit study, the atmosphere crackling. 'So, have you actually been to see the nature reserve for yourself yet?'

'Not yet, but that's something I intend to remedy as soon as possible.'

'You ought to pay a visit,' I encouraged. 'I'm sure, being a writer, it won't fail to charm you.'

My heart hammered against my ribs as Dexter continued to study me. *Why did I sound like a cartoon mouse all of a sudden?*

Deeper sunlight swept across the room, sifting through Dexter's black hair and highlighting its shots of dark red. 'So, when can you take me to see it?' Dexter's eyes refused to leave my face.

There was a charged silence, except for the odd distant clacks from a couple of magpies outside amongst the trees.

Dexter continued, undeterred. 'I think us going to see the nature reserve together would take on far more meaning, don't you agree?' He glittered at me from under his sooty lashes.

I felt like I was struggling to breathe.

I couldn't resist. I found myself agreeing, as though I were being hypnotised. 'Yes. Yes. Of course. That makes sense.'

I adjusted one of my earrings for something to do. 'You should see for yourself how beautiful it is.'

'Then how about this evening? That's if you haven't got anything else on?' Dexter was expectant.

I disguised the excited breath in my throat by swallowing.

Dexter's generous mouth softened into a smile. What was going on inside my head?

'So, see you this evening then?' he asked.

What should I do? Say no? Suggest he go up to the reserve alone? But he wants to see it for himself and he's showing a genuine interest in it, would it look childish not to go with him?

I set my shoulders and hoped I appeared far calmer than I felt. 'That's fine by me.'

'Good. I'll give you a call a bit later on this afternoon and you can let me know when to come and collect you.'

I departed, negotiating the last few steps of Hawk West Hall with Dexter framing the grand entrance. I didn't dare look back at him over my shoulder.

As soon as I heard the stately creak of the oak doors closing, I let out a long, cool rush of air.

I clambered back into my little Mini, grateful that I had a moment to compose myself. My stomach was exploding with butterflies.

I knew what I was doing was risky – dangerous, even – allowing myself to be enticed by Dexter. But I realised that right at this moment, despite my previous insistence that I could resist him, I suddenly wasn't so sure.

Chapter Thirty-Four

The high street soon slid into view, all winking shop windows, swinging baskets of flowers, and ornate lampposts.

I parked the car and returned to Paper Roses. Two departing customers nodded at me in greeting as I held the shop door open for them to pass.

Cate was on her phone, head thrown back and laughing at something Lucy was telling her. When she saw me, she waggled her fingers in greeting and rounded off the call. 'See you soon, babes.'

I asked her how Lucy was and if she had managed OK while I had been gone.

'Lucy's good and business has been steady.'

When I asked her if she'd managed to have her lunch yet, Cate confessed that she hadn't. I pointed at the shop door. 'Well, go and get some now. You couldn't pick me up a chicken salad wrap while you're out, please?'

Cate threw on her denim jacket, which she picked up from the back of a chair. 'Sure.' She looked at me. 'Are you ok?'

'Why?'

She narrowed her black eyes. 'You seem a bit… distracted.'

When I didn't argue the point, she led me through to the kitchen and ordered me to sit down. 'OK, spill.'

I dropped my bag onto the floor with a thud and explained about Dexter.

Cate listened, inclining her head like a beautiful tropical bird.

'You like him. A lot.'

'Who?'

'Tom Hardy. Who do you think I'm talking about?!'

Now it was my turn to throw my head back and laugh. Somehow, it didn't sound convincing, even to me. 'Me? Like Dexter Grayling? Don't be daft!'

Cate folded her arms and sat back, like a seasoned interrogator.

I squirmed. 'Why are you looking at me like that? I just think if he's keen to help with the cause, then we would be foolish not to let him.'

A tiny, knowing smile bloomed across Cate's lips. The sight of it made me wriggle in my seat.

'Uh-huh. So, you're taking our handsome author up there this evening?'

'Yes.'

When Cate continued to examine me, I flapped my hands. 'It's only to let him see for himself how stunning the area is. Dexter made a point of asking me to go with him.'

'Just the two of you?'

I tried to look nonchalant about the whole thing. 'That's right.'

Cate digested this with a huge dollop of cynicism. She rolled her eyes. 'Right. Of course. So there are no other people around here who could have taken him on a tour of it?'

I jumped to my feet, eager to end this conversation. 'I'd better get on. Sorry again for leaving you this morning on your own. Now go and get some lunch.'

'No problem.'

I had begun rifling through the post, which Cate had gathered up and propped beside the till, when she poked her head back around the shop door. The bell tinkled above her spiralling curls. 'Promise me you will be careful.'

She held up one hand as I prepared to answer her. 'I know what the reserve means to you – to us all – but I don't want to see you getting hurt.'

'Cate! It's just to show Dexter the reserve! I'm not asking him to marry me.'

She made the hand gesture again. 'You know what I'm saying, don't you?'

I blanched and attempted to appear ambivalent about the while situation.

'Keep all that in mind, won't you, Elle? You've had enough to contend with over the last year and what with Lloyd too.'

Then she vanished out of the shop in a flap of denim jacket.

Chapter Thirty-Five

I texted Dexter and asked him to drop by Paper Roses at 6:30 p.m.

Cate had departed for home by that time, but not without another knowing look and a dire warning to stay away from Dexter's evil clutches.

'You make him sound like Dick Dastardly.'

Cate pulled in her lips. 'That's putting it mildly.'

'So does that make me Penelope Pitstop or Mutley?'

Cate laughed.

I busied myself by swinging the shop door sign to read *Closed* and assured her that there was nothing to read into it. 'Dexter won't be able to appreciate how gorgeous the nature reserve is until he goes up there and sees it first-hand. That's all there is to it.'

My eyes softened at the thought of the bowing trees, silvery ribbons of streams and the hedgerows throbbing with wildlife. The prospect of taking Dexter there, a place that carried so many blissful memories, caused my stomach to ripple. I tried to dismiss it. 'I haven't got an ulterior motive, you know.'

Cate hitched up her collar. 'It's not your motives I'm worried about.'

Her words reverberated in my ears while I hovered on the step of the shop, waiting for Dexter to arrive.

'Hi there.'

I spun round. Dexter was a few feet away, with his car like something out of a futuristic TV series, glinting beyond the pedestrianised area. I snuck a look at my watch. It was just before 6: 25 p.m. He was early.

As I walked towards him, I struggled not to appreciate his sculpted shoulders in the white T-shirt he was wearing. He was also sporting what appeared to be new designer jeans in navy blue. On his feet were a pair of beige and black Dior sneakers.

I had dashed back to Pebble Brook over lunch to collect a change of outfit, which was an electric-blue vest top, loose checked shirt, my old jeans and my battered walking boots. I'd secured my hair back in a ponytail.

I must have looked so scruffy compared to what he was adorned in.

'Am I overdressed for a ramble?' he asked, sensing my appraisal of his high fashion.

I pulled an apologetic face. 'Maybe a little. Something tells me you didn't buy that footwear in the local supermarket.'

Dexter raised one foot and waggled it. 'If they get dirty, it's my own fault.'

He nodded at what I was wearing. 'You look…'

'Scruffy?'

His voice softened. 'No. Not scruffy. You look pretty. Very natural.'

I found myself savouring his compliments before Cate's warning jumped out at me from nowhere.

I rolled up the cuffs of my shirt a little more and checked my mobile was stashed in the rear pocket of my jeans. 'Thank you.'

I nodded over at Dexter's curvaceous car. 'I was going to

suggest we walk up to the reserve. It'll give you more of a feel for the area.'

Dexter blinked. 'Walk?'

'Yes. You know, it's when you put one foot in front of the other.'

A corner of his mouth twitched.

'Unless you don't feel up to it,' I teased. 'We country bumpkins know how delicate you townies are.'

Dexter grinned. It lit up his whole face. My stomach did a weird, fizzy thing.

'No need to worry about me, I can assure you, Elle. How long would it take us to get there?'

'About twenty minutes?'

He shrugged. 'OK. Let's go.'

It was as if the summer evening had been stirred up with a spoon. Dollops of lazy sunshine mingled with a light breeze. The air was filled with the sound of birds as we made our way up past some farmland and triangular areas of forest.

The main street and the houses of Fir Haven fell away, the stout chimney pots and slate roofs melting behind the growing bank of trees.

'How are you doing?' I asked after a pause, the air wafting over my face.

'You sounded just like Joey from *Friends* then.'

I laughed, wondering if he was trying to lighten the situation. 'I mean about your writing.'

Dexter's chest heaved. 'I'm fine about it.'

I blinked across at him. 'Sorry. That was a stupid question.'

He pushed one hand into his jeans pocket. 'No, it wasn't.' He fired a hand through his thick hair. 'I'm hating every minute of it. It's not getting any easier. My agent and publishers have been great under the circumstances, but they're becoming almost as frustrated about it as I am.'

'And what have you told them? About not you not being able to write at the moment?' I hoped the element of optimism I forced into my question might help to some degree.

We rounded a moss-encrusted wall which kept a field of sheep off the road. They looked like balls of candy floss.

'I've been trying to avoid speaking to them,' confessed Dexter. 'Or if I have had to talk to them, I've pretended I've been laid low with a bout of flu.' Dexter rolled his eyes. 'They will be referring me for scientific tests for having the longest spell of flu in medical history.' He cocked a brow at me. 'Did you laugh then?'

'No… OK, yes, a little bit.'

Oh god. There's that killer smile again.

I smoothed my ponytail. 'So why crime writing?'

His sea-blue gaze vanished somewhere into the distance for a few moments. 'I was diagnosed as dyslexic at school, but I found poetry seemed to make sense to me somehow.'

I listened as cows in the distance let rip a series of indignant noises.

'Maybe it was the rhythm, the word patterns… I don't know, but I found reading it boosted my confidence. Then my dad gave me a Sydney Sheldon novel to read when I was about twelve and that was it.'

His expression brimmed with enthusiasm. 'I knew then that I wanted to write stories of good challenging and overcoming evil. The hero triumphs over the bad guy, overcomes adversity, and wins.' He threw me a look. 'I found that I wasn't bad at it either.'

I smiled. He was attempting to be modest and not making a very good job of it.

I decided not to tell him at this point that I had sought out his books on the internet. I didn't want to appear like a groupie.

My first love was romantic comedies but his stories sounded

engrossing, so I'd found myself ordering his first two novels to read.

I risked another look up at him through the sunshine, taking in his fine, dark features and long legs. I realised where my thoughts were going and pulled myself together. 'Elsa said your parents are into horses? Sorry, that didn't sound right.'

Dexter flashed his white teeth again. 'You could say that. They own stables in the Cotswolds.'

I asked him if he had ever wanted to take over the family business. 'No. I love horses, but I always wanted to do my own thing. My younger sister, Marcie, works alongside Mum and Dad though.'

'You have a sister? That's lovely.'

Dexter nodded. 'And a younger brother.'

'Is he like you?'

'Not really,' replied Dexter quickly. He moved the conversation on, his aqua eyes hardening, before adopting a hopeful spark. 'I'd love to start my own stud farm here.'

I recalled the two photographs of stallions in Hawk West Hall. 'So I hear.'

Dexter gave me an odd look. Then a slow smile spread across his face. 'You've been chatting to a certain housekeeper.'

'I might have been.' I eyed him with curiosity. 'And have you always been a writer? What did you do before you became successful?'

Dexter pulled a face. 'I studied English at university in London, helped out my parents at the stables and drifted from job to job while I wrote my great English novel. I've been a barista, worked in a couple of restaurants, and taught English to some foreign students, just to support myself.' He gave me a wink. 'Then I got lucky.'

My heart sped up. Oh god.

We crossed a deserted part of the country road and climbed over an old wooden gate. 'This is a bit of a short-cut,' I explained, trying to sound matter-of-fact. 'And I think it's a more spectacular route.'

My enthusiasm growing, I turned around. 'And if you look back that way, you might see a glimpse of something you recognise.'

Dexter locked in on the faint sight of one of the sloping angles of Hawk West Hall. 'I didn't realise I was so close to the reserve. Wow!'

We moved on, our feet stepping in unison across the grass and twigs under our feet.

'And what about you?' he asked pausing for a moment to appreciate the spikey pine trees that waited ahead for us. 'Do you have any siblings?'

'No. I think my parents wanted more kids, but it just didn't happen for them.'

I could see the admiration in his eyes as we moved closer to the reserve. The forest of sage and emerald green had that effect.

He pulled up. 'That must have been awful for you losing them both like that.'

I sighed. 'It felt like it was all happening to someone else. At the beginning, I think I spent most of my time in a shocked fog.' I managed a smile. 'If it hadn't been for my grandmother, my best friend Cate, and her partner Lucy, I don't know how I would have coped.'

Dexter paused, watching the strobes of light slice through the woodland and stream down on both of us. 'And that's why you reopened the shop as Paper Roses? To keep busy?'

'Partly that and partly to make them proud of me.'

Dexter's blue eyes shone. 'I'm sure they were very proud of you anyway.'

I turned away, pointing towards a large brown tourist sign with the words, 'Fir Haven Nature Reserve' emblazoned across it. A lump gathered in my throat. 'Here we are.'

I strode ahead, with Dexter taking up the rear. He examined

the protest placards which were growing in number day by day, planted along the entrance. Several more had been added, shouting the slogans, 'Fir Haven: It's in our Nature!' and 'Fir Haven: It's Only Natural!'

'They love their reserve,' he remarked.

'I think you will too when you see it.'

We arrived at a small wooden gate. I unlocked it and gestured for him to step through first. 'I hope you're ready for this.'

The gate led out onto a path strewn with chocolate-coloured bark. On either side, the woodland spread out her branches, as though she were showing off a sumptuous ballgown. It was a tangle of ancient trunks, topped with assorted plumed leaves that stretched like a glossy canopy over our heads.

We walked on, with me inwardly betting he would be able to appreciate the mystery and beauty of this place every bit as much as me and the rest of the other Fir Haven locals did.

The path snaked downwards, with the woodland now opening out onto a vista of wild hills, peppered with lilac heather. From behind me I heard Dexter murmur, 'Oh my god!' and my chest zinged in delight.

'Oh, you haven't seen anything yet.'

I took a turn to the right and stopped. From our viewpoint, I indicated downwards and told Dexter to take a look. He took a couple of steps in his designer sneakers and peered down the slope of the hill. His eyes gaped at the flashes of the three streams criss-crossing like silver ribbons which rose up to greet him.

'It's beautiful,' he breathed. 'Really beautiful.'

I beamed, comforted by his genuine appreciation. 'Come on.'

As the water bubbled and coursed over the stones, I advised him to follow me, moving right into a denser part of the reserve. It was at this point that the tops of the trees closed in, creating a dark roof. Only fingers of light were able to poke through. There was the rich scent of fresh grass and damp pine needles.

'If we're quiet, we should hopefully see something.' I crouched down behind a large rock and Dexter followed suit. I was aware of his close proximity. He was wearing a delicious sea-fresh cologne. I fought not to inhale and trained my gaze on the distance.

'What are we looking for?'

'You'll see.'

I glanced down at my watch, willing this particular apparition to appear. The skyline, just visible in triangular snatches through the undergrowth, was twisting into an evening sky of tangerine. Only a matter of weeks and then the nights would start closing in.

Dexter, hunkered down beside me, spoke in a hushed tone. 'Did your parents used to bring you up here a lot when you were a kid?'

My lips twitched with recollection. 'They met up here as teenagers. My dad proposed to my mum in the reserve, over a haphazard picnic he had prepared for the occasion. Then they used to bring me up here for rambles and to show me the wildlife.'

Dexter listened, smiling and nodding.

'I'm sorry about this,' I apologised, taking another desperate look at my wristwatch. 'Sod's law but I think I've picked the one evening when— Oh, look!'

My hand shot out and squeezed Dexter's knee. *Oh shit! What am I doing?!* I yanked back my hand and dropped it down by my side. That was the second time my hand had lunged for him like that!

Dexter glanced down at where I had touched him. 'You don't have to stop on my account.'

I blushed and channelled all my attention elsewhere. 'There! Over there!'

I jabbed my finger to the left. 'If you look beyond that tall grass and through that cluster of buttercups.'

Dexter followed my finger before he locked on. 'I see it.' He let out an appreciative sigh.

A glimmer of satin beige coat flinched in our line of sight. As the slim, angular deer emerged from out of the undergrowth, she displayed a dash of white tail and a wet black nose. 'Keep watching,' I murmured. 'More might appear alongside her.'

As we crouched there, I could feel earthy dampness seeping into the knees of my jeans, but I didn't care. I was in one of my favourite places with Dexter.

Whoa! Stop, Elle! You're doing it again.

I gave myself a mental telling off and focused on the deer. She paused and angled her head over her shoulder. Following a few feet behind was a fawn, twitching and lolloping.

'There are more of them around here,' I assured Dexter, as he continued to appreciate them. 'Plus, there are foxes, badgers, and grey squirrels.'

As if on cue, a woodpecker interrupted me by hammering on a tree trunk somewhere nearby. The sound throbbed like a heartbeat.

The deer and her baby turned their velvet heads to the sound, before taking flight into the woods again. We watched them disappear in a flick of twig-like legs.

I could feel him looking at me as we huddled there.

Dexter sank down onto his bottom, appearing not to consider or care what effect the damp, dirty earth would have on his expensive jeans. His voice was laced with enchantment. 'This is a very special place. I can see why you love it so much.' He fired out his long legs and drank in the canopy of trees. 'This makes frivolous parties with people you barely know pale into insignificance.'

I gave him a small smile.

'All the vacuous hangers-on and the insincerity.' He flashed me a look. 'It's nice to get away from all of that for a bit.' Dexter's appreciative gaze trailed over the woodland. 'It would be even more inspiring if I could write!'

I lowered myself onto my bottom beside him and stretched my

legs out. 'I've got a good feeling that we'll find Linda Carlucci and all this will be over before you know it.'

'You think?'

'I know.'

He tipped his dark head back, staring upwards at the patches of evening sky.

I twisted myself round more to look at him. 'Dexter, it seems to me that both of us are fighting for something that means a lot to us. You want your writing ability back and I want to save this place.'

Dexter's loaded gaze locked with mine. 'So does that mean you believe it's a curse?'

I felt as if I were melting as he looked at me. 'Let's say I'm more open-minded about it than I was.'

'And the things that mean a lot to us,' he said, flicking me a look from under his lashes. 'How are we going to put them right?'

I pushed myself upright, reminding myself of the emotional harm I could find myself in if I allowed my growing feelings for Dexter to spill over. 'We work together.'

I dashed some earth from the front of my jeans and then threw a couple of leaves at him, which made him smile. 'And we don't give up.'

Dexter's eyes never left my face. 'I like the sound of that.'

Chapter Thirty-Six

Dexter and I spent more time strolling through the abundance of long grass that was tipped with wild flowers, catching tantalising glimpses of the wildlife.

Maybe it was the ability to escape from the misery of his writing drought for a while or perhaps it was the calming trickle of the streams. Whatever it was, Dexter was the most relaxed I had ever seen him.

As we meandered back out of the reserve and down the country lanes towards the high street and Dexter's car, he stopped. He seemed oblivious to the grass stains smeared across his designer footwear.

The sky was growing a deeper shade of tangerine and puffs of dark cloud were masking the last trickles of light.

'I want to help, Elle. To save the reserve. In any way I can. Even more so now I've seen for myself how spectacular it is.'

I nodded, my heart leaping. His T-shirt was now off-white and his black hair was ruffled, the local countryside spread out behind him like a patchwork cloak of emerald greens and earthy browns. He looked like a rugged hero who'd just stepped out of a historical romance.

I battled to keep my attention in check. 'That would be wonderful. Thank you.'

We set off side by side again, down the sloping lane towards the town. It glinted through the trees, all angular tiled roofs and sparkling windows with the church spire twisting up into the burnt-orange evening.

'You're such an optimist, aren't you?' he asked with a tinge of amusement.

I let out a hollow laugh. 'Well, if we don't have hope, what else is there?'

The high street opened out now in front of us. The shops all closed hours ago, the assorted business huddled behind their *Closed* signs and pulled-down blinds. From where Dexter had parked his car, I could see Paper Roses.

I noticed Dexter was looking down the road at my shop too. 'You should be very proud, Elle.'

I tried not to get distracted by his kissable mouth. This was crazy. I was letting myself think wild thoughts and imagine unspeakable things. 'Thank you.'

We both hovered until he produced his car keys from his jeans pocket. 'I'm more than happy to go public about the reserve. I'll say I'm supporting the cause to save it.'

I pulled open the passenger side door, staring across at him over the top of his glossy ghost-grey car roof. 'Dexter, I don't want you to feel coerced into doing it.'

He flashed me a look that made my stomach squirm. 'That isn't it at all.' He indicated his hand up the road, back towards the nature reserve. 'When I saw how beautiful it is for myself and you showed me how special it is… well, how could anyone not be touched by it?'

We remained frozen to the spot on either side of the car, staring at one another as a couple of vehicles streaked past us. I was relieved to sink into the passenger seat. I faffed around for a few seconds, pretending to get myself comfortable.

I forced my attention out of my side window, while Dexter slid on his pair of mirrored sunglasses and manoeuvred the car out of its parking space. 'Home, madam?'

'Yes please.'

I insisted on turning on the car radio. I wanted to fill my head with music rather than all the churning thoughts about the man sitting next to me.

The wooden gates leading down past the brook to the house were open, so Dexter eased his car through them and down the incline.

'You could have just dropped me at the top of the lane.'

'I could have done that, but it wouldn't have been very gallant.'

I smiled over at him. 'Thank you for agreeing to come to the reserve and for saying you'll lend your support.'

I swung open the car door and stepped out, my walking boots only just visible in the fast-descending dark.

'I'll speak to my PR people,' said Dexter, who had lowered the passenger side window and was leaning across to talk to me. 'They can advise us on the best way forward with this.'

'I really appreciate it.'

Dexter shrugged his solid shoulders. 'Anything to help.'

His clear blue eyes shone out of the car. I hoped my face wasn't betraying the roller coaster my insides were riding. 'I'll get onto Fir Haven Radio and follow up the appeal broadcast for information on Linda.'

There was another electric pause, with only the revving of the car engine breaking the heavy silence.

'Night, Dexter,' I faltered. I performed an awkward wave and strode off down towards the house.

The carriage lights either side of the entrance glowed like little bursts of sunshine and there was a sliver of light escaping from underneath the kitchen blind. No doubt Gran was rustling herself up a mug of hot chocolate.

I fished about in my back pocket for my door key and Dexter started to throw his car into reverse.

'Elle! Oh, Elle!'

My grandmother must have heard me arrive back. She had jerked open the front door and was dashing towards me, breathless and wide-eyed.

I threw my arms out to steady her, panic welling up. 'What's wrong, Gran? What is it? Aren't you feeling well?'

She clung to me, staring at Dexter over my shoulder. He must have seen the commotion in his rear-view mirror and killed the engine. He swung open his car door and strode towards us. 'Is everything ok?'

'There's someone here,' Gran gasped.

I stared around me. 'What?'

She pulled herself out of my embrace and blinked up at me, her light-grey eyes startled. She was trembling. 'I think we've got a prowler.'

Chapter Thirty-Seven

Before I could say anything, Dexter was marching past us and into the house.

'Dexter! *Dexter!* What are you doing?' I yelled after him, my concern for his safety escalating. 'For god's sake, be careful.'

Grandma stared at his disappearing back. 'Young man, it could be dangerous!'

We both went after him, my grandmother huddling deeper into her knee-length cardigan. Dexter was already making quiet strides in his soiled sneakers through the hall. 'Did you see someone?' he whispered, inspecting the sitting room before crossing into the kitchen.

Gran shot me a panicked look. 'I thought I did. I mean, I was sure I heard something.'

While Dexter insisted on bounding up the stairs to check the bedrooms, I squeezed Grandma's arms. 'Did you actually see anyone, Grandma?'

Her cheeks flared with colour. 'Well, if you mean did I see someone in the house in a black ski mask, then no.'

'So what or whom did you see?'

'I'm not sure.' Her face crumpled and I gathered her up into my arms again.

Dexter came back down the stairs towards us. Gran turned around to look at him. 'I definitely heard some sort of noise.'

'But did you actually see someone here?' asked Dexter gently.

Grandma lowered her eyes to the hall carpet.

Dexter and I swapped charged expressions. *Oh god.* I hoped my Gran was all right. It wasn't like her to be confused about anything.

We made our way back outside. The kitchen light was throwing out a pool of yellow onto our feet. 'I think a noise spooked her,' I hissed out the corner of my mouth. 'It could have been anything.'

'I may have had an awful fright, Elle, but I'm not bloody deaf!'

'Sorry, Gran.'

Dexter buried a smile at my assertive grandmother. 'I'll check around outside the house.'

'There's really no need,' I assured him.

Dexter shook his head. 'I really would rather do it. It would give me peace of mind, at least.'

I stared up at him. 'All right. Thank you,' I said, 'but you're not going on your own. We're coming with you.'

One of Dexter's dark brows rose. 'Are you worried about me?'

I ignored Gran's expectant expression as she witnessed our verbal exchanges.

'Not at all,' I snorted far too quickly. 'I just want to make sure you don't avail yourself of the family silver.'

My grandmother ordered Dexter to wait there while she scurried to the left side of the house and reappeared moments later with a glinting garden spade.

'Here,' she said to Dexter, thrusting the handle at him. 'Just in case we need it.'

Dexter studied it with an arch of his brow. 'Thanks.'

Grandma and I bunched up together behind him as we took the first tentative steps around the back of the house.

There was a high hedge at the rear of the garden, with my mum's rockery all shadowy in the dark. The only light we had was from the rear kitchen window, spilling onto the grass.

Dexter produced his mobile and used the flashlight, swinging it this way and that. Everything was tranquil, with only the odd flutter from birds preparing to nest for the night.

'Everything seems fine,' I commented in a low voice, guiding my grandmother around.

The three of us made our way back down the lawn, using the light from Dexter's mobile and were just reaching the front of the house when there was a crashing noise from somewhere up the right-hand side.

I gasped and Grandma's speckled hands fluttered to her throat. Dexter ordered us not to move and raised the spade. There was a cacophony of running feet, the snapping of twigs and branches, and then a blur of white headlights.

A tall figure had darted away from the house and into the undergrowth. Whoever it was must have concealed their vehicle there. They leapt into the driver's side and then a large, dark, clunky four-by-four was thrown into reverse and screeched off into the night.

Dexter ran after the vehicle, but it was rushing away at speed. The silhouetted woodland swallowed up the car and it vanished.

'Did you get a look at the registration?' I yelled, clinging onto Gran's trembling arm.

Dexter drew to a stop, gulping for air. He dropped the spade down by his feet. 'They'd covered it up front and back.'

'I knew I didn't imagine it,' murmured Grandma to herself. 'I had a feeling there was someone there.'

'I think we should call the police,' I said, cuddling my grandmother. A chill charged through me. Goodness knows what they wanted, and what might have happened if Dexter and I hadn't returned when we did didn't bear thinking about.

'I think you should too,' agreed Dexter. 'There was so sign of any strange vehicle when we got back, so they made sure it was well out of sight over there.'

We hurried back towards Pebble Brook.

'What's that?' quavered Gran's voice. 'Over there?'

She hurried past Dexter and me, one shell-pink painted nail shaking as she pointed at the open front door.

A crumpled white sheet of paper was lying face down on the front step. It hadn't been there before.

My gran was eager to see what it was, but when she reached it, her fingers became hesitant and hovered above the paper. She gave herself a mental shake, snatched it up, and unfolded it, her eyes scanning the page.

'What is it?' I asked, apprehension squeezing my chest. 'Grandma?'

She paled, her mouth drawing into a severe line. She offered the note to me to read.

'Intimidation,' she managed, her expression a mixture of anger and fear.

Chapter Thirty-Eight

THE RESERVE CAN'T BE SAVED.

The words shouted up at me.

Dexter put his hand out to read the note too and I passed it to him. His blinking blue eyes scanned the typed black words.

Grandma stood at my shoulder, the shock of what had just happened failing to diminish her spirit. 'Whoever it is, they're wasting their time.'

'I agree,' I said, nodding my ponytail. 'We must have rattled them if they took the time and trouble to come up here.'

I stared back up the lane, my heart jumping as I visualised the car and its occupant taking off into the night. 'They could be dangerous though.'

'Tish!' snorted Gran, struggling to sound blasé about the whole thing. 'I admit I was unnerved when I thought it was an attempted burglary, but now I know it's just some idiot who doesn't want us protecting the reserve, that puts a different light on things.'

She accepted the note back from Dexter.

Around us, the darkness was like spilt ink and the only spots of colour now were from the house and the diamond sparkles of water in the stream as it rode over the stones.

'Well, whatever their motive, I think we need to report this to the police,' said Dexter, looking to me for affirmation.

Grandma let out a 'Harrumph!', but didn't argue the point.

'We should,' I agreed. 'Just in case there are any repercussions.'

'This isn't the Bronx, darling. The worst crime that's been committed in Fir Haven of late is Audrey Dunbar painting her front door that hideous shade of lime green.'

Dexter moved to speak, but Gran's gimlet gaze made him reconsider. 'Elle will tell you that this town is a peaceful place.'

'Then all the more reason to report it,' I answered, indicating the note gripped in her hand. The fact that the local crime rate was non-existent made this evening's events take on a far more concerning edge.

I answered Grandma's defiant expression with one of my own.

'All right,' she sighed. 'We'll ring Phil now.'

Dexter's brow creased. 'Phil?'

'Phil Drysdale is our local bobby,' I added by way of explanation.

Dexter took a moment to process this. 'You've only got one copper around here?'

'And very good he is too,' answered my Gran protectively. 'I know his grandfather very well.'

As we went back into the house to ring Phil at the local station, I caught Dexter's appalled expression. 'One police officer?' he repeated.

'What did you expect? A full SWAT team in riot gear?'

Police officer Phil Drysdale came quickly and took copious statements from the three of us, while Gran insisted on making him tea. He also took details of the 'getaway vehicle' (although we were limited in what we were able to tell him).

'It's a pity it hasn't been muddy around here,' muttered Phil, pacing backwards and forwards into the undergrowth and then back out and onto the top of the lane. 'They would have left tyre marks then.' He glanced around. 'I'll ask some of the other bobbies in the neighbouring stations about the vehicle description and see if anything similar has happened in their area.'

I shot a glance at Gran. It didn't sound to me like we stood much chance of finding out who the person was.

When Phil had gone, leaving words of reassurance, Dexter rose up from our buttery leather sofa. 'I'm taking you ladies home with me.'

'Now there's an offer you don't get every day,' twinkled Gran. Dexter flashed her an irresistible smile.

I hugged myself. 'No. Sorry, I mean no thanks. That's very kind of you, Dexter, but we'll be fine.' No way was I returning to Hawk West Hall

I had to keep my distance. My feelings were developing fast for Dexter without sleeping in close proximity to him. The very thought of it triggered my mouth to dry up.

Things between us had to be kept on an even keel. I swallowed and set my shoulders. I didn't like this. I didn't like the feelings that he was stirring up inside of me.

I was relieved when Gran agreed with me. 'Thank you very much, Dexter, but I'm not having yobs drive me out of my own home either.'

Dexter blinked those ebony lashes of his. 'OK, ladies. Then you leave me no alternative but to stay the night here.'

'What?!' My mouth hung open.

'I can sleep on the sofa,' he reasoned. 'I'm sure that idiot won't come back, but it will give us all peace of mind if I stay over.'

'There really is no need,' said my grandmother with appreciation. 'You've done so much already.'

Dexter dismissed her praise. 'Not at all, Clara.'

I attempted to interrupt. 'That's really kind of you, Dexter, but we'll be just fine.'

'It's not up for discussion, Elle.'

It was now Gran's turn to brook no further argument. 'Well, thank you. That's very thoughtful of you. However, if you're staying here tonight then you're not sleeping on the sofa. We have a guest bedroom upstairs.'

I whirled round, widening my eyes at her in a silent appeal. *No. This is not a good idea.* I was trying to quell the concoction of emotions Dexter was firing up inside of me. Him sleeping under the same roof as me...

'It will only take a minute to put on fresh bedding and the room has a small en suite shower,' she added.

Dexter risked a glance over at me before speaking to Gran again. 'Are you sure?'

'Absolutely.'

My head snapped between my grandmother and Dexter until I had to stop for fear of developing a crick in my neck.

'Then it's settled.' Dexter smiled, studying me with a challenging glint in his eyes.

Chapter Thirty-Nine

I forced a smile and excused myself from the sitting room. Gran was heading upstairs to the linen cupboard. 'Why did you agree to let him stay?' I whispered.

We reached the top step and she performed an airy shrug. 'He insisted, and anyway, it will be nice to have a bit of eye candy around the place for one night.'

'Grandma!'

She winked at me as she pulled open the linen cupboard door. 'Now, where is that pale-blue stripy set of bedding? You know the one I mean.'

I frowned at her. 'Why are you going to so much trouble?'

'And I could ask why you went to so much effort to prevent him from staying?'

My cheeks blossomed. 'I'm not. I wasn't. I just don't think it's a good idea.'

Gran located the bedding and started to drape it over her arm, but I took it from her and hooked it over mine instead.

'Why is that?' she asked.

'Sorry?'

'Why don't you want Dexter staying here?'

'Come on,' I muttered, avoiding her question. 'Leave this to me. I'll make up the bed and get Dexter a clean towel.'

I lay in bed that night with the brook murmuring in the dark and the intermittent sound of Dexter moving around in the guest bedroom just a few feet away from mine. Because of where it was, every creak and footstep imprinted itself in my chest.

I attempted to banish the tortuous visions of him lying there, his shock of raven hair against the pillow. Eventually I fell into a fitful sleep and awoke the next morning to the babbling of the kitchen radio from downstairs. I was sure I could hear Gran and Dexter chatting.

I slipped on my mint and white cotton bathrobe over my pyjamas and studied myself in my bedroom mirror.

Good God. I couldn't let Dexter see me looking like I'd just fought a grizzly and lost.

I snatched up my bristle brush from my dressing table and fired it through my hair before securing it at the nape of my neck in a bun.

I eased open my bedroom door. I could hear low voices coming from the kitchen. Sticking one foot out, followed by the other, I dashed down the hallway, my dressing gown flapping behind me and dived into the upstairs bathroom unseen. I splashed my face, gave my teeth a quick brush and pinched some semblance of colour into my cheeks.

As I padded down the stairs and headed towards the kitchen, I could hear Gran's throaty laugh at some story Dexter was regaling her with. I hovered by the open kitchen door.

Wait. Is that crispy bacon and fried eggs I can smell?

It was, going by the desperate grumble coming from my stomach.

The sight that greeted me as I tapped into the kitchen was one of blissful domesticity.

Grandma was flipping over sizzling rashers of bacon in a pan, while Dexter was tending to thick slices of golden toast. Both of them were also showered and dressed. Gran was in one of her linen trouser suits in a Chinese style print. Dexter's hair was still damp from his shower and he was wearing fresh clothes consisting of a charcoal V-neck T-shirt and pale-grey jeans.

He caught my puzzled gaze at his clothes. 'Good morning. Hope you slept OK.' He indicated his outfit. 'One of my employees dropped by with clean clobber first thing this morning.'

Sure enough, my muzzy thoughts recalled hearing the faint thrum of a car engine earlier.

'Cooked breakfast OK for you, darling?' asked Gran. 'Did you sleep well?'

I pulled my robe tighter around myself. 'Yes, that smells good. As for sleeping, it was a bit on and off after what happened.'

I reached up to my bun and fiddled with it. I hoped I looked presentable. 'How about the both of you?'

Gran hesitated. 'I've had better nights, but having this young man here did make me feel a bit more secure.'

Before he could answer, Dexter's phone vibrated beside him on the breakfast bar and he excused himself to take the call in our sitting room.

As soon as he disappeared past me, I hurried to speak to my grandmother. 'What is all this in aid of?'

'What? Oh, this?' she lowered the spatula as the delicious rashers of bacon popped in the pan. 'Well, it's not every day you have a handsome author for breakfast. And he was so brave and gallant last night.'

'Yes,' I agreed, my eyes trailing after Dexter. 'Yes, he was.' Thoughts were thrashing around inside my head again.

I promised myself I would go and take a shower as soon as I'd eaten some breakfast. It would help to get things into perspective. At least I hoped it would. My emotions regarding Dexter were beginning to tangle me up in knots.

Dexter's feet tapping back across the wooden kitchen floor interrupted me.

'That was my PR team,' he explained. 'I left them a message to give me a call back. They'll be issuing a press release at noon today, publicly announcing my support for the nature reserve and condemning the proposals for development.'

My heart lifted. 'That's great. Thank you so much.'

'I'll say it is,' breathed my Gran. 'That's very good of you to do that, Dexter.'

He shrugged away our appreciation. 'It's my pleasure. You're helping me with Linda Carlucci, so it's the least I can do.'

He paused, stuffing his mobile into the back pocket of his jeans. 'And anyway, I wanted to do something after seeing for myself how stunning that area is.'

Grandma fetched three plates that were warming in the microwave and we all settled ourselves on the stools to eat. I had been so distracted by Dexter's presence in our house that I hadn't paid any attention to the time.

I offered my watch a cursory glance while I munched my last slice of buttered toast, thick with a layer of amber marmalade. I did a double-take. 'Shit! I'm going to be late for work!'

Gran was disapproving. 'Language, Elle!'

'Sorry.'

Dexter's lips flickered with amusement. 'You're the boss. You can be late.'

I jumped from my stool. 'I am, but I don't want to appear like I'm not committed to my own business.'

I was about to race towards the downstairs shower room when my eyebrows sprang upwards at Dexter's words. 'You're one of the most committed people I know.'

Silence descended in the kitchen; the scent of cooked breakfast still detectable. 'Thank you.' I hoped my voice was steady. 'And again, what you did last night...'

Dexter batted away my compliment, his eyes refusing to move away from my face.

I then spent the next ten minutes in the shower, my skin prickling with the knowledge that I was naked while Dexter was only a matter of feet away.

Dexter left Pebble Brook just as I was leaving for Paper Roses. He was returning to Hawk West Hall and Gran said she would join me in the shop today. I was relieved. I didn't want her at home alone after last night's incident. I also suspected she wanted to use the time to grill me about Dexter!

As we opened up the shop, she plucked our digital radio from the kitchen out of her hessian shopping bag.

'What's that for?'

'So we can listen to the news,' she said. 'We might get blanket coverage about the reserve, now that Dexter is getting involved.'

We had a brisk start to the day, with a flurry of Londoners in to buy some gifts for relatives, and a trio of young mums looking for a suitable present to get for a retiring school teacher.

By the time we had wrapped their various purchases in sheafs of pastel-coloured tissue paper and received their thanks and grateful goodbyes, the lunchtime national news bulletin was about to be broadcast.

My nerves rattled as the newsreader gave details of a new government policy on tackling internet abuse, the memorial service taking place for a head of state in the Middle East, and the proposed price increase for postage stamps.

'Maybe it's a busy news day,' I began, only for Gran to cling onto my arm as the polite-sounding newsreader began the final news story for the hour. 'And, finally, well-known crime writer

Dexter Grayling has surprised and delighted his legions of fans by announcing his support for a local nature reserve in Scotland.

'The future of Fir Haven Nature Reserve, in the west of Scotland, is under threat from development but Mr Grayling, usually known for not only his gritty novels but also his lavish lifestyle, has released a statement this morning, in which he said: 'This area of outstanding natural beauty is at the heart of the Fir Haven community and needs to be protected. I didn't realise how breath-taking it was until I saw it for myself and, upon hearing from a dear friend what it means to her, I wanted to publicly express my fierce opposition to any plans for harming that area, now or in the future.' A spokesperson for Atticus Development, declined to comment.'

Then a different voice took over the airwaves. This time, a bubbly weather presenter began to deliver the forecast.

Grandma's smile was wide. It was lovely to see her like that, compared to the trembling white version of her from last night. 'At least this will highlight what's going on up there and bring it to far more people's attention.' Her optimism flourished. 'And with any luck, it will let those developer idiots, and that cretin they had deliver that note, see that we're not going to just slink away.'

I had begun chatting to a couple of Gran's friends, Hilary and Stephanie, from her book club, who had brought in a poster they had designed 'Protect Nature – Protect the Nature Reserve' for me to display in the front shop window, when Dexter emerged through the door.

'Did you just hear the news bulletin?' he asked. 'I caught it in the car.'

I found myself flapping around several sheets of tissue paper underneath the counter. 'We heard it too. It was great. Thank you.'

Gran, Hilary, and Stephanie surrounded Dexter, buzzing with appreciation. 'Thank you, young man,' said Hilary as she looked up at him and flushed.

Dexter's white smile lit up his face. 'I haven't done anything.'

'Oh, you have,' insisted my grandma. 'You have such a high profile and you're publicly backing our cause.'

Dexter lifted his gaze from the three admiring ladies to me. 'I hope I can help. I'd like to.'

A hint of an amused smile fluttered at the corners of my grandmother's mouth as she watched us.

'That would be great,' I said, struggling to keep my voice light. 'The more people we have on board, the better.'

'Oh, excuse me.' Dexter waggled his ringing mobile in the air. He darted back outside the shop, making the doorbell rattle after him.

'I didn't realise he was so handsome,' breathed Stephanie. 'Those gossip column photos don't do him justice.'

I was asking Gran if she thought placing the poster on the front door would be better, rather than in the window, when Dexter burst back through the door. His bright-blue gaze, which moments before had been almost playful, was thunderous. 'Where's the loyalty? Where's the appreciation?!'

Hilary, Stephanie, and Gran stared at him, alarmed.

Dexter realised he must have frightened them and apologised, but his hard stare continued. I beckoned him through to the kitchen. 'What is it? What's happened?'

Dexter rubbed at his chin. 'That was Angie, my agent. It seems my publisher's patience has finally run out.'

'What do you mean?' I encouraged him to explain, although I could hazard a guess at what he was going to say.

His voice was flat, almost resigned. 'They've given me six weeks to present them with my next novel.'

Apprehension grew inside of me. 'And if you don't?'

Dexter's broad shoulders hunched. 'If I don't, they will terminate my contract with immediate effect.'

Chapter Forty

Dexter was so deflated.

I moved a bit closer to him. 'But they can't do that! All the successful books you've had and the loyal readers you've got… Don't they count for anything?'

Dexter let out a long rush of air. 'It doesn't look like it. You're only as good as your next book and, seeing as I've not met two of their deadlines now, that hasn't helped either.'

'But you had started work on your next novel before all this Linda Carlucci thing?'

I heard the shop doorbell jangle through the crack in the kitchen door.

'Yes, I had. I was about halfway through my first draft when all this happened.' Dexter carried on talking in despondent tones. 'Although my publishers were delighted with what I had written so far of *Killing Time,* they were growing increasingly frustrated with me to finish it.' He shot me a panicked look. 'Angie's done a fantastic job so far of buying me some extra time, but I get the impression that even she is getting fed up now.'

Dexter slammed his hand down hard on the kitchen table top.

'How the hell can I tell them the truth? Everyone will think I've lost my mind!'

He sank down into a nearby chair, his tall frame hunched with worry under his charcoal T-shirt. 'Not being able to write, Elle… it's like a living nightmare.' He blew out a cloud of air. 'I feel like I've lost a part of me and I have no idea how to get it back.'

My stomach sank at the hollowness in his clear blue eyes.

'I know the press portray me as some sort of self-absorbed party animal, and maybe I was like that, but I feel like I've changed.'

'Maybe?' I teased him, trying to raise a smile.

It worked for a few seconds.

I lowered myself into the chair opposite, while Grandma served another customer and bid farewell to Hilary and Stephanie. 'The radio appeal gets its first airing this afternoon and I bet we get something from that,' I cajoled, mentally crossing my fingers. 'Someone must know something about where she is.'

Dexter pushed his legs out under the table and waggled his trainers. 'The longer this goes on, the more pessimistic I am.' He rose to his feet. 'I'm going to head back home. Take a walk and try to clear my head.'

'Stay positive please, Dexter, and listen out for the radio appeal on Fir Haven Radio at 3pm.'

Dexter managed a nod before disappearing out of the shop. He didn't look positive at all.

Lunchtime saw a late flurry of members of the local Women's Institute, asking us if we would be prepared to donate a few raffle prizes in order to raise money for the nature reserve campaign fund.

I was more than happy to help and packed up half a dozen

paperweights, four notebooks, five assorted picture frames and two pen and pencil sets in silver and rose gold.

There had been no more news from the police about the prowler and the note they had left. Whoever they were, they had vanished into the night and not left any clues.

I ventured to the baker's a while later and fetched a toasted tomato and pesto panini for both Gran and me. 'I've never seen Dexter so despondent,' I said, as I picked over my lunch.

My grandmother made sure the *Closed for Lunch – Open Again in Thirty Minutes!* sign was up on the door, before surveying me across the Formica table. 'Have you spoken since this morning?'

I shook my head. 'I've tried calling him a couple of times, but his phone keeps going to voicemail.' I took a thoughtful bite of my panini. 'And even if I reached him, what could I say?' I stared at the glass of water beside me. 'If I could get my hands on Linda Carlucci right now!'

As soon as the words burst out of my mouth, I reddened.

Grandma angled her head to one side. 'Well, that wouldn't be very helpful, since you're trying to get the curse lifted – not extended indefinitely!' She examined me. 'You really like him, don't you?'

'No!' I snatched up my glass of water. 'I just feel a bit sorry for him.'

'Uh-huh.'

From through in the shop, I heard the landline ring from behind the counter.

'I'll go,' I insisted, rising to my feet. 'You sit and have your lunch.'

That afternoon, I tried on three more occasions to ring Dexter, but he didn't pick up and his voicemail kicked in. An uneasy sensation stole over me. It wouldn't have been so bad if it felt like we were getting somewhere with looking for Linda Carlucci, but we still had nothing to go on. It was all so frustrating.

I was sure she would reappear again after her and Dexter's confrontation, but there had been no more sightings of her in the local area.

Grandma was exchanging pleasantries with a little girl and her mum, who had promised her one of our new animal-shaped pencil cases. There was much debate over whether the fox design or the badger one was the best, as I carted Gran's digital radio from the back of the shop and plonked it on top of the counter.

I swivelled the control button until it read 'Fir Haven Radio'. I lowered the volume of my iPod, which had been playing some of Gran's favourite Ella Fitzgerald songs. 'I hope this appeal works. We're getting nowhere at the moment.'

Grandma flapped her thigh-length, cream cardigan. 'Have faith, sweetheart.'

The local news came to an end and then the presenter announced there would an appeal for information.

'Ms Elle Cassidy of Fir Haven is appealing for information regarding the whereabouts of a Mrs Linda Carlucci. This is an urgent matter and therefore it would be appreciated if any information, however insignificant it may be, be passed on as quickly as possible.'

The presenter then went onto detail an eyewatering reward being put up by Dexter, which would lead to locating Linda.

I had made sure that Dexter's name wasn't included in the appeal. He had enough to contend with, without having the national press getting hold of the story. The appeal concluded with my email address and mobile phone number.

The broadcast finished as quickly as it had begun and the local presenter began his 3pm afternoon show, with a blast of Sir Elton John.

I clicked the radio off again and resumed Ella Fitzgerald. My chest jumped as my mobile rang in my handbag. I rummaged under the counter to find it. Dexter's name sprang out of the screen. 'It's Dexter,' I explained to Gran.' I bet he just heard it too.'

I started to ask how he was, but as he spoke, I felt my expression transform from expectation to one of stunned hurt and biting disappointment.

'I've been thinking, Elle. Things aren't working out for me here.'

I clutched my mobile hard. Confusion took over. 'What are you talking about? What do you mean?'

There was a pause long enough to make my stomach clench.

'I'll still support the nature reserve.'

'But what?' I fired back. My heart pirouetted to the floor with a sickening thud.

There was a grim silence before he managed to answer. 'I've decided to sell Hawk West Hall and move back to London.'

Chapter Forty-One

'But you can't,' I stuttered. 'You can't give up. Not now.'

'Elle, my writing career is going into freefall.'

'Yes, but running away isn't the answer. We need to resolve it.'

'I'm not running away.'

Gran vanished into the kitchen to give me some privacy, patting me on the hand as she went.

My heart felt as though it were withering in my chest. 'Didn't you just hear the radio appeal? I think that will work.'

Dexter's anguished sigh travelled into my ear. 'I did hear it, but what are the chances it will bring any results?'

My breath pricked at the base of my throat

'You don't know that it won't,' I argued as calmly as I could. 'And say you do go back to London. You still wouldn't be able to write.'

He paused. 'Maybe a change of scene might help.'

My shoulders slumped further. He seemed like he'd already made up his mind and our lack of success so far was doing an excellent job of exploiting his concerns.

I battled to sound optimistic. 'Let's see what happens with the radio appeal. Give it a bit longer before you make any rash decisions.'

He mulled it over, the agony in his voice tugging at me. 'OK. Let's see what happens, but right now I'm not holding out much hope.'

My eyes burned into my mobile for the remainder of the afternoon, but there were no exciting calls from locals with any leads or helpful snippets of information we could go on, in order to locate Linda.

On the email front, I did receive one from a man claiming to have seen Linda Carlucci and Elvis shopping together in the frozen food aisle at the local supermarket, but that was the extent of it.

Gran did her best to allay my pessimism. 'But Dexter sounded so down,' I said, flopping down onto the stool behind the counter. 'And now he's talking about selling Hawk West Hall and going back to London.'

I could feel my heart juddering at the prospect.

The very thought of Dexter moving back to London filled me with a cloying, dark despondency.

'It's not good news, I'm afraid,' blurted Mr Monteith, appearing from the antique shop next door and interrupting my thoughts. His cherubic face was red and he was tugging anxiously at his buttoned-up waistcoat in the shop doorway. 'It seems that we won't be able to stop so-called progress.'

Foreboding clung to me. I didn't like the sound of that at all. 'What is it, Mr Monteith? What's going on?'

Grandma, standing beside me, rolled her pale eyes. 'For goodness' sake, man! Just say it before I have a coronary!'

I noticed him deliver a narrowed glower at my Gran. 'I've been told by a contact at the council's planning department that permission has already been granted for work to go ahead at the reserve.'

My fingers clutched at the edge of the shop counter. Any shreds of optimism I was hanging on to were falling away fast. 'No! They can't have done! For what?'

'Luxury holiday homes for townies.'

Panic and disappointment crowded in on me.

'And that's not all,' he added, dashing one hand over the top of his thinning silvery hair. 'The work is due to start in the next few weeks.'

Chapter Forty-Two

I turned to my grandmother, my stomach churning. Images of the reserve, its throng of trees and streams desecrated by bulldozers, pushed their way to the front of my mind. I felt sick.

Gran lowered the volume on the iPod, which was pumping out a jazz medley. 'I can't say I'm that surprised.'

I sank down onto the stool by the till, dejected. 'Everything is unravelling.' I stared out of the shop door at the sun-tinted trees. 'We've had no luck on the Linda Carlucci front and now the reserve is set to be destroyed.'

I couldn't conceal the splintering hurt registering in my voice. 'And now Dexter is talking about going back to London.'

Grandma touched me on my shoulder. 'This isn't my Elle at all. You've never accepted defeat in your life, just like your father.'

I rubbed my arms, concealed under my lacey vanilla top. 'Maybe I'm getting more sensible in my old age.'

The next couple of days limped towards the weekend and Friday came around, bringing with it the start of August. The local school children had two weeks remaining before they returned after their summer break and already parents were dropping in to begin stocking up on stationery essentials for the new school year.

There had also only been a couple of texts from Dexter asking how Gran and I were. He then said he would be back in touch once he'd got things moving with having Hawk West Hall valued.

I bit back the pain in my chest. I couldn't face texting him back and prolonging the inevitable.

I busied myself with a stocktake, while Cate had insisted on coming in to give my gran a much-needed break.

Cate finished polishing some of the paperweights and stood up in the window. 'I wish you'd stop talking, Els. You're giving me a headache.'

I pulled an apologetic face. 'Sorry. I'm miles away at the moment.'

'You're telling me.'

I couldn't help it. There had been no leads from the radio appeal about Linda and the nature reserve seemed to be doomed. But what could we do? Was there anything we could do?

And to top it all off, Dexter looked like he would be leaving Fir Haven.

Cate stepped down from the window display and sauntered over in her indigo capri pants and loose lilac shirt. 'I take it still no news on Linda?'

'Not a thing.'

I could see Cate was doing her best to think of and say something positive to me. 'Don't get all despondent yet. You know what some folks round here are like. They could be contacting the radio station now or about to email you with something useful.'

I cocked a disbelieving eyebrow at her, even though I appreciated her support.

'What? Why are you looking at me like that? I'm serious.'

I knew Cate was only trying to boost my flagging morale, but I didn't think even Keanu Reeves could put a smile on my face right now.

She looked at me out of those concerned dark eyes of hers. 'Please be honest with me. Now, I know you're not going to like my next question, but I'm asking it anyway.' She paused. 'How much of this is about the reserve and how much is about Dexter?'

I whipped my head back to fiddle with a half-open box of pencil sharpeners in the shape of pink fondant cupcakes. The pain and disappointment of Dexter quitting Fir Haven was growing. I knew it was crazy, but the more I tried to ignore how I was feeling, the worse it got.

I scooped out more of the cake pencil sharpeners. Why the hell had I let myself get into this position?

I kept my flushed expression focused on the novelty sharpeners in my hands. Cate didn't push the matter. The loaded silence answered her question.

Pictures of the reserve bobbed into my mind. I couldn't give up on it, even though things were looking bleak. Not yet, at least. And I needed to keep busy and stop my thoughts from going where they shouldn't.

'I'm not giving up on the reserve,' I said, finding my voice again. 'Not yet.'

Cate's eyes softened like melted dark chocolate. 'That's the spirit.'

'And I'm going to focus more on this place,' I added for good measure. 'I think I've been letting Paper Roses slide a bit with everything else going on.'

Cate shook her dandelion ball of black hair. 'No, you haven't. Not at all. You've just been trying to juggle too many balls at once, that's all.' She flicked me a sideways glance. 'So, what about you and Dexter finding Linda Carlucci?'

I shrugged. 'His answer seems to be to run away.'

I switched on a weak smile as two grey-haired ladies clattered in through the shop door.

The rest of Friday afternoon was busy, but in my head it limped along.

Once 5pm came around, Cate reached for my leather jacket hanging on the back of the chair in the kitchen.

I frowned at her. 'But we don't normally close till 6pm.'

Cate's stare challenged me to get into an argument with her. 'You've been like a wind-up clockwork toy all afternoon. You haven't taken a proper lunch break and if you've mopped this floor once, you've done it at least three times.'

I stuck out my lip. 'I like to be busy.'

'Yes, I know but there's busy and there's driving yourself into an early grave…' Horror reared up in her voice, when she released what she'd just said. 'Shit! Shit! Sorry!'

I laughed and dismissed her apology. 'There's no need to tip-toe around me, Cate.'

She pressed her lips together. 'Will you please go home now? Soak in the bath, pour yourself a glass of something chilled.' Cate gestured her arm around the shop. 'I'll close up for the night. Lucy's coming here to meet me anyway. We thought we might try that new wine bar in town. You know, the one with the glitterball and the 1970s 'Staying Alive' inspired dance floor.'

I gave Cate an appreciative hug. 'A long soak in the bath sounds heavenly.'

I threw my leather jacket over my arm and hitched up my shoulder bag.

'You could always come with us into town.'

The prospect of sitting there, sandwiched between Cate and Lucy as they made eyes at one another, filled me with dread. Talk about a spare part. 'Thanks for that, but I just want to chill out this evening.'

As I was about to leave, Lucy appeared at the door, her red hair like a shiny curtain. She was dressed in a white ankle-length dress. When Cate saw her, her face broke into a wide smile. She enveloped her girlfriend in her arms and they exchanged a lingering kiss.

'Good day?' Lucy asked, as she embraced me.

'Good from a business perspective,' I smiled, hoping I sounded more upbeat than I felt.

Cate delivered a knowing look to Lucy, who acknowledged it with the briefest of nods. They had obviously been discussing my various dilemmas but I didn't mind. Cate was only concerned for me.

'And what about you?' I asked her. 'Accountancy thrills aplenty?'

Lucy slipped off her red cardigan and draped it over the back of the chair behind the counter. 'It's as enthralling as ever. Got some new clients though, so I guess I can't complain.'

'But she still will,' interjected Cate with a playful grin.

Lucy offered her girlfriend a withering look. 'We can't all design frivolous jewellery for a living.'

'If you can call it a living,' replied Cate, to which Lucy smiled but appeared preoccupied.

Cate studied her. 'You OK?'

Lucy coloured. 'Yes. Fine.'

I clicked open the shop door. 'I hope you two young ladies have a lovely evening. Gran's offered to help out in here tomorrow, Cate, so no need to come in.'

'You sure?'

I nodded and Cate appeared pleased. 'That'll be handy. I've got a commission for a set of teardrop bridal earrings I need to finish off before next week. September wedding.'

I stepped out of the shop, the pale evening light lazily wafting over the top of the shops. 'Thanks for being here today, Cate. What with everything going on, I needed the moral support.'

I started to make my way out onto the pavement, when Lucy

emitted a groan. 'Shit! Shit! Nope. I can't do it. I promised myself I would, but I can't. Bugger it!'

'What do you mean?' I asked.

Cate's brows arched. 'What are you talking about?'

Lucy's voice was filled with conflict. 'I wasn't going to say anything – professional ethics and all that.'

Cate blinked at her. 'What is it?'

Lucy sighed. 'Right. So, I've been asked to set up a trust fund for a local Italian woman. It's all hush-hush, like something out of a daytime soap.'

It took a few moments for my addled brain to catch up. 'Hold on. Did you just say Italian?'

Cate widened her black eyes. 'Bloody hell. What's the name, Luce? Can you tell us?'

Lucy shook her red hair. Her wide steel-grey eyes were agonised. 'I'm sorry, but I can't. Client confidentiality.'

Oh my god. Could it be Linda Carlucci? I attempted to steady my bubbling optimism. 'Can I have a guess? You don't have to tell me.'

Lucy chewed her bottom lip. 'I can't. I wish I could.'

Cate placed both her hands on her girlfriend's slim shoulders. 'This is really important. It would mean a lot to Elle.'

Lucy's freckled nose creased in agony. 'I know. You did tell me what happened.'

Cate's understanding eyes searched Lucy's. 'You don't have to tell us, sweetheart. Just nod or shake your head if we happen to guess correctly.'

Lucy swivelled her pained expression from me to Cate and back again. She made a deep, resigned sigh. 'I knew I shouldn't have said anything. If I lose my career over this...!'

Optimism swelled inside of me. 'Thank you. So, Lucy,' I began, 'Is this Italian name by any chance, Linda Carlucci?'

She screwed up her face. 'Oh, for pity's sake!'

Cate and I observed her as she stole a breath. There came a

brief nod of her red hair. It was so brief, we were at risk of missing it.

'Bloody hell! It is! It's her!' Once I'd finished hugging and thanking her, I bathed her in what I hoped was my most appealing smile.

She groaned, folding her arms. 'I take it that means you would like her address as well?'

Chapter Forty-Three

Once Lucy had texted me Linda Carlucci's address and warned me again that if it came back to bite her on the arse, she would make my life a living hell, I bundled her into my arms.

Once I'd almost cut off her air supply and planted a kiss on her cheek, I hurried away, reeling with excitement.

My mind was frothing over. I had to speak to Dexter. OK, so he sounded as though he'd made up his mind about going back to London, but he should at least know we had acquired Linda's home address.

If he was adamant about leaving Fir Haven, then there might be a chance that his writing problems could be resolved before he left.

I would just have to confront the fact that he didn't feel about me the way I did about him.

Remember, Elle, you can't help who you like. Mum's words of wisdom drifted through my mind as I made my way back to my car. A crushing sensation came out of nowhere again, sending me into a tailspin.

Tears stung the corners of my eyes. How I wished Mum was

here right now. She always knew the right words to say at the right time, whereas Dad wouldn't say much but embrace me and reassure me everything had a habit of working out in the end.

I got to the end of the high street in a blur and stared down at my car keys jangling in my hand.

Steeling myself, I lowered my bag to my feet in the car park and reached for my mobile. My fingers hovered over my list of contacts. Why was I hesitating? What was the problem with ringing Dexter to tell him that at least we had an address for Linda now? It was a start.

I raised my face up to the icy-blue sky, searching for an answer. What if he thought I was trying to make him stay? I rubbed at my forehead. Good grief, this was bloody ridiculous! No wonder Mum always used to say I had a habit of overthinking things.

I imagined my mum talking to me in that soft, measured way of hers. 'Imagine the situation in reverse. What would you want Dexter to do? Would you want him to tell you?'

It was a no-brainer.

I rang Dexter's mobile. I could leave a message. Half expecting his voicemail to kick in, as it had done the past few days, I began to mentally concoct what I was going to say.

But then Dexter greeted me with a hesitant, 'Hi, Elle.'

I swallowed and began to tell him about where Linda Carlucci lived.

He was shocked and speechless for a few moments. Then he asked where I had got this information, but all I would say was that a friend of mine had come up trumps. I wasn't prepared to drop Lucy in it and risk her career.

His voice ricocheted from surprise to hesitancy, but he asked if I was OK to go up to Linda's home right away. 'I guess there's no point in hanging around.'

'Fine by me. Just give me half an hour to get changed.'

I ended up snatching a shower, freshening up my make-up, and throwing on my most flattering jeans and scoop-neck cream top before I heard the unmistakeable growl of Dexter's car as it slid down the lane towards the house.

Gran was out, having left a cryptic note saying she was going for dinner and would be back a bit later.

I clambered into the passenger side. Dexter's mouth softened. 'Hi.'

I smiled back, my stomach flip-flopping around.

'Well,' he announced, flicking his indicator to the right, 'I've already programmed the address you gave me into the sat-nav.'

My attention fell on the black screen jutting out of the dash display. 'So I see.' A red dot blinked, indicating where we had to drive to.

I allowed the subtle hum from his car radio to puncture the silence for a few seconds. 'So, your plans for returning to London going well?'

Dexter's stubbled jaw remained impassive. 'I'm having Hawk West Hall valued next week and I've already been in touch with a couple of removal companies for quotes.'

I fought to keep my voice light. So he was serious about leaving. 'Right. Good.' I trained my eyes on the woodland sliding past the window. Tears were lingering, but I jutted out my chin and refused to look at him.

'I really do appreciate everything you've done to try and help me. I just think that after everything, maybe it was a mistake to leave London after all.'

'Well, you have to do what you think is right.'

Dexter's handsome profile remained focused on the road ahead. I didn't want to ask this question, but it was pressing down on my chest like an immoveable object. I cleared my throat. 'So, if this Linda Carlucci lead proves to be successful and your writing capabilities return…' The rest of the sentence lodged in my mouth, but I forced it out. 'You're still leaving?'

Dexter drew the car to a smooth halt at a set of traffic lights. He appeared troubled. 'Yes. Even if my writing talent doesn't come back.'

What was he running away from? Why was he quitting his new life here?

'And what would you do? Back in London, I mean?' I was struggling to digest all of this. I didn't want to. It was pummelling my chest.

Dexter threw me a charged look. 'Probably go to the Cotswolds for a bit and help Mum and Dad and my sister with the stable business.' He put his foot down on the accelerator as the traffic lights dazzled green. 'Writing is my life, but if I can't do that anymore then at least I can focus on the horses.'

We wound our way round the country roads that took us beyond the carpets of lush fields and overhanging trees, which reminded me of emerald petticoats, flirting in the breeze.

He had made his mind up. No matter what happened now.

'Things,' he said, 'are getting overcomplicated. I never foresaw any of this.'

I forced out a laugh. 'Well, how could you? It's not every day you have a curse put on you.'

Dexter checked both ways at a quiet junction and eased us across it.' I guess that's true.' He took a considered breath before he spoke again. 'You know that I have this certain image.'

I knew what he was alluding to. You only had to google his name to see reports of his various parties and extravagant book launches.

'I suppose I've trapped myself inside that persona now.'

'But no one is trapped. You can be someone else, if you really want to.'

A flicker of a smile crossed his features and then evaporated as fast as it had appeared. 'My agent often reminds me that my image helps to sell my books. That and my considerable writing talent, of course,' he added with an eyeroll. 'That is, when it's not being obliterated by mysterious Italian women.'

'Well, I'm sure we're on the cusp of sorting all this out,' I replied, willing my voice to sound positive.

We drew up at another set of lights, surrounded by more woodland that opened out to reveal the roof of a house rising through the treetops.

'Thank you, Elle,' said Dexter. 'Whatever happens, thank you for trying to help. I won't forget it. And, like I said, I won't forget about the reserve. You can still rely on my support.'

I forced another smile. 'Thank you.' My heart stuttered in my chest like a faulty car engine.

The red dot on Dexter's sat-nav flickered like crazy in front of us. 'Nearly there!' I said with forced positivity. 'Come on, let's go and see what Mrs Carlucci has to say for herself.'

Chapter Forty-Four

The address Lucy had given me for Linda Carlucci was Fiore Cottage. It consisted of an old farmhouse in the middle of nowhere, cast adrift between Fir Haven and the next town of Tarran.

The red dot of Dexter's sat-nav had throbbed on the screen, confirming that this was indeed the correct address.

The farmhouse sat on an incline, surrounded by thick spruce trees either side. It was constructed of washed-out white stone and possessed a sleepy air. The roof was angular and grey tiled, and two crumbly chimney pots sprung out of it on either side.

The sash windows were thirsty for a lick of paint around the sills, but the red front door appeared to have been installed recently.

My hand reached up for the door-knocker. Dexter was solemn.

'Are you all right?' I asked him.

He considered my question for a moment before nodding. 'As all right as I can be, until we get this sorted.'

'Come on,' I urged. 'Standing here doing nothing isn't going to achieve anything.'

Apprehension was emanating out of him. I realised I wanted to hold him; to assure him everything would be ok; that his appetite and ability to write would come back.

But then visions of London and an empty Hawk West Hall bolted through my mind. It would be foolish of me to allow myself to feel anything more for Dexter, when he was leaving.

I had to try and put a stop to my feelings here and now. Easier said than done.

I realised I hadn't knocked on the door, as I was so consumed by my thoughts, so Dexter did it instead.

We waited, squinting around at the mounds of cut grass and a wave of wildflowers springing out of the chocolate-coloured earth. There were no vehicles parked nearby, so I did wonder whether there might be anyone at home.

From inside the farmhouse, a dog barked. Dexter and I swapped hopeful glances. We waited a few moments longer, but there was no reply.

'She's not in,' surmised Dexter, the charged glint in his eyes beginning to dim.

'If she isn't here, then we could find somewhere to grab a coffee and come back.'

'Good idea. I just hope she hasn't gone out for the evening.'

I peered upwards at the chimney pots, silhouetted against the scudding clouds. 'Then we try again tomorrow.'

Over the intermittent barking of the dog, Dexter studied me. 'Thank you.'

'What are you thanking me for?'

'For all this.'

I stared straight ahead at the closed front door, not daring to make eye contact with him. 'I'm a sucker for lost causes.'

'Gee, thanks.'

After a few more seconds, Dexter growled with frustration. 'This is a waste of time. She's not in.'

I folded my arms. 'OK, let's go and get a coffee and come back in a short while.'

We were striding back towards the car when a flicker of movement from behind one of the floral lemon-coloured curtains caught my eye and made me draw up.

Dexter frowned as I spun on my heels and returned to the door. 'What is it? What are you doing, Elle?'

'There *is* someone in. I saw those curtains move.'

'Maybe it was the dog.'

'Then it's eligible to go on *Britain's Got Talent* if it can stand on two legs and twitch a curtain like that.'

At least that made Dexter smile.

I knocked this time. When they failed to answer again, I cleared my throat and spoke to the closed door. 'I'm sorry to disturb you, but we wondered if we could have a quick word with Mrs Linda Carlucci, please? We understand she lives here.'

The door remained closed.

One of Dexter's dark brows arched as I refused to accept defeat and leave.

'We would really appreciate only a few moments of your time,' I said more loudly.

I turned and looked again at the window where I had seen the curtains flicker. This time, I was certain I caught sight of a flash of gold on a hand. A ring or bracelet perhaps?

But still no one came to the door.

Dexter heaved a sigh and stalked back to his car. 'Come on, Elle. Let's go.'

The sight of his broad shoulders slumping like that in defeat fired me up even more. Not giving much thought to what I was about to say next, I folded my arms again in defiant mode and remained on the doorstep. 'Now look, this is very important, otherwise we wouldn't have tracked you down and taken the trouble to come all the way up here.'

I planted my feet on the second step. 'Our visit will determine whether someone ends up leaving Fir Haven and abandoning their career, so we really do need to speak to her.'

Still, my words were met by only the grumpy growls and barks from the dog behind the door.

'Fine,' I ground out, striding away from the front door. 'We'll be back to see you again. We're not giving up.'

It was only when Dexter's car keys ignited the unlocking system on his car that a sound travelled down to us. The front door creaked open to reveal a short, slim, dark-haired woman in an ankle-length rose-pink dress and aubergine cardigan.

Dexter froze.

It was Linda Carlucci.

Chapter Forty-Five

Her tanned, lined face was bursting with agitation. 'What do you want?'

From behind her came a skirmish of ragged terrier. The dog stood by her leg and wagged its tail like an out-of-control boat rudder.

Dexter and I strode towards her.

I bent down and patted Mrs Carlucci's dog, which seemed to irritate her further. 'Calm down, Brando!' She frowned. 'I asked you what you wanted.'

Dexter stepped forward. 'I'm sorry to trouble you, Mrs Carlucci, but I don't know if you remember me.'

Her creased bottle-green eyes widened at the sight of Dexter. She stared at him like she had done before and paled. 'You're the idiot who tried to run me over.'

Beside me, Dexter's apprehensive features had transformed themselves into ones of contrition.

'Could we come in please, Mrs Carlucci?' I asked. 'It would only be for a few minutes.'

She gripped tighter onto her door handle. 'No. I'm just getting ready to go out.'

She must have registered our disappointment. Then she nodded her head. 'Oh, I see.' She tilted her chin up in defiance. 'That's why you're here, isn't it?'

Dexter and I did our best to feign innocence, but failed.

Linda Carlucci clutched at the door, still focusing most of her attention on Dexter. Her green eyes kept raking over his face. 'You want me to lift the curse.'

Linda Carlucci saying those words aloud, while a thrush in a nearby tree wagged its tail and let rip a series of excited chirrups, gave me a start.

I spun around to Dexter beside me, shamefaced. I had doubted him. Even up until this point, there had been a shred of disbelief in me, which struggled to accept the notion that this woman had indeed cursed him. But now, hearing her say it, made me stifle a gasp.

His eyes pleaded with Linda Carlucci. 'Please will you lift this thing? I can't write. I'm struggling to even think of ideas, let alone find the motivation to put pen to paper. I feel like my life as I know it is slipping away from me.'

Linda dragged her mouth into a tight line. 'Men like you are selfish. You think only of yourself. You do what you want. You're reckless and it's the people you leave behind who have to pick up the pieces.'

'He's changed,' I broke in, 'or at least he's doing his best to.' I gestured to Dexter beside me. 'I've seen another side to him. Really, I have.'

I dared not risk another look at Dexter as the evening sun sifted through his thick shock of black hair.

'So are the rumours true then?' batted back Linda. 'That you're planning on leaving Fir Haven?'

Dexter didn't reply.

'But that's what men like you do, isn't it, Mr Grayling? The posturing and the big gestures. I've met men like you before.'

My brows dipped. What did she mean by that?

'You haven't changed at all,' she croaked, backing further into her hallway. She continued to look at Dexter with a haunted expression.

Then the door banged shut and her dog made a few barks of protest.

We stood, wild-eyed at what had just taken place. 'Bloody hell,' muttered Dexter, stumbling away from the door.

I wrapped my arms around myself as a keen breeze began to pick up and coil itself around me. I didn't know what to say to him. Her reaction had been ferocious and uncompromising.

'We have to think of something else,' I said to him across the shining smoky-grey roof of his car. 'I'm so sorry I doubted you about the curse thing.'

He flicked his hand to dismiss my apology.

'If we can do some digging into the Carlucci family, maybe that might throw up something useful.'

'Elle.' He sighed as he said my name.

Warming to my theme, I carried on. 'I don't know about you, but didn't you think she was going a bit off-piste just now?' I bit my lip. 'Mrs Carlucci sounded like she was referring to someone else then and not you.'

'Elle!'

Dexter's raised voice startled me. He pressed his fob and the car flashed and bleeped. I got in and watched him slam his driver's side door. 'I know Linda Carlucci said I'm running away, but I'm not. At least, that's not the whole reason I'm planning on going back to London.'

I felt a sliver of apprehension. 'What is it?'

He rested one arm on top of his steering wheel. I could see he was debating whether to confide in me.

'Dexter. Please tell me.'

He let out a rush of air and searched the middle distance

through the windscreen. 'I can't lie to you or deceive you, Elle. It wouldn't be fair and you deserve so much more than that.'

I watched him turn his attention back to me, an agonised flint in his eyes. 'I've got a little girl back in London. A daughter.'

Chapter Forty-Six

His words hung in the air, suspended between us.

'A daughter?' I repeated.

Dexter gave the briefest nod.

'Do you mean you moved up here to escape from your responsibilities?'

Dexter was insistent. 'No! It's not like that.'

I could feel my heart splintering and shattering. I had thought I was beginning to know him. What an idiot I had been! Had he got someone pregnant and then abandoned her and the baby to come and live up in Scotland? Or had he got someone pregnant and only just discovered he was a father? No. Surely not.

I shifted away from him in my car seat. 'Have you had a crisis of conscience now, Dexter, is that it? Has Mrs Carlucci struck a nerve?'

'Yes. No! Elle, you've got it all wrong.'

I dismissed his half-hearted attempts at an explanation. I had been doing everything I could to help him with this curse and yet, here he was, forced into a confession that he was a father to a little girl, albeit a distant one.

We remained seated in the stationary car, with the light slowly vanishing behind the hillside.

'How old is she?' I asked after what seemed like an eternity, in a strangled voice I didn't recognise.

'Five.'

I scrambled to make sense of what he was telling me. 'And what's her name?'

'Nadia. She lives with her mum.'

I flicked my gaze back to Linda's cottage. 'That's a lovely name.'

Dexter turned on the ignition and we were soon gliding away and back towards town. I felt like my emotions were being spun in a tumble drier.

Dexter's voice was hesitant. 'I'm sorry. I should have told you sooner.'

We drove back in comparative silence before he pulled to a stop at the brow of the lane that led to Pebble Brook. The outside carriage lights were on, sending a honeyed glow into the darkness.

'I thought I was getting to know you, Dexter.' My voice tailed off. 'And don't concern yourself with the nature reserve.'

'But I promised I would. I'm more than happy to lend my support.'

'There's no point.' I reached for the passenger side door handle. 'You won't be able to do much after you leave.'

I climbed out, feeling idiotic. I held onto the open door. 'I don't understand why you came to Scotland, if you've got a daughter in London.'

Dexter blew out his cheeks. 'It's complicated.'

I shut the car door and heard the thrum of his car engine behind me as he drove away.

Disappointment lumped in my throat, while I delved into my bag for my front door key. 'Complicated?' I murmured to myself. 'That doesn't even begin to describe it.'

The next couple of weeks heralded mid-August and the local school children returning after the summer break.

I had already started browsing through catalogues, identifying suitable stock for Christmas.

That was a terrifying prospect in itself.

Fir Haven saw a tinge of frost on the colder mornings. And I still felt all knotted up inside about Dexter.

I couldn't blame him at all for wanting to go back to London, especially as he had a child there. But why make such a big thing of wanting to remain in Scotland?

He was still leaving, according to the local gossip hotline. There was talk of one of Glasgow's most prestigious estate agents having been spotted up at Hawk West Hall. I swallowed hard at the prospect and then felt ashamed and selfish. He belonged with his little girl.

Perhaps Linda Carlucci's harsh words had made him realise he needed to be a proper father and to stop being so focused on himself? If so, I couldn't fault him for that. I had no right to.

Dexter had rung me briefly a couple of times and sent the odd text, the last one of which had said he was taking part in a crime writing festival in the Lake District for a couple of days.

To be honest, I was unsure why he had felt the need to ring me at all.

Cate and Grandma were sympathetic, but both expressed understanding for his plight as well as mine. 'I bet he doesn't really want to return, but what with his daughter being there and all this Linda Carlucci carry-on, he probably thinks it's the best solution all round,' suggested my gran.

And so, with a heavy heart, I threw myself into Paper Roses even more than usual.

I also treated myself to a new cream and gold bedside lamp and fluted buttercup-yellow curtains for my bedroom, and popped my treasured photos of Mum, Dad, and Gran in new dark-wooden frames.

I had just arrived at the shop, huddled under an umbrella against an early morning shower, when my mobile rang in my bag. This was perfect timing!

I found the key and stumbled through the door. I fired on the shop spotlights to see Gran's expectant smile leaping out at me from the phone screen. 'We need to do something,' she gabbled, not bothering with her usual chit-chat and pleasantries.

'Gran, please slow down. What is it?'

'It's the nature reserve. I've just had a call from Morag at the council.'

A thud of dread punched me in the stomach. 'And?'

'It's not yet official. Morag is risking a lot by letting this out.'

I gripped my mobile. 'Go on.'

'It's not looking good,' said Gran. She sighed. 'There have been a few delays due to red tape, but Atticus Development are planning an official announcement within the next couple of weeks.'

'And the start of the work?'

Gran paused. 'Apparently six to eight weeks' time. They want things underway by Halloween at the latest.'

My heart sagged further as Gran's words rolled over me. 'I hate to say this, but I think we may be fighting a losing battle.'

Chapter Forty-Seven

How the hell could they justify this?

What on earth was possessing them to ruin the nature reserve, in order to throw up an array of holiday homes?

I already knew the answer of course: money.

Despite the protests and the vocal opposition, the council were intent on their mission. Pictures of Dexter leaving crowded in my mind too. Even his public support, which had garnered the attention of the national and international press, hadn't seemed to result in success. Atticus Development were bulldozing over the wishes of the local community in more ways than one.

More images flitted around my mind, of Mum, Dad, and me larking about up there. We would watch the robins flit from branch to branch in winter and admire the butterflies in spring, which were like mini rainbows hovering above the flowers. Then there were the swans gliding along on the surface of the water. Dad would scoop me onto his shoulders and march along laughing, while I squealed in delight and grinned down at Mum.

I blinked a few times and held my mobile tighter to my ear.

I forced a smile at a customer, who clattered through the shop door and began browsing our ruby anniversary cards.

I whirled on my heel, a grim determination overtaking me as I visualised my parents again and what they would have made of this terrible news. What would they have done? Would they have just rolled over and accepted defeat?

The future of the reserve did look grim, but the fight wasn't over yet.

I could feel my chin hardening as I spoke to Gran. 'If Atticus Development think this is over, they are much mistaken.' I steeled myself for the battle ahead. 'There's no way we're giving up now.'

'But, darling, the council have said it's a done deal.'

'I don't care, Gran.'

I dropped my voice lower, watching the customer agonise over a card depicting a waltzing couple and another featuring two champagne glasses. 'I've got an idea about how we can fight back.'

Grandma listened for a moment. 'All right. I'll pop by the shop at lunchtime today and we can talk more then.'

Lunchtime came around with a phone call from Cate, volunteering her services in the shop, but I told her things were manageable and I would give her a shout if I needed her help.

To be honest, I was relishing the time to think, with only the quiet, candy-coloured interior of the shop, soft music, and the golden tinged lights for company.

Grandma materialised just before one o'clock with a Tupperware box of turkey and salad sandwiches, a couple of shiny red apples even Snow White would have envied, and two pots of strawberry yoghurt. She also insisted I put up my *Closed for Lunch* sign, which I rarely liked to use. Her pointed frown brooked no argument.

We vanished into the kitchen and settled ourselves with our

lunch at the table. I didn't feel hungry, but forced myself to eat. I knew if I hadn't, my grandmother would have force-fed me.

Once the sandwiches had been eaten and we finished the crunchy apples, Gran asked me about my plans for more protesting against the development. 'So, Elle, what is your cunning plan?'

I reached for my yoghurt and peeled back the lid. 'I'm going to organise an autumn fair here in the main street.'

Grandma's neat eyebrows sprang upwards. 'Go on.'

I gave my yoghurt a thoughtful stir and explained my idea of having marquees lining the length of the cobbles. 'There will be baking stalls and local artists can sell their crafts. We could have a representative from the birds and animal protection charities and also from the Woodland Trust.'

I took an excited mouthful of yoghurt while my ideas gathered momentum. 'We could have speakers from the environmental lobbies and any local councillors or officials who are opposed to what's going on.'

I reached across the table and clasped her hand in mine. 'I know there are no guarantees, but we can't give in, Gran. Not yet. If we could just get enough money together to put in a counter offer on behalf of the community… or if they won't accept that, we threaten court action. If we have enough money at our back, that won't be an issue.'

Her light-grey eyes sparkled out of her cat-like face. 'We won't go down without a fight.'

'Exactly! And who knows? If some big company or organisation got to hear about what we're doing, they might pitch in financially as well.'

She dabbed at the corners of her mouth with one of two mustard-coloured napkins she'd brought with her. 'What timescale were you thinking of for getting this all organised?'

A blush crept up my face. 'I know it will be tight, but three weeks at the most.'

'Three weeks?!'

I tried to soothe her concerns, although underneath my positive exterior, my heart was charging around my rib cage. 'It's doable,' I assured her. 'It really is.'

I clasped my hands together. 'I've already started emailing marquee hire companies and nature organisations, asking about volunteers to come and do talks. Because the bulk of the wedding season is almost over now, the marquee company said availability is good.' I beamed at her. 'And I've spoken to Cate and she jumped at the chance to support it and have her own stall there, to sell her jewellery.'

Grandma started to speak but I was on a roll. 'And, bless her, she hasn't wasted any time alerting several of her arty friends too.'

I enthused about the interest she had garnered that morning from a potter, a handbag designer, and an old friend of hers from college, who makes her own soaps. 'And that's just for starters!'

My voice trickled away when I noticed Gran's odd expression. 'What is it? Are you OK?'

Her eyes softened further. 'I know what you do, Elle, when you're hurting. You do this.'

'I do what?'

She frowned at me. 'Precisely what you're doing right now. Throwing yourself into your work. Keeping busy. Occupying your mind so you have little time to think about other things.'

I knew she was referring to Dexter, but didn't say.

'I'm fine!' I blustered. 'I like keeping busy.'

'Yes, but there's busy and then there's going manic.'

I scraped back my chair. It was almost two o'clock and time to reopen. 'I promise you I won't go crazy, OK?' I moved towards the shop door to open up again. 'I'll give the local action group a ring and let them know what I'm planning too. I'm sure they'll want to get involved with this.'

I eased open the shop door. 'Come on,' I smiled. 'It's time to get back to work.'

Chapter Forty-Eight

The next morning saw a deluge of rain that slid over the cobbles and chased down the windows of Paper Roses.

Grandma had insisted on helping me out in the shop. 'My book club has been cancelled and I'm not in the mood to meet up with Muriel McTaggart. All she talks about is her grandson becoming a surgeon!'

The short journey from my car to the shop had still been a miserable experience, so we shook the rain from our umbrellas and stuffed them into the stand by the door.

I spent the next couple of hours emailing the marquee hire company about the quotes they had supplied me with, ringing contacts at the Woodland Friends organisation for guest speakers, and garnering local interest from artists.

It was so gratifying to know that there was so much enthusiasm and passion for what I was trying to do.

Gran encouraged me to focus on plans for what I had labelled the Nature Reserve Knees-Up. 'I'll look after things in here. If I need you, I'll tell you.'

The dank grey weather had delivered a few more customers than I had anticipated, which was good. I had a feeling it was more the comfort of escaping from the Scottish weather, rather than a burning desire to buy a glittery paperweight or a stationery set.

I was just draining the remnants of my tea while I crouched over my laptop in the back of the shop, when I heard the doorbell ding. Gran's voice drifted through to me from the counter.

'Hello, young lady. And what can I do for you?'

Whoever gran was talking to, didn't reply. I heard her feet tap across the shop floor. 'Are you lost, sweetheart? Where's your mummy?'

I scraped back my chair and made my way out, my curiosity well and truly piqued by the conversation.

In the middle of the shop floor stood a little girl, hunched in a buttercup-yellow waterproof jacket slick with rain. Tufts of dark hair were poking out from under her hood.

As I got closer, I could see she was wearing sparkly jeans and a pair of pink trainers. My grandmother was bent over, encouraging her to talk but without success.

'Hello,' I smiled, crouching down in front of her, so I was at eye level. 'I'm Elle. What's your name?'

She blinked her saucer-like corn-blue eyes back at me.

Gran and I exchanged glances.

The little girl finally pushed her hood back from her head, revealing her hair to be tied up in a curly ponytail. 'I'm five.'

'Wow!' I grinned. 'You are a very grown-up girl.'

She puffed out her little chest at the compliment. 'My favourite colour is purple and I like unicorns and glitter.'

'I love glitter too,' I grinned at her.

'Where's your mummy and daddy, sweetie?' questioned Gran again. 'Have you been shopping with them and got lost?'

She considered the question and shook her head. 'I didn't come shopping with my mummy and daddy.'

'Well, who did you come out with?' I asked with a smile. 'You didn't come out on your own, did you?'

She cocked her head and listened to the soft tones of the panpipes playing from my iPod. 'No, I'm not allowed to go to the shops on my own.'

'Nadia! For goodness' sake! You mustn't run away like that!'

Elsa, Dexter's housekeeper, barrelled through the door, puffing and red-faced. *Nadia?* My eyes grew as I realised who the little girl was.

Elsa waggled her wet umbrella at the child. 'I only turned my back for a moment to buy a newspaper and when I looked around again, the little mite was gone.'

Grandma sympathised with Elsa's panicked state, but I couldn't drag my eyes away from the cute little girl gazing back up at me.

Nadia. The thick, dark hair and sea-blue eyes were unmistakeable. This sweet little thing was Dexter's daughter.

Chapter Forty-Nine

Questions buzzed around my head.

What's Nadia doing here? Didn't Dexter say he was returning to London to be with her?

Gran looked at Nadia and then at me with dawning realisation. I could see her slotting the pieces of the jigsaw into place. She too must have deduced who the little girl was.

Gran offered another friendly smile at Nadia and Elsa. 'You're both soaked through. How about a nice hot drink to warm you both up? There's some hot chocolate and marshmallows through the back.'

Nadia broke into a gap-toothed grin. Elsa rolled her eyes. 'This one could charm the stars out of the sky.'

Just like her father.

While Elsa showed Nadia our array of unicorn erasers we had begun stocking, Grandma and I slipped through to the kitchen. 'Dexter's daughter,' she said, filling up the kettle with cold water.

I glanced at her out of the corner of my eye. 'But what I don't get is why she's suddenly come to Fir Haven? Dexter said she was one of the reasons he had decided to move back to London.'

Gran listened as she fetched a jar of marshmallows from the

cupboard above the sink and unscrewed the lid. 'Look, darling,' she began in a low voice. 'Please don't be offended by what I'm about to say. I'm only thinking of you.' She placed the jar down on the sink top.

Nadia's giggle travelled through to us from the front of the shop.

'Believe me, I can appreciate what you see in that young man. He's very good-looking, intelligent, and charismatic.'

I toyed with my bangle. 'I can sense a "but" is coming.'

Gran delivered an empathetic smile. 'But he's also very famous and you don't know much about him – well, apart from what you read in the gossip columns.'

I let out a low, hollow laugh. 'Ain't that the truth.'

The kettle bubbled behind us and clicked itself off.

'That's what hurts the most,' I confessed after a pause. 'I thought I was getting to know him and then I hear he's heading back home.'

I moved towards the kitchen door and peeked out at Nadia and Elsa. Their heads were huddled together, exclaiming a scented watermelon pencil while the rain persisted in streaming down the shop windows. 'When he told me he had a little girl, I found myself trying to make excuses for him.' My smile was tight as I turned back around. 'But now I'm beginning to doubt whether I ever knew him at all.'

I gestured to Nadia. Conclusions thrust themselves to the front of my mind. 'I've been so stupid. I thought that removal van was him getting ready to leave, but perhaps it wasn't. What if Dexter arranged for Nadia's things to be transported up here, so that she could get used to spending time with him?'

'You don't know for sure,' Gran insisted.

'Well, everything seems to be pointing that way.'

'And what about the Carlucci curse?' pointed out Gran, scooping hot chocolate into two mugs. 'Where does that fit in?'

I let my hands fall back down by my sides. 'Maybe Dexter

thinks that being a good father – or being seen to be – is the way to break it.'

Gran's brows angled. 'I don't follow.'

I watched her pour the steaming hot water into the mugs. The powder transformed into two pools of swirling milky chocolate. 'Perhaps Dexter is out to prove what a good dad he is in order to get the curse lifted. He wouldn't leave Fir Haven then.'

'Oh, surely not,' Gran tutted, scooping out some marshmallows and dashing a sprinkle of them on each of the two mugs. 'Using his own daughter like that? Bringing her here, just for his own ends?'

The thought chilled me too. Even considering the notion made me flush with embarrassment.

Gran took the mugs of hot chocolate into the shop for Nadia and Elsa to enjoy. I admired his sweet little girl with the snub nose and rosebud mouth.

I didn't want to even contemplate it, but perhaps Dexter Grayling had played us both.

Chapter Fifty

While Nadia occupied herself with rearranging my display of tartan bookmarks, Elsa sat by the counter and gratefully sipped her drink.

Neither Gran nor I quizzed her about Nadia. We waited to see what she might divulge, which, to her credit, was very little. No doubt Dexter had insisted she sign some sort of confidentiality agreement when she began working with him.

She must have noticed our meaningful glances at one another as we admired Nadia's quirky giggle and glossy black hair.

'She's up visiting,' was all she would offer in a protective rush. 'Her mother is a friend of Mr Grayling's.'

I managed to push a smile out. 'That's lovely. I'm sure Nadia will love it around here.'

Grandma added, 'You'll have to take her to the nature reserve. I fear it won't be here for much longer.'

Elsa gasped and clutched at her mug of half-finished hot chocolate. 'Oh, please don't say that. If it's up to some of that council lot, her generation won't have a clue what a roe deer is.'

Sensing she was the hot topic of conversation, Nadia glanced over her shoulder at the three of us and twitched her nose.

'Yes, well,' I ground out with determination, 'the fight isn't over yet.'

The rain had vanished by the time Elsa had finished her hot chocolate and coaxed Nadia back into her yellow jacket.

I dropped down in front of her, keeping my hands behind my back. 'Here,' I offered, handing her two of the unicorn erasers and a fluffy pink pencil case. 'These are for you. Now, no more running away from Mrs Bennett, all right?'

Nadia's eyes popped and she clutched the gifts in both hands. Elsa whispered something into her ear. 'Thank you, Miss Cassidy,' she sing-songed.

'Elle. Just call me Elle.'

'OK.'

Gran escorted them to the shop door.

'I'll take missy here to the playpark for a little while,' said Elsa. 'It's been a bit fraught up at Hawk West Hall of late.'

Gran shot me an eyebrow raising look. 'Oh dear. Why's that then?'

Elsa waited till Nadia was hopping from foot to foot on the shop step and admiring her new pencil case. She dropped her voice so the little girl couldn't hear. 'Mr Grayling is having issues with his agent and publisher. I have to say, I haven't seen him writing much recently.'

Elsa collected her umbrella from the stand and fastened it up.

'Anyway,' smiled Elsa, disappearing out the shop door. 'Thank you again for the hot chocolate.'

Chapter Fifty-One

Arrangements were beginning to come together for the autumn fair.

I'd honed in on Saturday 1st September, which was a little over a week away now and, although a tight timescale, was doable.

The last thing I wanted was to allow the protest momentum to slide.

The end of the week arrived in a flurry of confirmatory emails for a dozen stalls, as well as a list of the crafts, art, and baking that would be on sale.

The local businesses were looking forward to a surge in footfall that day, thanks to the event being held along the main street.

September was on the horizon and was often a pretty time of year in the town, what with the leaves transforming into firebrand shades and the sky managing to deliver sleepy sunshine. There was also the seasonal hint of what was to come, in the shape of air promising the scent of pumpkins and fireworks, before Christmas descended.

The thought of the impending festive season pressed down on me. This would be our second Christmas without my parents.

I'd always loved our family Christmases. Pebble Brook would

be decked out like a snow globe, thanks to Dad stringing lights over every conceivable surface. He would even twist them around nearby trees so that they blinked and winked. Their gold and silver reflections would shimmer in the water that flowed past. Mum, meanwhile, would produce beautiful festive wreaths bursting with berries, cones, and twigs, which she would suspend from the doors and windows.

I stared past my laptop, clicking my mouse far harder than I meant to.

Cate, having relieved Gran of her shop duties for the day, waved goodbye to a departing customer. She turned around in the doorway, her dark eyes assessing me. 'Everything OK?'

I forced a smile. 'Of course. Why do you ask?'

She moved towards me and peered over my shoulder. I was in the middle of crafting an email to two children's entertainers, Top Hat Tom (a clown on stilts), and The Magical Matilda, a drama student who not only performed magic tricks but was also a talented face painter. At least being able to combine the two with her would save a bit of money out of our nature reserve fund, which all the local businesses had kindly donated to.

Both entertainers had confirmed they could make the 1st, so I was arranging arrival times.

All my fellow businesses had been so very generous with their donations, but in order to stage the event properly, we had no option but to spend that bit more.

I hadn't told anyone, not even Gran, but I had already put in £5,000 of my own money and intended to inject a bit more into the fund, if we needed it. Well, it was actually some of the money Mum and Dad had left me in their will. I knew they would understand.

I turned my attention back to Cate.

'I don't want you making yourself ill,' she warned. The concern was evident in her smoky voice.

'I'm fine. Really.'

The way Cate twitched her red-slicked lips let me know she didn't believe a word I was saying. 'You're taking on far too much after everything that's happened.'

I flicked my plait. 'Rubbish!'

Without saying anything, she reached across and pulled my notebook and to-do list away from me to examine it.

'What are you doing?'

'Well, I'm not about to break into song.'

I sighed with irritation.

'Your eyes look like two fried eggs, Elle. Go and get some fresh air.'

'But what about the shop?'

'What about it? It's not going anywhere.'

I was about to argue, but thought better of it when Cate interrupted me. 'I'll sit here and do some of this and then if anyone comes in, I can attend to them.' Cate lifted a finger and pointed at the shop door. 'Go! Now! Take a breather.' She shrugged her shoulders. 'It's almost lunchtime anyway, so we shouldn't be swamped. Take your mobile and I'll ring you if things turn ugly.'

'OK.' I laughed in surrender. 'Thanks. I won't be long.'

I slid on my cream leather jacket and pushed my mobile and purse into my pocket. The clouds were skimming along the sky as I walked. I wasn't too sure where I was headed, but it was great to escape from that blinking laptop screen for a few minutes.

The other windows along the main street glinted their assorted displays of wedding cakes in the bakery window and the grocer's displayed trays of fresh fruit and vegetables in a colourful rainbow.

My reflection wavered in the windows as I ambled past. My dark-brown eyes were blurry and my skin looked paler than normal. I thrust my hands deeper into the pockets of my fitted black jeans.

'On your lunchbreak?' asked Mrs McVicar, one of the local

charity shop volunteers. She was hurrying up to me, all belted coat and coiffed red hair.

'Just getting some air on Cate's insistence.'

Mrs McVicar nodded. 'Lovely girl, Catherine.'

I hid a smile. Cate disliked her Sunday name. Even her parents didn't call her Catherine. Mrs McVicar was the only person who did. 'Yes, she is.'

I was about to resume my walk when Mrs McVicar moved closer to me, adopting a conspiratorial air. 'It's all happening up at that author's house.'

A weird concoction of emotions took over while I stood there, with just the faint drone of a car in the distance. 'Is it?'

Mrs McVicar's alert navy-blue eyes shone with knowing. She leant in and cast her attention around, as though scoping out the area for snipers.

'That bonnie wee lass whose visiting up there at the moment, is a friend's daughter by all accounts.'

Nadia. She's talking about Nadia. Of course, that would be the official line. I assumed not many people would know Dexter had a little girl. I nodded along with her. 'Yes, I believe so.'

Mrs McVicar pressed on, still in possession of some juicy bit of gossip by the looks of it. 'Well, he hasn't let the grass grow, as my mother, God rest her soul, used to say!'

I hoped I was feigning mild interest. In reality, my stomach was sinking. I tilted my chin up and tried to appear casual. 'Oh? Why's that then?'

Mrs McVicar looked like she was sucking vinegar. 'A tall brunette. They've been seen together around town and in The Salmon & Swan. I think it's the wee girl's mother.'

She disarmed me with a cheery smile. 'Tell your gran I was asking after her. Cheerio now!'

Chapter Fifty-Two

I made my way back to Paper Roses in a numb fog, melancholy thoughts skittering around my head.

Cate was tapping away at my laptop, her black lashes batting while she concentrated on the screen. 'I've just rung those two kiddies' entertainers to confirm their arrival time on the first. That was a quick walk! I told you to take a proper break.' Cate pushed her chair back. 'What is it?'

I feel so bloody stupid!

Cate insisted I sit down while she attended to a harassed-looking mother with two little boys.

Once they had departed with their purchases, Cate darted back behind the counter. 'Right. Spill.'

And out it came in a torrent of embarrassment, about the arrival of a statuesque brunette up at Hawk West Hall. 'I wouldn't be at all surprised if she's Nadia's mum.'

Cate read my face with her huge black eyes glowing under the shop spotlights. 'I took one look at you and I could see how upset you were.'

I dropped my gaze to the floor and examined my pink and white Converse trainers. 'All this is self-inflicted, Cate. That's what's making me feel so stupid. I promised myself I wouldn't get involved or hurt again and now look at me!'

'Well, if it's any consolation, I can see what you see in him – and I'm gay, for pity's sake!'

I managed to laugh, despite my heart sagging in my chest.

Cate's hair spun out of her red, dotted headband. 'You don't need a mess, Elle, and you certainly don't need any complications.' She fired me a mischievous look. 'Maybe he does deserve this curse after all!' She rested her elbows on the counter. 'Whatever his motives are for bringing his daughter to Fir Haven, you don't need to get involved.' She paused. 'I'm not saying he isn't trying to be a good father, but we don't know what's going on.'

I sank back in my chair and pushed out my legs. Cate was doing her utmost not to say what I had been thinking. Was there a chance Dexter had brought Nadia here purely to show Linda Carlucci that he wasn't the arrogant, selfish cretin she thought he was?

I glanced across the shop and out through the glass panel of the door. When would I ever learn? I'd thought I was beginning to get to know the real him.

Just goes to show how wrong you can be.

Cate slapped her hands down on both knees of her denims. 'Right. Onto something far more interesting. Would you like the good news or the good news?'

'Go on.'

She flashed her bright-white smile. 'Have I ever mentioned to you that one of Lucy's new clients is Dean Ellwood?'

The name marched through my mind. 'Isn't that the folk singer who's been getting a lot of press coverage recently?'

Cate beamed with self-congratulation. 'The very one.'

Enthusiasm radiated out of her. 'Lucy has mentioned our plight with the nature reserve to Dean Ellwood personally. She makes a point of getting to know all her clients well and it turns out he's very big on environmental issues.'

My excitement rose.

'Lucy spoke to him about your autumn fair and Dean has offered to appear for free!'

I let out a squeal. 'Are you kidding?!'

Cate grinned back. 'Nope. He said he would be delighted to lend his support and that the publicity of him playing in aid of the reserve won't hurt sales of his new album, which is due out at Christmas.'

This good news diluted my pain about Dexter, allowing me to at least temporarily revel in this terrific development. 'You do know you have one hell of a girlfriend there.'

Cate's gaze glittered. 'You don't need to remind me.'

I charged headlong into the next couple of days, making sure the local paper had all the necessary information to cover the Nature Reserve Knees-Up and that everything from the market stalls, the local traders and bakers, to the children's entertainers and representatives from the environmental groups and wildlife protection societies were in place.

I posted regular updates on the Paper Roses website, as well as our Twitter, Facebook, and Instagram accounts, to make sure the word spread far and wide. Cate even used her artistic talents to create a poster for the event, which fellow shop owners were only too happy to display in their windows.

Atticus Development had gone silent, however, which did concern me. It was as if they were toying with us, waiting to see what our next move would be, before they made theirs.

It was now only a week until the autumn fair took place and the Saturday late August sky had been bulging all morning with the prospect of rain. I hovered on the step of Paper Roses and silently pleaded to the heavens for better weather one week from today.

The trees on the opposite side of the cobbles were carrying faint dashes of gold, amber, and claret and as the first fat raindrops fell, they spun the few fallen leaves down the road like little boats.

From over my shoulder, I heard my mobile erupt in my bag.

'Don't worry, lovey. I'll get it,' called Gran.

I turned and headed back in, an enquiring look on my face and a bemused expression on hers. She spoke in hushed tones. 'That's the management team of Dean Ellwood. They want to know if he can drop by after lunch today to take a look around.'

I grinned. 'Of course.'

'They apologise for the short notice, but he's been busy dropping his latest single – whatever that means.'

I laughed at her frown. 'It's just a fancy way of saying the record has been released, Gran.'

She rolled her eyes and handed me the phone. 'Why couldn't they have just said that then?'

Once I'd chatted with his PR person, Laura, I put my phone back in my bag and let out a long rush of air. 'Oh God. I hope he's impressed.'

'Impressed with what? He's coming here to help save our nature reserve, not buy a house!'

Thank goodness I had my wonderful gran to keep me sane!

As it was the weekend, the shop was busier than usual. We dealt with passing customers, as well as giving people a verbal update on the autumn fair and also popping further bulletins up on Paper Roses' social media sites.

I ordered my grandmother to take a break and she agreed, on the proviso that I too would have a proper lunch, if she brought back two of the warmed golden chorizo rocket and tomato rolls from the bakery.

I would have preferred not to have closed on a Saturday for lunch, planning instead to capitalise on weekend trade, but one charged stare from her brooked no further argument.

I swung the door sign to closed and we sat in the back, savouring our warm lunch and chatting over cups of freshly brewed tea. We chatted about everything from the current novel she was reading for book club to what we wanted to give each other for Christmas. Gran had just told me about woodland-scented festive candles she'd spotted on the internet, which she thought might sell well in the shop, when I glanced down at my watch. 'Bloody hell! It's almost 2 p.m. already! Dean Ellwood will be here any minute.'

Gran cleared our crumb-strewn plates and I rinsed the mugs before darting into the bathroom to tidy myself up. I neatened my ponytail, which I'd curled messily earlier that morning, and reapplied my rosy lipstick.

I had just emerged from our staff toilet and was straightening the lavish bow of my pearl-coloured shirt, when the door dinged open.

Dean Ellwood was alone. I had expected his entourage to accompany him, but instead he hesitated with a lopsided smile. He was attractive in a slouchy sort of way. 'Elle Cassidy?'

'That's me.'

We shook hands while he appreciated the interior of Paper Roses through a pair of warm hazel eyes that complemented the colour of his shaggy red hair.

He apologised again for turning up so suddenly, but I dismissed it. Grandma offered him tea or coffee, but he declined with a charming gap-toothed smile. 'I'd love to, but I'm a bit tight for time.'

I pointed towards the street outside. 'Then let's go. I'll show you where we're holding next week's shindig and I'm more than happy to answer any questions you may have.'

'Sounds good.'

We stepped out onto the cobbles. Thankfully, the rain had moved off, leaving only a faint glisten on the pavements and trees; lemony sunshine was stippling through the branches now. At least the elements were showing Fir Haven for what it was: a pretty corner of Scotland, cradled by superb woodland and rolling fields.

I explained about the stalls that would be there next Saturday, selling everything from shiny glazed cakes to handmade jewellery, and the enthusiastic children's entertainers who would be meandering about to keep the little ones occupied.

I then spoke of what the reserve meant to everyone in the area.

Dean agreed. 'It's beautiful. I did some research on the place after Lucy told me what was happening.' Then he went onto mention its historical links. He'd really done his homework.

'If I'd had more time today, I would have loved to have gone up there again for another visit.'

I blinked up at him. 'You've visited the reserve already?'

With a big, shy smile, he confessed that he had. 'I've actually bought a place just outside Tarron and when I was checking it out on Wednesday night, I took a drive over there.'

Snapshots of the neighbouring town, with its rocky harbour and long tradition of family-owned fishing vessels, leapt into my head. 'And what did you think of the reserve when you saw it?'

Dean's twinkly eyes burned with intent. 'I think it deserves to be saved. It's stunning.'

We wandered side by side along the main street. 'The locals and the businesses here are so fired up about saving the reserve.' I gestured towards the back of the wide street. 'I had thought your stage would be good over there. Please say if you don't agree.'

Dean stopped, his navy and white trainers slapping over the damp cobbles. 'That's great. I'll be able to work the crowd from there.'

I hope there will be a crowd, I thought to myself, crossing my fingers behind my back.

Dean asked what time I would like him to arrive with his band. 'The earlier the better, so we can get set up.'

But my concentration was suddenly failing.

A familiar figure was moving to my right on the other side of the road.

It was Dexter walking hand in hand with an animated Nadia.

My heart jolted as he smiled down at her. Then he glanced up and noticed me.

His happy expression dissolved.

He paused, a fidgeting Nadia by his side, and appraised Dean.

Then a plummy female voice rang out. 'Dexter! Look at this!'

A tall brunette emerged from the jeweller's at the foot of the road, all legs and ankle boots. I watched with morbid fascination as she tottered over to him and linked her arm through his.

'Mummy, Mummy! Can I get some banana ice cream please?'

The woman turned her attention to Nadia. 'Ice cream doesn't contain many nutrients, sweetheart. How about some frozen yoghurt instead? Yum!'

Nadia pulled a disgruntled face while Dexter continued to stare across at me, his expression unreadable.

They were like a perfect glossy family that had just stepped out of a magazine. I swallowed my pain and from somewhere deep inside, managed to drag up a faint smile.

The brunette, Nadia's mum, began talking to Dexter again. When she realised he wasn't paying attention to her, her eyes followed his across the road.

Pain and longing swallowed me. 'I'd better get back to the shop,' I managed, returning my attention back to Dean. 'We can discuss things more there.'

Dean and I moved off, making our way back to Paper Roses.

Dexter watched us go.

Chapter Fifty-Three

My grandmother was one of the most perceptive women I knew.

She kept glancing over at me as Dean Ellwood spoke enthusiastically about the autumn fair.

I managed to smile and nod in the correct places, delighted by his enthusiasm, but annoyed at myself for even allowing Dexter headspace.

Dean departed from Paper Roses and I escorted him back to his car, a Mazda affair in electric blue. Gran was loitering by the shop door when I returned.

'What's wrong, Elle?'

I rubbed at my face. 'Not much gets past you.'

'And you've only just realised this?'

I forced a small smile.

One of the young girls who worked as a junior in the local hairdresser's darted in to buy a birthday card for her auntie and once Gran had served her and observed the girl's flash of black denim skirt swish out the door, she stared me down.

She didn't have to ask me anything. The simple gesture of her firing up her eyebrows made me cave. Out it came in a painful rush about having just seen Dexter, Nadia, and the little girl's mother, strolling along. 'You should have seen the three of them together, Gran.' I bit back the stabbing hurt. 'Nadia looks so much like the two of them.' They had been a picture-perfect family scene, like something out of a Benetton advert.

Grandma listened, not making any initial comment. But the more I could hear myself churning it over in my mind, the more painful it became.

It was what it was. Dexter had a gorgeous little daughter who needed him, either here or back in London. And the arrival of the girl's mother, I should have seen coming.

But what would I have thought of him if Dexter had told me about Nadia and then admitted he didn't want anything to do with her? At least he seemed to be making a concerted effort to be a good father. I couldn't fault him for that.

The arrival of Nadia seemed to be having a positive effect on him too. The Linda Carlucci curse even seemed to have been pushed into the background, as far as Dexter's priorities were concerned. Nadia should come first. That could only be a good thing.

Surely he was being genuine and not playing at being a dad to try and break the curse? My skin flushed. I felt ashamed for even contemplating such a thing.

Grandma moved to speak, but I straightened the bow on my blouse and raised one hand. 'I'm fine, Gran. Really. It did give me a jolt seeing them all together as a family like that for the first time.'

My grandmother's face was riven with concern. 'Elle.'

I jumped to my feet, pushing back my chair. 'If they decide to stay round here, I'm just going to have to get used to it. And I will.'

I clapped my hands together and forced a smile. 'Right. I've still got lots to do before next Saturday.'

The week of the run-up to the Nature Reserve Knees-Up was frantic.

I found myself getting up earlier each morning with the birds fizzing in the trees outside. Every day I arrived at Paper Roses at the same time as the newspaper shop cranking open its shutters, so that I could get a head start on ensuring final preparations were in order, before opening at 9 a.m.

Cate and Gran were invaluable, taking it in turns to assist me in Paper Roses or insisting on making follow-up phone calls to everyone involved in the fair, from the stallholders to the bunting suppliers. At least this gave me some respite, so I could concentrate on the shop for a while.

By Wednesday that week, I possessed a final list of the stall sellers and the musicians (Dean Ellwood headlining) and where they would be pitched along the main throng of the street.

Cate had taken it upon herself to update the Paper Roses Twitter feed and our other social media accounts with what was happening and Gran had roped in several of her book club and bridge-playing buddies, to hand out homemade leaflets Cate had helped me with at the local train station and in the park.

Fir Haven Radio had already made several mentions of the event in the last few days and was sending a reporter along on Saturday. Our local newspaper had been very supportive too, covering all the background to our opposition to the development and they were also despatching a photographer.

I found myself leaving Paper Roses after 6 p.m. each evening that week, longing for a long soak in the bath. It was lovely, lying there in the warm lavender-scented water. I would light one of my favourite scented candles and as I watched the small flame weave around by the bathroom mirror, I felt a small pang of pleasure from knowing I'd been working hard.

I had been so preoccupied, especially over the last week, that only occasional snapshots of Dexter's handsome face came back to me. I waggled my toes in the bath, pushing them up and down in the lapping water, as a picture of Dexter, Nadia, and the striking brunette burned itself into my brain again.

Nadia was adorable. If things had been different, then goodness knows what might have happened.

I gave my head a fierce shake and splashed some of the bath water up against my face. *Good grief!* I must be even more exhausted than I thought if I was imagining myself assuming the role of Nadia's step-mummy!

I sat upright and reached up to my hair, tightening my topknot.

Dexter had made no attempt to contact me since I'd seen him, Nadia, and her mother together. Rumours were rife that he had abandoned his plans for selling Hawk West Hall and that he was intending to remain in Fir Haven after all. They must have decided to make a go of things together for Nadia's sake.

The prospect of that sent my heart spinning down to my toes. Hopefully, I wouldn't have to see much of him from now on anyway.

I let my body sink lower under the bath water again. 'Right! Enough wallowing!' I said out loud. My main priority right now was ensuring that Saturday was as successful as I could possibly make it.

Chapter Fifty-Four

The bunting flapped above our heads, in triangles of various shades of blue and green. The hired stalls, constructed out of white canvas and wooden shelving, hunched side by side down the centre of the main street. Above us, the sky was pearly grey, but the temperature was mild and faint traces of September sun were beginning to wriggle through the trees.

Vans were parked at the top of the pedestrianised walkway and I watched the stream of stallholders buzzing backwards and forwards, collecting boxes of their wares to sell. Everything from sparkly cupcakes, topped with blue sugar roses, to silky chiffon scarves and woollen handbags were being laid out with great care.

About halfway down the line of stalls was Cate. She was draping her jewellery over a series of large polished stones. Beside her was Lucy, all red gleaming hair and adoring smile.

I hurried over to marvel at the swathe of spangly earrings which dripped from a makeshift gold ribbon Cate had strung either side of her stall. 'All of this looks beautiful.'

Cate grinned her appreciation. 'I think you might be a bit biased.'

Beside her, Lucy rolled her eyes and touched her girlfriend's arm. 'I've known this woman for three years and yet she still can't take a compliment.'

Around us was the buzz of voices – van doors clanging and the odd rumble of a mobile phone. I took a moment to gaze down the parade of shops, their sleepy windows stirring in the early Saturday morning light. 'I just hope we get a good turnout.'

Lucy took a sip of her coffee. 'It's going to be better than good, Elle. It's going to be phenomenal.'

I rubbed my sweaty palms down the front of my faded jeans. I wished I could be as confident.

From further up the cobbles, I heard more commotion and spun round.

Dean Ellwood was emerging from a black transit van with a couple of his band members. He strode towards us, an appreciative smile on his curious face. 'So, this is where it's all happening?'

'I certainly hope so.'

He gestured to the makeshift stage, which a few of his roadies, who had arrived much earlier, had already got set up in preparation for him. On hearing Dean arrive, they emerged out from behind the two columns of white canvas background and Dean high-fived them, before they all exchanged a few jokes.

I glanced down at my watch. Crikey! We only had about an hour or so till the fair was due to start! 'I'd better get back to Pebble Brook and have a shower.'

Cate insisted there was no need. 'You've brought a change of clothes with you, I take it?'

I nodded that I had. 'I wasn't going to bother showering again, but I've been dashing about so much.'

'In that case, let yourself in to our place,' said Cate, reaching into her bag and handing me their flat key. 'You can get showered and ready at ours and it means you won't have to schlep back to Pebble Brook.'

The relief on my face must have been evident. I didn't fancy driving back to Pebble Brook now, just to have to make the drive back again.

'Thank you! You're a star!'

I'd brought my change of outfit, thinking I could throw it on right before the fair began at 10 a.m., but the prospect of freshening up was growing more appealing by the minute. What with my jangling nerves about the whole day, I didn't exactly feel fragrant.

I dived back in to Paper Roses to collect my change of clothes, satisfied at least that the arrangements so far seemed to be going well.

All we had to hope for now was the local people supporting us!

I jumped in and out of Cate and Lucy's shower cubicle before blasting my hair dry and throwing on my clean outfit, which consisted of an ankle-length sky-blue dress sprinkled with cream stars and with ruched sleeves and matching kitten heels. I had also brought my vanilla denim jacket to throw on over it, if the weather got a bit cool, and my navy trainers if my feet started to protest.

I rough dried my hair and toned down my pink complexion with my arsenal of foundation and loose powder. I finished off with a sweep of my autumnal-coloured eye shadow, a flick of black mascara, and my favourite pink lipstick.

Then I hooked my hair behind each ear and gathered up my dirty clothes from that morning.

Cate and Lucy's en suite bathroom in their flat led out into their gorgeous bedroom. It was an eclectic mix of their two characters, with Cate's love of bling evident on the scatter cushions, picture frames, and mirror surround. Lucy's rustic influence could be seen in the burnished shades of the curtains, landscape paintings, and distressed furniture.

I locked up their apartment and adopted a brisk pace as I headed back to the main street.

As I rounded the corner, I drew up. A fizz of delighted adrenalin pumped through me when I saw that the road and pavements outside Paper Roses and the other shops was a sea of mingling people.

Toddlers were hoisted on top of their dads' shoulders; there were teenagers milling around in front of Dean Ellwood's makeshift stage, anticipating his appearance; children were clustering around the baking stall, admiring the array of cupcakes, muffins, and scones for sale.

Some of the local ladies were flitting between the knotted chiffon scarves, knitted handbags, and Cate's jewellery, while animated representatives from the animal and bird conservation societies were answering questions and referring to leaflets set out on their respective stalls.

I turned to my left, feeling my smile widen. One of the children's entertainers was parting the crowd as he balanced on stilts, his glittery top hat winking under the September sun.

To his right, the magician was bending down and chatting to an entranced little girl, who gasped when the performer threw her hands behind her back and produced a posy of plastic flowers. A waft of bagpipes travelled over the heads of the crowd.

I picked up my pace, happiness and relief coursing through me. Surely the council and developers couldn't ignore such a groundswell of support for the reserve? Maybe there was still a chance that it could be saved? I just hoped this amount of people converted into a considerable sum of money.

The air was filled with chatter and the scent of toffee apples, hot chocolate, and roasted nuts as I got closer to Dean Ellwood's stage. There was a twang of guitars and a series of high-pitched squeals from a throng of teenage girls.

As the triangular blue and green bunting fluttered, Dean gave me a big grin before launching into his first song. I smiled back, finding myself tapping my booted feet and nodding my head in time to the music.

Some of the fair attendees were carrying placards with the words 'Hands off our Reserve!' and 'No to Ruining our Nature!'

All the work and the worry, all the concern that this event would be a flop and would achieve nothing, ebbed away at the sight of the crowd.

Even if, heaven forbid, the nature reserve didn't survive – and a large part of me refused to even entertain the notion – at least the community would go down fighting.

I ignored my fleeting pessimism and concentrated again on Dean Ellwood. He was whipping up the growing crowd in front of him.

'Hello.'

I stared down to see Nadia standing by my leg, looking up at me out of eyes like blue buttons. Her dark hair was swinging past her shoulders in a cute French plait.

Images of Dexter swam before my eyes as I looked down at the little girl. I dropped down to my knees in front of her. 'Hello, you. I hope you haven't run off again.'

She offered a cheeky smile. 'I'm going to buy a toffee apple with sprinkles.'

'Well, that's good to hear.' I cocked a cynical eyebrow at her.

'I like dolphins. They're my favourite.'

I admired the way her lashes tilted upwards. 'More than unicorns?'

'Not as much, but dolphins are cleverer.'

'I like them too. They always seem to be smiling, don't they?'

I wondered if she had come along to the fair with Dexter and stood up, scanning the heads of the crowd. It would be far better if he wasn't here. Perhaps Elsa had brought her. Or her mother.

I lowered myself back down to her height. 'Sweetheart, you didn't run away from Mrs Bennett again, did you?'

She cast a wary look down at her pink desert boots. 'I got a bus.'

I tried not to smile at how serious she looked. 'Nadia, there are no buses from where you live.'

'Well, I got one. It was purple and had flowers on it.'

I noted her petulant lip. 'People will be worried about you. Very worried.'

She kicked a stone on the cobbles. 'No they won't. Mummy and Uncle Dexter have been arguing again.'

Uncle Dexter? Why was she calling him that? The little one couldn't know he was her father. Perhaps they were waiting until she was a little older before telling her. My heart zinged in sympathy for her. Arguing? No. *Don't go there. It's none of my business.*

'I'm sure they weren't arguing,' I answered softly. 'But even if they were, that's what adults do sometimes. But it has nothing to do with you.'

Nadia glanced at the people wandering past us, clutching banners, crafts they had bought, or savouring roasted chestnuts. 'Mummy said we had to come up to Scotland because she needed more money from Uncle Dexter.'

'Nadia! What have I told you?!'

I sprang upwards. Elsa was hurrying towards us, her voice a concoction of relief and annoyance. She wasn't her usual jovial self. She managed a harassed greeting. 'Hi, Elle. How are you? Nadia, not again! Now, come with me. Sorry!' She took hold of the little girl's hand to lead her away.

Needed more money? What did that mean? Was Dexter worried about news getting out that he had a young child? Did that mean he was paying Nadia's mother money to keep her quiet?

Thoughts cross-crossed through my head. Or was the woman just capitalising on the fact that she had a child with him?

Elsa adjusted the collar of Nadia's pink corded jacket. 'Thank you for taking care of her, Elle.' She didn't meet my gaze. 'Again.'

The little girl gave me a cheery wave as Elsa began to guide her away with a promise of taking her to see a tower of Nutella brownies.

Goodness only knows what was happening up at Hawk West Hall right now.

Chapter Fifty-Five

I spent the next hour assisting Gran at our Paper Roses stall before we decided we would take turns to serve so that the other could have a casual wander around the fair and soak up the atmosphere.

The footfall was amazing. 'Perhaps we should stage these events more often,' joked my grandmother.

'Let me think about that… no!'

I had just offered to relieve Cate from her jewellery stall so that she could go and fetch some lunch for her and Lucy when Elsa meandered past, clutching Nadia's hand.

The little girl was chomping on a princess cupcake and had a cuddly robin tucked under one arm, which she must have purloined from the exhibition stall featuring wild birds that could be seen at the reserve.

Nadia waggled the bird at me with sticky fingers. 'I'm going to call her Rhiannon.'

'That's a lovely name.'

Lucy, who finished serving two teenage girls and wrapping the earrings they had bought, followed me out from behind the canvas to say hello to Nadia, but Elsa encouraged her to move on. 'Come on, young lady. You haven't seen the magician yet.'

Lucy folded her arms, puzzled. 'What was all that about? She couldn't get the little one away quickly enough.'

We watched her and Nadia get swallowed up by the crowd.

'I've no idea,' I confessed. 'Elsa might be concerned Nadia might say something she shouldn't.'

Lucy pulled a face. 'These bloody celebrities!'

Lucy began adjusting Cate's display of wood and shell-encrusted necklaces, which were draped over some driftwood. 'The wee one has probably already heard or seen something she shouldn't. Kids don't tend to miss much.'

As a few more potential customers appeared, Lucy's face took on a flash of panic.

'Don't worry,' I assured her. 'I'll stay to help you out until Cate reappears.'

'Thanks, Elle. I owe you one.'

While Lucy accepted the money for the various purchases of Cate's jewellery, I wrapped what they had bought in small silver gift bags.

I was chatting to Lucy and Cate, who had returned with two takeaway cappuccinos and two packs of sandwiches, when I sensed someone hovering by Cate's tree-inspired fashion rings. I looked up. 'Can I help you?'

I was confronted by a pair of startling light-blue eyes.

Dexter mustered an apprehensive smile. 'Hi.'

Beside me, Cate and Lucy edged to one side. If they were trying to afford us some privacy, it was going to be bloody difficult, seeing as the whole town was present.

I hoped he couldn't sense the adrenaline charging through me right now.

His black hair had grown a little since I last saw him and was furling at the collar of his pale-grey shirt. It suited him.

Shit! Why did he have to turn up today? I knew I had

impressed upon him the importance of getting more involved in the community, but now the idea was much less appealing.

I opened my mouth to say something – what, I wasn't quite sure – when Elsa and Nadia materialised behind him. Elsa observed Dexter and me for a few moments.

There was a prickly silence. Nadia was performing some sort of skippy dance by her side.

Relief flooded me that I could at least chat to Nadia. 'Did you enjoy your cupcake?' I asked, eager to say something – anything – to fill the silent void.

'It was great,' said Nadia, licking her fingers, 'but it wasn't big enough. I'm still hungry.'

Despite my heart quivering at the sight of her father, I grinned. 'Well, I'm not surprised. You are a growing girl.'

She nodded, her French plait waggling. Then she grew bored of talking to me and turned her attention to her cuddly robin.

'Elle.' Dexter saying my name made my chest flutter. 'There's something I need to—'

'Why did you walk off just now?'

All our heads swung round to Nadia's mother. She clip-clopped over towards Cate's stall, draped in a navy jacket with brass buttons, a cream T-shirt, and stonewashed jeans. Her shoulder-length brunette hair was secured away from her face with a red Alice band.

'Shelley, I didn't walk off,' answered Dexter. 'I've been doing the same as you. Browsing the stalls.'

The woman's lightning-strike look at me was brief but charged. 'I can see that.' She flashed her pouting gaze around. 'I would have been more than happy to provide my expertise to the stallholders. I used to be an executive visual merchandiser before I became a celebrity.' She offered Dexter a coy look.

'A what?' whispered Cate to Lucy.

'I think she means a window dresser.'

Dexter glowered at her and turned back to me. 'Elle, I really do need to talk to you.'

I blinked in surprise as Shelley's manicured hand shot out and rested on Dexter's arm. A look of brief panic flashed across her face. 'I don't think that's a good idea, do you?'

My attention rocketed back and forth between them. *What on earth is going on?*

I noticed the disapproving pinch of Elsa's features.

Elsa squeezed Nadia's hand and caught Dexter's eye. An undecipherable look was exchanged between the two of them. He hesitated and sighed. 'Right.' He turned and began to walk away, but then whirled round. 'Shit! It's her! Elle! It's her!'

I moved out from under the flapping canvas of the stall. 'Who?'

Dexter bounded back up towards me. I gasped at the sensation of his warm fingers wrapping themselves around mine as he pulled me along. 'Dexter! Hang on! What on earth?!'

Shelley's kohl-lined grey eyes hardened at the sight of Dexter holding my hand. 'Dexter! What the hell are you doing?'

But he was ignoring her, tugging me along behind him through the array of protest placards, chattering families, and past the fluttering canvas stalls. He gasped over his shoulder as we picked up speed. 'Elle, I just saw her! She's here! Linda Carlucci!'

Chapter Fifty-Six

Several people swung round in curiosity as Dexter tugged me past them at speed. 'Slow down, Dexter! For goodness sake!'

'I've got to speak to her,' he panted over his shoulder. 'I've got to try and reason with her again.'

I picked up my pace, shouting apologies and offering embarrassed smiles to the bemused locals. I could see a figure ahead, moving steadily. She was wearing a chocolate-and-white-printed headscarf and a pair of outsized Jackie Onassis sunglasses. When she slid a look to her right, I recognised her proud profile. It was indeed Linda Carlucci.

'What are you going to say to her?' I rasped, as Dexter's hold on my hand sent a lurching sensation through me. 'You can't just accost the woman.'

Dexter's eyes flashed back at me. 'I'm not too sure, but I need to at least try.'

He stopped short, making me bang into his broad back. I stared up at him. He seized both of my hands in his. 'Sometimes you only realise what you've lost when it's taken away from you.'

Dexter scanned my face. His attention slid down to my lips and hovered there.

A ragged breath lodged itself in my throat. What was he talking about? Was he referring to us? Or was he talking about not being able to write? Or did he mean losing Nadia?

I forced my attention away from him, searching for Linda Carlucci's current whereabouts. She had left the throng of the fair now, leaving behind the numerous stalls and buzzing chatter.

We moved off again, catching sight of her approaching a white Ford Ka. Keys shone in her hand.

'Shit! She's leaving!' groaned Dexter. 'Come on!'

My hair flapped behind me as we bolted side by side now, along the pavement. The afternoon September sun had made a cursory appearance and was sliding off the top of her car like melted butter.

'Mrs Carlucci,' I called, taking gulps of air. 'Please!'

She turned around, swiping off her sunglasses. She narrowed her sage-green eyes at Dexter. 'Oh, it's you.'

Dexter drew up in front of her.

Linda Carlucci drank him in. There was an odd flash of something in her expression. 'I've got to go,' she stammered. 'I've got a client coming for a tarot reading at 3 p.m.'

Dexter implored her again. 'But can't you just spare a few moments? Please!'

Linda Carlucci unlocked her car. Her hand appeared to tremble. 'Sorry, but I'm busy.'

Dexter ploughed a hand through his hair. 'Can't you give me a few moments just to hear me out?'

She jabbed the car key further into the driver door lock and whirled round in her dark-brown boots. 'I think it's appalling what you're trying to do!'

Dexter's confusion was obvious. 'Sorry?'

'That little girl,' she snapped, cranking open her driver's side door. 'Everybody's talking about it – how you're using her to try and get your curse lifted.' She must have noticed Dexter's discomfort. 'Or should I say, *your daughter*.'

Dexter stiffened. 'Who told you that?'

'Well, it wasn't me,' I insisted. 'You told me in good faith and I would never break a trust like that.'

Dexter's jaw clenched at Linda. 'You don't understand the situation at all.'

Linda Carlucci folded her arms. Several silver bracelets clattered against her speckled wrist. 'Oh, Mr Grayling, I think I do.'

Her eyes bore into Dexter, shards of sadness lodged in them. Her voice cracked before she turned her ire on me. 'You wondered the same, didn't you, Ms Cassidy, about why his daughter has suddenly arrived in Fir Haven?'

There was an awkward pause.

I flicked the briefest glance up at Dexter, but before I could answer he was staring down at me from under his arched black brows. 'You thought it too?' He let out a hollow laugh. 'You thought I brought Nadia here deliberately, for my own ends? To save my own skin? Wow! My reputation really does precede me then.'

I let my hands rise and fall. 'I'm sorry, Dexter. I would be lying if I said it hadn't crossed my mind.'

Dexter dragged a hand across his stubbly chin. 'I thought you could see another side to me. You never treated me any differently, even though I had all this fame nonsense going on.'

A rising tide of guilt was promising to swamp me. 'Dexter, I'm sorry. But when Nadia appeared out of the blue like that, surely you can understand I was sceptical, especially after all that's happened?'

He shook his dark head at Linda Carlucci and me. Pain cluttered his eyes. 'You have no idea about the real me, or about my life. None at all.'

Then he strode back towards the fair to collect his daughter.

Chapter Fifty-Seven

I didn't even bother to watch Linda Carlucci drive off. I walked briskly back along the pavement after Dexter.

Nadia was helping to serve customers at Cate's stall when the pair of us returned. There was an awkward silence.

Cate and Lucy had Nadia sandwiched between them and were giggling at Nadia's impersonation of Donald Duck. Shelley, meanwhile, had treated herself to three handbags and two chiffon scarves.

Their smiles faded when they saw Dexter and me.

'Where the hell have you been?' erupted Shelley. 'I was about to contact the police! I've just had to use my own credit card!'

Dexter's eyes rolled.

Elsa, examining some pots of honey on a nearby stall, meandered back over.

Dexter managed a wink at his daughter. 'Come on, monkey, let's go.'

'But, Uncle Dexter, I want to stay and help Cate and Lucy!'

Brooking no argument, Dexter outstretched his arms and scooped a sulky Nadia into them. 'Thanks for keeping her amused.'

'No problem,' said Lucy. 'She's such a cutie pie.'

Elsa studied Dexter. 'Mr Grayling, Nadia is having such a lovely time. Don't you think—?'

Dexter swung round. Nadia's arms were draped around his neck. 'I'll say what's best for her!'

Elsa's cheeks burned, but she maintained a dignified silence.

'Elsa,' managed Dexter, shame now scrawled across his face. 'I'm so sorry. I shouldn't have snapped at you like that.'

Nadia put her arms out to Elsa and she crawled into them. They had a brief cuddle and then walked off, hand in hand.

'Are you all right, Elsa?' I called across the sound of bagpipes and laughing children. She didn't turn around.

'Of course she is,' barked Shelley. 'I wouldn't worry about her.'

My eyes burned into her as she wobbled away, weighed down with purchases. Dexter was already striding off.

Cate and Lucy turned to look at me, having observed all the fractious exchanges taking place right in front of them. Lucy pulled a face, muttered 'Bloody celebrities!' again and moved off to help serve someone enquiring about one of Cate's ring designs.

My mind lurched back to the hurt clouding Dexter's Caribbean-blue eyes when he realised I'd doubted his motives for bringing Nadia to Scotland.

But what had he expected? He hadn't exactly rocked up in Fir Haven and made a favourable impression from the get-go!

A combination of guilt and hurt pushed down on my shoulders. I returned to the Paper Roses stall where Gran was sitting down having a rest and a couple of our recruited student helpers were wrapping up snow globes for customers.

At the top of the road I could make out Dexter, now a blur of black hair. Shelley was teetering behind him, trying to catch up. 'Couldn't we have stayed a few more minutes, Dex? There was another handbag there that would have matched those new leopard-print heels I bought last week.'

Elsa, her head bowed and chatting to Nadia, stopped again on the pavement and delivered another glance down at the fair, before they all vanished from sight.

Chapter Fifty-Eight

I spent the remainder of that Saturday afternoon attempting to enjoy Dean Ellwood's set. He had originally only planned to play in the morning, but had received such a rapturous reception that he and his fellow musicians decided to stay on.

Gran had witnessed Dexter stalking off and once I'd explained everything, she insisted I take a break and have some lunch. I sat picking at a gourmet chicken burger and salad, which Gran had bought for me from one of the food stalls.

Dexter hadn't even been prepared to hear me out! At least he could have granted me the courtesy of explaining.

I managed a few more forked mouthfuls of lettuce and tomato under the watchful eye of Gran, before sliding the remainder of it into a nearby bin.

Grandma frowned. 'You barely touched that.'

I shrugged off her concern. 'I've got too much to do. The local paper and radio station will be here soon.'

By the time they arrived, the Nature Reserve Knees-Up was in full throttle.

Children were scampering around, their faced painted like tigers, zebras, and butterflies. The air carried a concoction of barbecued food and scented candles and there was laughter and chatter rising up from the crowd. Placards were waved and thrust around, demanding that the reserve be saved.

Dean Ellwood did an excellent PR job, chatting to the reporters about the reserve and how an area of such historical and environmental importance deserved to be saved.

The entertainers mingled with the families, handing out balloons moulded into the shapes of animals and birds, and the representatives from the wildlife organisations drew rapturous applause for their impassioned speeches about the abundance of creatures which inhabited the area.

Gran emerged at my shoulder as the first of the families began to drift away during the afternoon. 'You did a wonderful job, darling.'

I linked my weary, satisfied arm through hers, smiling and thanking more people as they said goodbye and headed home. Sleepy youngsters were slumped against shoulders, their painted faces smudging their parents' clothes. The weary stall holders began to pack away their stock.

Dean Ellwood appeared, his pale eyes twinkling. 'What a day! You deserve huge congratulations.'

Gran disappeared to chat to a couple of people she knew, while Dean pushed a hand through his tangle of red curls. 'The guys are just loading up the van.' He paused. 'That wasn't Dexter Grayling I saw earlier, was it?'

I felt my skin prickle at the mention of his name. 'Yes. He lives locally.'

Dean was impressed. 'Wow! I love his books. That last one he wrote about a series of murders in a museum was terrific.'

As more locals wandered past, bidding us good afternoon, there was the sound of flapping canvas while the stalls were dismantled.

'If there's anything else I can do to help with your campaign, please let me know. I mean it.'

'Thank you. That's very kind of you.'

He handed me a flash business card in black and gold. 'My mobile number is on there.'

I accepted it, avoiding the prolonged gaze he was giving me. 'I'll let you know how things go, Dean. And thank you so much again.'

I risked a look up at him. He was sporting an understanding smile. 'Sure thing.'

That evening, I soaked in the bath with an array of scented candles while the bathroom window clouded up with steam.

Now all I had to do was hope that we had created enough momentum and raised a significant amount of money so we could fight what Atticus Development were planning.

As for Dexter, well, that ship seemed to have well and truly sailed.

Chapter Fifty-Nine

As I opened the shop with Gran the following Monday morning, I couldn't help but look over my shoulder at the main street.

It was odd to think that only two days ago it had been a seething mass of people, with the bunting and the sound of sizzling food and Dean Ellwood's vocals rising up towards the roofs.

Now it was its usual self again with the September light pouring over the cobbles like clotted cream.

As she fussed around, Gran noticed me looking out through the front window of the shop. 'You did a fantastic job, darling.'

I turned to smile at her. 'And we did well. The takings far exceeded what we thought. But one event won't be enough, Gran.' I gave her a hopeful smile. 'I was thinking of asking Dean Ellwood if he might consider recording a song and dedicating some of the proceeds to saving the reserve.'

At that moment, the shop doorbell tinkled, signalling the arrival of Angus Ronald, one of Grandma's old friends from her school days. His grandson was about to start university and he wanted to give him one of our fountain pen and pencil sets as a good luck gift.

Gran plucked several options from the glass cabinet behind the counter and Angus perused each one in turn, murmuring his appreciation.

I was about to open the mail when I was distracted by the shop door opening again. Joshua Boyd barrelled in.

I felt myself go rigid. *What does he want?*

He tugged down the jacket of his ink-blue suit. His near-balding head was shining almost as much as his temper-induced cheeks. 'This farmer's market nonsense on Saturday won't make any difference. Your loyalty to the reserve is commendable, but it won't achieve anything.'

I noticed Grandma's hands grip the edge of the counter. 'It was far, far bigger than a farmer's market and much more successful.'

Joshua Boyd tried not to reveal his irritation. 'Well, I'm not here to debate the issue over a few stalls selling hot dogs and scented candles.' I could feel myself bristling. 'I'm here to make a proposition.'

Angus Ronald, who had abandoned his perusal of the fountain pens, flicked Gran and me a loaded look.

I felt my jaw clench. 'Like sending thugs round to people's houses to intimate people?'

Angus turned to Gran. 'Clara, what's this about thugs? Is everything all right?'

She nodded. 'Yes. It's fine. I'll tell you later.'

Joshua Boyd shrugged. 'I don't know what you're talking about,' he replied airily.

I felt my dislike for him ramp up even more. 'Of course you don't.'

Joshua Boyd glanced around at Paper Roses and sniffed. 'If the development were to, say, invest in the future of this little business of yours, perhaps you could see your way to embracing our plans.'

The audacity of the man! Had I heard him correctly? I shook my head in disbelief. 'You're trying to bribe us?'

Joshua Boyd adjusted his red silk tie. 'Not at all. I mean, in this precarious economic market, I would have thought any extra financial injection would be welcomed.'

'Not as a bribe!' I snapped. 'How dare you even think I might consider such a thing.'

Joshua Boyd's hooded eyes sharpened. 'You're being a very silly young lady.'

Angus stepped forward; his shoulders squared under his checked jacket. 'That sounded like a threat.'

Joshua Boyd eyed Angus for a few moments. Then there was a flicker of realisation. 'I know you.'

'Angus Ronald. I own Calder Fern Farm. I'm also an ex local councillor, like Mrs Blackmore here.'

Joshua Boyd's fat fingers reached for his tie again while he processed this revelation.

'And I can tell you,' continued Angus, emboldened, 'that we still have powerful contacts. We also don't appreciate attempts at blackmail.'

Realising he had thrown his weight around without thinking of the ramifications, Joshua Boyd backtracked. 'There was no blackmail. It was merely a generous offer of investment.'

I glowered at his audacity. 'Yes, to someone who is ardently opposed to this horrific plan.' I planted my hands on my hips, my heart pumping. 'You're wasting your time, Mr Boyd, and I want you to leave. Now.'

He retreated back towards the shop door. 'You're making a terrible mistake, Ms Cassidy. By Christmas, you'll be wishing you had accepted that offer.'

The three of us glared at him disappearing out of the door, his suit jacket rustling behind him.

Grandma stared at Angus. A bloom had overtaken her cheeks. 'Thank you for your support.'

'Not at all. What are friends for?'

I eyed them both with interest. I suddenly felt like I was intruding on something.

The latter end of Monday was quiet, but the tranquillity was welcome after the charged exchanges that morning with Joshua Boyd.

Grandma insisted on cashing up at the end of the day, while I jotted down a series of ideas for future events to support and raise money for the reserve. At the top of my list was approaching Dean Ellwood about his offer of further help.

I looked up from my notebook to where Gran was on the other side of the counter. 'Angus was very alpha male this morning.'

I noticed her speckled hands hover for a moment over the till. 'Yes. Yes, he was very supportive.'

I concealed a grin. 'I think he likes you, Gran.'

'I should hope so! We've known each other for sixty years.'

'You know full well what I mean, Grandma.'

She pushed a lock of her bobbed hair back behind her ear. 'He's a dear friend, Elle. Nothing more.'

I wanted to pursue my line of enquiry, but my grandmother was wearing a steely look of concentration as she continued adding up the day's takings with her calculator.

I decided I would select my moment to continue this conversation at a more conducive time.

I ordered Gran to take herself off home a bit earlier than normal, as she was eager to finish the last thirty pages of the book club novel she was reading. 'It's lovely when you can lose yourself in a good book.'

She swished on her belted maroon coat. 'Oh, it's not that, love,' she groaned. 'It's an awful bloody story! I could only manage the first three chapters and then I found myself losing the will to live.'

As Gran beetled out of the door, she added with a cheeky smile, 'At least that bossy old bat Nora Witcombe won't be selecting our next read.'

'Whose turn is it next time then?'

Her glittery-eyed grin told me the answer.

'And what book do you think you'll choose for the group then?'

'Something racy, with lots of erotic sex. That should put Nora's pacemaker to the test. See you back at home soon, darling!'

I laughed and shook my head at my incorrigible gran's disappearing figure.

I flicked off the shop lights and had turned the door sign to read *closed*. I was just reaching for my bag under the counter when there was an urgent rapping on door.

It made me jump.

I peered through the main shop window.

Elsa Bennett, Dexter's housekeeper, was hopping from foot to foot on the step. I checked to see if Nadia was with her, but she wasn't.

Oh no. Don't tell me that little girl has taken off on her own again.

I unlocked the door to be greeted by Elsa's anxious expression. 'I'm sorry to turn up like this but I need to speak to you, Elle.' Her blue mac rippled as she moved. 'It's about Dexter.'

The mention of his name made my heart hammer harder. I knew I shouldn't get involved again. Snatches of Dexter's hurt expression, the pain burning in his blue eyes, jumbled together in my head.

Elsa lingered on the step outside Paper Roses. She could sense my reluctance. 'Please, Elle. It's very important.'

A few discarded leaves danced past us on the cobbles.

There was a pleading look in her dark-grey eyes.

Ignoring the screaming warning klaxons going off inside my head, I gestured to Elsa. 'You had better come in then.'

Chapter Sixty

I locked the shop door behind Elsa and indicated for her to go through to the kitchen area.

She watched me switch on a corner light in the hope it might lift the atmosphere a little. The evenings were beginning to get darker a little earlier, now that autumn was knocking on the door.

I lowered myself into the chair opposite her at the table. 'So, what is it?'

She laced and unlaced her hands together. 'I know Dexter gives the impression that he's some sort of indestructible force and that very little affects him and, yes, he did used to be like that.'

'And now?'

She sank back in her chair. 'Two young ladies have come into his life and have changed all that.'

What she was saying triggered a pang of pain. 'That's good,' I forced, fighting to sound pleased for him. 'He and Shelley and Nadia—'

Elsa's greying brows arched. 'Who? No, I'm not talking about that money-grabbing madam!' A glimmer of a smile melted across her pink-frosted lips. 'I'm talking about you, Elle. You and Nadia.'

My stomach made a whooshing sensation. 'What?'

Elsa gave her head of crisp white waves a guilty shake. 'I've worked for Dexter for almost seven years now. I know him better than he thinks I do.' She rubbed her powdered forehead. 'I know I promised to keep his counsel and be discreet, but he's making such a huge mistake with Shelley.'

'She is Nadia's mother,' I pointed out. 'And Dexter is her father. He's trying to make a go of things for the sake of that little girl. You can't fault him for that.'

I expected Elsa to agree with me, but she didn't. Her expression was pained. She shuffled in her seat and let out a sigh. 'But that's the whilc point. There's something you should know.'

She flashed me a meaningful look. 'Nadia isn't Dexter's daughter.'

I frowned. 'Sorry? I don't understand.'

Elsa knotted her fingers together and concentrated as she spoke. 'Nadia is Jay's child. Jay is Dexter's younger brother.'

I turned all this information over in my head. 'But... but Dexter said she was his.'

Elsa shook her head. 'He's her uncle, but he acts more like a father to her than that wastrel Jay ever did. Jay didn't want anything to do with Shelley when he discovered she was pregnant, so Dexter stepped up to the plate and provided for them both.' She gave me a small smile. 'He's been there for both of them ever since.'

Thoughts flapped around my head like wild birds.

I slumped back in my chair, trying to unscramble it all. So... he was the little girl's *uncle*.

'Dexter insisted on financially and emotionally supporting Shelley Horgan during her pregnancy and once Nadia was born. Then it continued.' Elsa flicked me a look. 'Dexter didn't want it getting out about what Jay had done. He was appalled by his brother just cutting and running like that, so he stepped in.'

I took a few moments to digest what Elsa was telling me. 'Who knew? Who knows?'

'Only members of Dexter's "inner sanctum" know about Nadia. So just his parents and the immediate members of his management team. Oh, and me.'

I took in the surroundings of my shop for a moment, shock and surprise overtaking me again. My heart filled my chest for Dexter. What a caring and altruistic thing to do. 'But why has Nadia come to Fir Haven with her mother?'

Elsa's scepticism was evident. 'According to Shelley, Nadia would benefit from a more rural education when she starts school. She also told Dexter that neither of them was happy where they were living.' She let out a grunt. 'How she couldn't be happy in that gorgeous townhouse in Chelsea – which Dexter bought her – is beyond me.'

Elsa sighed and carried on. 'Shelley has been ringing and video-calling Dexter, telling him how much Nadia was missing him. So he caved in and told Shelley to pack their things and come to Scotland.'

I glanced out of the open door to the shop, which only a couple of hours before had been bustling with customers.

I was trying to slot all this together, piece by piece. So Dexter made sure he was involved in Nadia's life and was giving her all the love, security, and attention she needed – what she should have been receiving from her proper dad. He had made sure he was there for Nadia when her own father, his younger brother, had refused to. 'Where's Jay?'

'Now there's a question. The last we heard, he was auditioning for bit parts in a couple of US soaps. When he isn't doing that, he's bumming around on the beaches in California with his surfboard. He isn't remotely interested that he has a lovely little daughter.'

Elsa carried an air of disbelief. 'It's so strange how two brothers can be so different.'

She ran one finger over the top of the table. 'When I joined Mr Grayling's employment seven years ago, I had to sign a confidentiality agreement.' She paled as the realisation of what she had just divulged to me became apparent. 'He can't know I've told you,' she pleaded, sparks of panic rearing suddenly in her alarmed eyes. 'I could lose my job and I love it so much.'

I patted her hand. 'You have my word I won't tell anyone, Elsa. You've trusted me and I won't betray that.'

As the light faded more outside the shop windows, the kitchen grew cosier. 'And I take it the press don't know about Nadia?'

'Absolutely not. He didn't want her put in the spotlight, especially after his books became so successful. He thought that if word got out he was taking responsibility for his niece after Jay took off, Nadia could become a curiosity piece, thrust into the limelight.'

I nodded as I began to realise that there was a side to Dexter I hadn't even glimpsed. 'I can understand that.'

'I think, in a way, Dexter does think of Nadia as his, despite everything.' Elsa's expression softened. 'He's been more of a father to her than that brother of his ever has.'

A wave of emotion for Dexter took me by surprise. She was such a gorgeous and sweet little thing. She was lucky to have him. All the bravado, the wild parties, the swaggering arrogance, designer clothes, and glitzy book launches… behind it all, he had been doing this.

Elsa spoke again, her voice now wistful. She dragged my attention back. 'I could never have children and when my Kenny passed away… well, I felt like a huge part of me had died with him.'

She flashed me a glance. 'I can't imagine working for anyone else, other than Dexter.'

'Did you have any idea that the advertised vacancy was with him when you applied?'

'No. The advert was a large one, but it was very discreetly worded and the contact details were for a PO Box number.' A trace of a wistful smile passed across her face. 'Mr Grayling interviewed me. I thought what a handsome, intelligent young man he was but there was something else about his demeanour. He was guarded.' She gave a casual shrug. 'I know this might sound soft, but I suppose, over time, the more I got to know him, the more I started to look on him more like a son.'

My heart contracted for her. 'That's lovely, and it seems to me as though he looks upon you as one of the family too.'

Her jowly cheeks pinged with a tinge of colour. 'I thought he did.'

'What do you mean?'

She held my gaze. 'Dexter used to confide in me. He told me all about Nadia not being his and he admitted he was supporting the little one and that Shelley woman.'

The way she spat out Shelley's name, made me blink hard. 'But?'

Elsa regarded me out of pale, inquisitive eyes. 'Dexter talks about you a lot.'

My chest heaved. For something to do, I began twisting my ring around and around on my right hand. I knew Elsa was waiting for a reaction. All I could manage was an unimpressive, 'Does he?'

Her pale-pink lips twitched. 'Very much so.' Her mouth lifted at the corners. 'I get the impression that our Mr Grayling hasn't met a young woman like you before.'

'What? A mouthy Scottish woman, obsessed with local nature and stationery?'

Elsa hitched a cynical eyebrow. 'No. A woman who knows her own mind and who doesn't want to be with him solely because of who he is and what he has.'

I took a gulp of air. 'Who said I wanted to be with him?'

'Your eyes do. Every time you see him.'

Her words stung me in the chest.

'That's why I don't understand why he won't confide in me this time,' said Elsa with concern. 'I know something's wrong because I haven't seen him writing anything for weeks and weeks now.'

I couldn't conceal my surprise. 'So Dexter hasn't told you anything then? About his writing drought?'

She shook her ball of white waves. 'Any time I ask him about his writing, he gets tetchy and brushes it off. He says it's a blip and that he'll get over it. But I've never known him like this before. He's always so creative. Writing is his life.'

So Dexter hadn't told Elsa about Linda Carlucci and the curse. I sat there, conflicted, internally arguing with myself about what I should do.

'I blame this Shelley,' she muttered. 'It was always Dexter she had her eye on. Jay was the substitute.'

I listened as Elsa divulged details about Shelley's extravagant spending habits and her tireless efforts since Nadia's birth to ensnare Dexter. 'No wonder the poor man can't write his novels when she's hanging around, always trying to get her claws into him or spending his money.'

Wild ideas converged in my head, tripping and falling over each other. Dexter must have his reasons for not telling Elsa about his writing problems – embarrassment probably, as well as fear she wouldn't believe him – but she had come here and opened up to me. It was also obvious that she only had his very best interests at heart.

Dexter would be furious with me, but I was doing it for him. I allowed my fingers to trail across the Formica surface of the kitchen table. I had to tell her. It was only fair. She had confided in me about Nadia not being his daughter. 'There's something I should tell you. About Dexter.' I paused. 'Dexter's case of writer's block has nothing to do with Shelley.'

She frowned and leant forward. 'So what is it to do with? Oh God, he's not ill, is he?'

I rubbed my nose. 'No, nothing like that.'

Blowing out a cloud of air, I steeled myself and began to explain something to Elsa which, up until recently, I had refused to believe myself.

Chapter Sixty-One

It was therapeutic, telling Elsa all about Dexter and Linda Carlucci and what Dexter had been experiencing following the near collision with us in his car.

I realised, as I was talking, that my explanation sounded crazy. Elsa's bewildered expression compounded that.

I finished speaking and rubbed at my forehead. 'So there you have it. I know it must sound ridiculous.'

Elsa's dazed grey expression drifted from me to the kitchen walls and then out to the silent shop floor and back again.

'I'm telling you the truth,' I insisted.

Elsa knotted her hands in her lap. 'Good grief. Well, I've never seen Dexter like this before. He's had bouts of frustration with his writing, but not as prolonged or as tortuous as this.'

Outside, the Monday evening light was seeping into twists of grey and amber.

'I don't expect you to believe everything I've told you, Elsa, but I do want you to know I have no reason to lie to you.'

Her hands, sprinkled with a dose of freckles, clasped and unclasped themselves on top of the table. 'I know that.' She thought for a moment. 'Have you spoken to this Carlotta woman since?'

'It's Carlucci. And yes, I have. Both Dexter and I have tried to reason with her.'

'And no luck?'

I shook my head. 'She wouldn't listen. She seems to have made her mind up about him. I think she thinks Dexter hasn't realised the error of his ways.'

Elsa shot forward in eagerness, her buttoned blouse rustling as she moved. 'Then I suggest we go and see her together.'

'But they can't be!' I choked. 'They're not giving us a chance to fight back.'

My grandmother rested her head against the back of her favourite armchair later on that evening. 'According to Kay's granddaughter, who works in PR for the developers, the council are intending to come back with an alternative proposal about the reserve.'

A kernel of optimism started to flourish. Grandma noted the flash of hope in my face too. 'I wouldn't get too excited if I were you, darling.'

My optimism shrivelled. 'I don't like the sound of this.'

'They're apparently going to put forward some proposition that if the locals agree to buy the reserve, the council will consider pulling the plug on the deal.'

My heart banged. 'How much are we talking?'

Gran eyed me steadily and announced a figure that made me cough.

'You have got to be joking! The folks of Fir Haven don't have that sort of money.'

Gran sighed as the carriage lights in the sitting room cast a sleepy hue around her. 'We know that and so do they. They're playing with us.' She let out a sigh. 'I can't believe I'm saying this, but I think we might have to face up to the possibility that the reserve might not survive.'

The following day was a busy one in Paper Roses.

Cate offered to help out, but I knew she had a last-minute bracelet to finish for a bride, which had been commissioned by her anxious groom. Grandma, however, was more than happy to step in, though by late afternoon I could tell she was desperate to get into her slippers with a glass of something chilled and catch up on the latest mini-series crime drama which had her riveted. 'Do you mind if I slip away a bit earlier this evening, darling?'

I shook my plait. 'Of course not. I'm more than happy to close up.'

She watched the raindrops chasing each other down the windows. 'Are you out this evening?'

'No, not tonight.'

She loitered for a moment, while she belted up her red raincoat. She appeared hesitant, opening and closing her mouth for a few seconds.

'Is there something wrong, Gran?'

'No! No.' She gave me an odd smile. 'So, usual time home then?'

I folded my arms. 'Gran, are you sure you're all right?'

She responded a little too quickly. 'Yes. Absolutely. Of course I am.'

I was debating what could be going on when she delivered a swift kiss to my cheek and vanished out of the shop. Her sky-blue umbrella disappeared along the rain-slicked cobbles as she made her way back to her car.

I was still wondering whether she was feeling all right when my mobile rang from under the counter. I reached for it, not recognising the mobile number glowing up at me.

It was Elsa.

After exchanging a few pleasantries, she lowered her voice. I could hear the odd door closing behind her. Then came random snippets of Shelley's voice from somewhere in the background. She must be ringing from Hawk West Hall. My heart performed an odd thud. 'How is Dexter?'

'He's all right, considering he's got Imelda Marcos breathing down his neck.'

'And Nadia?'

'She's as wild as ever,' answered Elsa with affection. 'But adorable with it.' There was a pause. 'I'm getting more worried about Dexter. He can't carry on like this.'

Concern clutched at me too. 'Is he OK?'

'He's pretending he is. I overheard him talking to his agent and publisher on a conference call this morning. They were threatening him with breach of contract proceedings for not turning in his latest novel. Then there's Shelley making all sorts of financial demands on him.'

I could hear Elsa's footsteps shuffling along the tiled hall floor, then there was a sharp click of a door.

'I've just gone somewhere a little more private.'

'Where?'

'The cloakroom.'

I couldn't help but smile at the picture of Elsa talking to me whilst concealed by Dexter's military coats and leather jackets.

'I'm really concerned,' continued Elsa. 'He's becoming so despondent, Elle.' She swallowed. 'I think we need to try again with this Carlucci woman. Would I be able to pop round to yours this evening?'

I found myself nodding, even though Elsa was unable to see me. 'Yes. That's a good idea.'

I glanced down at my watch. 'If you could drop by Pebble

Brook around 7:30pm, that would give me enough time to get something to eat and freshen up.'

'That's perfect,' she enthused into my ear. 'I'll see you then.'

My insides were squirming as she ended the call. Dexter needed our help and fast, but what we could do was anyone's guess. All I knew was that we had to try something – even if he didn't want my help anymore.

I finished tidying up and closed the shop before driving back along the rain-splashed country lanes.

I did my best to focus on the music crackling out of my car radio, but Dexter kept looming large in my mind.

I gripped my steering wheel and flicked my indicator to turn left at the junction. Through the wall of trees ahead of me, I caught a tantalising glimpse of the sharp gothic-style roof of Hawk West Hall.

My stomach flipped over and over. Dexter had made his decision to be there for Nadia. It was an honourable one, but from what Elsa had been saying, that adorable little girl and her mother came as a package.

Shelley had her sights set on becoming Lady of the Manor and it was Dexter who Elsa said she had always harboured true feelings for. Jay had been the consolation prize. Despite all this, I knew I had to help Dexter in any way I could. And the best way to do that was to make sure he got his writing ability back.

I trundled down the steep incline that was stained with licks of rain.

As I got closer to the house, my eyes were drawn first to the shafts of porch light that were throwing themselves out in front of my tyres. Then I noticed a car I didn't recognise, parked beside my gran's little Polo.

It was a vintage Jaguar XJS in metallic sapphire blue and looked like it had been plucked from the set of *Mad Men*.

I drew to a halt beside it and snatched my shoulder bag and laptop from the passenger seat. As I locked up my car, I peered in at its whipped-cream interior and walnut dashboard.

Gran must have a visitor. I didn't know any of her book club or bridge tribe owned such a gorgeous car.

I stopped. Bloody hell! What if it wasn't an innocent visit from a friend, but something sinister instead?

My imagination fired itself up and I tried to quash it.

Nevertheless, I found myself delving into my shoulder bag for my mobile. The front door was locked. I opened it and, once inside, reached for Dad's old golfing brolly in the stand. I unhooked my shoulder bag and lowered it to the floor, together with my laptop.

From the sitting room, I could hear the faint rumble of Dean Martin crooning 'Amore'. I pushed off my converse trainers and edged towards the sound.

The double doors were closed, but through the glass I could see Grandma sitting opposite Angus Ronald. Their hands were reaching across to one another and they were sharing a chaste kiss. They sprang apart like embarrassed teenagers when they saw me.

I concealed a smile, not wishing to embarrass them any further. 'Hello.'

Angus jumped to his feet. 'Good evening, Elle. Er… I was just visiting Clara here.'

I folded my arms and pinned my grandmother to her seat with a fake stare. 'Oh, I can see that.'

So that was the reason behind all her earlier questions about what time I would be home! She had arranged a secret rendezvous with Angus.

Grandma moved to adjust the volume of Dean Martin on the CD player and narrowed her eyes at my suggestive wink.

I held my hands up in playful surrender. 'Please don't on my account, Gran. I'll leave you two alone.'

They both began to protest, but I closed the sitting room doors behind me and vanished into the kitchen. Seconds later, my blushing grandmother appeared. 'I should have told you, lovey, but it really isn't a big deal.'

I dismissed her explanation. 'It's none of my business, Gran. If you want to bring strange men back to our house…'

She moved to protest, caught me grinning, and slapped my arm instead. 'Stop teasing me, young lady.'

I fetched a pan from the cupboard below the hob. 'Have you two lovebirds eaten yet?'

'Yes. I made myself something before Angus came over.' She hesitated. 'We're just taking things slowly.'

'Oh, I could see that.'

She nudged my elbow. 'That was our first kiss.'

My hand hovered over the pan handle. 'So is this your first date then?'

She flushed and studied her loafers. 'It's our third.'

'Third? Why didn't you tell me?'

Grandma trailed her baby-pink nails along the edge of the granite worktop. 'I don't know. I suppose I felt a bit silly at my age.'

I brushed off her explanation. 'You're never too old for romance, Gran. And it's not as if you're trying to replace Grandpa.' I took her speckled hands in mine and gave them an affectionate squeeze. 'You've been on your own for twelve years now. He wouldn't want you to be lonely.'

We stood, exchanging knowing smiles until I remembered that Elsa was coming over in around an hour. I divulged to my grandmother what was happening. 'I can cancel her. I don't want to spoil your evening with Angus.'

'Nonsense. There's no need at all.'

I fired up the plate on the hob and reached for a saucepan and a packet of boiled rice.

'We were going to go to my quarters and watch an old Gregory Peck film that's on this evening.'

'Your quarters?' I repeated, with a teasing raise of an eyebrow. 'Are you sure you don't need a chaperone?'

Once I had eaten my dinner of a chicken stir-fry, I threw on my slouchy off-the-shoulder pink jumper and faded jeans.

I had only just tied my hair into a messy top knot when Elsa's pillar-box red Ford Ka pulled up in front of the house and I welcomed her in.

Grandma and Angus were wandering out of the kitchen clasping fresh cups of tea and they exchanged pleasantries with Elsa.

'We're just going to have a catch-up,' I explained. 'About Linda Carlucci.'

Grandma smiled and started to move after Angus, but he must have caught some of our conversation and stopped. His dark-blue eyes took on a pensive spark. 'Dear me. That's a name I've not heard for a long time.'

I pulled a face. 'I think she's a rather infamous character.'

Angus took a sip of his tea. His soft, open features grew hard. 'You can say that again. There've been more stories and rumours about that family than there were about the Borgias.'

Gran shot me a look.

'You know her then?' asked Elsa.

Angus nodded. 'You could say that. Linda Carlucci almost became my sister-in-law.'

A surprised gasp escaped from my throat. From behind him, Gran was wide-eyed. 'Really, Angus? I never knew that.'

Excitement climbed inside me. 'What can you tell us? If there's anything at all, it would really help.'

Angus clasped his mug of tea tighter in one hand. 'It's not really something my family used to talk about.'

Gran patted his arm. 'I think Gregory Peck can wait. Let's go into the sitting room.' She led the way, with Angus following behind and Elsa and me at the rear.

Elsa nervously smoothed her hair. We were both channelling so much optimism. Hopefully Angus could supply us with something useful, which might help us talk to Linda Carlucci again. I didn't want to get too optimistic, but at least this was looking promising.

I indicated for Elsa to take up one of the armchairs beside me, while Angus and Gran seated themselves on the sofa opposite. 'So, what are you able to tell us, Angus?'

He hesitated, shooting an alarmed glance at my grandmother next to him. *Oh no! Don't tell me he's already experiencing second thoughts about talking to us.*

Sensing his apprehension, Elsa offered Angus an encouraging smile. 'It's to help a friend of ours,' she volunteered. 'Elle has been struggling to get any information. Other people round here seem rather reluctant to tell her much.'

Angus's weathered face broke into a brief, dry smile. 'Now that I can understand.'

He placed his mug of half-drunk tea onto a coaster on the glass coffee table in front of him and dived one hand into his back trouser pocket.

The three of us watched him flip open his leather wallet. Gran frowned, straining to see what was occupying his attention. His eyes clouded over while he gazed down at a photograph. Then he handed it over to me.

I gasped at the black and white photograph of a handsome man, leaning against a wall. I studied it for a few moments longer.

I turned to Elsa, noting her surprise as she looked at it too. 'That's your brother?' I managed, struggling to take my eyes off it.

Angus nodded. 'My older brother.'

I took in his waistcoat, long legs in drainpipe trousers, and head of thick black waves. He had a teasing smile.

Elsa clutched at the wallet. She passed it back to me. 'Dexter,' she faltered, saying aloud what was circling around and around inside my head. 'He looks like Dexter.'

Chapter Sixty-Two

4th August 1964

'I don't want you out in the car tonight, Ross.'

'Oh, don't start all that again, Linda.'

Ross Ronald held his fiancée's slender, honey-coloured arms between his hands. 'I've already had a lecture from Angus. I'll be careful.'

Linda wasn't at all reassured. She removed her bare arms from Ross's hands and rubbed them repeatedly. These odd sensations and dreams she had been having recently were becoming more and more frequent, more vivid and more troubling. They would bleed into one another, like raindrops mingling with splatters of bright paint.

Linda's engagement ring – a square white diamond on a gold band – winked in the afternoon sunshine.

That same tide of panic was rising up inside of her again. She tried to swallow it back, but her pleading thoughts had other ideas. 'Don't do it, Ross. Pull out of the race. No one will think any the less of you.'

Her voice died as she picked up on the resolute cut of his jaw.

Ross stared ahead, watching a sprinkle of shoppers meander around Fir Haven's main street. 'Bloody Cameron Lomax will!'

Linda ran her agitated hand through her backcombed brunette bob.

'Cameron Lomax is an arrogant idiot!' She blinked her kohl-lined eyes at her fiancé. Why couldn't he see sense and refuse to take part?

Ross's chest heaved with frustration. 'Why do you think he's such an arrogant idiot? He's like that because he's so used to getting everything he wants, when he wants it.'

Ross's wide blue eyes scanned Linda, whose growing desperation triumphed over her failing attempts to sound calm. 'Please. Be the better man, Ross. Tell Cameron you won't race him.'

His lips tightened. 'No. I'm doing it.' He offered her a reassuring smile. 'We belong together, Linda. I'm going to race that idiot and then we'll leave Fir Haven. We can start our lives over together somewhere else. We can get married; have a family.'

Linda's shoulders sagged under her mint-green flared dress. Ross noticed. He detected tears swimming in her eyes. 'Trust me. I will be careful.'

She didn't answer. She was too busy drinking in every detail of the dark, pensive features of the man she loved.

Ross took his hand and traced it around the side of her face. 'I hate it when you have these horrible dreams.'

But that's it, *Linda screamed inside, nuzzling her cheek against Ross's warm palm. She was experiencing more of them. And they weren't just dreams anymore.*

The atmosphere in the sitting room was palpable.

Grandma jerked her head to look at Angus beside her. 'But you always said Ross was killed by a hit and run driver.'

'That was the official line.' He explained to our shocked and bewildered faces, that Cameron Lomax was the son of Don Lomax.

Angus's expression grew grim. 'Don was the local police sergeant at the same time.'

I could see Gran considering what Angus was telling us. 'But wasn't the story round here that Cameron Lomax experienced some sort of breakdown after a family event and left here to recover elsewhere?'

Angus eyed her from under his silvery brows. 'That was the story that was put out at the time and I suppose it was partly true.' Recalling what had happened to his younger brother triggered a cloud to pass over his distinguished features. His voice faltered. 'I was told he hit the accelerator at that sharp bend near the reserve. He lost control.'

'And this Cameron Lomax blamed himself?' chipped in Elsa, sitting in the chair beside me. 'Is that why he left Fir Haven?'

Grandma placed one hand on Angus's arm. 'It must have been guilt, I suppose,' he said.

Thoughts fizzed in my mind. 'Angus, may I see your photo of Ross again please?'

He tugged his wallet back out of his trouser pocket and handed it over to me. I stared down again at the black and white photo. It could have been Dexter standing there, with his challenging gaze. My head began to whirl with assumptions.

I recalled Linda Carlucci's initial reaction to seeing Dexter that first time, when he had screeched into the main street in his growling sports car; the way she had stared at him as though he were some sort of apparition. Was that why she had been like that with him? Why she had been behaving the way she had? The way her woodland-green eyes had grown in her face when she saw him standing there; the sudden paleness of her olive skin. Then there had been her various comments about knowing 'men like him'.

Not only did he bear a close resemblance to Ross Ronald her late fiancé, but he'd been behind the wheel of a fast car too. It had brought all those terrible, painful memories screeching back.

I whirled round, an excited timbre in my voice. I pinned Elsa to her seat with my wild-eyed stare. 'I think that might be why Linda Carlucci did what she did to Dexter.'

Angus swivelled his sweep of white hair between me and Elsa. 'What is it? What has Linda Carlucci done?'

Grandma pulled an apologetic face. 'I know this is going to sound rather silly, Angus, but Dexter Grayling – the crime writer who moved here recently – well, it appears that Linda has put some sort of curse on him. Or so he believes.'

A pensive Angus flexed and unflexed his fingers. 'It doesn't sound silly at all. Goodness me. I always thought the stories about the Carlucci family were just gossip or spiteful locals making up lurid tales.'

There was a considered silence between the four of us. Inky darkness was descending, so I rose and clicked on the sitting room lamps, which bathed us all in lemon-hued light.

'So, what now?' asked Elsa. 'Elle, you said you've already tried to appeal to Linda Carlucci's good nature and it didn't work.'

I sat down again, rubbing my knees in contemplation. 'But that was before we knew about her relationship with Ross.'

I turned back to Angus. There had to be another way. I hoped I wouldn't offend him by asking such a delicate question connected to the death of his brother. I leant forward.

'Angus, I hope this doesn't upset you, but you don't happen to know where Cameron Lomax is now, do you?'

Chapter Sixty-Three

'I know Cameron Lomax lives somewhere in Glasgow now, but I don't know his precise address,' explained Angus.

I could feel my optimism deflating, until he added that one of his gardening club friends still kept in touch with him – at least he had up until a couple of years ago. 'I wasn't pleased about it, but you can't dictate to people who they socialise with.'

Noting the urgency in my eyes, Angus gave his friend a call on his mobile and after a few moments of exchanging pleasantries, asked him for the address of Cameron Lomax.

Angus ended the call. 'Charlie's off home now and is going to text it to me as soon as he can. He's at his allotment at the moment.'

Angus broke the expectant hush that had fallen. 'I never wanted to come across Lomax again. I knew Charlie was aware of his whereabouts, but I couldn't face the prospect of setting eyes on him after what happened to Ross.'

The four of us sat hunched together, making a concerted effort not to stare at Angus's silver mobile perched beside him. Angus described his brother, saying how sensitive and creative he had been and that he'd had ambitions to study at Edinburgh Royal

College of Art, when there was a ping from his phone. 'We were very close,' he added wistfully. 'But very different too. I think I was always perceived as the sensible, boring one.'

Angus peered down at the screen and nodded with quiet satisfaction. 'Charlie has sent his address.' Then he asked for my number and forwarded Cameron Lomax's address to me.

'Thank you, Angus. I'm sorry to have asked.' I showed it to Elsa beside me. She read the screen and nodded. If Elsa was in agreement, we could go tomorrow and pay Cameron Lomax a visit. There was no time to waste.

Dexter's writing career hinged on this.

If I was right and Linda Carlucci was festering, hanging on to painful memories, then as long as she did so, Dexter's career was over.

'What do you think his reaction will be?' asked Elsa a little later, shooting me a sideways glance. 'Cameron Lomax.'

I watched her clamber into her car as the stars pricked the sky above Pebble Brook. 'I honestly don't know. I'm hoping he'll be willing to speak to Linda Carlucci and that she will agree to see him. But that could be a long way off.'

'Maybe if Cameron Lomax were to talk to her… apologise… explain what happened that night Ross died. It might do some good.'

I wasn't sure about any of it right now. If Cameron Lomax did agree to talk to us, I wasn't sure what our next course of action should be. Linda Carlucci seemed to be carrying around so much resentment and heartache, even after all these years, and seeing Dexter's resemblance to Ross had brought it all hurtling back for her.

I had lived here for twenty-nine years and yet I had never heard stories about the Carlucci family. Was it because locals were embarrassed about how they had been treated? Was it down to their lives having been tangled up in some way with the Carlucci's'?

Was regret and embarrassment a large part of it?

I munched on a white chocolate cookie and fired up my laptop.

Gran had gone to bed and Pebble Brook was surrounded by the blackcurrant darkness.

I dashed some cookie crumbs from my pyjama bottoms and leant forward. The neon glow from my laptop screen illuminated my face.

My fingers tapped *Cameron Lomax* into the search engine and I slumped back. I didn't know what I expected to see or find, but what flickered up in front of me still came as a surprise.

I scrolled down, ignoring the images of a twenty-something Cameron Lomax on holiday in Ibiza and a forty-year-old Cameron Lomax who lived in New York and sold real estate. The Cameron Lomax I was searching for wasn't either of them.

Then my attention flitted to a couple of photos of an intense-looking older man. He possessed a prominent forehead and an enviable sweep of salt-and-pepper, collar-length hair.

One photograph appeared to have been taken at a formal dinner. He was dressed in a penguin suit and had a rather starchy expression.

The other picture was of him seated on a varnished bench in what looked like an art gallery. There was a grand Cavalier-style painting behind him in a gilded frame.

I tapped on the link that accompanied the picture to discover it was a newspaper interview undertaken with him a year ago.

Was this him? My brows crawled upwards. This Cameron Lomax was a successful art dealer.

I began to read the article and within the first couple of paragraphs, it confirmed that he was originally from Fir Haven. It also stated that he was 'a fit and energetic man in his seventies'.

It must be him. This must be the Cameron Lomax who had been involved in Ross Ronald's death.

I greedily carried on reading. His responses to the journalist's questions were considered and thoughtful, but he made no more reference to his home town, only that he was a great admirer of the late and local nineteenth-century artist, Stratford Miller, and that he and several other rival art collectors were hoping that his first work, *Little Town*, would be discovered one day.

I focused again on the interview, reading a few paragraphs about Cameron Lomax's career and his particular passion for the Romantic period.

I bit my lip and snatched up my half-eaten cookie from its plate. My stomach swirled with anticipation. Something told me our conversation with him wasn't going to be easy.

We parked a few feet away from Cameron Lomax's address. It was a steel-grey apartment block, overlooking the extravagant shops and eateries of Merchant City. It appeared to have been a church at some point, before having been converted into swish apartments.

The windows were long and narrow, twinkling out of the grey brick.

A man walking his springer spaniel gave us a quizzical look as he marched past my stationary car.

Cate and Gran were taking care of Paper Roses, so at least I had no concerns about the shop. Right now, all I could think about on this dull Saturday afternoon in September was Linda Carlucci and Dexter.

The newsreader on the car radio finished talking about waiting times in the NHS. I was about to click it off when she moved on to the last item. 'And, finally, there have been reports that the painting *Little Town*, by the Fir Haven artist Stratford Miller, has been discovered at a local residence in the Scottish town.

'Details are sketchy, but the Glasgow Museum of Art have confirmed that the mysterious piece has been found, but no further information on its whereabouts, who came across the painting, or who owns it, have been released.'

I switched off the radio and widened my eyes at Elsa. 'Wow. Someone will be very happy today after finding that. I bet whoever it is won't be going in to work this morning.'

Elsa sighed. 'No doubt it will end up in some shadowy room belonging to a mega rich businessman.'

'Let's hope not. There are a lot of people who would love to see it in the flesh.'

I slapped my hands on my legs in a decisive gesture. 'Are you ready to do this?' I asked, reaching into the back seat for my bag.

Elsa unclipped her seatbelt. 'Well, we won't get anywhere if we keep sitting here.'

The air was tinged with the whispers of bonfires and damp leaves as I locked up my car and we both walked up to the main entrance.

I pulled up the address Angus had texted me to double-check we were about to buzz the correct flat number. 'Flat six,' I murmured to Elsa. She located it and pressed the button.

We both swapped nervous glances as the sound of the buzzer zinged. There was no reply for several seconds.

Then a 'Hello?' crackled towards us. It was a cultivated female voice.

I cleared my throat. 'Good afternoon. I wondered if we might speak with Mr Cameron Lomax, please?'

There was silence for a moment. 'Who am I talking to?'

'I'm Elle Cassidy and with me is Elsa Bennett. We're from Fir Haven.'

'Fir Haven?' repeated the disembodied voice, faltering. The

woman took on a more confrontational edge. 'Why are you so interested in speaking to my husband?'

Elsa's eyebrows took on a life of their own as she looked back at me. I detected the hint of a Swedish accent in the disembodied voice.

'It's about something that happened in the early 1960s,' I said. 'A tragic accident involving a Mr Ross Ronald?'

'Who is it, darling? Who are you speaking to?'

A male voice could be heard now, floating behind her.

'He's not here,' barked Mrs Lomax. 'And we don't know anything about any accident.'

I tried to appeal to her again. 'Mrs Lomax, we won't take up much of your husband's time.'

'Are you deaf?' she snapped through the intercom. 'He's not here at the moment and even if he were, we don't know anything.'

She stopped talking for a few seconds to recover herself, but this time Elsa jumped in. 'Mrs Lomax, we wouldn't be here if it wasn't important. There is a young man whom I work for. His name is Dexter Grayling.'

No response.

Elsa straightened her posture and carried on. 'I think of him more like a son.' I could hear the emotion in her voice. 'He really does need your husband's help.'

Mrs Lomax's frustration threw itself into overdrive. 'Now, look! I'm getting tired of this. For the umpteenth time, we don't know anything and if you don't leave right now, I'm going to call the police.'

I sighed and looked to Elsa for inspiration. Her expression was as grim as mine. 'Thank you for your time,' she said, rolling her eyes. We listened as a loud click signalled that Mrs Lomax was gone.

I slumped against the brickwork of the building. 'Now what?'

Elsa bit the inside of her cheek. 'We need to move on to Plan B.'

'Which is?'

'I don't know. I hoped you might have one.'

Frustration gnawed at me. Cameron Lomax was there. We heard a man's voice. So why had she lied and said he wasn't? She must be trying to protect him. But from what? And why?

We both accepted defeat with no good grace at all, glowering up at the apartment block while we made our way back down the path and to my car.

'It was obvious Cameron Lomax was there,' I said across the black roof to Elsa. 'She must have known we heard him.'

Elsa tugged open her passenger side door. 'It's like she's trying to protect him.'

'Yes, but from what?'

'From myself.'

We both jumped and whirled round.

A panting man was hovering a few feet away from us on the pavement. He snatched a few gulps of crisp, cold air. He looked conflicted and confused, as though he was still debating whether he should be there or not. I recognised him straight away from his photographs on social media.

'I'm Cameron Lomax,' he managed. 'You said you wanted to talk to me.'

Chapter Sixty-Four

Cameron Lomax led Elsa and me back up to the apartment block and took us to the right and down a polished hallway.

The woman, who I presumed was his wife, stood open-mouthed as her husband edged past her. We followed, offering her apologetic nods.

'Cameron!'

He stopped. 'What, Ingrid?'

'What do you think you're doing?'

His tanned, lined face hardened. 'Come on through.'

He gestured to their sitting room, which looked out over the stippled roofs and winking domes of the Glasgow skyline.

The room was all dark wood and cream walls and reminded me of a library. There was an expanse of burgundy carpet and the odd abstract painting on the walls, beside other more traditional works of sinewy men and women wreathed in sumptuous cloth. It was a really eclectic mix. 'This is my wife, Ingrid.'

He pointed to the two-seater Champagne-coloured sofa and Elsa and I sank onto it under Ingrid's chilly stare. 'You don't need to tell them anything, Cam. You're not under any pressure.'

Cameron Lomax's deep-grey eyes flashed back at her. 'I know I'm not, darling.'

He waited until we were settled opposite him. 'You don't need to stay, Ingrid. You've heard it all before.'

Her mouth grew pinched. 'Why are you doing this, Cameron?'

He threw her a weary look. 'I want to.'

Discomfited, she pushed her too-long blonde fringe out of her suspicious eyes. 'No, it's all right. I'll stay.'

Ingrid Lomax lowered herself down beside her husband on the other sofa and rearranged her long, thin legs which were encased in red jeans.

Cameron leant forward, angling his plume of greying hair, and Ingrid clasped one of her hands around his.

He managed a faint smile and then he began to speak. 'I was in love with her,' he admitted, sharing an apologetic glance with his wife.

It took me a moment to realise who he was talking about. 'You mean Linda Carlucci?'

Cameron nodded briskly at my question. He raised his eyes up to the apartment ceiling, with its swirling cornice details. 'I don't know what I was trying to prove. Or to whom.'

He blanched at the memories he was dragging up again. 'I should never have challenged Ross Ronald to that stupid bloody race. You have no idea what pain and regret I've been carrying around with me for the last fifty-nine years.'

He swallowed, not looking at Elsa, me, or his wife for a few moments.

'It was a stupid race that went wrong. It was a race that I instigated. And because of that, Ross lost his life.'

Cameron Lomax finally raised his troubled eyes. 'I was jealous of him being with Linda and so I wanted to humiliate him. But he saved my life. He stopped my car from crashing…'

His voice faltered.

Elsa and I detected the regret and searing pain behind the

words as he struggled to recall the tragic events from that day. 'God only knows what I was thinking,' he ground out, gripping Ingrid's hand tighter. 'I was an arrogant sod, trying to prove something to myself.'

I shuffled forwards on the sofa.

'It should have been my car that crashed into the tree that day and not his.'

Chapter Sixty-Five

Ingrid clutched tighter at Cameron's fingers. 'You don't have to say any more.'

He trailed his hands over hers, before looking back up at Elsa and me. The words sounded claggy in his mouth. 'Ross died instantly. He saved me by using his own car to slow my out-of-control vehicle. But Ross hadn't spotted a large puddle further down the road.' He swallowed, his eyes clotted with the memory of it. 'He lost control as he went through the water and struck a tree. We weren't wearing seatbelts – people didn't back then – and Ross broke his neck.'

Elsa spoke next. 'I'm so, so sorry. What happened in the aftermath of the accident?'

Cameron's guilt-ridden expression shifted towards the Glasgow landscape piercing the horizon. He took a few moments to sort the events in his head.

'My late father was a respected police officer in Fir Haven, with many valuable connections. There were very few witnesses to what happened and so my father ensured the incident was recorded as a tragic accident. Nothing was attributed to me.' He shook his head. 'I'm not proud of it.'

'And Linda?' I asked.

'She never forgave me, and who could blame her? She was about to leave her house to come up and watch the race when the police arrived and told her what had happened.'

Cameron wrung his hands together. 'I tried to tell her. I really did. But all she saw when I tried to apologise, when I tried to explain, was the man who killed her fiancé.'

The more Cameron revealed, the more the fog cleared.

I shifted beside Elsa.

'Mr Lomax,' I began, wondering what was the best way to frame this next question. 'Please forgive me if this sounds strange, but were you ever aware of any stories about Linda or her family?'

Cameron's gaze was loaded. 'Are you referring to the rumours about her grandmother having some sort of ability and it being passed down to her?' His mouth twisted at the corners. 'Yes,' he answered at length. 'The town was awash with rumours about her and her family; that a couple of them were able to inflict curses on people.' Then his expression turned cloudy again. He turned sideways to look at Ingrid. 'There were some folks, of course, who dismissed it as utter rubbish and idle gossip.'

'And how about you?' I asked.

He shrugged. 'She said my guilt would be punishment enough. And she was right.'

Once Cameron Lomax finished talking, we all sat for a moment in quiet reflection.

The anguish and remorse he was still carrying around with him was rivered on his ghostly face. 'It was me who called that bloody race. And I only did it because I was a stupid, immature idiot.' He struggled to look at us. 'Linda told me that they had been planning on leaving Fir Haven together after the race.'

Elsa spoke beside me. 'What if we told you that someone else was suffering now, because of what happened that night, and perhaps you might be able to do something about it?'

Cameron's thick brows dipped. 'Who is it? What's happened?'

Elsa leant forwards; a pleading look on her face. 'How would you feel about coming back to Fir Haven to talk to Linda? Perhaps you could tell her what you've just told us?'

We flinched as Cameron leapt to his feet. 'I'm sorry but I'm not going back there. I can't face it.' He began to prowl up and down in front of us.

Ingrid rose and indicated their apartment door. 'I think my husband has been more than helpful.'

'But, Mr Lomax,' I began, 'a man is suffering. A good man. His career – his future – is in jeopardy because of this curse.'

Elsa's expression was pleading. 'I know this is going to sound ludicrous, but we think she's put a curse on the crime writer Dexter Grayling.' Elsa continued talking. 'As Elle has just explained, his writing is his career and it is now at stake.'

'I sympathise, I really do.'

I thought we were making progress, but disappointment hit as Cameron Lomax strode towards his apartment door, with his wife following behind. 'I've done all I can.'

Ingrid began to usher both of us out of the door, but I paused and jotted down my mobile and shop telephone number onto the back of an old scrap of paper located in my bag. 'Just in case you change your mind.'

The sound of his wife banging shut their door reverberated at our backs.

Chapter Sixty-Six

Our drive back home was solemn.

Elsa stared empty-eyed out of her passenger side window at the traffic winding its way around the city. 'That went well.'

I sighed and offered the buildings flashing past a cursory glance. So what were we supposed to do now? What should we do? Cameron Lomax was refusing to help us. If he had agreed to see Linda Carlucci again and tell her how sorry he was… If he could explain what actually happened that awful night… My heart sank.

I had been daring to hope that Cameron would agree to return with us, but it was evident that even after all this time, his memories and his guilt wouldn't allow it.

Pessimism invaded me. I knew what all this could mean.

Dexter would want to return to London with Nadia and Shelley, to escape from Fir Haven and continue with his role of surrogate dad. And it was obvious Shelley had ulterior motives.

The prospect of not seeing Dexter again made my heart twist.

'Elle?'

Elsa saying my name made me blink. 'Sorry. Just mulling a few things over.'

'I could see that.'

I slowed down at a set of traffic lights as the late Saturday afternoon sun flitted across the autumn patchwork of fields and the cows grazing there.

'So what do we do now?' she asked.

I glanced in the rear-view mirror. My forlorn hazel eyes stared back at me. 'I don't think there is anything else we can do. You heard Cameron Lomax. He doesn't want to relive it all. He struggled talking to us about it, as it was.'

Elsa clutched her patent handbag on her lap. 'Elle, I realise I've only known you for a short while, but in that time I've seen what a determined young woman you are.'

I managed a smile and experienced a flicker of relief as the wooden painted sign proclaiming 'Welcome to Fir Haven' emerged over the brow of the country lane. 'It's in the genes.'

'In that case, I don't understand why you're giving up.'

'I'm not giving up, Elsa. I'm simply being realistic.'

She pulled a face.

'What was that look for?'

She nestled herself into the passenger seat and appraised me out of her thoughtful eyes. 'Please forgive me for being blunt, but that sounds like an excuse to me.'

I sucked in a cloud of air through my teeth, not taking in the tangled beauty of the nature reserve as we flashed past. I felt a pang of guilt. I had been so preoccupied with Dexter's predicament that saving the reserve had taken a bit of a back seat of late in my priorities, but I was determined to address that again.

My thoughts were drifting again, so I pulled them back to Elsa. 'An excuse?'

Elsa's usual placid expression was now a challenging one. 'I think you don't want to risk losing someone else who means a lot to you.'

I opened my mouth to argue the point, but Elsa was having none of it. 'I'm not blind, young lady. I've seen the way you look at Dexter and the way he looks at you.'

'But—'

'But nothing. Believe me, he has feelings for you. He just won't admit it to himself because of all that's going on with Nadia, Shelley, and his current inability to write.'

I approached Pebble Brook, so that Elsa could retrieve her car. I killed the engine and turned to face her. 'Dexter is dealing with so many issues right now,' said Elsa. 'He's doing all he can to be a good father figure for Nadia, but he's trying to work out how to let Shelley down gently in the process. And what with his writing career under threat, he's in a tough place.'

My stomach performed a loop-the-loop.

Elsa shuffled round in her seat, her thick raincoat rustling. 'There must be something else we can do. I can't give up on him and I know you feel the same, even if you don't want to admit it.'

My mouth twitched in a faint smile. 'You are a very persuasive lady.'

'My Kenny used to say I was a professional nagger.'

Silence descended again. I knew I couldn't just stop. I'd promised Gran I would try to help Dexter. Now Elsa was relying on me too.

I threw my hands up in the air. 'OK. We won't admit defeat just yet.'

An idea breezed into my mind. It was another long shot, but my dad always used to say they were the best kind. I trained my eyes on Elsa. 'There's one other suggestion, but it might not work. In fact, chances are, it won't.'

Elsa's round expression flickered with optimism. 'Well, anything's worth a shot. I like a challenge.'

Chapter Sixty-Seven

The stream by Pebble Brook glistened as while I described my sketchy plan to Elsa.

As I spoke to her, I could feel my optimism crumbling. Saying it out loud was different to forming it in your head. 'I know the likelihood of this working isn't good, but what else can we do?'

Elsa stared out of the windscreen and I trailed my hands around the steering wheel. Whether Dexter decided to stay here or return to London, I knew I had to help him, whatever he chose to do.

Elsa was thoughtful. She let out a sigh. 'You should see him. He's not the young man I've grown to know.'

My heart lurched.

'The Dexter Grayling bravado has well and truly slipped.'

I switched on my car engine again and parked up my Mini beside Elsa's car.

Elsa gathered her coat around herself, thanked me for the ride back and picked up her bag from the footwell. She clambered out and hovered there. 'But he's wonderful with Nadia.'

My insides twisted over. Had Gran been right? Had I

deliberately fought against how I felt for him because I couldn't face the prospect of losing someone else I loved?

'Elle? Are you all right?'

I forced a stray hair back behind my ear as I climbed out and locked up my car. 'Yes. Yes, I'm fine, thank you.'

She regarded me with narrowed eyes.

'So,' I said, examining her over my car roof. 'What do you think of my suggestion?'

'I agree with you. Anything is worth a try.'

'When do you think we should do it?' I asked.

Elsa hovered on the spot, giving Pebble Brook an appreciative glance. 'The sooner the better. If Shelley has her way, Hawk West Hall will be crated and packed up by the end of the week.' She pursed her lips. 'I overheard her ranting at Dexter last night about some apartment in Mayfair. She was saying there are a couple of excellent private schools there for Nadia.' She locked eyes with me. 'The way I see it, she knows how you and Dexter feel about one another and she wants to get him away from here as soon as she can.'

I watched Elsa rifle in her bag for her car keys.

It was best not to involve Dexter for now. The last thing I wanted to do was raise his hopes again, only to see them dashed.

Images of Dexter standing at a side window at Hawk West Hall conjured themselves up in my mind. There was a lost look to his handsome, pensive features. He appeared almost resigned as he stared out over the tops of the trees.

My heart flipped over.

In my imagination, Nadia appeared by his side and stretched up for his hand. He ruffled her hair and scooped her up into his arms. Together, they stayed by the window with the mini Juliet-style balcony, observing the ravens diving from branch to branch.

I buried a lump of emotion.

What Elsa and I had agreed to do was a long shot in the extreme, but if we didn't try, we would never know.

With one last picture of Dexter and Nadia huddled together in my head, pointing at the birds, I waved at Elsa and watched her drive away.

Chapter Sixty-Eight

Elsa rang me later that evening and said we could set off the next morning at 9 a.m. 'Is that convenient for you, Elle?'

'Not a problem. I'll ask Cate and Gran if either of them can cover the shop for me.'

Elsa's voice was low. She explained she was ringing me from the kitchen at Hawk West Hall. I could detect a weary smile creeping into her voice. 'Nadia should carry a government health warning. She never stops.'

I thought back to Dexter and Nadia at the Nature Reserve Knees-Up, their dark heads huddled together.

I noted Elsa's tone change. 'As for Dexter, he's just cancelled a series of TV and magazine interviews. He's even pulled out of a mentoring project for up-and-coming new crime writers.'

I struggled to dismiss negative thoughts. My parents always taught me that it was worse not to attempt something. If it didn't work out, then at least you had no regrets.

I caught sight of my anxious expression in the hall mirror. I would speak to Gran now and then ring Cate. 'I'll come and pick you up at 9 a.m.,' I said to Elsa, relieved that things were moving.

'But I'll park a little up the lane from Hawk West Hall so no one sees me. Just keep a look out for my car, OK?'

Cate assured me she could make it into Paper Roses for a couple of hours first thing when I called her to explain, so that just left Gran to speak to. 'Do you think it will work?' my grandmother asked with a modicum of doubt.

I shrugged. 'I guess we'll know soon enough.'

I started to rise from the sofa. 'Oh, I've had some more thoughts about how we can protest the sale of the nature reserve. I was thinking of holding a competition and launching it on the Paper Roses website.' My enthusiasm started to climb. 'There could be a five-pound entry fee and all proceeds can go to our nature reserve fund.'

My hands began flapping with excitement. 'I thought we could ask people to write a love letter to the reserve. It holds so many special memories for local people – wedding proposals, children taking their first steps up there, that kind of thing.'

I hovered over Gran, trying to assess her thoughts on it. 'I'm sure we would receive a lot of entries.'

I stopped talking. Gran's expression had fallen. 'What is it?'

She steeled herself. 'It might be a bit too late for that, Elle.'

I sank back down in my chair. Apprehension gripped me.

'I received a phone call from Marjorie while you were on the phone to Elsa.'

Part of me was willing her to continue, while the other half didn't want to hear what she had to say. Trepidation sizzled through me.

'The sale of the nature reserve is going ahead next week.'

I experienced one of the worst night's sleeps I'd had since losing Mum and Dad.

My thoughts were on a merry-go-round that refused to stop.

First, they would latch on to Dexter and the prospect of him leaving, and then they would veer to the nature reserve. I couldn't accept that nothing more could be done to save it.

The local council were selling it to the highest bidder and that was Atticus Development. They weren't prepared to wait for a group of enthusiastic but poor locals to scrape together a meagre sum and counter offer. The prospect of ostentatious getaway second homes for the affluent sent a chill through me.

I got up at 6am the next morning, showering robotically, and had an early breakfast, even though I didn't feel at all hungry.

Gran hadn't appeared yet, so I threw on my walking boots, fleece, and jeans. Once I'd secured my hair in a top knot, I collected my phone and walked the fifteen minutes to the nature reserve. Even though it wasn't lovely weather, the plumes of trees discarding their leaves and damp swishing grass still looked magical in the smoky light. It would soon be October and more and more bare branches twisted their branches like elegant flamenco dancers.

A wood pigeon burred above my head. I found a large rock and settled myself down on it. A blur of grey squirrel shot up a tree trunk a few feet away.

As I buried my cool hands in my fleece pockets, so many thoughts jostled in my head. My eyes misted at the memories of me, Mum, and Dad traipsing about up here in our wellington boots.

Then I imagined my parents as teenagers, sheltering under the green umbrellas of the trees and exchanging clumsy kisses.

Mum's description of how my dad almost fell over just before proposing to her and temporarily losing her engagement ring in the process, made my lips flicker. 'The silly sod was so embarrassed,' Mum had laughed in that throaty way of hers I loved so much. 'He told me he was looking for his contact lens,' she would grin, nudging Dad in the ribs. 'I would have swallowed that, except your father didn't wear contact lenses!'

I shifted on the rock, laughing into the lining of my fleece. I scanned the landscape. I felt as though I knew every knot on every tree trunk and every pale stone in the brook.

At least I still experienced that same love for the place, that same familiarity, whenever I came up here. As for the town and the impact the Carlucci family had clearly had on the local community over the years, that was beginning to skew my perceptions.

The way that poor family had been treated by certain members of the community left me with a shifting sense of guilt. It had been like a ripple effect, tossing a pebble into a mirror-still lake and observing the water reacting and moving in response, touching each ring.

I breathed in the fresh, earthy scent and the festive smell of pine needles.

Even though the future of the reserve seemed a foregone conclusion, I couldn't give up.

Not yet.

I walked back to Pebble Brook, my pink-and-cream fleece keeping me cosy as I strode home.

Today felt like our last chance to appeal to Linda Carlucci. If this didn't work, I feared it wasn't only the reserve I was going to lose.

Chapter Sixty-Nine

'Ready?' asked Elsa beside me.

'No.'

She attempted a smile. 'I'm not either.'

We both remained sitting in my Mini Cooper S, blinking out at Linda Carlucci's farmhouse cottage the next morning. A ghostly September tinge was clinging on to everything. I was sure I could smell pumpkins and fireworks already.

I tugged my car keys out of the ignition and attempted to still the roller coaster careering around inside my stomach.

'Come on,' I urged, patting her hand. 'We won't know if we don't try.'

We made our way up to Linda Carlucci's cottage, our nerves jangling like church bells.

We knew our options were narrowing and if this didn't work, I was struggling to think of any other alternative.

Elsa paused on the grassy path and gazed up at the chimney stack and short silky curtains hanging at the windows. 'I know he can be a cantankerous sod, but I am very fond of Dexter.'

'I know you are. I see the affection you have for him every time

I look at you.' I smiled encouragingly. 'Then let's do all we can to help him.'

I started to walk towards the front door.

'Elle.'

I stopped and spun round to look at her.

'You mentioned to me before that you began helping Dexter because your grandmother asked you too, despite your protestations at the beginning.' She flashed me a look. 'Is that still the case?'

Pink flipped in my cheeks and I fiddled with the strap of my shoulder bag. 'It did start off that way.'

'And now?'

I knew I couldn't conceal my feelings for Dexter any longer. 'Now… it's grown into something so much more.'

Elsa gave a satisfied nod. 'Sometimes you just have to accept what your heart is telling you.' She took a steadying breath. 'OK. Let's go.'

We moved in step together and arrived at the red front door of Linda Carlucci.

Right now, all I could think of was getting this right.

I knocked, hearing yaps and barks from the hallway. Elsa and I swapped a hesitant glance.

The door eased open a sliver. Linda Carlucci's disapproving face appeared. 'Can I help you?' Her expression hardened. 'Oh, it's you again.'

'Please, Mrs Carlucci,' I began. 'We really do need to speak to you.'

Elsa took a step forward. 'I work for Dexter Grayling as his housekeeper. I see every day what a terrible effect this is having on him.'

'And I can attest to that,' I broke in, my desperation rising.

Linda Carlucci's leafy-green eyes flashed like an exploding firework. 'Driving the way he did is dangerous. He could have killed someone. Or himself.'

I noted her swallowing back a look of pain and bit my lip. Her sentiments rang true with me too. 'That's what we want to talk to you about.'

She squinted against the morning light. 'I don't understand.'

My heart pumped faster. It was now or never. 'It's about Cameron Lomax.'

Linda Carlucci let out an audible gasp. One hand fluttered to her chest and rested there.

'We know,' confessed Elsa gently after a beat. 'We know about you losing Ross that night during that race.'

Linda swallowed and clung to the door, her knuckles growing white.

Sympathy for her swam through me. 'We've been to see Cameron Lomax. We spoke to him.'

Linda's haunted expression shot past us and out to the thicket of trees that sheltered her cottage.

We waited while what we had just told her sank in.

Her shoulders dropped under her black scoop-neck top. 'You saw him? You spoke to him?'

'Yes.'

Her chest rose and fell. She pulled her attention back to us. She hesitated, before opening her front door wider. 'You had better come in.'

Chapter Seventy

I bent down and patted Brando.

Linda's expression was strained, preoccupied even, as she showed us the way down her dimly lit hall and into her sitting room of dark swirly carpet and assorted paintings. It was an array of romantic opulence, boasting everything from scenes of Venetian bridges to the Piazza Santa Croce in Florence.

Brando sank down by Linda's feet while she perched on the edge of an amber-and-gold armchair. The room carried an air of the Italian Renaissance about it. I didn't know what I had expected, but it wasn't this.

As the exterior of the old farmhouse cottage was more like something from a Highland croft, it was like stepping from one century into another; from one culture to another.

Her voice was filled with incredulity when she finally did speak. Her eyes glittered. 'How did you track him down?'

'It was rather accidental,' confessed Elsa. I nodded, but decided not to elaborate for now. I wanted Linda Carlucci to open up to us, to tell us her side of things, and why she had inflicted the curse on Dexter. There would hopefully be enough time to explain to her about our discoveries and us talking to Cameron Lomax. Right now, all that mattered was Linda being open and honest.

Linda Carlucci was rubbing the knees of her slim grey trousers so much, I thought she might burn a hole in them. 'You know he killed Ross? My Ross?'

My heart stilled for her. 'We are so sorry, Mrs Carlucci. It must have been awful.'

Elsa was sympathetic. 'You and Ross were engaged to be married, is that right?'

Linda's hands continued to rub up and down against her trousers while she crouched there. 'We were planning on leaving Fir Haven together; starting our lives together elsewhere. That was until that heartless maniac, Cameron Lomax, challenged him to some stupid race and killed him!' She shook her head, tears gathering. 'Do you know Ross deliberately gave me the wrong starting time for the race because he didn't want me to be there?' A lump appeared in her throat. 'I should have been there.'

Elsa paused. 'Did Cameron Lomax tell you that he caused Ross's death?'

Linda's gaze was contorting into one of increased pain. 'He didn't have to. Everyone knew what a nasty troublemaker Lomax was.'

Elsa couched her next question as she delicately as she could. 'Did Cameron ever try to explain to you what happened that night?'

I watched Linda rub Brando behind his furry beige ears. 'He tried to speak to me several times, but I knew the truth. All he was concerned about was saving his own neck.' Her back went ramrod straight. 'If it hadn't been for that conniving police officer father of his, he wouldn't have got away with what he did.'

I shuffled forwards a little. 'Mrs Carlucci, there are a couple of things you should know.'

Her slim mouth, adorned in strawberry-red lipstick, pursed. 'I know everything I need to know about that man. I lost my Ross so many years ago and yet I can still recall that night in minute detail.'

'I'm sure you can and again, we are so sorry. But there's something you don't know.'

Linda's eyes narrowed with suspicion as I explained how Ross had died saving Cameron. Her kaleidoscope of expressions twisted from incredulity and anger to pain.

Elsa jumped in when Linda's body language indicated that she was about to erupt. 'We've been to see him and he is still haunted by what happened that evening.'

Linda's hands scrambled for the arms of her chair. Her fingers tightened around them. 'I don't believe you. Even after all this time, he won't take responsibility for what he did to Ross.'

Concern pumped through me. 'Mrs Carlucci, I realise this is a big ask, but would you be willing to speak to Cameron Lomax face to face?'

Elsa and I jumped back in our seats. Linda was on her feet, with Brando gawping up at her. 'You've fallen for his lies as well.'

Elsa disagreed. 'Mrs Carlucci, we haven't fallen for anything. Cameron Lomax has been affected by what happened to Ross too. If you would just consider talking to him, it might help both of you…'

She strode towards her sitting room door and pointed at the way out. 'I want both of you to leave. Right now.' She flashed me a hot look. 'You're just here saying all this to get that boyfriend of yours off the hook!'

Knowing there was no point in trying to debate the point, Elsa and I rose from the sofa and moved reluctantly to her front door. Despondency got a tighter grip of me.

Linda kept Brando behind her leg while she hustled us out of her cottage.

My desperation was biting. Before I could think straight, my thoughts tumbled out. 'Mrs Carlucci, is that why you placed a curse on Dexter?'

She was about to bang the door shut, but hesitated. 'What are you talking about?'

I knew Dexter's future was teetering on the brink. There was no time to waste. 'I know he almost hit you in his car, which I agree was dreadful, but it wasn't the only reason you took umbrage with him, was it?'

Elsa shifted beside me on the doorstep, as if to say, *Careful, Elle, for goodness' sake!*

Frustration was hissing inside my head. What did I have to lose? I swallowed any doubt and carried on. 'I saw a photo of Ross.'

Her eyes widened.

'He looks a lot like Dexter.'

A mist of tears glistened in her eyes.

'He's talking about leaving Fir Haven – Dexter, that is,' I carried on, emotion balling in my chest. 'He can't take any more of not being able to write. He feels like he's lost so much purpose.'

'He wants to continue to be a good father figure to Nadia and he seems to think that he won't be able to do that here, if he can't write,' added Elsa.

Linda's mouth twitched with defiance. She raised her chin. 'That's the child I saw him with?'

'Yes,' confirmed Elsa, who went on to explain that Nadia was in fact his niece, and how he had assumed responsibility for her.

Linda listened, her eyes widening at this revelation.

'Please, Mrs Carlucci,' I begged. 'Dexter has grown to mean so much to both Elsa and me.'

A bloom of optimism promised to bud. Linda hesitated as she held her front door open, conflict battling its way through her eyes. But then my hope was crushed. 'I'm sorry, but I can't help you.'

'But, Mrs Carlucci, if you would just agree to speak to Cameron Lomax—'

'I lost the love of my life,' she faltered. 'Nothing will ever change that.'

Elsa and I were left standing on her step with the bang of her front door ringing in our ears.

Chapter Seventy-One

My insides contracted on seeing Elsa's desperate expression.

'That's it. We're all out of ideas,' she said. She buried herself deeper into her quilted jacket. 'That woman,' and she indicated to the closed door behind us, 'is still trapped in 1964 with her grief.'

Elsa marched back towards my car. 'She won't listen to reason, Elle.'

I could see her chest rising and falling in frustration. 'I know Dexter can be an arrogant bugger at times, but he has changed for the better.' She paused and flicked me a look. 'And that is thanks to you.'

I forced a smile, even though despondency was pressing down on me.

Elsa watched me pluck my car keys from out of my bag. We both got into my car and sat for a few moments, with a faint wash of morning sun lighting up the sky that surrounded Linda's cottage.

I was going to lose Dexter, even though he wasn't really mine to lose. My fingers furled and unfurled themselves around the steering wheel.

'Even if Cameron Lomax told her face to face what really happened that night, I don't think she would listen,' said Elsa.

I thought about that. Would it even work, if I could make it happen? We were running out of time. But it had to be worth a try…

Elsa's brows fenced as she watched me fetch my mobile from my bag on the back seat. 'What are you doing now?'

I found the number I was looking for in my purse and began dialling it. 'I'm doing what you just suggested. We have to.'

'What suggestion?'

I locked eyes with her as the ring tone at the other end drummed in my ear. Concern pulled at my insides. What if they weren't there? A voice inside my head begged them to answer.

After several seconds, however, I heard Ingrid Lomax's voice. 'Hello?'

Still baffled by what I was doing, Elsa leant forward in the passenger seat and mouthed, 'What?!'

I hesitated. *Oh god. What am I doing?* My stomach pirouetted. I couldn't say who I was again. She wouldn't speak to me. But I had to do this, for Dexter's sake.

Elsa stared at me, puzzled, as I proceeded to disguise my voice by putting on an English accent and pretended to be from the local doctor's surgery, insisting that Cameron Lomax was due a blood pressure check.

Ingrid Lomax hesitated. 'But I thought he had that done a couple of months ago.'

Shit! I swallowed a ball of panic and fought to stay in character. 'No, that was his cholesterol.' I could feel beads of perspiration collecting on my forehead.

Please be there, I repeated silently to myself. *Please be in.*

Ingrid paused. 'Oh, right. Yes, hang on a second and I'll fetch him.'

When she put down the phone, I let out a long breath that

sounded more like a balloon deflating. Then Cameron came to the phone.

In a deeply apologetic gush, I explained it was me. 'I'm sorry but I needed to speak to you.' Not giving him an opportunity to interrupt, I told him where Elsa and I were and what had just happened. 'Please can you help?' I begged. 'Linda is refusing to listen to us, but if you spoke to her, I think it would make all the difference.'

I could make out Ingrid's irritated tone in the background and her persistent, 'Cameron! Who is it? Who are you talking to?'

'Please, Mr Lomax,' I said again, my voice cracking. 'A man's happiness rests on this.'

Elsa gestured for me to pass my mobile to her. When I did, she puffed out her cheeks and tilted up her chin. 'Mr Lomax, you said you would do anything to change what happened to Ross.' She shot me a glance and carried on. 'We know that isn't possible. But you can change the future of someone else for the better.'

My hands fidgeted as Elsa talked to Cameron Lomax. I was unable to sit still.

'And I think it might even go a little way towards helping you and Mrs Carlucci.'

When there was no response, Elsa handed back the phone. She slumped in her seat, defeated, and stared out of the passenger-side window.

'Mr Lomax,' I stuttered. 'Enough people have suffered over the years. I don't believe you would want that to continue.'

There was silence.

Trepidation crawled over me. 'Mr Lomax? Are you still there?'

'Yes,' he croaked. 'I'm still here.'

I adjusted my mobile against my ear and stared in desperation at Elsa.

I felt as if I were wading through treacle. 'Mr Lomax, we are sitting outside Linda Carlucci's house right now. We did all we could to convince her of what happened to Ross, but she won't listen.'

I blinked back pictures of Dexter leaving. 'Three lives were ruined that night. Do you really want a fourth to be ruined too?'

I hesitated and bit my lip. *Oh shit!* Was that too strong? What if I had blown any chance we had of reaching out to Cameron Lomax?

Silence prevailed again and my frustration took over. I lowered my mobile. 'I think he's hung up.'

Elsa's chest heaved and she patted me on the hand. 'You did your best, Elle.'

'I blew it.'

'Hello? Are you still there?'

Cameron Lomax's voice buzzed out. Elsa and I stared back at one another. I hitched the phone up to my ear again, my heart zooming. 'Yes. Sorry.'

Cameron lowered his voice. Was it because he didn't want Ingrid to overhear?

'All right,' he said after an agonising pause.

I blinked and repeated 'All right?' like an idiot.

'I'll come back to Fir Haven and speak to Linda Carlucci.'

I let out a gasp of shock and relief and whirled round to look at Elsa. 'Thank you, Mr Lomax. Thank you so much.'

Realising it was good news, Elsa clapped her hands together and beamed.

'I realise there are no guarantees,' I said, anticipating what he was about to say next, 'but it might go some way towards helping you too.'

Cameron's voice took on a dark inflection. 'This will be the first time since the accident that I will have been back to Fir Haven.'

'Well, if it's any consolation, I think it's a very courageous thing to do.'

He admitted he was terrified at the prospect. 'But I'll do it,' he rounded off. 'You're right. There have been enough people affected by my stupid actions that night.'

Cameron then explained he couldn't come tomorrow, but that he would make it on Wednesday.

In a shaky stunned voice, I repeated Linda's address so he could write it down. Then I gave him the address of Paper Roses. 'But come to my shop first,' I suggested. 'Elsa and I will accompany you.'

'I think that would be best,' admitted Cameron. 'I have a feeling this conversation isn't going to be easy.'

Chapter Seventy-Two

Cameron insisted on driving the three of us to Linda Carlucci's cottage.

It had been such a covert operation that I felt exhausted and it was only half past nine in the morning.

Cameron had arrived at Pebble Brook just before 9 a.m., as had Elsa, who had driven down and parked by the house.

I had decided not to tell Gran what was happening for now. I didn't want to upset her in light of her history with Linda's brother, Lorenzo, and I also worried she might tell Angus. There would be plenty of time for that afterwards.

So I had hovered by the front door of Pebble Brook after getting up earlier to breakfast and shower, before waiting for the arrival of Cameron and Elsa.

Elsa was sitting in the back of Cameron's white Vauxhall Grand Land and I was occupying the passenger seat. He parked a little way down the narrow drive so we were shielded by some of the trees.

The autumn sky was a rinsed-out blue this morning, complementing the myriad beige and gold leaves. A trail of smoke danced out of Linda Carlucci's chimney pots.

Our plan was to arrive early so we stood a better chance of her being at home.

The interior of Cameron's car was cosy and warm, with its squashy black interior and heated seats. We all exchanged nervous glances before Cameron set the car in motion again and parked a few feet away from the cottage.

Silently closing our respective car doors, the three of us walked together up to the red front door.

Cameron's collar-length greying hair and craggy features were set off by the ankle-length black coat he was wearing.

I hitched up the collar of my navy Burberry jacket and wished I could bury myself so deep in its quilted lining that I could disappear.

What if this is the worst idea I've ever had? What if Linda refuses to talk to Cameron? Or decides to attack him with a pitchfork? Maybe only I've succeeded in making matters worse, rather than better?

We reached Linda's front door and Cameron fell back into position behind me. I heard Brando's now familiar bark.

There was a rattling of the door chain and Linda Carlucci emerged, her dyed-black hair tied back at the nape of her neck in a low ponytail. She was wearing a pair of loose-fitting trousers and tunic in smoky grey.

Her woodland-green eyes hardened at the sight of us. 'Oh, not again. I really don't know what else to say to you, Ms Cassidy—' Her brittle voice vanished at the sight of Cameron, who stepped up beside me. She scanned his face. A few seconds dragged. 'Oh god.'

Linda's age-spotted hands reached for the door. She steadied herself, paling. 'What the hell do you think you're doing, bringing him here?'

Wild-eyed, she turned on Elsa and me. 'Whose idea was this? Don't you think I've been through enough?'

Cameron tried to regroup but his expression remained

stricken. 'Linda. You have no idea of the guilt I've been carrying around these years.'

Her voice hardened. 'It's no more than you deserve! You killed Ross and then that corrupt father of yours covered it all up.'

Cameron's shame was evident. 'My father should never have done what he did. I never asked him to. I'm so sorry. But you need to know the truth about what happened.'

'I know the truth,' she wailed, scooping up Brando and cradling him in her shaking arms. 'You took Ross way from me. You ran him off the road. *You took everything away from me!*'

Cameron shot her a desperate look. 'I should never have arranged that race, Linda, but I swear I didn't drive him off the road.'

Linda Carlucci began to close the door, but Cameron rammed his foot in the way and it stayed open. I reached out my arm, trying to calm him, but he was determined.

Cameron's desperate silver eyes clouded with remorse. 'It was me who should have died that night,' he wailed into the countryside air. 'Ross died saving me.'

Chapter Seventy-Three

Linda's rich green eyes glistened. 'What are you talking about? You killed him!'

Cameron's drawn mouth tightened. 'I didn't. I swear.' He took a gulp of cold air. 'I should never have suggested that race to begin with. You have no idea how much I regret it.'

'Then why did you?' she screamed. 'Why?'

Cameron rubbed his freshly shaved cheek. Shame shone out of him. 'Because I was jealous.'

Linda's words were full of scorn. 'You? Why? The spoilt brat son of the local police sergeant? What the hell did you have to be jealous of Ross for?'

Cameron looked to me and then to Elsa. Now he had started this conversation – which he knew was fifty-nine years in the making – he knew he had to continue.

We remained on Linda's doorstep, the three of us huddled there in front of a stunned Linda.

'Because,' he struggled, flashing Linda a glance charged with guilt, 'I was in love with you.'

Shock and confusion reared up in her. She made a strange

gasping noise. 'What are you talking about? You were always vile towards me. Spiteful, even.' I noticed the scent of freshly brewed coffee and lavender air freshener coming from inside her hallway.

Cameron blanched at the memories Linda was dragging up again. They were all ones he knew he had to confront. 'That's because I was a self-centred little bastard who couldn't admit my feelings.'

Cameron's shame made him flinch in the ethereal woodland light. 'It was easy for me to hide how I felt about you, and lash out at Ross instead.'

Linda's hand reached for the crescent moon necklace dangling around her neck, her trembling fingers grasping it.

'Please, Linda,' said Cameron taking another step towards her. 'I know I have absolutely no right to ask this of you, but I'm desperate.' He cleared his throat. 'I need to tell you the truth about what happened that night.'

She appeared lost somewhere, as though she were struggling to find her way back. Maybe she didn't want to.

'You ought to know the truth about the man you were going to marry.'

Linda blazed back at him. 'Don't you dare tell me what kind of a man Ross was!' She blinked and straightened her shoulders. 'I knew him better than anyone.'

Cameron's increasing desperation was evident. 'I know you did and you always will.' He swallowed. 'But I do need to talk to you. Please, Linda. May we come in?'

Her bewildered expression travelled from Cameron to me and then Elsa. Linda straightened her tunic and, after an agonised pause, took a few steps backwards. She gestured for us to enter.

Brando weaved around my legs as Elsa, Cameron, and I sat down.

Elsa took up the seat next to me on the sofa and Cameron sat on an old solid armchair.

The air in the sitting room was warm, but we kept our coats on. Cameron flapped open his long coat. The open log fire hissed and spat in the grate.

Linda swallowed and pinned Cameron with her jade stare. 'So?'

Cameron studied his polished black brogues. He dashed one hand over the top of his grey-tinged hair before recalling the events of August 1964 with alarming clarity.

He described the powder-blue sky and how it was at odds with the roaring of their car engines. He spoke of them both doing all they could to conceal their nerves, in the hope of psyching the other out. Then he moved on to the race itself, as they vied for the lead side by side down the country lanes. 'It was as we were nearing Turnpike Trail that I began to lose control of my car and the brakes failed.' He gathered himself. 'Ross must have seen the trouble I was in and instead of capitalising on it, he sped up and used his car to stop mine.'

He paused, risking a look at Linda's shocked expression. 'And he saved me.'

His shoulders sagged at the memory. 'Ross used his car to slow me down, but there was a pool of water on the road.'

Linda's stricken face made him look away. 'His car spun… There was nothing he could do… I shouted at him! I tried to warn him!' Cameron closed his eyes for a few seconds. 'There was a screech of tyres and a smell of smoke… before Ross's car hit a tree.'

Linda clamped one hand over her mouth and sat rigid in her chair. She was milky white.

I jumped out of my seat and went into her kitchen, banging cupboards open until I located a glass and filled it with water.

I hovered by her side while she took a few reluctant sips. When I was certain she was a little more composed, I resumed my seat next to Elsa.

'So… Ross saved you?' she croaked, clinging on to the glass of water like a life raft.

Cameron nodded. 'And there's not a day goes by that I don't feel guilty about it.'

Linda's green eyes were flecked with pain. 'But why didn't all this come out before?' As soon as she asked the question, her jaw set. 'Of course. Your father.'

Cameron's long, craggy features blanched. 'I should never have gone along with it, but my dad was, to put it mildly, a very persuasive man.'

Cameron shook his thatch of thick side-swept hair. 'I should have spoken up, but Dad gave me his 'I'm a pillar of the local community' speech. He said he could lose his career.'

Linda placed her glass of water on the stout little table by her chair. Her movements were slow; deliberate.

'I'm so sorry,' said Cameron. 'If I could change what happened, I would.' He indicated to Elsa and me. 'We can't do anything about that night, but we can stop someone else suffering because of what I did.'

Cameron shifted in his chair, knees bunched up under his coat. 'Please, Linda. Please don't punish someone else because of what I did, or because you lost Ross.'

'I'm doing no such thing. You don't know what you're talking about!' Linda snapped.

Cameron's Scottish lilt was soft and imploring. 'I think you do.' His expression was beseeching. 'Please don't punish someone else, just because he reminds you of Ross.'

Linda looked like she was about to say something and then decided not to. She clamped her wobbling mouth shut.

'I think,' ventured Cameron, 'that you are doing this to Dexter Grayling because he inadvertently brought back all those terrible memories for you and I understand that.'

The sitting room was silent, except for the panting of Brando and the intermittent spitting of the logs on the fire.

Then came a quiet swallow and a sob. The sound was pure anguish and bottled-up pain. Linda Carlucci was crying for Ross again, after all these years and for what might have been.

Chapter Seventy-Four

I got up and moved towards Linda to comfort her.

Her head was bowed and her dark hair was falling around her crumpled face. Brando was snuffling at her feet and gazed up at his mistress with concern.

Linda raised her tear-cluttered eyes and I slid my arm around her and gave her a reassuring hug. She smelt of citrus perfume.

'This must sound awful,' she struggled, 'but I felt so resentful towards Ross. So angry.'

I held her for a few more moments, until she was able to gather herself again. 'We were going to get married. We had everything mapped out and then he goes and takes part in that stupid race.'

I resumed my seat next to Elsa. Cameron was looking on.

'I didn't mean for things to turn out the way they did. I just wanted to humiliate him,' Cameron admitted.

Linda shook her head. 'But instead he saved your life.'

There was a quiet pause before Cameron ground out, 'I wish to God he hadn't. I didn't deserve it.'

Linda continued to hunch in her chair, struggling to comprehend everything Cameron Lomax had just told her.

'Mrs Carlucci,' I said, hoping my next question wouldn't make her retreat back into herself again. 'Your ability… your power… whatever you want to call it. How did it start?'

There seemed to be a battle going on inside of her, about whether she wanted to talk about it. She shifted in her chair before leaning down to ruffle Brando's coarse beige coat. 'That particular gift, if you can call it that, was passed down to me by my great-grandmother, Maria. Lorenzo and Marina, my brother and sister, escaped it.'

Linda rubbed the solid wooden arms of her chair. 'I didn't want it. I didn't want the responsibility of it. But when my family were treated with disdain by some of the locals, I found myself reaching for the one thing I knew I could control.'

Robert Masters and Marina. She wanted to hit back at him for breaking her sister's heart. Protecting your family and the ones you love. I could understand that.

Elsa spoke. 'Mrs Carlucci, this curse you placed on Dexter Grayling… He doesn't deserve it.'

Linda listened while she fiddled with the strap of her wristwatch.

She sighed, allowing her fingers to soothe Brando's velvety ears.

'Dexter is a good person underneath all the gruff and bluster,' assured Elsa. 'And I've seen him with Nadia. He's devoted to her.' She flicked me a look. 'And he *has* changed. For the better.'

Elsa offered me a small caring smile. 'Elle has changed him.'

Linda didn't say anything. She swivelled her attention from Elsa to me and back again.

'Linda.' Cameron, who had been observing our conversation, broke in.

She bit her bottom lip while she watched a blackbird hop along the top of the hedge outside her sitting room window. The silver crescent moon necklace was nestled against her freckled crêpey skin. 'I was living in the Lake District before I returned here. My husband died. Things changed.'

We all offered our condolences, but Linda carried on. 'I was in an unhappy marriage. Steven wasn't a bad man, but he could be selfish and cold. He was a farmer and expected me to adapt to that way of life; to embrace it.'

She continued to fondle her pendant. 'After Steven passed away, I knew I had to return here. Being married to him showed me what I would have had with Ross.' She confessed that being free of her late husband meant that she'd felt able to come back and be close again to the man she still loved. 'I even reverted back to my maiden name.'

She gazed down at Brando by her feet and then back up at the three of us. Her attention locked on to me.

She nodded as though convincing herself of something and cleared her throat. 'Can you take me to him? Can you take me to see Dexter Grayling?'

Chapter Seventy-Five

It was the oddest collection of people I'd ever seen, piling into one car: a stationery shop owner; an art collector; the housekeeper of a crime writer; and an Italian lady with special powers.

Cameron made sure we were all settled before driving away from Linda's cottage. The air in his car was expectant.

I was again sitting in the front passenger seat, while Elsa and Linda occupied the back.

To break the expectant silence, Cameron reached for his digital radio and clicked it on. I had already given him Dexter's address at Hawk West Hall and he entered it into his sat-nav.

Hawk West Hall emerged on the screen, identified by a red dot. My stomach performed an impressive series of forward rolls.

I felt as if I had been awake for hours, despite it only being 11 a.m. I glanced over my shoulder a couple of times at Linda, but she didn't appear to notice. She was too preoccupied, her misty green gaze boring into the back of Cameron's groomed head.

Elsa shuffled uneasily beside her, making the odd remark about the countryside. Linda struggled to reply. She was clearly too busy fighting to comprehend the situation she now found herself in.

Cameron's attention reverted to his backseat occupants. 'I understand the nature reserve is up for development.'

I sighed. 'Yes. Developers are planning to build lavish second homes on it for the townies.'

He shook his head, indicating right past a farm and down an avenue of burnished trees, weighted down with tiny red berries. It reminded me of Christmas. 'I read an article about it in the national press. Isn't Dexter Grayling supporting your cause?'

'He is,' I confirmed. 'So too is Dean Ellwood, an up-and-coming folk singer, but it doesn't seem to have made much of a difference.'

Cameron listened, drawing up at a set of traffic lights. They glowed green and we moved off again. The countryside glided past in an endless flow of dry-stone walls and frost-stirred fields, until the sign for the nature reserve materialised over the brow of the hill.

I turned my head to check on Linda, who recognised the area as the place where Ross and Cameron had raced. She swallowed and blinked out of the window.

I almost couldn't bear to look out of the car window. Goodness knows how much longer the nature reserve would be there.

Hawk West Hall's Rapunzel style turrets poked through the mish-mash of trees.

As we approached, Cameron examined his sat-nav screen. 'That's some area of land your Mr Grayling owns.'

The irony of Dexter being 'My Mr Grayling' was not lost on me. 'It used to be the council offices.'

'Of course it did,' nodded Cameron. 'I thought it seemed familiar.'

We got nearer and the sight of the tall iron gates made my heart swish. Cameron drew to a stop in front of the intercom and

Elsa clambered out and entered the security code before resuming her seat again beside Linda.

Linda appreciated the impressive manor sprawling in all directions under the chilly morning. Elsa shot her a concerned, sideways glance. There was the sharp sound of buzzing and then the gates slid open to let us in.

'Are we ready?' I asked the car occupants.

Linda Carlucci looked hesitant but she nodded.

Chapter Seventy-Six

'What the hell is going on?'

Shelley's piercing eyes, daubed with winged eyeliner, were leaping out of her face like sharp blades.

She swooped on Elsa as we entered the hall. 'You've been gone hours!'

From behind her came Dexter, clutching Nadia's hand. My breath stuttered in my throat.

When he saw our odd little group, he stopped dead. 'Elle?'

I took a few steps towards him, my long velvet boots clipping on the tiled floor. 'Mrs Carlucci wants to talk to you.'

His powder-blue eyes swept over me. I could feel my heart rattling. Then a cacophony of emotions travelled across his handsome face.

'Are we having a party, Uncle Dexter?' piped up Nadia. She shot me a cheeky grin. I winked back at her.

'We might have a party,' I said to Nadia, 'once we've had a chat with Uncle Dexter.'

'Yippee!' she squealed, hopping from foot to foot. Her dark bunches bobbed either side of her head.

Shelley's irritation was evident. She turned to Dexter, swishing her brunette waves. 'Can't we ask them all to come back another time, Dexy? I thought we were going to that fusion restaurant for lunch.'

'Mr Grayling?' Linda's stilted voice rang around the hall.

Looking like a seven year old who had just come face to face with Father Christmas, Dexter ushered us all into his office. 'Please. All of you, come in.'

Shelley stepped to one side, gawping as the four of us filed past her. When she came to me, her expression hardened.

'Shelley, would you take Nadia into the gardens for a little while please?' asked Dexter.

She took her daughter's hand, muttering something about it being 'too bloody cold' before guiding Nadia away.

We all lingered in Dexter's office, assisting him to move chairs and the small sofa. He looked amazing in a pearl-coloured cable-knit jumper and black jeans, but there were traces of melancholy under his heavily lashed eyes. I think even I had underestimated how much of a toll all of this had taken on him.

Cameron Lomax started to talk, but Linda Carlucci interrupted. 'It's true,' she gushed. 'I did place a curse on this young man.'

A combination of relief and apprehension flooded over Dexter's face.

'That day,' she started, 'when you sped into Fir Haven in your car… you reminded me of someone. Someone I lost.'

'And that loss was down to me,' added Cameron Lomax.

Dexter sat behind his desk, his brows rising and falling. One minute he was blowing out air, the next gulping it in as Cameron Lomax explained again about that fateful August night in 1964, before Linda took up the rest of the story.

At times her attention drifted, weaving in and out, but she managed to compose herself.

I nodded encouragingly at her as she described the loss and anger she still felt and how the sight of Dexter in his fast car, who reminded her so much of Ross, had made her lash out in pain. When she finished talking, a sense of relief enveloped her.

I watched as Linda's right hand snaked up to her crescent moon necklace and she touched it for the briefest time. No one else seemed to notice except me.

Dexter rubbed his stubbly chin. His eyes swam while he comprehended everything Linda had told him. 'I'm so very sorry for your loss,' he managed. 'It must have been awful for you. And then when I came speeding into town like that…'

Dexter's broad chest rose and fell as he spoke to Cameron. 'And I appreciate you being so honest, sir. It can't have been easy for you coming here either.'

Cameron dragged a tired hand through his greying waves. 'I think there's been enough misery. But it's really down to these two ladies that we are here.'

Linda Carlucci flicked a brief nod of agreement.

Dexter was bewildered. His gaze softened as he looked across the desk at me. 'You did all this for me?'

Elsa slid me a small smile. A pink blush rose up from my neck. I couldn't think of a pithy reply. My heart was making far too much noise as it thundered in my ears.

Without taking his eyes away from me, Dexter asked, 'And the curse?'

Linda murmured. 'It's gone now.'

It was like watching all of Dexter's troubles fall away. His shoulders relaxed and an audible rush of air escaped from his chest. 'Thank you.'

In fact, there seemed to be a collective sigh of relief in all of us, as the birds pitched in the sky outside and the lunchtime sun sent triangular shadows through the window.

'There's something else,' erupted Cameron, making us all start. He got to his feet, pushing both his hands into the pockets of his long military-style coat. 'The nature reserve. Well, I've been thinking about that and I think I might be able to help.'

Gathering himself, Cameron paced up and down. 'I'm an art collector – and I've been lucky enough to be quite successful. I'm fortunate that I am in a position where I can help Fir Haven hang on to the nature reserve. I've been involved in a number of successful art transactions over the past few years, buying and selling some remarkable paintings, and the commissions have been very generous.' Cameron hesitated, choosing his words carefully. 'It won't make amends for what happened, but…' His voice faltered and faded.

I sprang up from the sofa. 'Are you serious?'

'Very.'

I buried a squeal. 'But you can't do that! I mean, it's wonderful of you, but we couldn't possibly ask you to do that.'

Cameron dismissed my protestations. 'You aren't asking me. I'm offering. And I want to fund a memorial,' he added, his voice growing thicker. 'A memorial dedicated to Ross Ronald. It will be erected at the entrance to the reserve.'

There was a collective intake of breath. We all swivelled to look Linda Carlucci, poised but silent in her chair. She cleared her throat and blinked back hot tears. 'Thank you.'

Dexter clapped his hands together, still bewildered by it all, but with new light in his eyes. 'Right then. There's no time to waste.'

He began firing up his PC. 'We need to contact Atticus Development and the council. Fast.' He started pressing his mouse. 'We need to make them an offer they can't refuse.'

'But what if it doesn't work?' I asked, hating myself for not sounding positive.

Dexter's determination was evident. 'Oh, it will. We'll make sure of it.'

We sat, bubbling with enthusiasm, as Dexter demanded to be put through to the chief executive of Atticus Development first of all. After delivering a teasing outline of a proposal, John Gerrard agreed to come to Hawk West Hall to discuss the matter face to face. 'Oh, and I suggest you bring a representative from Fir Haven Council with you,' added Dexter.

Dexter rounded off the call and confirmed that Joshua Boyd from Atticus Development was attending too.

My stomach swirled around like whirlpool. 'When?'

'Tomorrow morning at 9:30 a.m.'

Cameron asked if any of us knew of a decent local bed and breakfast. 'And if there's somewhere I can buy a shirt and tie for the meeting tomorrow too, that would be helpful. I might as well just stay local and that will save me driving back here tomorrow morning.'

Dexter refused to hear of it. 'You must stay here tonight. It's the least I can do.'

Cameron gave Dexter a shadow of a smile and a firm handshake. 'Thank you. That's very kind of you.' He gathered himself together, verbally running through his plans. 'I'll ring my wife now and tell her I won't be home this evening,' said Cameron.

Dexter sought assurance from Linda that she was all right with attending the meeting. 'We are all involved in this,' he said. 'Every one of us, in one way or another.'

We all filed out of Dexter's office in something of a daze over what had just taken place.

'Elle.'

I was aware of Dexter standing right behind me.

I turned to look at him, my chest fizzing.

'I don't know what to say to you.'

'You don't have to say anything to me, Dexter.'

He reached out and cupped one of my hands in his. Bolts of excitement rattled though me like an express train. 'We need to talk.' His eyes lingered a little longer than necessary on my mouth.

'About you going back to London?'

'Yes.'

My heart shrivelled. What was I expecting him to say? He felt such a responsibility to Nadia, and the fact he did was one of the things I loved about him. He had to do what was best for her.

I forced my lips into a smile. OK, so I was losing him, but at least I'd been able to help put something right before he departed. I struggled to remain composed, trying not to engage with the pain stabbing at me.

'Can we can tomorrow, after the meeting?'

I pushed out another smile. 'That would be good.'

I should have felt elated that night. There was still hope for Dexter and me, surely? Why had he insisted that we needed to talk?

Instead, a sliver of worry gnawed at my insides. I didn't want to entertain the fact that I could again be losing someone I loved and, if that was the case, there was nothing I could do about it.

Chapter Seventy-Seven

Gran ushered me out of Pebble Brook just before 9 a.m. the following morning.

I pulled at the pussycat-bow of my candy-pink blouse. 'I'm so sorry for deserting the shop again and leaving you and Cate to hold the fort.'

Gran dismissed my concerns. 'Listen, young lady, what you're doing is far more important. The future of our town is at stake here.'

She gave me a supportive grin. 'Now go and knock 'em dead!'

Dexter had decided to hold the meeting with Atticus Development and the local council in his library.

I didn't even realise he had one, until Elsa escorted me into it. It reminded me of Beast's library in his castle. Cherry-wood shelves glowed with polish, housing all the modern classics like *The Great Gatsby*, *Animal Farm*, and *To Kill a Mocking Bird*.

There was a long, narrow table surrounded by several high-backed chairs in a Charles Rennie Mackintosh design, and a black and white zebra-style rug thrown in front of the smouldering fireplace. In the middle of the table was a gorgeous floral display of orange and amber germini, sunflowers, and assorted grassy fronds. The colours reminded me of winter, all burnished nights, autumnal leaves, and pumpkins.

It was a formal but comfortable setting, with a pitcher of water and glasses set at each place, together with paper and pens.

I smoothed down my knee-length navy skirt. Right now, I didn't know whether I felt more nervous about seeing Dexter again or taking part in this crucial meeting.

Elsa indulged me with an encouraging smile. 'You look lovely, Elle. Very professional.'

I rolled my eyes. 'I feel almost as sick as I did when I was about to sit my driving test.' I glanced around. 'No Shelley or Nadia this morning?'

Elsa pulled a face. 'Shelley said she has an urgent appointment with her manicurist.'

'And Nadia?'

Elsa broke into a fond grin. 'Eating all the cereal in my kitchen. Josie, one of the cleaners, is fussing over her.'

The sound of feet tapping across the hall drew my attention towards the library door.

Cameron Lomax and Dexter entered, talking in hushed serious tones. When Dexter saw me, he stopped talking. 'Hey.'

'Hey back.'

His face broke into an appreciative smile. He moved towards me, but Elsa, who had disappeared out of the library, reappeared. 'So sorry, but Linda Carlucci is here.'

Seconds later, Linda made her way into the room. Cameron appeared awkward when he saw her again, as if all his long limbs were suddenly too big for his body.

Her hair was drawn back at the base of her neck in an Eva

Peron style bun and she was wearing a knee-length beige woollen dress and boots.

She nodded at everyone as she hovered by the table. I approached her with a small smile of welcome. Her lips flickered. 'Thank you for letting me see I couldn't continue the way I was.'

I squeezed her hand, which was poking out of the ribbed sleeve of her dress. Her eyes flew to the library door. 'Atticus Development and the council are here now too?'

Dexter, resplendent in a three-piece navy suit and mauve tie, nodded. 'Please come and take a seat and we can all introduce ourselves. Then we can begin.'

'You don't have that sort of money,' scoffed Joshua Boyd at the hastily assembled meeting. 'All your efforts are to be applauded, Ms Cassidy, but I would be very surprised if baking stalls and raffles have raised the amount we are talking about here.'

I narrowed my eyes across the table. 'The local community have dug deep to try and save the reserve. We have been doing all we can.'

I wanted to wipe that supercilious smirk from his round face.

'But the fact remains that you simply can't make an offer to buy the reserve from the council without the necessary funds, which you clearly don't have.'

From beside me, Cameron Lomax coughed. 'And you know that for a fact, do you?'

Joshua Boyd toyed with the pen in front of him. 'Well, no, of course not, but the amount of money we're talking here—'

Cameron cut him off mid-sentence. He smoothed down the gold silk tie which Dexter had lent him. 'One of the first rules of business: always research the competition.'

He sat back in his chair.

Joshua Boyd, his boss, John Gerrard, who was seated beside

him and the council representative, a stork-like lady by the name of Una Groves, shuffled in their chairs.

Cameron leant forward. 'I am an art collector. I own a number of very high-profile pieces of artwork.' He scanned everyone at the table. 'I take it you've heard of the local Fir Haven artist Stratford Miller? Well, one of his paintings, *Little Town,* was recently discovered by a local gentleman by the name of Robert Masters. It was handed down from generation to generation in his family and when his brother passed away recently he discovered it amongst his possessions in his attic.' A small smile hovered on his lips. 'Mr Masters was all set to donate it to a local charity shop but he happened to hear a radio interview with me and made contact.'

I froze in my chair, recalling the news item about the discovery of the painting on the radio while Elsa and I had sat in my car outside Cameron's apartment that day.

Robert Masters? His name rang like a bell in my head. So it was his late brother who had owned it? I let out a tiny gasp of shock and tried to refocus.

The three officials made uncomfortable murmurs at each other.

Cameron continued to explain. 'I was thrilled to buy it from him. In fact, you could say it was a team effort. When I told Robert of the importance of his discovery, he insisted that he sell it to me for a modest fee under the proviso that it be auctioned and the proceeds go towards saving the reserve.'

Cameron smiled gently at our stunned faces gawping at him from around the table. 'He said we should be working together to support the efforts of the Fir Haven community.'

My heart pummelled my chest. So, Robert Masters' brother had held on to this elusive painting for goodness knows how long and now he was indirectly helping to save the reserve.

There were more grunts and tuts from the suits who were present, but Cameron seized on their disquiet. 'My plan is to have the painting auctioned as soon as possible and all the proceeds from the sale will go towards purchasing and maintaining the nature reserve.' He then announced a figure he was confident *Little Town* would achieve at auction. 'In fact, that's a bit of a conservative estimate.'

Una Groves's small eyes grew big. She flicked her ash-blonde fringe out of her eyes. 'So, let me clarify, Mr Lomax. You are saying you want to purchase the nature reserve.'

'But we've already got interested parties on board for those homes,' choked Joshua Boyd. 'High-profile names! What are we going to tell them?'

'You can tell them,' said Dexter, 'that there is alternative land available, still in Fir Haven.'

I frowned at him. What was he talking about? There was no other alternative land that could be used. Or at least, I wasn't aware of any.

Everyone observed Dexter rise out of his seat and stroll across to the library window. He pointed across the swathe of grass beyond a high fence decorated with climbing vines. 'Over there is land I also own, which I had intended to develop as stables but I've changed my mind about that.'

My heart banged. 'Dexter!' I gulped. 'What are you doing?'

He smiled broadly and gave me a wink. 'It's secluded but has beautiful views, as well as not impacting in any way on the nature reserve or the surrounding wildlife.'

Joshua Boyd's flaming cheeks threatened to explode. 'This is ridiculous! We've already released the specs of where we will be building.'

John Gerrard ignored his underling. He eyed Una Groves's optimistic reaction with interest. Then he turned to Dexter. 'What figure are we talking, Mr Grayling?'

Dexter smiled coolly. 'I know exactly what my land is worth, Mr Gerrard.' Dexter scribbled an amount on a piece of paper and thrust it across the table.

John Gerrard blinked. 'That's quite a sum, Mr Grayling.'

'It is. But I am more than happy to negotiate on that amount for my land, as long as the reserve is sold to Mr Lomax.'

Josh's bald head glowed with frustration, but both his colleagues were too busy salivating as they debated the offer.

'There's one other thing,' remarked Cameron, flashing a wary look further up the table to Linda Carlucci. 'I intend to commission a memorial to a local man, Ross Ronald which will be erected at the entrance to the reserve. I take it there would be no council opposition when it comes to making preparations for that.'

When Una Groves enquired more about the memorial and why it was being dedicated, Cameron urged Linda to explain.

She did so with deep emotion but also a great deal of clarity, and flashed Cameron a brief nod when she had finished.

Una Groves smiled sympathetically. 'That sounds very fitting.'

My head, whirling between the half a dozen faces at the table, was struggling to comprehend everything. 'So… it's a deal?' I asked, my palms clammy. 'The nature reserve is safe?'

John Gerrard beamed with self-congratulation. 'We have a deal.'

There were exclamations of relief and delight all round, together with firm handshakes, before assurances were given by one and all that the necessary paperwork would be drawn up as soon as possible.

Elsa escorted the visitors out of Hawk West Hall, unable to conceal her delight, even though Joshua Boyd continued to make grumpy protestation as they clambered into his boss' Jaguar. He only fell silent when John Gerrard told him to 'button it' and that he could seek employment elsewhere if he was unable to reconcile such a 'forward thinking business proposition'.

Cameron and Linda faced each other in one corner of the library. 'I hope we can work together on a suitable memorial for Ross,' he said. 'I realise things will never be easy between us and that's down to me.'

Linda didn't disagree. 'I would like to be involved in any way I can, though.'

'Elle?'

I had been gazing out of the library window, forcing back happy tears knowing that the nature reserve was now safe and that all the precious memories the locals had wrapped up there were protected too.

Dexter had removed his suit jacket and was standing there like a hero from a 1940s drama in his white shirt and waistcoat. 'Can I have a word?'

He guided me across the hall and into his study. He closed the door behind us. I hoped my voice didn't betray how much my insides were twisting, standing so close to this wonderful man. 'I can't thank you enough for what you did in there.'

He flipped his shoulders. 'I had to help. I wanted to.'

'But the idea of starting your own stud farm meant so much to you.'

My insides melted as he took a few deliberate steps towards me. 'Since my books started selling, all I've come across, for the main part, are people who want something from me. That was, until I met you.' His black lashes cast a faint shadow across his cheeks. 'What you have done for me, Elle; how you fought for me…'

My dark eyes locked with his, which were like the sky outside the window – clear and deep, like an azure sea. I was unable to look away. I didn't want to ask this question, but I had to know. 'London?' I asked, hoping I was managing to conceal the trepidation I felt.

'What about London?'

'Well, now you can write again, you can do what you want and live where you want with Shelley and Nadia.'

Dexter blinked down at me. 'I'm not going anywhere, Elle. That's what I was driving at yesterday. I want to be where you are.'

I swallowed, my heart fluttering like a cage of wild birds. 'But I thought when you mentioned London, that you were planning to go back home?'

'Being with you is home now.'

He took both my hands in his. 'I have been such a dick. I was frightened to admit I was falling for you. That day when I left Paper Roses whilst you were on the phone... that was when I started to realise how I felt about you and I had no idea how to handle it.'

I tried to reconcile what he was telling me. 'But what about Nadia and Shelley?'

My skin sizzled as Dexter's long tapered fingers moved to caress the tops of my arms. I could feel the gentle imprint of his fingers through the chiffon of my sleeves.

'I spoke to Shelley last night. She knows I will always be there for her and Nadia, but not in the way I think she was hoping for.' His hypnotic eyes never left my face. 'I told her the truth – that I've fallen for you.'

My heart lurched. My voice was cracking. 'And how did she take it?'

'Not very well at first, until I showed her a brochure of a new five-bedroom detached house I've just bought in Edinburgh to rent out. When I told her she and Nadia could stay there rent-free, I think that sweetened her mood, especially as it's just ten minutes' walk to the shops.'

His face broke into a grin and I found myself grinning back. My head was buzzing with everything that had happened, but it all felt so wonderful. Seeing the spark back in his eyes made my breathing pick up pace.

'At least them living in Edinburgh means I can still see Nadia and be her favourite uncle.' He paused. 'Come to think of it, I'm her *only* uncle.'

'So, what now?' I smiled, my heart juddering. 'I guess now that you can write again, you'll want to crack on with completing the first draft of *Killing Time*.'

Dexter was appalled. 'There's something far more important I need to do first.'

And as Dexter's lips claimed mine, all I could think of was how important it was to enjoy every moment with the ones you love.

Epilogue

15 June 2023, Fir Haven Nature Reserve

There was a swell of people from the local community gathered around the leafy entrance to the nature reserve.

Ahead of us, as we blinked out of sunglasses, was concealed the memorial to Ross Ronald. It was shrouded under a long, silky blue cloth, only giving the odd tantalising glimpse when an occasional breeze decided to lift the material.

Standing beside Dexter and me were Elsa, who was holding Nadia's hand, Linda Carlucci, and Cameron Lomax with his wife, Ingrid. Behind them were Cate and Lucy, unable to contain their excitement about their forthcoming wedding which was to be held here at the end of the month.

I heard footsteps behind me. It was Gran and Angus, their arms linked as they murmured their appreciation of the weather.

While the others talked in hushed tones, Angus made his way over to Linda and offered her words of comfort. After all, they had both felt the loss of Ross so keenly and, had he lived, they would have become brother and sister-in-law.

It was as if the heartaches of the past, though not forgotten, were being addressed and dealt with for the sake of those who had been lost.

The town was saying sorry to the Carlucci family – and not before time.

Angus moved up to stand beside the concealed monument, clutching some words he had written on a piece of paper. He blew out a puff of air, offering a shaky smile to my grandmother. She replied with an encouraging thumbs-up.

'Thank you to everyone for coming. You will be relieved to hear I don't intend to say very much.'

There was a ripple of laughter.

'But I do want to thank some very special people who have made this memorial to my brother possible.'

Angus reeled off a series of names, which included me, Dexter, and Cameron. Then he turned to Linda in the crowd, hovering there in her long mint-green dress and fitted jacket. 'I also want to say thank you to Linda Carlucci, the love of Ross's life. Even after all these years, your love for one another is as enduring and as special as this place.' He indicated the swell of swaying trees behind him. 'And it seems fitting that today, on what would have been Ross's seventy-seventh birthday, we reveal a memorial to his brave actions that night in August 1964.'

I was aware of Cameron Lomax lowering his greying head and Ingrid tightening her grip on his hand.

As Angus moved to take one of the corners of blue cloth, Cate leant towards my ear and whispered, 'I hope me suggesting the sculptor doesn't backfire. I feel personally responsible.'

Lucy, beside her, rolled her eyes. 'I'm sure it will be beautiful, Cate. Stop worrying.'

Angus tugged at the blue cloth and it slid off… to reveal the figure of a young man, his head bowed as he sat engrossed in a book.

There was a collective gasp of appreciation.

One of Cate's friends, the sculptor Robbie Glover, who she had got to know at art college, had created it using thick varnish, bronze resin, clay, concrete and a mould. It was beautiful, a life-sized romantic interpretation of Ross Ronald

Underneath the sculpture was a bronze plaque on which was written:

DEDICATED TO THE BRAVERY OF ROSS LIAM RONALD
BORN 27 JANUARY 1942
DIED 4 AUGUST 1964
ALWAYS LOVED – NEVER FORGOTTEN

Linda's emotional green eyes melted at the sight of her beloved Ross, brought so tenderly back to life.

Angus, too, was enchanted by the touching memorial. He stood for a moment, marvelling at the way the artist had captured his brother's pensive and handsome profile.

Cate moved past me and approached Linda and Angus, both tearfully admiring the statue of a man who still meant so much to each of them for different reasons.

'Robbie was sorry he couldn't be here today. He has a deadline for a commission for the Scottish Parliament, but he told me to tell you that the memorial is waterproof. All it needs is the occasional wipe down with a damp cloth dipped in soapy water.' Cate smiled up at the bronze statue. 'That should keep it in tip-top condition.'

'I'll do that,' insisted Linda, one hand reaching out to stroke the impression of Ross's angled cheek. 'I'd like to, Angus. If that's all right?'

Angus nodded and smiled. 'Of course, it is. Ross would have wanted that too.'

While the local newspaper journalist took photos of Ross's sculpture and the assembled crowd, Dexter clapped his hands together. 'Excuse me, ladies and gentlemen, if I could have your attention for one moment, please?'

Heads swivelled round under the June sunshine.

'You are all more than welcome to come back to Hawk West Hall now, where afternoon tea is being served out in the grounds.'

Thanks were offered, as the locals ebbed away to collect their cars for the short journey to Dexter's. I started to follow them when Dexter caught me by the wrist.

'Have you got a minute?'

We hung back, smiling and exchanging pleasantries with the last of the stragglers, until it was just the two of us left standing within the shadow of Ross's bronze sculpture. There was the heady scent of wild flowers and the throb of birdsong.

'Is everything all right, Dexter? Are you worried we won't have catered for enough people, because Elsa and I erred on the side of caution and the catering company is very good...'

My eyes widened as he placed one long, slim finger against my mouth to silence me. 'This place carries so many memories for you, Elle.'

'It does,' I sighed. 'It always will.'

Dexter eyed me in my stripy maxi dress. Then he swallowed and gave the pocket of his ocean-blue suit trousers a reassuring pat. 'Well, hopefully I can add to those memories.'

My hand flew to my mouth as Dexter proceeded to go down on one knee in front of me on the grass. He held up a small white leather box.

He slid open the lid, revealing the most gorgeous white-gold willow-diamond ring. Wispy vines of precious metal entwined towards the marquise buds in the centre.

Happiness and shock hammered in my chest.

Dexter continued to kneel, searching my face with his electric-blue eyes. 'Nadia insisted that she help me choose it. It reminded us both of the reserve.'

My heart was skipping with love for this man.

'So,' he said, an edge of apprehension creeping into his voice, 'I don't want to rush you, Elle, but it will be dark in a few hours and my knee is getting a bit damp.'

I laughed, throwing my arms around his neck and inhaling his familiar scent of citrus body wash. I seized his mouth with mine, kissing his lips over and over, almost sending the two of us toppling backwards.

Dexter broke into a megawatt grin. 'I take it that's a yes, then?'

Acknowledgments

Huge and grateful thanks as always to my wonderful editor at HarperCollins, Jennie Rothwell, for her patience, flair, and expertise!

Thank you also to all the team at One More Chapter and HarperCollins who are such a talented and dynamic group of people.

My ongoing thanks and appreciation to my amazing agent, Selwa Anthony, and to the fab Linda Anthony. I'm very lucky.

And love always to Lawrence, Daniel, Ethan, and Cooper.

As Elle says in the story, enjoy every moment with the ones you love, seize happiness when it comes your way – and never let it go.

Read on for an extract from The Christmas Highland Lodge

Chapter 1

I offered a smile to the elegant, ice-cool blonde woman who had just entered the shop and was admiring our latest range of rose-gold tinsel and matching baubles.

I glanced down at my to-do list, which was making its way to the bottom of the pad. I still had a couple of suppliers to chase up. We hadn't received the order I had placed for illuminated holly wreaths, and the ceramic penguin and robin decorations had arrived smashed to bits in the bottom of the box.

All around me, fairy lights dazzled and there was the warm, festive scent of cinnamon emanating from our Christmas pot-pourri for sale.

I was just about to ring the ceramic decoration suppliers and ask for them to arrange delivery of ones that weren't like a Mensa jigsaw puzzle, when I realised there was a customer on the other side of the counter, waiting to be attended to.

'Excuse me? I love these tear-shaped baubles. You don't happen to have any in silver?'

I snapped my attention back to the woman who had entered Christmas Crackers just a few moments ago. 'I think we may have some through in the stock room. Would you like me to check for you?'

She scooped up an eclectic mix of the two-tone rose-gold and lilac baubles. 'If you wouldn't mind, that would be helpful. Thank you.'

I hurried towards the stockroom, located at the rear of the shop.

Christmas Crackers was located on Craig Brae high street, stationed between the local optician's and the card shop.

It was a sweet little place, with two huge, bevelled windows, covered in fake snow and tinsel, with a tree and a couple of illuminated Christmas cottage decorations.

The counter, a huge, old-fashioned mahogany affair on the right, greeted you as soon as you stepped inside the door and running down either side of the length of the shop was a number of matching wooden shelves and hooks, displaying everything from snow globes and festive table decorations to advent calendars and holly wreaths.

It used to be the local ironmongers until Mr and Mrs McIntosh decided to retire and sell the business just over three years ago to my boss, Vivian Sangster.

After completing my degree in interior design at the Glasgow School of Art, I worked for a couple of different department stores in the city for a few years. I ended up being able to indulge my love of Christmas by using my imagination and creating eye-catching window displays, which I loved doing but especially at my most favourite time of the year.

I glanced around the stockroom with a frisson of excitement. Only a matter of months now and Mrs Sangster would be retiring, heading off to the States and selling the business to me, as she had promised. I beamed from ear to ear.

I located the surplus baubles stock, marked up in sturdy silver boxes on the shelves in the stockroom and tapped back down the wooden floor of the shop, carrying several silver baubles. The wintry November sunshine shot through the shop window, making them sparkle even more. 'How are these for you, madam?'

She beamed, displaying, large, white teeth. 'Perfect. Thank you so much.'

'Which ones would you like?'

'Oh, I'll take all of them. I've got three trees to decorate.'

Three?! Wow!

I tried not to stare at her as I prepared her purchases. I wondered where she lived and how big her house was, if she was going to be decorating three Christmas trees. Perhaps she was a day-tripper or was visiting for a few days?

I didn't recognise her.

Perhaps this well-dressed, middle-aged woman was a new weekender? I smiled to myself. That would please Mr Clarkson, the caretaker down at the town hall. He was always grumbling, 'Aye, all these darn incomers pushing up the prices of the properties in the area,' and, 'parking their bloody great SUVs all over the place, like they've been abandoned.'

While I reached for some of our embossed Christmas Crackers red and green tissue paper to wrap her purchases in, the woman appreciated her surroundings. 'You have a beautiful shop. Are you the owner?'

I retrieved one of our large, glittery bags from under the counter and secured it with blue and green tartan ribbon. 'Thank you. No, it's not my business – well, not yet anyway. I'm the manager at the moment.'

I proceeded to explain to her about Mrs Sangster retiring and how I would be buying the business and taking over.

She nodded over at our white and gold wooden Nutcracker soldiers. 'Well, it's gorgeous. I could spend a fortune in here.'

'Oh, please do!' I joked, accepting her credit card.

While I processed her purchases, she pointed to the window and then the shelves, groaning with assorted festive gifts and decorations. 'Do you do all of this? The displays?'

'I do. It's a labour of love for me. I studied interior design.'

The woman laughed. 'Well, it's stunning.'

'Thank you. That's very kind of you to say so.'

She cocked her head to one side, making her blonde hair swing around her jawline. Her expression was open and intrigued as she studied mine. 'You must love Christmas then.'

'I'm obsessed,' I admitted, blushing. 'I always have been.' I indicated to everything that surrounded us, from the ornate, scented candles, infused with berry and vanilla, to the gingerbread tree decorations and the rainbow waterfall of tinsel, cascading down from the racks. 'Every day I come to work, it's like stepping into Christmas all over again. It's the most magical time of the year and I never tire of it.'

I let my attention fall on our miniature Christmas trees for sale, complete with dinky white lights, that I had lined up behind her. 'It seems like at Christmas, anything is possible.'

I was aware the woman was staring at me and I let out a self-conscious cough. 'Sorry! I'm prattling on. If you stay here any longer, I shall start boring you about Christmas traditions in Italy and Scandinavia.'

She grinned, hitched her shoulder bag up and clutched her purchases. 'Not at all. It's so refreshing to hear someone so enthusiastic and in love with what they do.' She flashed me an intrigued look. 'So where have you worked before? And where do you get such innovative ideas from?'

'I used to work for Canterbury's, which was like a Scottish Harrods – I'm sure you will have heard of it.'

'Indeed, I have.' The woman smiled, apparently impressed. 'And did you create gorgeous displays like these for them too?'

'That's very kind. Thank you.' I blushed. 'I certainly tried. I used everything from tinsel animals to scented candles to create scenes which were like something out of a children's picture book.'

I lowered my voice, even though there were no other people in the shop. 'The owners, Barbara and Stratton Canterbury, were forward-thinking, approachable and open to any and all suggestions about how to make their store the biggest and brightest in Glasgow, so they gave me free rein.'

I smiled as I thought about my job and how much I had enjoyed it there. 'I loved working for them. But when Canterbury's began to lose money as people cut back on their luxury purchases, they had no option but to economise and that meant their generous staff quota had to be addressed. I was one of the members of staff who was let go, two years after I joined them.'

The blonde woman nodded. 'That must have been awful.'

'It was, but luckily Mrs Canterbury tipped me off about a new store across the other side of the city, Sanders, who were looking for someone with my skillset to turn their drab, average window displays into something magical.'

The woman listened with interest and seemed to be on the verge of saying something else, but we were interrupted by Mrs Sangster sweeping in.

The woman thanked me again and then departed the shop with a wave of her gloved hand.

'Everything going well?' Mrs Sangster asked, resplendent in her long berry coat and white winter scarf. The glistening from the ruby fairy lights strung along the shelves behind her cast a soupy glow on top of her yellow-blonde hair. Vivian Sangster was a very well-preserved lady in her sixties, who had dabbled in fashion modelling for a bit during her younger years and enjoyed telling everyone.

'Business has been very steady.'

'Good.'

She hovered around, her attention alighting on the blue and silver fluffy robin redbreast I'd propped up by the cash register. We had received a job lot of them a few days ago and I was hoping that by positioning one there, they might start to sell.

The sound of Elton John stepping into Christmas began to play from Alexa.

'I've been having a think about when I buy the shop,' I enthused, coming out from behind the counter. 'There is a new magazine coming out next year, which will focus on Scottish women in rural communities. I'm going to drop them an email.'

Mrs Sangster's expression shifted. Her fingers tweaked the cute little bird's knitted winter hat. 'Lottie, I need to talk to you.'

I was on a roll and carried on. 'And I've already had a word with Mrs Crill and she said she would be happy to start making edible Christmas cracker decorations which I can sell and we can share the profits—'

'Lottie!' Mrs Sangster's sharp voice made me start.

She dragged a hand over her blonde bouffant. 'This is very important. I should have spoken to you sooner. I'm so sorry.'

She clipped towards the shop door in her boots and spun the red and white painted sign hanging from it, to say *Closed*. 'Come through to the office.'

Oh God. Was this about those broken ornaments? No. It wasn't about Mum, was it? My mother worked behind the counter for a few hours each week, helping out, and loved it almost as much as I did. She had been doing such a great job too.

Mrs Sangster stalked ahead of me. I followed her through to the office.

An uneasy feeling was taking hold. What did she want to talk to me about?
